THOMAS

A SECRET LIFE

A Novel

by A. J. B. Johnston

This book is a work of fiction dramatized from a historical viewpoint. All of the characters, organizations and events portrayed in this novel are either products of the author's imagination or are used fictionally.

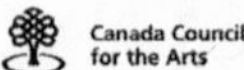

Cape Breton University Press recognizes the support of the Canada Council for the Arts, Block Grant program, and the Province of Nova Scotia, through the Department of Communities, Culture and Heritage, for our publishing program. We are pleased to work in partnership with these bodies to develop and promote our cultural resources.

Cover design by Cathy MacLean Design, Pleasant Bay, NS
Cover image: *Vue du pont neuf à Paris* / anonyme. - N°INV=RO 795 ; 1521 (Ro).
Toulouse, Musée des Augustins, photo : Daniel Martin.
Photo of A. J. B. Johnston by Chris Reardon Photo
First printed in Canada

Library and Archives Canada Cataloguing in Publication

Johnston, A. J. B.
Thomas : a secret life : a novel / A.J.B. Johnston.

ISBN 978-1-897009-74-1

I. Title.

PS8619.O4843T56 2012 C813'.6 C2012-903184-4

The font used in this manuscript is Garamond, which would have been familiar to all French readers in the 18th century. Claude Garamond created the typeface in the 1540s for the French king François I. The French court later adopted Garamond's Roman types for their printing. When Claude Garamond died in 1561, his punches and matrices were sold to a printer in Antwerp, which enabled the Garamond fonts to be used on many printing jobs throughout Europe. The only complete set of the original Garamond dies and matrices is at the Plantin-Moretus Museum in Antwerp, Belgium. Today, the Garamond typeface is regarded as eco-friendly because it uses less ink than many other fonts.

Cape Breton University Press
P.O. Box 5300
Sydney, Nova Scotia B1P 6L2 CA
www.cbupress.ca

THOMAS

A SECRET LIFE

A Novel

by A. J. B. Johnston

Cape Breton University Press
Sydney, Nova Scotia, Canada

For Elinor

La nuit est la mère des surprises.
– Pierre Claude Guignard, *L'École de Mars* (1725)

1

Departure

Vire, Normandy

December 1712

The boy struggles in the dark, kicking at the panting vision of dogs running through his head.

The dogs are in a woods, this Thomas knows. He knows them as shadows, long-stretched shadows a-running on wintry wastes, lean hunters bent on prey.

Yet where is their prey? There has to be prey. There always is. For these are dogs, forest dogs, and they run like this only when there's prey. If Thomas can't see it, it must lie ahead. Deeper into the sentinel forest than the boy can yet see. Perhaps there will come a clearing, if a clearing these dense woods allow. It is hard to imagine. The black branchless trunks loom like a phalanx of thick oars and masts standing up straight. No, that's not right. The trees are wooden soldiers. Dark soldiers whose furred canopies link arms overhead. There is only enough space among this wooden army's legs on the white ground below for the dogs to run and weave in a ceaseless onward file.

The snow in the dense woods is thin, a crisp covering of white hiding what the boy's ears make out under the dogs' drumming paws as the crush of last autumn's dried leaves. Powdery bursts of white kick up as they run. Quick rise and long fall, the disturbed snow makes a second slow tumble to the frozen ground.

There might be a moon, there must be a moon, how else can he see what he sees? Yet there is no hint of sky's lantern nor any stars penetrating this forest of dark trees. Thomas twists and extends. He stretches long where he lies, sightless hands clenching then uncurling to understand. Then it comes to him: there's something special about these woods and these dogs. This is a course being run, and it's running through the heart of the land.

A sudden wind, a dark gust, pushes into the woods. The dogs' fur ruffles and the snowy cover underfoot turns a cold winter's deep blue.

The drum beats on, tireless legs all a-whirr. Rasps of hot breath in Thomas's fearful ear. A rhythm of wants and needs. With a shiver, a shiver from his head to his toes, it's made clear. These dogs, these blood-driven dogs, they're not dogs at all. Nor hounds on a chase. They're tongue-dangling wolves in a forest where it's Thomas who is the prey.

Run and rasp, run and rasp, the hungry wolves pound the frozen ground. Rasp and run, he hears them coming on. Behind him, beside him, and he's running too. He's running but they're close. No, closer than that. He smells the lick of their foaming breath and knows they are near. His limbs, his only hope of escape, they start to freeze up. Thomas turns to face them as they come on the run.

Run and leap, run and leap, leap and…

"Maman!"

The blanket is kicked off. Sent into the air of the *grenier* then fluttering to the cold floor.

"Maman!" shouts the boy again, struggling to come round, to send away the sights and sounds of the dark woods and their wolves on the run. "Oh, please, please come now," he implores the air above him, more a prayer than anything else.

Thomas is shivering, his skin wet from the dream. He is frozen where he is, curled on the narrow attic bed. The blanket is out of his trembling reach, sprawled on the floor beside him not even an arm's length away. His body has taken over, his mind cannot think. The *grenier* awash in the colour of spilled milk that's coming from the little window on the other side of his room.

—

Ashes and embers, the fire is out. Thomas peeks from beneath a weight of blankets, arms round legs, hands clasped tight.

Motionless in the dark, eyes wide and round, Thomas feels a hand smoothing the covers. Oh yes, her hand. His mother's hand. She's pressing through the wool blankets on his chest and shoulder too. Even when the pressure lessens Thomas knows where the hand has gone, to twist the frayed edge of the woollen cover, threads his mother's fingers play round and round. His own hands slide up to find more heat between his thighs.

Above the bed, through the tiny window that peers out upon the chimneys and rooftops of the town of his birth, comes the still milky light of an unseen moon. It paints the room pale and sickly. Thomas gives a start. The mother's hand returns, to his hair this time. She pushes her boy's head gently back down to the bolster.

To the exposed wooden beams above the bed in his coldly lit room, to the chilled air that draughts across his attic space, Thomas asks the question that's been troubling him of late. "Am I bad or good?" He does not say the words aloud, yet his mother feels his young frame tremble and sees his lips move in silent mouthing.

"There, there," she whispers. "Everything's all right. Back to sleep you go."

Thomas is not so sure that's what he wants. Not quite yet. Sleep was where he'd been when a dream turned into a nightmare. A race through the woods that he couldn't let come to its end. That's why his mother is there beside him, seated on the edge of his bed. She has one hand upon his back, rubbing a circular path. The other is tousling the hair upon his head. She told him that she climbed the stairs to answer the shout. He did not at first remember the shout, though it made sense that he might call out after he'd seen what he'd seen.

To soothe the child, her only boy, Marie came up to this his room, the coldest in a cold and wintry house, up at the top of the second set of steps. Too old at twelve to be calling out his mother's name, Thomas was yelling it nonetheless and Marie answered it as she always does. Each time she leaves the huddled warmth of a husband's bed and sets her feet on boards so chilled she has to pull on thick wool socks. The socks now wait on the chair beside her side of the bed just in case, just in case her little boy cries out in his sleep. Off she went, socks pulled on, grabbing a blanket from the armoire as she hurried past.

"The moon," was all he said in a tiny voice when she opened the door. She came and bent over him, covering his slim trembling frame with the blanket she'd brought and Thomas's own that had been kicked to the floor. She pressed the covers to his body and leaned on him so he'd feel her weight and so she could transfer some of her heat. "The moon," he whispered once more before he closed his eyes and wished he could undo the vision of his earlier sleep.

Marie didn't ask what it meant, "the moon," and Thomas didn't say. It was enough that she had come.

It is not the first time he has awoken and called for her. It is the third time in a month. The third time since the weather turned cold, cold enough to keep snow on the rooftops of Vire and on the ground. She wonders, was it the same dream, always the same dream? She doesn't know and won't ask. She doesn't want to encourage him to be so troubled by such a foolish thing. The moon. Marie shakes her head. Despite his twelve years, old enough for many boys to start acting like men, learning their fathers' trades, Thomas is nowhere near ready. He should be showing more interest in their family business. A cloth merchant is better than many other trades, why can't the boy see that? Marie does not know why her only son is so late. In her dark doubt and swirling worry, she still gives in, rising in the dark to answer Thomas's cries when they come.

"Won't grow up" is how Marie's husband, Jean Pichon, put it once. They were in the kitchen. He cast an accusing look in her direction. She shrugged it off and hid the wince, but she knew that he was right. Jean Pichon's sleep is never troubled by foolish fancies. There are only two sides to her husband when they're in bed. One is the stiffening twixt the legs; the other is worries of shipments of cloth gone astray. No, that's not true, there's a third side, the one that allows him to go deep asleep and snore like some kind of machine. Of late, the money worries are the most frequent. It's become no easy matter to pay the bills of the household since the run-in with La Motte, the town's perpetual mayor. Stupid business that, taking on Vire's mightiest pillar.

Her husband should have known you cannot win when you go against a superior. Tilt against a pillar hard enough and the roof can come down. Which it did, only not on Renaud Brouard sieur La Motte as it was supposed to but on Marie and Jean, found guilty of calumny, La Motte saw to that. So now there are pressures on Jean Pichon's cloth-selling business like never before. Which, Marie muses, taking her hands away from her son to rub them together for a bit of warmth, means her husband has to have a vent for the way things turned out. Thomas, it seems, is that vent. Jean Pichon doesn't often put it in words that Marie is coddling their only son, but then he doesn't have to. Marie knows just by looking at her husband's downcast face that that's exactly what he thinks. He blames the boy's disappointingly slow path to manhood on her side of the family. The first-born, on the other hand, eager and obedient Anne, she takes after my side, says Jean Pichon's appraising look.

Marie exhales deeply as she glances round Thomas's moonlit attic room. It's so bare. Yet it's not because of the setback in the family business that her son's room looks like it is fit for a monk. No, it's more than that. It's because her son wants to be a priest someday. He's never admitted it; he may not even know it yet himself, but Marie sees that's how it is. Her boy chooses to live at the top of the house in a cold and nearly empty room. It's a stark and simple preparation for his later path. That's why he has so few pieces of furniture up here. There's the small bed in which he lies and where she is seated and there's the old armoire against the far wall, barely visible in the gloom. Closer at hand is the rickety desk with its lone candlestick on top. And a couple of chairs. The wash basin and then the battered oval rug on the floor. She can't see his chamber pot. It must be beneath the bed. Surely to God he is not one of those boys who pisses in the fireplace rather than in the pot, just because it saves him the time of taking out the pot and dumping it in the street. No, Marie shakes her head, not Thomas. Her nose would know if he'd ever done that, and he hasn't. He's a special boy, destined to be a priest.

Marie closes her eyes. The warmth that comes when the lids slide down is a comfort. Not much of a comfort but better than none at all. She thinks her husband is of course right, about her coddling Thomas. Yet what can she do? We're all the way we are, are we not? Me. My boy. There's nothing we can do to be someone else. And that's how Thomas is: soft, sensitive. One day he'll be a wonderful man of the cloth. That's why she comes to him now, so that that later day will arrive. Fate is fate. All we can do is give it a helping hand.

"The moon," Marie mouths, opening her eyes once again. The room is still a pale ghost, though brighter than before. The moon must be marching on, closer to the frame of the small window. "The moon," she repeats as softly as she can, wanting to know why her son's eyes were wet with fright when she first came into the room. She lays a hand upon his head once more and tries to caress away the recollection. "Oh, help us Lord," she mouths with upturned face, staring at the beam above her head. Is this son of mine afraid of the moon with its unearthly light? She musses the boy's long brown hair and issues a yearning sigh. How she wishes this moon-frightened son of hers might find some strength. Stand up on his own two feet. Grow a backbone. Those are things her husband, Jean, has said. Become a man. Marie shakes her head. A mother's hopes may well end in disappointment, that she knows. It's the curse of having hopes at all. Though in Thomas's case, his slowness about making his way in the world can be forgiven if in the end he does become her shining priest.

Thomas hears his mother sigh. He twists his head her way to see if she is all right. He senses that she's puzzled by what he said when she came into his room. He'd near shouted out "the moon" when he should have said "the dogs" or truth be told "the wolves." The moon was nothing more than the source of light in his room, and in the nightmare as well. Yes, it had to be the moon's glow that painted the snow-covered floor of the sentinel forest first cold white then an even colder blue. "Maman," he says, wanting now to explain. The spinning head, the throbbing heart, are gone.

"Shoosh," Marie says. "Shoosh. It's all right. You're all right. Be quiet and try to go to sleep."

Thomas does as he is told. Yet he wonders how long it's been. How long has she been sitting with him, on the edge of the narrow bed? Minutes? Or could it be an hour or more? He's warm now beneath the blankets and the comfort of a portion of her weight. He shifts to see his mother's face. Her eyes are closed as if in prayer and yes, the lips they are moving though there is not much he can hear. He catches just enough to recognize the usual prayer, an invocation to Him on high. Well, to the entire Trinity and of course to Mary too. Thomas once used to say that very prayer himself – even as recently as a few months ago – yet he does not anymore. He no longer hears the call he once heard. In fact, he's no longer sure he ever did. He now thinks it was his imagination, an imagination shaped and willed on by the very woman seated on his bed. Thomas knows she wants a priest and that means it must be him. His older sister can only be a nun, and they have no other children.

So she'll come to understand that he has lost the Church's call. She will, will she not?

No, she can't or she won't. Thomas rolls over. He knows it's true. He's stuck. Still, he's glad she came when he called. It was a troubling dream.

Thomas listens to the rise and fall of a mother's mumble, a prayer sent to the attic ceiling and the sky above. He knows his Latin and what the words mean. Nonetheless, he chooses not to hear any meaning but instead something like a running brook. The words are the stones in that stream.

Thomas understands that such prayers repeated low and often are a comfort. Well, they're a comfort for her, his mother, and many others. Mostly women, it comes to him. He's never seen or heard his father in prayer. The man hardly goes to church. Why is that? Because women are the ones that have the babies, Thomas decides. That gives them the connection with the blessings of God, for children come from Him.

Is this something I think myself or something I've been told? Thomas's eyebrows rise and his mouth makes a shrug.

Past his mother's elbow, an elbow he notices is poking nearly out through a frayed portion of her chemise, Thomas makes out in a squint the rest of the tiny attic room. He sees his table, the one with the wobbly back leg. He pictures the leather-bound volume that lies inside the desk's only drawer. The book is his, a gift from his father. Well, hardly a book and not much of a gift. From an auction six months ago: "thrown in with the rest" was what Father said that day, tossing it Thomas's way. Not in a mean way, not at all, but it was not handed over carefully the way Jean Pichon gave big sister Anne the glass paperweight a moment earlier. Father said it was "of value" because it came from Venice, made by the Jews. "They have some secret," he said with a knowing nod of the head. Anne's gift fit in her hand and it was bluish green with specks and swirls. She keeps it in her bedroom window where it catches the sunlight for the hour or so it shines on that part of the house. Thomas's gift, the two book cover boards, tossed not handed, has never seen the sun. It stays in the desk drawer where Thomas keeps it. The only light it catches is from a candle's glow at night when Thomas has reason to take the thing out of its hiding place.

So be it, thinks Thomas beneath blankets turned warm and the weight of Mother's moving hand upon his back. Of the two gifts, he supposes he is happier with the one sent his way. A book it really isn't, just two hard covers held together by what once must have been a complete spine. That spine is now threadbare thin and ripped here and there. Still, the boards are solid. And they have endpapers coloured with swerves of mauve and cream. Thomas keeps his verses between the boards of that book long gone, for he a sometimes secret poet is. When words come to him he sets them down upon paper he's taken from his father's ledgers, sheets severed with a razor, carefully done. He knows not to take too much or too often. Waste not, want not is a lesson he's learned more than once. Father would tan his arse if he found out what he's been doing, if not for the stolen paper then for the slyness of the taking. So Thomas does not ask or tell.

His limbs are suddenly heavy under the blankets and he feels his thing begin to grow. He tenses his entire body to make it stop, and shifts his weight to release the urge his legs have to move. Thomas is able to face the window now, its moonlit glow having lessened and the light in the room gone dull and flat. It is no longer the moonlight of his dream. Gone are the snowy woods and snarling wolves on the run.

Marie lifts her hand as her son rolls over, lowering it when he settles again to rest. There comes from her a soft sigh, then a shiver. The single thin blanket wrapped round her shoulders is not enough anymore. She tells herself that since her boy has settled down she'll soon be able to go back to her husband's bed two flights of stairs below.

Thomas purses his lips and shoots his breath spiralling upward. The wisps writhe in the moon's faint glow. One puff then another uncoils toward the sloping roof. Seen through the haze of exhale, the other mother, the heavenly one engraved on paper and suspended above the mantle, begins to wear a veil. The boy stays silent but mouths a few lines.

Virgin, Virgin, on the wall
See me here, sweet and small.

Mother Mary keep me warm.
Guard me from the other's storm.

The verse brings to his lips a contented smile. It's something he came up with a few weeks ago and he likes to say it from time to time. Because it's his, and his alone, he finds it more of a comfort than the routine prayers the church teaches everyone to say.

Thomas's mother, the real woman not the one on paper in the ghostly air, leans forward. She catches her son's full lips at the end of his verse, his face in a crinkle. Clearly, her boy is past the scary dream. She ceases caressing his shoulder. At once Thomas shifts to lie upon his back. He returns her gaze. Her face, the dark mouth and black eyes, is the one face he has always known. His sometime wish, never spoken to anyone, is that there would be but the two of them in this the house they share with Jean Pichon and sister Anne.

A cloud must blanket the unseen moon, because his mother's face goes dark. Thomas closes his eyes and lets his head roll away. Marie's seated body shifts, making ready to rise. First though, she rubs both hands together to generate warmth. Then she looks again at her son's face in profile, the angelic nose and the now shut eyes. How this boy needs her so. Yes, he needs time to grow up into a man, but he must be sheltered until that comes about.

The lift of Marie Pichon's body off Thomas's bed does not come right away. She stays despite the hour and the chill, the thin blanket pulled tighter still round her cold shoulders and back. Then all at once, with a breath sucked in, she stirs and straightens. She is up and across the room. Thomas opens his eyes to see. He catches the hesitation and the last look from the doorway. An instant later his mother's footfalls flutter down the stairs.

The moon emerges from hiding. Like before, when the nightmare was fresh, the celestial body lights up the room. To Thomas, now warmed, the brightness is a summons, no longer a threat. The running hounds and dark woods are all gone. He wants to see what's beyond the glass panes. He eases from beneath the weight of blankets, clothed in only a chemise that descends to just below his bony knees. Socked feet – he sleeps with them on – slide across the battered floor. Here and there, a few lifted slats click his advance. Thomas doesn't want the sound to carry below. His mother might think him a fraud. So he jumps over to the nearby rug and slip-slides the old oval woven mat across the remaining boards.

He propels himself over to the little mirror his mother gave him a few months ago. She said it was important always to present himself in the best possible light. How he tied back his hair in a queue, how he kept his hands and face clean, these things mattered. To become a priest he had to start looking and acting the part.

Thomas squints at the reflection of his face. Where the mercury has not faded and been scraped away on the glass, two large dark eyes stare back. He wonders what secrets those eyes might one day hold. He knows there's not much hidden behind his boyish face yet, but he aspires to change that as he goes along. Yes, he wishes that his face were leaner than it is now, and that maybe he had more than the one little thin line of a scar on his cheek beside his nose. He has to thank Jean-Chrysostome for that. Oh how Jean-Chrys used to love waving that stick of his, a stand-in for a real wooden sword. Thomas can't wait to get older and lose some of the softness and roundness he sees in his face, what his mother calls his innocent good looks. Father's mother, the nasty grande-mère who died last year, she put it differently. Thomas has to give the old biddy her due for that. She spoke the truth two Easters ago when she said to his father in a loud whisper in the kitchen, loud enough for Thomas to hear, "That son of yours, he's too pretty, you know. It's bad enough he has the temperament he does, but he almost looks like a girl." Thomas sticks out his tongue at the mirror. Yes, he would like what he hasn't yet got. He wants to look and act like a man.

The boy steps off the oval woven mat and steps over to the moonlit window. It surprises him, as it always does when he gets up at night, to see the town in something other than light of day. Vire on an especially moonlit night is anything but its ordinary self. The latest *couche* of snow, thin white with shadows of blue, gives crisp lines to rooftops and dormers. He quickly finds what before were just sounds: the wail of a west wind, in off distant ocean waters, and the moan of the tradesmen's swinging signs.

Vire by night, moon on high,
Yes I like and know not why

Thomas closes his eyes and squeezes them shut. He knows at once there is no point in keeping such an empty verse. "Tired," he mumbles. He blinks the lines away.

Left and right then up and down, Thomas scans the rooftops. His gaze comes to rest on the clock-tower gate. As always, it's the dominant shape from his window. It pleases the boy in a manner the rest of the town does not. It is so much taller than the jagged jumble. He likes its bulk and its shape, each of its segments set at a different angle atop the one below. The whole is a hulk of pleasing layered shapes. He especially likes how the high stretch on the vertical is ever so slightly turned to distinguish itself from the direction of the vaulted arch where it rests on the ground below.

A gust rattles the attic window, announcing a flotilla of dark clouds on their way from the west. Thomas hears fresh lines.

The crenellated walls are black tonight
And in the darkness each will find his sight.

Or should that be "his light"? Thomas shakes his head then makes a tentative nod. Yes, he'll change the ending to: "each will find his light." That decision brings a second and more decisive nod. There it is, right there in the verse, the answer to the question that's been on his mind. The one about whether he is good or bad. He has to find his light. He must jot the couplet down. He throws a glance toward the table where in the drawer he keeps his poetic pages out of sight. He's learned that it's important to get the words down right away. Verses come and go with a will all their own. It's only when he puts them down, on his razor-lifted paper taken from his father's sheath, that the lines really become his own. With the moon so bright he'll not even need to light a candle this night.

When Thomas pulls out the drawer to get his paper he spies the short length of blue silk he also keeps in there. He likes its feel when he has the itch. It allows him to make a spill into the chamber pot without even touching what he's not supposed to touch. He's in no mood for it right now, but maybe later on. He pushes the silk to the back of the drawer and picks up his sheets, then the inkpot and one of the two quills. He has to capture the lines he just heard.

April 1713

The boy rises early, before the others. He flexes his muscles with a stretch and a twitch, and gives passing thought to changing his chemise. He's worn it for two days, slept in it too, so he holds his arms above him and turns his head quickly to either side, sniffing the air. Not bad. There's a scent, but it's only his. It's a heaviness to the air that tells him he's doing fine. A couple of drops of orange water, a tiny bottle that is a recent gift from his mother, will add to and mask the natural perfume. Besides, the shirt is already warm to the body and therefore feels good. He'll leave well enough alone.

Thomas takes the breeches and socks off the nearby chair where he put them last night so dressing this morning would be quick. It takes but a moment to pull them on. Next he splashes his hands in the washbowl then brings up a bit of water to wet his face. There, he's done. He goes to the window to see what he should expect at this the peep of day.

No one is in the streets yet. There looks to be little or no wind. The sun is starting to do its work. The clock tower is a rosy glow. The slate shingles on the roofs across the way are gleaming. In the pale blue sky puffy white clouds are taking shape.

"As they should," Thomas says in affirmation.

The young man makes his way down the stairs carefully as he can. Silence does not come easily. Stealth from a growing body is difficult to find. Yet he knows he has to go slowly past his parents' room and next to theirs that of his sister too. The boards that squeak – the third and seventh steps – he avoids by stepping long and over. Nothing stirs from inside either of their closed doors as he stretches slowly past.

In the kitchen, which still carries the smell of onions, garlic and last evening's fire, when the chicken cooked on the turnspit, he bends to pick up his shoes. They are where he left them, hidden behind the pile of split firewood near the hearth. He will not slip them on until he's outside of the house, out on the stone steps that descend to the cobbled street.

Thomas goes to the heavy door that leads outdoors but his hand freezes on the latch. He turns to stare at a different door, the lightweight one that makes private a little space on the far side of the kitchen. The door does not look ajar, but he knows it likely is. He wedged a little wooden sliver into the mechanism yesterday afternoon. That was to prevent a complete closure and locking click. Shoes still in hand, Thomas moves toward the beckoning door, his steps long and carefully lifted across the kitchen's wooden floor.

He comes to the door of the servant's room without a squeak from the floorboards beneath his socked feet. He waits for the thumping in his chest to slow, for controlled breathing to come. His ears pick up the tick of a distant clock, the one in the salon, beyond the quiet kitchen. Yes, it's true, he thinks with a frown, tick-tock. Time does not wait. Hurry. Must.

The touch upon the jimmied door becomes a careful push. The lightweight wooden door opens a bit. He makes it wider still.

Thomas peers into the waiting shadow. He makes out the rosary hanging from a nail on the facing wooden wall. And there's the shelf with its basket of wool in billows and coils of blue and red. Nothing has changed since the last time he peeked in, nearly two weeks ago. His eyes shift to the chair, where a long white ribbon lies unfurled on the seat. That is new. Best for last, Thomas lowers his eyes to take in what he has really come to see.

Servanne is sprawled on her back. The last time he dared put a piece of wood in the door latch to her room, so he could steal a glance at her sleeping self, she was facing the wooden partition wall. Before that, a month earlier, she was on her stomach. Always is she draped by the same solitary cover, an old white blanket with the blue fleur-de-lys resting on her hips. Thomas thinks Servanne treasures the blanket because it carries the recollection of some lost love, a soldier or a tradesman who had lain with her and maybe come and gone the same night.

In truth, it is the only blanket Servanne has in her room. It is the only blanket Thomas's parents have given the seventeen-year-old who does the household cleaning. Some nights the cover is enough to keep her warm, sometimes it is not. Such practicalities do not occur to the thirteen-year-old boy peering at her through the haze of morning lust. All he can think of is her face and form. She has a body that curves like a serpent through his waking thoughts and sometimes turns up in his bedtime dreams. He's used his silken cloth more than a few times thinking of how he'd like to touch her intimate seat. He'd like nothing better than to join her right now beneath her blanket frayed and worn.

One arm, the left, rests on the bolster, close to Servanne's face; the other is out of sight. Her hair seems darker than usual to Thomas in the room's dim light. It is thick and undone, and looks to be the colour of his mother's. He blinks away the resemblance. The servant's face is pretty, full and puffy at this hour, a sleeper's look. Her smell, or rather the smell of the room, is the scent of morning. No, Thomas corrects himself as he looks on. The scent he's picking up is coming from the bundle of lavender hanging from a string above her bed.

He holds his breath as he pulls Servanne's door back to nearly shut. He has other fish to fry this morning and scurries across the kitchen floor. A click, a pull, a step and he is out of the house, the door pulled shut behind. Only now, safely out, does Thomas fully exhale. He lays his shoes upon the top step, slips them on then leaps to the cobbles. He is away.

The leather soles of Thomas's shoes slap through Vire's *enclos*, the air heavy with the weighted moisture of the rainy night just past. He avoids the channel in the centre of the street, containing as it does the late-night emptying of dozens of chamber pots from all along the street. Some turds are always worse than others. He wants to look somewhere else, and keep his nose high and away, but as he hurries along it's hard not to glance down at the stinking mess people cast away.

His head is full of purpose. He knows just where he's going and why. He follows the familiar route, though it feels anything but ordinary at this time of day. A peal of bells begins from one of the cloistered orders. It's *lauds*, or no, maybe *prime*. It depends on the hour. It is a ringing reminder of why he no longer wants to be a monk or priest. Whichever call to prayer it is, down the rue du Pont Thomas goes, a street that at the moment he has all to himself.

He moves swiftly under the half-timbered overhangs of the buildings of the *enclos*. Every so often as he goes along he reaches out to touch a surface as he passes it by. It's a habit he has, though he does not know he does it. He could not say why if ever anyone pointed it out and asked point blank. It's just something that makes him feel at ease, reassured. He likes to make contact with the physical world around him as he goes by. Thomas brushes his hand lightly along the top of the bright red geraniums in the planter box of one house and next touches the dark heavy wood that frames the house on the corner. There's a cart up ahead, one left out in the street overnight. He'll tap that as he goes by as well.

The morning is warmer than he thought it would be. The dark stains and tiny puddles on the cobbles from last night's downpour will be gone by the time everyone else in Vire is up. The thought of all those risings makes Thomas pick up his pace. It won't be long before the town begins to stir, the masters in their beds and the servants at their chores.

The fountain of Esmangard comes into view. After the fountain comes the church where he is bound.

—

The twin doors are heavy. Of course they are, being so huge. Thomas admires the figures carved in wood. Their names he doesn't know, but they are holy heroes from the Bible, from some story about long ago. Each figure is kept from the others by dividing lines made up of long, thin crosses finely traced atop the wood. Thomas pulls hard to open the door on the left. He steps over the ankle-high wooden threshold and quickly pulls the door to close behind him. He stays put for six long breaths as he waits for the inside darkness to lighten a little, then takes two steps and reaches for the next door. This small interior door he imagines comes from a faraway forest, across an ocean or two. Brazil, he thinks. He has seen an engraving of some of their feathered Indians' visit to France. Tupinamba was their name, if he recalls. He remembers practicing pronouncing the name many times so he could say it right for the brother who taught him geography in school.

Thomas takes another breath and makes the next step, the one that carries him through the smaller doorway and within.

The air on the other side is much colder than outdoors. It tastes of age and dust. No surprise that, for it is exactly the suffocating quality of the church that he savours. Where once he believed everything the priests and the brothers told him, he no longer does. Oh some of it still sounds right, but not all. Nonetheless, he loves the smell of his Roman and Catholic apostolic faith and the feeling of completeness it brings.

Thomas swings left, in front of the baptistery. Pale shafts of light from unseen windows on high, faint lunettes, do their best to brighten the gloom. Thomas lifts his gaze to the immense arches that bear the weight of the upper reaches of the church, up where the spire points to heaven. Great round pillars, five times the girth of the boy, plunge to the level of the faithful. His shoes slap softly on the stone floor as he walks over the great slabs. Here and there the giant stones underfoot show the hollowing wear of all those who have walked in the church since before long ago.

When he was younger, Thomas recalls as he hurries deeper into the church, stepping from the central aisle over into the right transept, his mother once told him that this particular church – le Saint-Thomas – was named after him. Yes, *him,* her son, *her* Thomas. Yes, it's true. *He,* little Thomas Pichon, he is the Thomas the church's builders had in mind. They were leaving the Vire market at the time, when she told him that. He remembers it clearly. She had just purchased a dozen fresh plums. They were in her market basket beneath a linen cloth. He'd helped her pick them out.

"And," Marie said as she placed a hand atop her son's head, picturing him as the tall handsome priest he was sure one day to become, "that is why you have to be especially good. Do you understand that Thomas, *my* Thomas? This is *your* church."

Thomas thinks he nodded that he did understand, that of course he was taking his mother at her word. Is that not what mothers are to their boys: the source of every truth? So Vire's Saint-Thomas was named after him. He recalls that she kissed him on his cheek and then upon the brow. A week later, in catechism class, Thomas repeated what his mother told him, that the big church was named after him. There was a pause and a strange look came over Father Alexis's face. Then the priest slapped Thomas hard across the cheek.

Thomas did not tell his mother what happened, for fear she'd make a scene. Better take the slap, he figured, keeping the correction to her lie all to himself. But ever since that slap, he's been thinking his mother's idea of him becoming a priest is not for him. The church, however, the Saint-Thomas itself, is still a place he loves. He loves its darkness, its height and most of all its smell. Its scent is time itself. And if he gets up early enough on some mornings, he can have the place all to himself.

Thomas skirts another mammoth pillar. It never fails to amaze him how the aroma in Saint-Thomas is always the same, no matter the hour, the day or the season. Its air is always thick, filled with the weight of centuries. The boy wonders if it's that way to suffocate the faithless. Or perhaps to inspire its shaky believers, people like himself.

"Both," he mutters, nodding agreement.

"Dry as death," his father once said, on one of the rare occasions he actually came into Saint-Thomas. This coming weekend will be another such time, for a mortal sin it would be for anyone, men included, not to make the Easter communion. Anne will be on Father's right, no doubt, with Mother on the man's left. Thomas will be out on the end at his mother's distant side.

His eyes go to the closest of the Stations of the Cross, the one with the spear and sponge. Could his father be a heretic, Thomas wonders? Father Alexis has warned the boys, more than once, about the dangerous cult that calls itself reformed and Protestant. It survives in pockets here and there in Normandy, says the good father. "Despite the best efforts of the Church to reach them. We have an obligation to re-educate them. Or else." Father Alexis occasionally implores the boys to come forward if they suspect anyone of such errors. And the good father, shaking his finger at Thomas and the other boys, lets them know that if they keep quiet about heretics then it will be *their own* souls at risk.

Thomas gives a nervous twitch and glances down to the stone floor. He wonders whether he should tell his parish father the doubts he has about his family father, the cloth merchant Jean Pichon? But Thomas blinks the thought away as quickly as it comes. He starts to move again. After all, it is Jean Pichon is it not, who puts the roof over his and his mother's heads? Food on their table too. Not as good a roof as he should or could and not as varied a diet as he might, but still, it's better than no roof and no food at all. If Father Alexis were to discover and punish Jean Pichon as the heretical non-believer he likely is, it would only be worse for Thomas and his mother. And for Anne as well.

Things used to be better. That was before the family suffered at the hands of Renaud Brouard, sieur de La Motte. What exactly went wrong Thomas doesn't know, other than that his father spent a week in prison and lost a great deal of money as a result of trying to take on La Motte, the forever mayor of Vire who is also the judge of the bailliage court and the head of police. There's the lesson of an example in this. His father's mistake of trying to bring down someone above him Thomas vows not to repeat. Why couldn't his father see it for himself? That it's better to be *with* rather than *against* authority?

Thomas shakes his head to clear the slate and glances up, farther along the transept. This time it's a large painting that captures his gaze. A canvas as dark as it is huge. He comes to a halt and leans a shoulder against the closest pillar. The nuances of the tableau – the skull in one corner and the hourglass in another – do not interest him, not at all. He is taken instead by the crazed look on the saint's face, the body cloaked in a frayed brown habit and the eyes burning with some distant vision. Some victory off the canvas is clearly foretold. The chin is set and the black-red lips delight in exultation. The dog represents fidelity, Thomas knows that much, while the snake underfoot means temptation. The painted saint waves a sword, long and leaden. Thomas imagines he could be someone to do the same.

He continues on and in a few paces slips into a shadow. This is it, the favoured spot, the reason he has come. He looks round the little chapel. He has to make sure no one else is near, no one else is in sight. He is, as far as he can tell, alone. Except for the sacristan, of course, whose half-crippled scuff Thomas hears as a distant stirring off in the apse or over in the nave. He is fairly certain the sacristan doesn't even know that he is in the church. That's the idea. Thomas will have his private moment.

He comes as close as he can get to the base of the pedestal. She stands above him, aloof and cloaked in blue. The red skirt hangs in folds, stopping just above bare feet in sandals. At her waist and to her chest she holds the child, fat and naked in her arms. Her head is bowed, slender hands cherishing the infant, the only son she'll ever have. Thomas drops to his knees. He clasps his fingers and says the words he has come to say, and whispers them in a hush.

Virgin, Virgin, close and near,
Wrap me tight, calm my fear.

He seeks the heavenly mother's eyes. They're aslant again, a gaze not quite his way. He understands she's but a statue yet he yearns for her just the same. It isn't long before he feels his knees grow numb. This is what he needs; it's why he's come, the longed-for swirl and spin. His body sinks into the stone slab and at once he feels the rise. His eyes turn up in what has become his own version of holy prayer.

A hand moves along the line of her carved form, touching the cloak and hood that are coloured in shades of blue. The ecru chemise slips away. Her skin goes flush and warm, lips and cheeks run soft. The mother's eyes shift his way. There is a hint of smile. There comes a hand, a light brush under chin, a thumb that traces the firm line of jaw. She strokes his face with the back of her hand, then with the front. His child's face twists to wanted touch. The words come in spurts.

Comes an opening,
the chemise in folds gives up.

Nose to silken skin,
fingers curl and cup.

Veins faint, blue coursing,
a babe begins to sup.

The sun reaches into the sky, high enough to send its first rays through the lower windows of Saint-Thomas. Blue, green and crimson – the glazier's godly colours – splay across the granite floor. It is a quiet glow.

Thomas makes to stand. He hears the sacristan's footfalls coming close. It's time for first Mass, on this a holy day. He must away.

Summer 1713

The streets are awake. Hawk and cry, merchants shout their calls. It's market day and the people who work with their hands have practical matters on their minds. They are on their way to fill their separate needs: bread and vegetables, fruit and fish, gossip and chat. A jabber of voices swells around Thomas, along with a rumble of wheels on cobbles. Thomas closes his eyes for just an instant. He does not much care for the excessively sweaty perfume of those who toil more than he does, those who are brushing past him on both sides. He is after all a merchant's son, a cloth merchant's son at that. Not as high a rank among the trades as some others in the town, but nonetheless higher than all the people sweeping past him in this lot. And yes, Thomas admits he likely has his own smell, yet he covers it with rosewater, orange water or some other scent. At the very least, he doesn't smell like a goat. Thomas takes a shallow breath, more exhale than inhale.

He steps over to the side of the street. He recognizes many of these people, the other Virois. He doesn't know all their names, not in every case, but he can place their faces and their clothes and which occupation they practice. What he would give to live in a place where he would not know everyone and fewer still would know him in return. His future is unknown, as the future must be, but he's certain it won't unfold at this market or in Vire, or maybe not in Normandy at all. Just to show the world a little of this inner thought, Thomas decides to strike a pose. He imagines it to be the stance of a painter of note. He's too young still to see the absurdity of such pretense. He has none of the painter's tools or in truth the slightest aspiration to that profession. If there is an art that he does see as maybe being within his grasp, it would be the scribbler's toil. When Father Alexis circled some phrases Thomas had used on a history essay about Henri IV and wrote in the margin "Very well done," it made Thomas's chest puff out. It also made him think he had the gift to write. So, to let the smelly market people know that he is not like them, he puts hand to chin like he might be a sculpture. Then he adjusts his tricorn hat to give it first a jaunty then a rakish tilt. Thomas imagines he makes a pretty picture, someone far beyond his thirteen years.

He swivels his head, studying the way the ground slopes slightly down from where he's standing to the tree-lined market square below. A gentle grade, he observes, nodding as if he's come up with something new. Ahead, the packed earth of the square is dotted with what he guesses must be nearly a hundred awnings over an equal number of rolled-in carts. The rows appear ordered from his would-be artist's distance, and the square is filling with people. He too will descend to be among them soon enough. He has come to get some cherries, but he will wait a little bit.

Frozen in his foolish pose, Thomas does not hear them coming, the lads who are pointing at him and laughing at his awkward fake artist stance. The sudden whack on the back of his head buckles his knees and sends the tricorn flying.

"Oh my, lost your hat?"

The words, like the blow to the head, come from behind. Thomas spins round and finds a laughing face. It's the boy everyone calls Vinaigre. Thomas knows Vinaigre well enough. They were in the same catechism class a year or so ago. Sometimes they sat side by side. When they did, Thomas liked to correct or improve on Vinaigre's answers. Vinaigre didn't like it much but Father Alexis did, which is why Thomas kept it up. Vinaigre would breathe heavily out his nose whenever Thomas spoke up. Now when they walk by each other in the streets of Vire, if Vinagire doesn't give him a snub then it's a glare. Until now that is. Beside Vinaigre stands some other fellow who has his hands in his pockets and a stupid grin on his face. The grinning fellow is nearly a head taller than Vinaigre, who is already taller than Thomas.

Vinaigre and his friend come quickly forward, the one pinning his arms and the other leg-tripping Thomas to the ground.

"Tripped up?" says Vinaigre. "Or I suppose, it's *down* in your case." Vinaigre gestures with his hands like he's doing some kind of conjuring trick before placing them akimbo on his hips.

Thomas looks up at the two of them with a blank expression on his face. He rises to stand again, as slowly as he can, and as he does he feels his fingers forming into fists. He'd like to knock the triumphant smile clear off Vinaigre's face.

Vinaigre notices Thomas's reaction with an expression of mock fear. Then he lowers his arms to his sides and lifts and bobs his chin in a way that Thomas takes to mean "come closer and take a swing." Angered though he is, Thomas is not a fool. These two lads would make short work of him. He makes his fists uncurl. Next he finds an aloof look to put upon his face. He bends down to pick up his hat.

"Wind catch your hat?" Vinaigre taunts.

"Guess so," Thomas says.

He recalls that the only fight he has been in was nothing to brag about. The surgeon's son, Guillaume, jumped on his back as he was going down the rue du Pont with Jean-Chrysostome. The two friends were on their way to the *collège* for Latin class. Thomas responded to the sudden weight on his back – the arrival of the slender Guillaume – by bending low. The poor thing rolled right over Thomas, cracking his head on the cobbles. Face contorted, Guillaume got up and smashed Thomas in the guts then full in the mouth. Thomas stayed doubled over until Jean-Chrysostome held Guillaume at a distance and convinced the surgeon's son that the fight was done. Thinking of that episode, Thomas decides that this little knocked-hat incident with Vinaigre is not worth a fresh drubbing.

"Yeah, guess so," Thomas repeats. He whacks his hat against his thigh to rid it of any dust it may have picked up. He floats a forced smile, though it comes out more like a grimace than he can control.

"That's right," says Vinaigre. His chin is upraised as if he has just outwitted Thomas. "You guess so. Be more careful next time, right?"

Thomas nods but right away pretends he has better things to do. He shifts his gaze to the open street that leads down the incline to the market area below. He straightens his posture then re-positions the tricorn. He pulls it down tight and snug. No more jaunty angle for him.

Yet against his own thinking, he feels his chest puff out. His mouth opens to say something to Vinaigre. Something, anything. Yet nothing comes. So Thomas does the only thing he can: he spins and shows his back. He hopes the ruffians will not strike again, not at the tricorn nor at the vulnerable body below. Just in case, he braces for the blow should it come. The end result is that Thomas moves something like a scarecrow as he stiff-walks away. He would laugh to see himself so awkward and afraid, but happily he is spared any such sight.

—

Thomas tries not to look longer or more frequently than he should. An occasional glance across the aisle in the girl's direction is all he allows. He has to keep his observations within what he imagines his mother will think normal. They are after all in church and not at the fountain of Esmangard or in the market square.

Yet Thomas cannot resist. He cannot help but gaze and then gaze again at the girl seated across the aisle. Her row is only one row in front of his, a mere ten feet away. And most of the distance is open aisle.

Thomas pictures them with their arms around each other, the two of them wrestling across the stone floor of the church after the service has ended and everyone emptied out. They would knock the chairs this way and that as they rolled about.

Wisps of hair are peeking from beneath her Brussels cap. The dark green material of her dress is showing through the lace shawl that hugs her shoulders tight. When she inclines her head to listen to the priest or to offer the appropriate prayerful reply, the girl's neck is as slender as … Thomas searches for the right word. It does not quickly come.

From time to time the object of Thomas's attention turns his way, a fleeting backward glance. She pretends to be oblivious to his gaze, but he likes the look of her dark brown eyes, wide mouth and defined nose. He also likes the faraway expression on her face. He imagines she bathes in warm milk to make her skin look like cream.

If his mother were to catch him staring and ask him what it is he's looking at – Thomas has thought about this – he will say that he is admiring the girl across the aisle, that he's inspired by her devoted look. It's the simple truth, only explained in a mother's way. The deeper truth is that what's stirring in Thomas is not an admiration of piety but something else, something between his legs. It occurs to him that he would like to run his piece of silk along his urge. Thomas shifts in his seat at the thought.

"Stop it," his mother hisses, loud enough to make the woman two rows ahead noticeably flinch. "Stop it now," Marie repeats in a lowered voice. This time her hand squeezes the boy's knee to make up for the missing volume of her voice.

"What?" mutters Thomas, feeling the pinch.

His voice carries. Heads turn, including that of the woman two rows up. She takes the vocal disturbance as permission to turn full round. What she sees is an errant lad with a startled face who has done something wrong, something for which his mother has correctly inflicted a bit of pain. Before she turns back to face the front of the church the unknown woman sends an acknowledging nod to Thomas's mother. She wants to let Marie know that whatever she has done to the boy she approves and understands.

"Why? It's nothing," whispers Thomas leaning his mother's way. His face has turned crimson, and he clasps his hands across his lap to hide what's bulging, the buttons rising from his breeches.

The mother glances down and sees what her son is doing. Her head moves left and right as she gives the boy a withering, scornful look. Thomas, poor Thomas, wishes he were dead.

The drone from the front of the church continues, a mumbled Latin said too faintly and too fast for Thomas to follow, if he were the least bit inclined. Which he is not. It strikes him that the priest is in a rush. He must want the service over and done and him on his way to somewhere else. Thomas can understand that and wishes the priest would run through the words even faster than he is.

It is not long, not as long as he wants to hold back, before Thomas steals a fresh glance at the girl across the aisle. She and her slender neck and wisps of hair through the Brussels cap are still there.

To make time pass until the service is over, Thomas comes up with something new. He concentrates on his breathing, exhaling as much as he can before he slowly brings in the air that is new. His mother hears the long and loud ins and outs. She shakes her head but leaves him be. Her son's huffing is better than his staring at a girl and his bulging buttons. Marie Pichon closes her eyes in prayer.

It's only when there's a complete halt in the priest's words, when the cleric is climbing the steps up to the pulpit, that Thomas allows himself a stretch of the arms and gives his upper body just the slight turn it needs to take a fresh look in the girl's direction. Yes, she's still there, with her face uplifted in some sort of wondrous reverie.

"Thomas," comes a fierce whisper, followed by a sharp elbow to his ribs.

Thomas snaps his attention back to the front of the church, where the priest is now atop the pulpit, gazing wordlessly out to the congregation as a prelude to what he is about to say. The sermon begins, something about sheep that are lost and the shepherd who must go and save them from themselves. It is not long before Thomas sends his eyes down to his shoes and then lower still to the great slab of scuffed stone beneath his feet. Marie lets him be but wonders if this service will ever end.

Thomas, keeping his head bent low staring at the floor, goes over what little he knows about the girl a few body lengths away. He's seen her three times in church, yet nowhere else in town. He's learned that her Christian name is Angélique and the family name Tyrell, or maybe it's Tirell. He's not seen it written. But it sounds English either way, and that makes him smile. In Vire, of any name that's not been there for two hundred years or more people say the bearers have come from away. And away, with few exceptions, means England. The cursed godless land. For little Vire, the hilltop town of Thomas's birth, was once under the not-so-distant enemy's sway. English dogs, English pigs, English everything else. Well, who cares, thinks Thomas. He's feeling the pressure re-emerge in his breeches. He darts another look at the girl. She is dark and slender and holds herself erect. By the way she dresses and carries herself he guesses that she comes from a family background much better than his own, regardless of any English roots the family might have. Thomas goes back to staring at his shoes as they scuff the floor.

An audible sigh escapes Thomas's lips, which draws a curled-lip stare from Mother and a turnaround scowl from the woman two rows ahead. Thomas lifts his shoulders as his apology. He sees their heads shake left then right. He lifts a hand to hide the smile. Too late he hears a rustle, the sound of moving fabric. A moving shape, a darkening blur, passes on his left. Thomas twists to see. A bewildered look takes over his face. The pious Angélique Tyrell has up and gone, left the church before even the sermon or the service has come to an end. Thomas finds his feet and lifts his body to follow after.

"Sit. Sit down," fills his ears. The embarrassed mother's hand is pinching like a dog just above his knee.

Thomas sags. He does as he is bid. The opportunity is lost. He was going to give chase. Outside the church, his hand upon Angélique Tyrell's outstretched arm, gazing into her eyes, he was going speak to the girl. Instead, he kicks the floor. And kicks it again. Down the day. Down the mother and down the church as well. The opportunity, the day and maybe Thomas's entire life are ruined.

—

The cumulus clouds hurtle cross the sky, headlong into evening. One after another, each large and puffy, they follow a course to the west, over the bocage and on into what lies beyond. On the earth below, in grey and ancient cobbled Vire, the winds on high have little effect. In the walled town there is but the appearance of a breeze. Few leaves stir. The afternoon air does not move so much as it clings. The time is heavy, breathing golden warmth.

Thomas and Jean-Chrysostome lead each other out through the gate on the west side of town and along a trail that takes them to the crest of a hill, a dominant hill that overlooks the river. It's a redoubtable rise, steep and narrow. Thomas twists to face the trees ahead: chestnuts planted in parallel rows back when he was a little boy. He tries to follow the intersecting lines of their branches as the young trees angle upward. He pauses to study the clusters; tiny and tender green pods stand erect on stems. Jean-Chrysostome, known to Thomas as Jean-Chrys, follows the line of his friend's glance.

"Let's not be late, all right? It's surely getting on for four. We don't have time to linger."

"Suppose not. Yet it is *full*, is it not?" Thomas stretches the one word so that it lingers in his mouth. "The day, I mean."

"Yeah, come on. We'll be late." Jean-Chrys tugs on his friend's shoulder.

The two boys have come to the hill at the edge of their town for a reason. They're to meet a tall thin lad, an apprentice to the apothecary, who says he knows a way into the underground. The underground is a word and a place that makes the boys' hearts race. Thomas and Jean-Chrys have been hearing about Vire's subterranean passages as long as they can remember.

"The tunnels," an older boy once said to Thomas, "they're like heaven and hell." Thomas felt his neck spring back at such words. "Yeah," the fellow continued, unafraid of what lightning might next strike him dead, "because no one knows if they really exist." He winked at Thomas and chuckled like he'd made a clever joke. Thomas said nothing, but he stepped back from the blasphemous boy, just in case. Thinking about it later, Thomas agreed that heaven had to be questionable. It really did. How could any place have everything for everyone who ended up there? It was too good to be true. But hell on the other hand, well there was no doubt in his heart that it was real. Because there was so much wrong that people did that they deserved to answer for. Be punished for. Yes, hell was real, and it was hot, hotter than any day he'd ever sweated through. The devil's agents were going to give sharp pricks and pains to all the sinners, especially on their things. Thomas knew that because his thing did what it wanted, no matter how much he ignored it or tried to make it settle down. Even praying at night, kneeling on the floor by his bed, the disobedient thing wouldn't rest. Well, Thomas didn't want to go to hell. He wouldn't be able to stand the inferno. Or the pricking of his thing. He could not imagine how much that would hurt.

Thomas blinks away the troubling thoughts and reaches out to give a gentle shove to his friend Jean-Chrys. On this August afternoon, striding under the chestnut trees on their way to meet the apprentice to the apothecary, Thomas has no reason to think of hell. Instead, he shifts his focus to meeting this fellow who will be their guide to a half-whispered other world. That the apprentice is a stranger and tall, an older boy to boot, means that maybe just maybe he knows what he says he does.

According to the story repeated to Thomas, the apprentice told Jean-Chrys that he's already been underneath, down where the air is cold and damp. He says there are dark passages that twist and turn beneath Vire's green hill. He wouldn't tell Jean-Chrys where the entrance is, only that it was shrouded in thick cover. He'd gone inside but only about ten paces. He said he was barely able to squeeze through the outer rubble, and he tore his breeches pushing past. After that the passage opens up, but he could go no farther without a lantern. What he could tell was that the passage was tall enough, at least in the early part, to stand upright. Oh, and that the walls on either side were fieldstone, rough and wet. The floor was packed earth; it stuck to his shoes. All he could do in the blackness was listen to the sound of trickling water somewhere farther on.

Jean-Chrys relayed these bits to Thomas. Ever since, the idea of going inside the earth, down into the subterranes, has coiled through Thomas's mind. It's been a long wait, seven days, but this Sunday afternoon he finally gets to see for himself. He's guessing that the opening is going to be up on the ridge, hidden somewhere in the tumbled jumble of ruins of the ancient château, ordered destroyed by Cardinal Richelieu a hundred years before.

"He'd better still be there," says Jean-Chrys, wiping the sweat off his brow with the back of his hand. "He said he wouldn't wait past four. And it's almost four."

"Relax, will you? He'll be there. Unless…" Thomas picks up his pace with the introduction of doubt.

"Unless what?" Jean-Chrys halts their advance with a hand to Thomas's chest. "Unless I fell for a story? Is that it?"

"Didn't say that."

"Didn't have to."

The boys begin their march once more, even faster than before. Each feels trickles of sweat on the lower back and under the arms. It was a quarter of four on the clock-tower gate as they passed under it and that was a good ways back.

"Where do you think they'll lead?" Jean-Chrysostome nearly pants the words.

Thomas steals a breath before he replies. He has been thinking about this the entire week of wait. "A bishop, can't remember which one, is said to have erected them."

Jean-Chrys shakes his head.

"What?"

"You don't *erect* tunnels. You *dig* them."

Thomas grimaces at the correction. Yes, he chose the wrong word. He reaches round to rub his chemise hard against his lower back to absorb some of the sweat. "All right, a bishop *built* the tunnels so he could get away if Protestants ever besieged Vire."

"Who told you that?" says Jean-Chrysostome. "Father Alexis? 'Oh, Thomas, your eyes are so brown. You'll be with us one day. You'll be a wonderful priest'."

Thomas gives his friend a jab in the ribs with his elbow. He hates it when Jean-Chrys teases him about becoming a priest and being a favourite of Father Alexis. "He didn't say any such thing," begins Thomas, but he is right away cut off.

"There, he's there!" Jean-Chrys shouts. Then he catches himself and tries to remove some of the excitement from his voice. "The apprentice," he continues in a more controlled manner. He is pointing up ahead. "He's there. By the *donjon*."

Thomas sees what his friend has spotted first. A tall, thin lad, the apothecary's apprentice apparently, standing in front of the dense thicket that covers the *donjon*. Well, by what local people call the *donjon*. In truth, it's a heap of stones, ruins masked by bush and weed. Some dim memory of the long-ago fortification lives on in Vire so everyone still calls what is really rubble "the *donjon*."

The apprentice is not by himself. Two other boys are sitting nearby, atop the rubble, the boredom of their waiting evident in their poses. They straighten when they spot Thomas and Jean-Chrys coming out of the shadows of the trees. The smile of anticipation on Thomas's face disappears when he recognizes one of the two boys waiting with the apprentice. It's Vinaigre.

"Shit," mutters Thomas, breaking stride and slowing down.

"Hey," yells Vinaigre, recognizing Thomas. His eyes spin with delight. "It's the children's crusade."

Hoots greet the joke like a door slamming in Thomas's face. There is nothing worse than laughter at his expense.

Somewhere overhead a cloud covers the sun, dimming the colours of the day. Halftones replace sharp shadows. A flutter of starlings comes to ground behind the two boys. The birds sound their cry as they twist and angle their heads at Thomas and Jean-Chrys. Then they reclaim the air, the dismissing skirr of their wings filling the boys' ears.

Thomas has lost his mood. For a week he pictured this adventure and it was not like this. There was not to be so many, there was no Vinaigre. Thomas's legs have weights tied to them as he forces himself to close the distance with the others. The five boys exchange handshakes all round, though in truth it is really an exchange of nasty grips with each lad trying to impress and maybe hurt another.

"So," says Vinaigre, his grin resembling a weapon. The weapon is aimed at Thomas.

"So," says Thomas, resigned to take whatever is to come.

"So," says the apprentice to the apothecary, frowning at Vinaigre and Thomas, who clearly have some kind of bad history between them. "So," the apprentice continues, drawing up to his full height, "we … we're … we're all here."

The apprentice's stuttering brings raised eyebrows and exchanged looks. This is their leader? This is the one to get us underground? Thomas glares at Jean-Chrys. The eyes ask: why didn't you tell me the apprentice can hardly talk?

The apprentice sets off quickly to the left, and Vinaigre steps in right behind him. He raises his elbows to protect what is now his, second in command. He is followed in turn by his friend, Pierre, who is as large an oaf in Thomas's mind, since any friend of Vinaigre's is no friend of his. Thomas notices that

Pierre has a large mole on his cheek near his left ear. That entitles him to a different name. He becomes the lout with the mole. Jean-Chrys and Thomas follow in fourth and fifth positions of what is a column. In the silence of the next half-minute, the apprentice leads the boys through the shadows of overhanging trees to the far end of the ridge. They stop where there's a small clearing near a thicket. Suddenly, as if corks have been removed, there is an outburst of mutter and mumble. Not a word of the talk, however, is about the underground. Vinaigre's friend, the lout with the mole, leans forward to tell the others about the time he was in a wooded spot much like where they are right now. He was with a cracker girl. She let him put his hand under her skirt.

"Right up. Touched her seat and the scratch itself."

Thomas's and Jean-Chrys's heads snap back.

Vinaigre jumps in with a tale. He says he once got down on his knees and put his head up under a skirt. She said it would be all right so long as he didn't touch the cunny. So she held on to his two hands outside of her skirt to make sure. Vinaigre says he put his nose against the bristles. He raises his right hand, as if he were swearing an oath.

"What was it like?" asks Jean-Chrys.

"Roquefort," says Vinaigre. Everyone laughs in relief.

The leader, the apothecary's apprentice, is next. Thomas leans in to hear what he's going to say. When he leans closer he picks up a sharp odour of urine off Vinaigre, which makes him pull back. Thomas leans instead toward Jean-Chysostome. Jean-Chrys's smell is better, merely a hint of fresh sweat.

The apprentice knows he has to hurry with his story. His leadership of the group is on the line. So he goes as quickly as he can, jumping from words he can't handle to ones he can.

"One day … be-behind … the fo-fo-forge … demi-loaf … fresh it was … g-g-g-girl … wa … wa … wanted … a bite … … ca-came here, right here … she-she … ru-rubbed … my-my thing."

Four faces are trying to follow. No one is really sure what the fellow is saying.

"Sp- sp- spilled it." He is pointing to a spot to everyone's left. Four heads turn to follow the finger's lead. "Sh-she sp- spilled me there."

There is no comment, no talk, no laughter either. Everyone has understood. There is only silence and lowered eyes. And a subtle shift of five bodies away from the spot where the apprentice says he or the girl spilled his thing.

Whether or not the apprentice's story is true, or for that matter the tales from the lout and Vinaigre that preceded it, no one knows or cares. It's the idea that counts, for these are lads whose loins often rule their heads. Thomas and Jean-Chrys dart looks at each other. Their own little soldiers grew in warmth and size as they listened to the others talk, yet now that it's their turn to talk they can feel them shrinking back. The two boys exchange a second, worried look. Neither has a story about girls they've seen or known and no inventions come to mind. Thomas thinks of Servanne and Angélique Tyrell, but what kind of stories are they? So he fakes a yawn and looks up to the trees. Jean-Chrys's escape is to make as if he has to walk around for a minute, tugging at breeches that are now a bit too tight.

"We going underground or not?" Vinaigre raises both arms in impatience.

The gesture and the look on Vinaigre's face are a challenge. The apprentice recognizes that right away. Either he makes good on his promise to lead them into the subterranes or else Vinaigre is in charge.

"Ri- right." The apprentice's voice rises to meet Vinaigre's assumption of the lead. "Le- let's go."

—

"Phew," says one of the boys. The others follow with their own muttered sounds, all meaning the same thing.

The air inside is foul. Damp and heavy it pushes up their noses, the darkness making it stronger than it ever would be in light. It's not possible to put a name on it except to say that it stinks. Not of sweat or shit or animals, the way a street or yard can stink, but of some much oozier scent of the earth and ground itself. It's as if the mud and leaves and who knows what else have all merged in the underground and come to form a single smell. Yet bad as it is, it is not a smell that makes the boys reconsider what they are about. Hands across mouths and noses, they advance into the dark unknown that lies ahead. Thomas keeps his right arm and hand extended as he goes forward. He caresses the stones of the wall with every second step.

All Thomas can see in front of him are the back of Jean-Chrys's head and his shoulders, and not much of either. The only light source is the candle lantern held waist high by the leader at the front of the trudging procession. By the time its dim light makes it back to Thomas it is merely a faint amber glow. It is as if everyone is lit by an orange melon, if melons could illuminate.

The five boys are in the same positions they were in when they took turns squeezing through the narrow opening. Thomas is still in last. And with the flickering glow of the candle being the only light there is, everyone stays in place. No one wants to push and scramble. If the light were to go out, they'd … well, no one wants that.

The amber glow splays mostly forward and up, so only the leader really sees where they're going and even for him it's not as much as he'd like. The apprentice can make out only that their way ahead is surrounded on three sides by looming rock and stone, and that it's packed earth down where they trod. Like Thomas, but much less often, the other boys reach out to touch the stones jutting at them left, right and overhead. The touches are to calm the inner doubts. By touching and lightly pushing off, hands and fingers tell the rocks that the boys are expecting to come back out the same way they're now going in.

Here and there a few rocks shine in the dim lantern's glow. That's when the lantern light catches wetness running over a surface. The farther the boys go, the less the subterrane appears to be a man-cut tunnel. Only the entrance was chiselled and burrowed. That was obvious by the pits and grooves and drill holes in some rocks. Soon enough, however, it is clear that only the entrance shows evidence of the work of man. Farther in there are only long flat beds of upturned rocks, random in shape and size and each with its own band of colour.

The passage where the boys are treading narrows and widens at its whim. It is some natural fissure. So close do the dimly lit stones sometimes project and descend that the boys are required more frequently to duck and bend as they move along. Thomas mulls if he's the only one wondering if it's wise to keep going into this, a stinking, wet and buried world.

"Oh," comes a moan an instant after there's a thud.

"What?" Jean-Chrys's voice wavers. The other boys hear the worry.

The candle lantern halts up front and the boys following behind trudge to a stop. Thomas makes out that the lout with the mole, the tallest of the five, is rubbing his head with his hand. He must have hit the roof. Thomas gives him credit for not crying out in fear or in pain.

"You cut, Pierre?" Vinaigre leans in to study his friend's forehead.

Pierre examines the tips of his fingers. "No, guess not."

"Bend lower next time, bean pole," says Vinaigre. Then after a pause, speaking now to the apprentice holding the lantern: "Want me to take the lead? Just for a while?"

Thomas does not hear the reply, but the lantern does not change hands. It begins to move again with the apprentice still in front. The only sound Thomas can discern above the trudge is a trickle of water. It's not like there's a river or a stream. No, there are a hundred tiny drips all around. There must be seams or cracks with water coming in from all over, Thomas decides. He doesn't want to hear such noises. The wet pulse of whatever it is that resides beneath the earth is a troubling sound. Within his chest it feels like there's a hand starting to squeeze hard. The trickle of water gets louder.

"Far enough," comes a breathless voice.

Thomas recognizes that it's Jean-Chrys. His voice is far from his normal one. It's thin and wobbly, as if Jean-Chrys were trembling. Thomas reaches out to touch his friend. Yes, Jean-Chrys is aquiver.

"Time to go back." Jean-Chrys is speaking louder. The voice almost shrill.

The line of boys shuffles to a halt. The three up front crane over their shoulders. In the amber glow Thomas makes out three pinched faces.

"And who said that?" taunts Vinaigre. "You, I bet." His eyes fix on Thomas. "Little professor want to go home?"

Thomas feels a surge of heat well up inside. His mouth opens all by itself. "What so?" he says, his left leg vibrating like a guitar string. He puts a hand down to steady that uncontrolled part of his body. He hears a vibrato in his voice. "Maybe it's far enough."

Vinaigre smirks at the two boys closest to him. The apothecary's apprentice opens his mouth to give his leader's opinion but Jean-Chrysostome gets there first.

"No, it was me." Jean-Chrys's words come in a hurry, like he's running out of time. "Lantern. Candle. If it, if it goes out … way down here … we're … not getting out. Not get … we … we … let's start back." His voice trails off.

All eyes go to Vinaigre, whose face is more orange than before. The apprentice is holding the lantern right beside his cheek. Vinaigre is shaking his head. The lips, the eyes, they show disgust. In front of Vinaigre, though, Pierre, the lout with the mole, is mulling over a retreat from this chill and frightening subterrane. And the apprentice too, Thomas notices, he is peering through the glass of the lantern to measure just how much candle might be left.

"So, what say you," Thomas directs at the apprentice. "Our time is nearly up?"

"Go on," snarls Vinaigre. He uses his left hand to make a dismissive sweep. "No one's stopping you. Get. Get. But the lantern stays here. That's what we say. You two cunnies go back on your own. In the dark."

"Whoa," says Thomas, both hands upraised. He ignores the thumping of his heart. "Jean-Chrys is right. The apprentice and your friend, they think so too. If the candle burns down much more, we're … we're not …" Thomas shrugs to make his point. "It's going to be black down here."

Vinaigre glances to his left and his right. He receives in return weak shrugs from the apprentice and from Pierre. He takes that as an endorsement of his leadership. Thomas is dead wrong. The other boys don't want to turn tail. "What say you, boys," says Vinaigre, seizing the moment. "What say we leave these two girls right here. Who cares about them anyway?"

Vinaigre takes a step ahead, making contact with the apprentice. The leader is now holding the lantern as high as he can, out of Vinaigre's reach should he have ideas to try and take it away. Pierre snorts agreement with Vinaigre and sidles closer to his friend. They each place an arm around the other's waist.

The apprentice speaks, "I say le- le- let's ke- keep going on."

"That's right." Vinaigre leans in to Thomas and aims to place a finger on the cleft of Thomas's chin. Thomas bats the hand away before it gets too close. "Babies," says Vinaigre. He turns back toward the apprentice holding the lantern and nods to him that it's time to get moving, moving into the darkness of the subterrane still unexplored.

Thomas puts a hand on Jean-Chrys's shoulder, the sea of impenetrable blackness closing in as the lantern edges forward. Jean-Chrys blinks his sad eyes. The trudge and shuffle of the other three boys is moving away from them. The bouncing amber light is getting thinner and thinner. Another minute and....

"Wait," shouts Thomas, arms outstretched. He has to catch up to the only light there is; there is no other choice. He can't, they can't go back up the stony, dripping darkness without any kind of light. "Wait up."

"Wait," adds Jean-Chrys. His feet quick-scuff the dirt floor to catch up to Thomas, who feels the clutch of two desperate hands grabbing at the clothes on his back.

—

Time slows to the pace of an endless trudge. The five boys continue what has become something to endure. The heat in the clearing above ground was no guide to the cool air found below. Worse than the damp air is that other chill, the one that comes from going on in a closed-in darkness into God knows what.

In the rasp of breath and trudge of shoes in steadily wetter ground Thomas thinks he hears something else as he goes along. First it's a rhythm then it's a chant.

Bravura, brave boy.
Fear of black and blue.

Fortissimo, little friend.
Find out, find out what to do.

All at once, the ground beneath their feet changes. It's no longer firm with occasional spots soft and wet. Suddenly, it feels like ooze. A suck of muck comes with each horrible step.

"Wh- wh- what's that?" is the cry up ahead. It's the apprentice. His lantern is out chest high, way out in front of his body as far as he can extend. His free hand is over his nose. He's making a gagging sound. Vinaigre and Pierre halt alongside the leader, all three blocking the passage, their dark shapes swallowing the light. They crouch as one. Their heads swivel. Back and forth at each other and at whatever it is that lies just beyond their feet.

Thomas and Jean-Chrys stretch tall, but neither can see what it is that has stopped the others in their tracks. The amber lantern light up ahead is spinning back and forth across the passage's stone roof.

"Give me that." Vinaigre comes full height and grabs for the lantern, trying to wrest it from the apprentice's hand.

For an instant the glass and wood box is airborne. The lantern in freefall and the candle sputtering. The apprentice reaches out to catch it but is thrust back by Vinaigre. Just before the lantern hits the ground Vinaigre catches it by its metal ring. He rights the lantern and brings it to his chest. The candle regains its flicker, painting the rock sides and roof with dim amber waves. Vinaigre wraps the fingers of his right hand tight round the wire handle to make sure that such a drop or change of possession cannot happen again.

"Better," says Vinaigre, to no one in particular. He sucks a breath as he moves forward to examine more closely what it is on the ground that so horrifies the apprentice. Pierre, with the importance of his friendship with Vinaigre never stronger, pulls on the new leader's shoulder. Pierre's breath is as rapid as a dog's.

There on the ground just ahead of Vinaigre's feet, the flickering lantern lights up a tangled mass of something hairy and oozing. It's a carcass of ribs. It's hair and skin. It's something like meat only with bits of fat, hair and fur and all torn in a heap. A single dead glassy eye stares back at the lantern's light. Vinaigre and Pierre suck in their breaths, just as the apprentice had done. They follow a trail of yellowish mucus that is seeping out of the thing in a trickle across the ground. The sickening flow pools at their feet.

"God in heaven," mutters Vinaigre, swinging the lantern left then right.

Thomas and Jean-Chrys follow the quivering lantern light. When they see the bloody carcass they too gasp. Then everyone sees the solid rock wall face. This is where the exploration, where the subterrane ends. Whatever it was that brought the carcass here is eventually going to come back. They have come into some ferocious animal's lair.

Vinaigre spins round, the lantern held as high as he can. His flickery face is waxen, eyes filled with what to Thomas looks like panic. "Out," Vinaigre shouts, flailing the free arm at the bodies in his way. "Out of my way."

The apprentice and Pierre flatten against the sides of the subterrane, Vinaigre's lantern swinging past their startled faces. Thomas and Jean-Chrys are not so quick. The collision with Vinaigre is jarring. Elbows on chests and faces, knees on knees and thighs. There are oofs and grunts and curses before Vinaigre topples over an unseen leg. The sounds of the three boys tumbling – shouts and then the crush and snap of the lantern – come fast. The extinction of the candle's light comes next. It drains like water down a pipe. A total blackness, an impenetrable cloak, is thrown over every little thing. It's a deeper dark than Thomas has ever known before.

For a sliver of suspended time no one says or does a thing. There is only the trickle of water dripping. It's the same wet tick-tock that's been there from the start. But then the animal nature within each boy responds. It's one grabbing, pushing, shouting, reaching, blaming the other and whoever is in the way. Arms swim the air as if in water and the darkness is a stream. A desperate fight and crawl begins. On all fours it's everyone up, over and through all the others. Push and pull, scratch and punch and muttered threats. The sidewalls of jutting stones hit back when blind heads and shoulders and hands make contact. It takes only a few panic-stricken moments for a new regime, the reign of darkness, to establish itself. Vinaigre in front, Jean-Chrys next, followed by Pierre, then the apprentice with Thomas in the rear. Thomas tells himself that he picked where he is at, though if there were any light at all, the marks on his face and chest would reveal that he was put where he is. The hands, elbows and feet of four others have all left their marks.

—

"Still day," Vinaigre cries out. The other boys, each in his turn, express more or less the same surprise when they finally spot the narrow rock opening up ahead.

Everyone squeezes through in a hurry and heads for the sun-drenched clearing. In the deepness of late afternoon golden light the five boys stand with their faces upturned. It's as if they have reached a promised land. There are handshakes, back pats and conquerors' words all round. Even Thomas and Jean-Chrys join in the camaraderie, though Vinaigre makes a scowl at their approach and the weak grips of their hands. Thomas pulls his hand back after the slightest of contact, before he gets hurt. He steps away, and looks up to the sheltering chestnut tree. Two large grey birds are flitting from branch to branch, pecking at something to eat. Thomas pretends to study the birds. What he is really doing is wondering if this is how it will always be for him. A little apart. Of course, there have to be leaders and followers, yet will it always be him that brings up the rear? Is it possible to change the order of things in a life or is it set when you're young and there's no hope of a rise? What is it he overheard his father say to his mother: that he needed a backbone to survive? Can Thomas be different than he is?

He brings his focus back down to where he is standing, away from the chestnut and its food-pecking birds. Yes, he thinks, I'll be up near the front the next time. If not the leader then at least by his side. Unless, Thomas continues with a wince, glancing past Vinaigre, unless that leader is you.

"That's right," Thomas says aloud, but to no one at all. He walks away from the other four boys, and runs his hands over his ribs. They're hurting, but he's pretty sure that's all that's wrong. If something were broken, surely it would hurt more than this. No, he'll be all right. He's relieved just to be out. He looks back at the brushy area that hides the opening to the cave.

One of the birds he had been watching up in the chestnut tree swoops down, across Thomas's sight line then away up out of sight over the trees. It flashes into Thomas's mind that with a bit of luck he too, like the bird, will eventually be out of this place, out of little Vire. All he has to do is wait things out. Some kind of chance for a departure will emerge. His parents hint that they are making arrangements for him to go away to follow his studies. No doubt they still want him to become a priest. But he'll make them see the nonsense of that. Instead, he'll go study medicine, maybe even in Paris. Physicians have standing in the world. Maybe not as much as a priest in a mother's eyes, but they're better than merchants at least. He makes a face at his father's occupation. Cloth merchant, he nearly says aloud. Thomas shakes away his reflection and tugs at the crotch of his pants.

"What're you doing?"

Thomas spins round. He finds Jean-Chrys.

"Nothing. Just … just waiting for you, I guess." Thomas gestures in Jean-Chrys's direction. "How are you anyway? I mean, down … down underground. You all right?"

"Just glad we're out." Jean-Chrys summons a deep breath.

The two friends look over to the other three lads, who haven't yet moved from their chosen spot in the sun. Vinaigre is spinning some kind of story that has his two listeners paying rapt attention.

"Quite the guy, isn't he?" says Jean-Chrys. "He just takes charge."

"You, you admire Vinaigre?"

"No, no," says Jean-Chrys, taken aback by the instant anger on his friend's face. "Just saying, that's all. He takes charge." Jean-Chrys shrugs at the self-evidence of what he's saying.

"Let's get out of here," says Thomas.

"All right." Jean-Chrys reaches out to tap Thomas on the elbow, but Thomas elbows the seeking hand away. They turn their backs to the other three boys and start up the long hill.

"Hey!" It's Vinaigre. The cut of his voice puts a dozen small birds to flight from the top of one of the nearby chestnut trees. "Where you goin', girls?"

Thomas and Jean-Chrys look round over their shoulders, unwilling to turn any more than that. Jean-Chrys opens his mouth to say something to Vinaigre in return, but Thomas warns him not to with tiny shake of his head and a quick roll of the eyes.

"Home to Maman?" Vinaigre shouts. His chin is up, his head tilted back. The apprentice and Pierre laugh like they've turned into crows. "That's right, you'd better," Vinaigre adds for good measure. "Girls."

Thomas and Jean-Chrysostome look at each other, then at Vinaigre, their heads swivelling like owls. They keep their faces blank, intent on saying nothing. Neither wants to send an invitation for Vinaigre to come after them and maybe strike them down. They are comrades coming out of the underground no more.

"Let's get out of here," Thomas mutters through tightly closed lips. His clothes look like he tried to swim through muck.

Jean-Chrys nods agreement and the two are off. They run as fast as they can. At the top of the incline, where the beaten earth turns to finely crushed stone, they pause to look back, to make sure that neither Vinaigre or his allies are coming after them. No one is. Thomas raises an arm and makes what he thinks is a Roman salute, feet together, arm upraised. Vinaigre swats the air in return, but he stays where he is.

"Could've been worse," says Thomas to Jean-Chrys as they come to within a dozen paces of the town gate. He flexes his eyebrows, inviting his friend to comment.

"Yeah, it sure could've. We could've been trapped. I'm not going back down in there, I'm not."

"No," Thomas laughs, "why would you?"

"Yeah." Jean-Chrys hunches his shoulders. "Why would I? Well, I'm not, that's what. I'm not. I'm just saying I'm not going back."

As they pass under the giant metal-capped teeth of the great wooden portcullis, moving into the dark centre of the Martilly Gate, Thomas's thoughts are on the mistake that he made in the afternoon just past. It wasn't just that he went into the underground with an enemy like Vinaigre. No. Oh, true enough, that was part of it. But there was more to it than that. What he's decided he's learned is to never again put himself in a situation he can't control. Or if not control at least be able to influence.

"No, that's right." Thomas heartily slaps Jean-Chrys on the back. "Why would you ever go back into that animal's cave? Me either, Jean-Chrys, me either."

By the time the boys get to the square with the fountain of Esmangard, which is where they go their separate ways, the narrow streets of the ancient town are deep in evening shadow. To the townspeople who were not underground with Thomas and Jean-Chrys, it's simply the descent of another late-summer night. To the two friends, it's time to eat heartily at dinner and afterwards gladly go to bed.

—

Thomas runs the thumb of his right hand back and forth along the sliver of bread in his left hand. He has the piece as slim as he wants it, which he knows from experience can't be too thin. The bread has to retain enough stiffness so that it won't break or leave more than a few crumbs behind. The secret is to dip it in and pull it out on the count of four. The bread feels ready.

Thomas leans back to get a crick out of his neck and scans the surface of the table where he's been busy preparing his crust. It's a marvel how many crumbs the preparation makes. As always, he'll sweep them away once he's done. He likes to keep this little treat a secret, so no one knows what it is that he does.

He puts his head at a listening angle, just in case. He hears father and mother in the shop, as they always are this time of day. It sounds like they're with a customer.

As for Servanne, the seventeen-year-old servant who sleeps in the room off the kitchen, she must be out of the house. Thomas figures she's off doing laundry, which will keep her out of the house for a while. Meanwhile the cook, a day servant, has not shown up yet. She's always late. His sister, Anne? Who knows? She could be anywhere. Thomas hears only the tick of a distant clock and the faint footsteps of someone far, far away. He decides it must be his sister, somewhere upstairs.

Thomas takes a last look at his task. The honey jar on the tabletop and the sliver of bread in his hand. With a blink of his brown eyes to say go, he pushes his crust into the golden surface. The honey bends and yields, and Thomas smiles to see the semi-liquid spread up and round the bread gone in. He counts the seconds. More than four and the bread can come apart or at least leave too much of a trace. He's learned all this over the past few months, ever since he started dipping stiff bread in honey when no one was around.

"Three, four," he says barely aloud.

He jerks the bread out and leans down to reap his catch. Head nearly touching the tabletop he opens wide and just in time it turns out. The molten drip covers his teeth and his tongue. It's a slow advance of golden sweetness throughout his whole mouth. Thomas straightens, and runs his tongue everywhere, wherever the honey coursed its path. He smacks his lips then sucks the remainder of the bread to get anything that might be left. Then he chews the sliver till it's completely gone.

"Master," Servanne says softly, not wanting to frighten him, just let him know that he's been caught.

Thomas stiffens. The head turns slowly toward the voice.

"Yes," he says, face and eyes coming just far enough around to see the servant over by the turnspit. "Oh, Servanne." His cheeks flex with annoyance because he hears a trace of guilt in his own voice.

"Wondering if there's something you want me to do?" She keeps her head lowered, looking anywhere but directly at Thomas. "Here in the kitchen I mean."

Thomas turns full round. The first thing he notices are the moccasins, the Indian shoes, on the girl's feet. He remembers her telling him she bought them at an auction a few weeks ago. That explains why he didn't hear her coming, why he thought the steps were far away, maybe in his sister's room upstairs. He wipes his mouth with the cuff of his left sleeve. He pouts with his full lips in a pretence of deep thought.

"Anything I should see to in here?" she asks again. "Young master?"

"Not that I can think of."

Thomas straightens like he's a busy person with something to do. He makes a last sweep with the hand behind his back then steps away from the table to come closer to the hearth.

"Something funny, Servanne?"

"No, sir." The servant girl tightens her face. "Just looking forward to … well, what was it now? Gone like that. Empty headed, I am sometimes." Servanne averts her eyes from the boy and takes a long step in the direction of her little room. Then she stops. "I notice a bit of a mess. Crumbs, young Master Thomas. Over there." She points. "No, near the table. Someone's been in the honey pot. Dipping is my guess. Maybe you could see to cleaning that up yourself?"

"Yes, well then," says Thomas, blushing at the accusation and the smirk on Servanne's face. So she knows what he's been doing and is challenging him to come clean. He replies to her inquiry by hurrying past her on his way to the stairs and up to his room. The golden sweet swirl of the honey in his mouth is all gone.

Spring 1714

"Thomas," comes a voice from below.

The boy, going through the time of rapidly growing limbs and deepening voice, looks up. He is working on a verse at his wobbly desk in his attic room. He has been searching, without success, for a word to rhyme with the end of the second line. He has come up with a couple of possibilities – bevy and levy – but neither fits the sentiment he wishes to express. If he can't find one soon he'll have to recast the second line so that some other word comes at the end. That's because there has to be a rhyme with heavy, but the rhyme has to make sense.

"Thomas." The voice comes again, sharper this time.

Thomas stares at the door to his room. It's closed, which is how he likes it. It gives him time, not much but a bit, to put things away should he hear someone climbing the stairs. It doesn't happen often, though occasionally his mother or sister comes up to see what he's doing. Father doesn't climb the stairs because he doesn't have to. What he does instead is bellow from down below, like he's doing right now.

"Thomas. Do you hear me?"

"Yes, Father." Thomas puts down the quill. He stacks up his sheaf of papers and puts it back inside the empty book cover that he uses to contain and protect what he writes. Then he places the whole thing inside the only drawer of the desk.

"Come down, please."

"Coming." Thomas also puts the ink well and quill in the drawer. He prefers the surface of his writing table to be completely clean and empty when he's not seated there working on something. Uncluttered. Hidden away. That way, no one knows what he's up to and yet it only takes him a moment to bring things out. "Right there, Father."

Thomas spies the length of blue silk coiled up at the back of the drawer. It still comes in handy, and allows him to say no with a clear conscience when the priest asks him certain questions in the confessional. Do you ever touch yourself? No, Father, I do not. Except to relieve myself when I have to use the chamber pot.

Thomas glances at his little mirror and gives his dark-eyed reflection a friendly wink.

"Thomas! Down here now!"

He bends to the mirror and takes both hands to undo the black ribbon that has been tied round his long brown hair, keeping it tied in a neat queue. He shakes his head to unfurl what has been contained. He thinks the tumble of dark hair makes him a highwayman or a poet. Though if his nasty grandmother were still alive, she'd say it made him look even more like some untended peasant girl.

"Boy! Now."

"Coming."

He scuttles down the stairs, arriving on the ground floor with eyes wide and quickening breath. Tomorrow is March thirtieth, his fourteenth birthday. He hopes, no, he prays, that Father is calling him down to announce something of importance. He hears it in the voice, the way the man says "now" and "if you please." There must be news, big news on the way. And Thomas knows what he wants that news to be. He swells his lungs just before he steps into the salon. It must be that his parents have at last understood who Thomas is and what he has the potential to be. It took them long enough, did it not? For so long they would not let go of the idea that he should either follow his father into the family cloth business or else become a priest. Jean Pichon wanted the former while Marie made no secret she preferred the latter. Learn the clothier's trade or join the Church. Thomas could not tell them right out that he was not meant for handing over bolts of cloth to customers in off the street or for bestowing empty blessings on all sorts of unwashed in the Church. But now, he detects it in his father's urgent voice, they must have figured it all out for themselves. They must have learned finally that he has talents and ambitions to be more than a merchant or a priest. They don't know about his poetry, but they've undoubtedly come round to see that his second choice, medicine, is a good field for their son. They are right to think so. His rise in rank and standing will benefit them all.

Thomas takes another breath, shallow this time. He wants the news to be that they've made arrangements for him to study in Caen, though Paris would be better still. At the very least they have to agree that it will be best for him to get away from Vire. Thomas takes the step forward so he can be seen.

"Father." Thomas halts in the threshold to the salon. He is unable to hide a smile. It is such a relief that his parents have come round. Thomas offers an adult-like tilt of the head. It is how he has seen one man sometimes greet another, at least when it is equal to equal. Jean Pichon is standing by the first flames of the evening fire. How that man does love to warm his backside.

"Took your time."

"I am sorry, Father. Oh, good evening, Mother. I'm sorry, I did not see you at first."

"Yes," is all Marie says.

Thomas bows to his mother, Marie Esnault by birth, Madame Pichon by marriage. She is seated where she always sits in the salon, on the flame-coloured divan that came from her family at the time of her marriage to Jean Pichon. Its Hungarian stitch pattern is long since well-worn, overdue for re-upholstering. She often says she must have it re-done, but so far she has not. The financial setback suffered at the hands of La Motte has put any such expenditure on hold.

Thomas squints in confusion to see his mother looking grim. Her hands are clasped tight in her lap. Is that worry on her face or has someone died? No, Thomas decides, his mood rebounding, she is merely resigning herself to the fact that her son will not after all become a priest. Her sad face is in that respect a good thing, a confirmation that Thomas is about to get what he wants and needs. Mother will come round. She'll be proud of her physician son, yes she will.

"Me too, little brother."

Thomas cranes to his far right, where his sister, Anne, is feigning a yawn. She is standing half hidden between the dark green drapes that hang from near the ceiling down to the floor. Despite having spoken, the moment Thomas glances her way Anne turns around to gaze somewhere else. She pretends to peer out the window beside her, though Thomas knows she doesn't really care who is passing by.

"Sister," says Thomas, adding a roll of the hand such as a gentleman might offer to a lady.

He has no objection to her being there to hear the news. In fact, it's better this way. She might even be pleased for him. After all, everyone in the family stands to benefit from his rise and advance, even her. Reflected glory must be better than having none at all.

"Yes, well." Thomas turns an eager face to his father. He places his hands behind his back and plants his feet. He glances down to make sure there is a slightly angled turn to the calf of his left leg. It's the stance gentlemen adopt when at ease. Many a time Thomas has observed the stance in the square and along the streets, and he and Jean-Chrys practice it for fun.

Jean Pichon rolls his eyes and sends a pointed look his good wife's way. "Yes, well," begins the father coming back to study his son. The man spreads his thumb and forefinger and rubs them along his bristly brows. Then he clasps his hands together like he might be inclined to pray. "We've been looking out for you, Thomas. You know that, I think. It is our duty. It is. Speaking, talking, inquiring. For months now. For your future..."

"Yes, Father," says Thomas. Silently he repeats: Paris, make it Paris. Caen would be all right.

"Father Alexis says that you have an excellent—"

"Father Alexis?" Thomas's head snaps back. "What does Father … what does *he* have to do—"

"Let your father finish," says Marie from the divan. She flutters a hand like it's a handkerchief her husband's way. Her eyes avoid Thomas's darting glance.

What is going on, thinks Thomas. Is this sadness at his leaving Vire on his mother's face or is this something else? He straightens his legs. The gentleman's stance is no more. The son is confused. In desperation he swings to catch a clue from his sister over by the window. Anne lifts her cheeks and sends a shoulder rise. If she knows, she's not revealing.

"Father?" Thomas feels his left leg begin to pulse. It is not something he can control. "You, you were saying? I interrupted."

"Yes, thank you," says Jean Pichon and not one word more.

Husband and wife exchange expressions. Thomas follows the looks and thinks the faces are showing some kind of grim determination. Two sets of lips tightly pulled and eyes that match. Thomas feels the top of his head begin to spin. Someone is pulling a rope tight round his chest. A thought comes into his head, words he thinks he hears: this is what disappointment feels like. Thomas's eyes flash to his father. The man's bristly eyebrows, well-worn clothes and rough ways are an embarrassment to Thomas, but this is something worse. The man is going to let him down in some awful way.

"We know it's not your first choice, Thomas. No, it's not." Thomas is confused. It's not like Jean Pichon to use roundabout words. He usually talks straight and cold. "A life in the Church is something you'll thank us for one day." Jean Pichon halts. He looks over to Marie.

"The Church?" Thomas's face is one of incredulity.

"That's right."

Thomas is shaking his head. "No. Not the Church. Not after all I've—"

"After all you've what?" Jean Pichon's voice goes hard, like the expression on his face. "What? You tell me you little—"

"Husband, stop," says Marie. She is shaking her head, the face mournful.

"What? He's never tried to help out around here. In the shop. If he had, we might not...."

"Not now, Jean. Not now."

"All right." Jean Pichon rolls his eyes to the ceiling. "All right." He turns back to face his son. "We've not the means, Thomas. That's all. We cannot send you anywhere that would … that would be at our expense. Not for medicine, not for anything. Not since the troubles with … the bugger La Motte wiped us out."

The room goes silent. The only sound is a clock ticking in the next room. That and, to Thomas only, the grating sound of air going in and coming out of his hollow lungs.

He has the sensation he is back in the subterrane, in the darkness and not knowing if there is any way out.

"We're not made of money," he hears his mother say, though the words are coming from far away. "We never were."

Thomas is in deep, still water. He is wet all over; his clothes are completely drowned. The water is now up to his neck and it's climbing higher still.

"So the Church it is," his mother continues. "Really, in truth, you should be glad about it. Father Alexis says that …"

The water is above Thomas's head. The surprise is that maybe, just maybe, he doesn't mind. It'll be quick, it'll be over and that'll be it.

"The priest says you have a calling." Thomas recognizes that it's his father speaking now. Why won't he just stop? "Frankly, I don't see it, but who are we to argue with a priest. Besides...."

In the stillness of profound disappointment, Thomas turns slowly his mother's way. He wants to see her face. He remembers that she once was filled with love for him, he felt she really was. But he does not find his mother's face. She has it hidden. It's buried in her hands. He wonders why. Isn't this just what she wants? Him a priest and her excused from purgatory for some secret crime. Well, he now knows what that crime is. It's this. It's what she is making him do.

Thomas moves from his standing spot, his legs leading the way. He thanks his legs for that. He glances back at sister Anne, over by the curtains. That's a smile on her face, is it not? Oh well, it's all right for her and for Father and Mother to cast away his life this way. They can gloat all they want. But Thomas, the birthday boy, he has to go.

"Thomas," says his father, startled by what he sees, "don't you walk away. Not from me you don't."

Thomas is out the doorway of the salon.

"Where're you going? Hear me?"

The voice shouting behind Thomas is faint. What's clearer is the sound of his own shoes on the floorboards as he reaches for the door that is there to take him outside.

"You come back here. You'll stay if I say so. You hear me? Come back here. Don't you dare, you—"

—

Out through the Porte Neuve and into the evening, Thomas makes his way beyond the few makeshift huts and shelters of the very poor that the town's administration allows to stand on the southern edge of the outskirts of Vire. He is heading for the spot on high, where the ridge overlooks the countryside and the Vire River courses far down below. That's the best spot. The vista from there, Thomas says to himself on the way, is the only thing he'll miss when he's gone.

Thomas wends through the branches along the little-used trail to where he wants to be, up where the river can be seen directly below. That river is black at this late hour of the day, twisting through the valley of Vire. He imagines he can hear the sound of the water's passage down there, a pulsing ripple. In truth, he hears no such thing. What he thinks is the water is his future trickling away.

He comes to a halt at the end of the path, where the ground ends and the long, straight drop to the river below begins. Thomas lifts his gaze to the trees on the other side of the Vire. He cups an ear to listen once more, this time for the rustle of their branches. Though it is much too far, he imagines he hears the leaves twisting on their stems. It suggests the tremble of petticoats. It won't be long, he notices, looking up to the greying sky, before the valley disappears entirely in the darkness of the night. The sun has already sunk below the level of the trees on the other side of the river.

He wonders how far it is down to the river. Is that one hundred or two hundred feet? And how long might that be if one were to fall or to jump? Would it be the length of a prayer before he hit the rocks or maybe the water? Depends on the prayer of course. He doubts you could get it all said, even a short one. Your mind would not work very well once you'd leapt off into the air. Too much of an unknown, too much of a thrill. Would the impact hurt? He's not sure. It would certainly be different. They'd be sorry, his father and his mother, they'd be sorry for what they had done.

Thomas looks at his feet. His shoes are old and worn, scuffed and one of the buckles is askew. Thomas bends to correct the buckle, to get it just right. He straightens again and surveys the dimming scene. He takes a deep breath, one to hang on to and hold. He looks again at his feet, how firmly they are planted on the ground. He wonders if they really will obey him if he tells them to jump.

Thomas blinks away that thought and decides to study his hands. He holds them aloft in front of his face. He wouldn't want anything to happen to them if he fell. He likes his hands. They're good to him when he cradles the quill. And his face, he wouldn't want his face to get hurt in any fall.

There comes a whisper:

Advance soft shadow
    Down the dark wind

Deepen the twilight
Dust of the sinned

Thomas is startled. Those are not lines he's ever heard before and he likes them a lot. He pats his breeches to see if in a pocket there might be a pencil. There is not, but then he doesn't have a scrap of paper either. He could use his fingers and scratch the words in the dirt. He adjusts his legs and takes a deep breath. He closes his eyes, hands crossed on his chest. He wants the same words to come to him again.

Advance soft shadow
Down the dark wind
Deepen the twilight
Dust of the sinned

Shadow swing round
Out of the deep

Blanket this air
In

"Hey! Hey, Thomas."

Thomas opens his eyes. He looks down to the river, dark now in the gloom, then he scans back along the trail. There's a dark shape in the shadows, coming along between the trees. The shape is on the path and it's coming fast.

"Thought that was you. Whew. Ran all the way."

"Jean-Chrys, what … what're you doing here?"

"Your mother." Jean-Chrys bends over with his hands on his knees. He is sucking deep breaths. "Came to the house. Said you'd … you'd taken off. She was … worried I guess. And she asked me to search."

Jean-Chrys looks up quizzically at Thomas. Thomas makes a sour face in return. He didn't ask for this.

Jean-Chrys stands straight, his full breath back. "Getting late, you know."

"Yes, I know." Thomas studies his friend to see just how much he might know. About his parents and the Church and Thomas's walk to the edge of the ridge.

"Want to head back now? Together, I mean? Before it gets really dark. It'll be black out here and … well, maybe it's time."

Thomas doesn't answer at once. He studies Jean-Chrys, someone he's known forever. Well, since they both began to go to church and to school, and that was a long time ago. Then they've been to the *collège* together since then. He's not as good as Thomas in Latin and rhetoric, but he seems to have a knack for philosophy and mathematics. It strikes Thomas in the fading light that his friend has an uncomplicated face. It reminds him of a cherub as the painters make them out to be. All the rosy-cheeked boyishness is still in its place. And now, because of his run, Jean-Chrys is flush on the brow and the cheeks. He took no hat in his haste, so his hair is dishevelled, his curls here and there. And the eyes, well, they aren't asking Thomas any questions at all. They're simply smiling, happy to come help a friend.

Odd, is it not, that Jean-Chrys isn't the least bit curious as to why Thomas left his home with night coming on and why he came up on this ridge? Or if he is curious, then isn't it remarkable that he's not asking why? That, thinks Thomas, is surely what one should have in a friend. No prying, no bother. Thomas puts a hand on Jean-Chrys's shoulder. He pats him to tell him without words that he's glad that he came.

"What do you say?" says Jean-Chrys with a shrug. "Time to get back? Before the gate closes and we're locked out?"

Thomas pats his friend once more. "Yeah, guess so."

The two young men turn and begin to file silently back along the narrow trail. In a few minutes they will be back on the avenue of chestnut trees, which leads in turn up to the torch-lit town gate beyond. As Jean-Chrys leads the way, Thomas suddenly realizes with a start what he's just lost. Several lines of poetry he liked had come to him when he was alone, before Jean-Chrys came along and disturbed his train of thought. As he walks along Thomas tries to summon the poetry's return. Nothing comes, not a line, not a word. Thomas scuffs the ground, kicking dirt on the back of his friend's stockings and breeches.

"Hey. What're you doing? What's that?" Jean-Chrys turns full round.

"Nothing," says Thomas. His face is fierce in anger and disappointment but that face is not visible to Jean-Chrys in the near dark. "Nothing."

"Doesn't sound like nothing."

"It is. Go on, turn round. Let's get inside the gate."

—

Back at home, up in his attic room at his desk after a wordless entrance into the house followed by a rapid, silent tread up the stairs, Thomas tries one more time to recapture the lost words he heard up high on the ridge. The quill is in hand, ink from the well waiting to make marks on the forlorn empty sheet. Yet not a word, not a one answers the call. He cannot even remember what the lines were about, though he's certain they were pretty good. Something about the river, was it not?

Thomas puts the plume back into its well. It'll have to stay there for a while. He pushes back the chair and takes himself away from the table, over to lie on the narrow bed. Eyes gone large in concentration, he stares up at the bare wooden boards of the steeply pitched roof overhead. Still nothing comes, not a hint of a word. He shifts and tilts his head and stares at the engraving of the Virgin Mary pinned to the wood. He sends her a wordless prayer with the wave of a hand. Nothing comes his way in return.

Thomas closes his eyes and rolls on his side. He brings his knees up into a child's comforting curl. He wonders: maybe if he'd pushed Jean-Chrys off the ridge when he first arrived, maybe then the lines would have stayed.

II

Journey

Vire, Normandy

May 1715

So far it's just as easy as he imagined. The key goes in, the hand twists to the left and there comes the sliding sound and clunk. The door opens. Withdraw the key, step into the gloom, lower the satchel to the floor. Close the door softly behind. That's that. Now he's inside where he wants to be. It's so simple, why didn't he think of it before? Well, he did think of it before, two weeks before, but that was too soon to take this step. It's only tonight that is right because tomorrow is hurrying on its way. By the time the next day gets here, Thomas will be done and be gone.

—

It took a while for it all to come clear. A month and a half ago, just after he turned fifteen, Thomas asked his father if there was anything he could do to help out in the shop, with the customers or anything else. Just something to keep him occupied until he went into the seminary, a matter of months away. No ulterior motive, not when he said it, none at all. He simply wanted to show his father he bore no grudge, even if he still did. Little did he know where his reconciliatory contribution to the family might lead.

Jean Pichon was delighted. Thomas saw it in his face right away. Then he heard it in his voice.

"Surely! That would be good, very good," said his father, eyes a little treacly. Two firm hands grasped the son's elbow. They gave a long squeeze. "A clothier you'll learn to be. If only until you go off to the Church."

"Good then," said Thomas, "just show me what to do."

At the time there was no plan, no aspiration for anything untoward. Though, truth be told, Thomas did hope that maybe his good deed would somehow be rewarded. That's the way it's supposed to be, is it not? Good deeds find a reward? It took a while to see what that reward might be. When it made its appearance, Thomas was as surprised as he could be that his reward was a possible escape.

In the first week Thomas found out where nearly everything was in the shop and how it mostly worked. In the second week he stayed late one evening and observed how at day's end the place was secured. Father checked the windows and made sure both doors were locked – the one to the street and the one that connected to the house. At the end of the third week Jean Pichon gave Thomas the keys to do the lock-up himself. When he was done, Thomas gave his father back the two keys that were used. Jean Pichon told him to follow him into the kitchen. Thomas watched as his father lifted the lid off of a pharmacy jar and dropped both keys inside then put the lid back on. "No one would think to look there," his father said.

"No, of course not," Thomas replied. "Very smart." He noted with a little smile that the hiding spot in the pharmacy jar was only two containers down from the honey pot into which he used to dip crusts of bread.

Thomas's eyes grew a little more bored each day to see how the hours and days of his cloth merchant father's life ticked by. Luckily, he thought more than once, such a life was not in the cards for him. He still had no plan for what that future life might be and how he was going to avoid the Church, but he knew that at least he wasn't going to be spending his weeks, months and years in this little Vire shop. Maybe a life wearing a cassock would not be so bad after all.

One morning toward the end of his third week of working in the shop, while he was folding and putting away bolts of the horrible brown wool cloth, Thomas felt something odd. It was like a thought only there were no words. It was more of a sensation, right in the back of his head. Though he didn't know what it was, he felt it had to be pursued, whatever it was. He took the sensation to be the forerunner of some thought or idea. Or maybe it was a longing, though his longings usually began in his breeches and this wasn't one of those. Whatever it was, Thomas felt that something was coming and when it arrived he would pay attention.

The following week Thomas glimpsed for the first time what that sensation had portended. He was putting away the least expensive bolts of fabric – brown drugget, brown flannel, dark blue flannelette and green serge – when the arm-waving Madame Couperin came in from the street. As always, she wanted to look at the latest cloth. Something about a dress she wanted to have made. Thomas's father looked after the lady with as much deference as he could. It struck Thomas as funny that the man could be so obliging to customers yet so unyielding to his own blood. No matter. After Madame Couperin left the shop, having purchased ratteens of wool mixed with cotton, Thomas glanced over to his father to ask how many ells the lady had taken. That was when Thomas saw his father bend over beneath the little corner counter that no one ever used. It looked like he was putting something away down there because he was out of sight a whole minute or two. When his father stood up again, the hands were empty and he was glancing around as if he'd just done something secretive. Curious, Thomas idled over to where his father was.

"Just wondering," he said, tendering a shrug as if he didn't really care, "what it is you put down there a moment ago …" Thomas pointed under the corner counter where his father had just been busy. "I didn't know there was anything under there."

Jean Pichon held up a hand to stop his son from saying another word, and the eyes narrowed. Then he relaxed and gave his son a wistful smile.

"It's out of sight for a reason. It's where I keep it all. The money, I mean. A strongbox."

Though there were only the two of them in the shop, Jean Pichon was whispering.

"And this," he said, pulling on a rawhide string that ran round his neck, one Thomas had always thought held a religious medal of some sort, "this is what opens the lock."

"Oh," said Thomas, blinking. He knew the locks to the shop and where those keys were kept, but he'd not realized there was any kind of strongbox. Of course, the money people paid for the fabric had to be kept somewhere, didn't it? "Might I look? Under the counter, I mean?"

Jean Pichon studied his son for an uncomfortable moment then nodded slowly. He checked the empty, quiet shop once more for good measure. No, there were no customers, no one who might see.

"No harm there, I guess." But Jean Pichon went over to bolt the door to the street – just for as long as this was going to take – just in case. Then he came back to the corner counter and bent down behind it and pulled out what looked to Thomas like an ancient wooden box. The thing was the size of a large loaf of bread, one of the big round six-*livres* loaves, if such loaves were baked rectangular not circular in shape. There were two metal bands around the box and a large padlock in the front.

"Heavy?" Thomas asked.

"See for yourself."

Thomas crouched down and prepared to summon all his strength. It turned out he didn't need to be Hercules. The box did have weight, but he was able to lift it. He smiled at his father as he demonstrated his feat of strength, jostling the box and holding it at waist height. He could hear the sound of coins stirring within.

"Used to be heavier." Jean Pichon gave a knowing look. Thomas recognized that his father was referring to the hated La Motte. But for that mistaken crusade, taking on the town's most powerful man – a thought Thomas keeps to himself – why he might be heading off to study medicine in Paris after all.

"Yes, I suppose it was." Thomas felt the underside of the box with his left hand. There were what felt like small cracks and holes in the underside of the old thing. In one spot a finger went through far enough to touch the coins within. "Don't you think it's a bit … old?" Thomas nearly said "fragile" but thought better of it.

"Of course it's old. It has character. But the lock's not. Have a look. That lock will never be picked."

"Let's see."

Thomas laid the strongbox on the top of the counter and spun it to check out the lock on the front. Sure enough, the iron lock was large and imposing, and looked like it was only recently manufactured. Thomas sent an acknowledging look to his father, who responded by tugging on the rawhide string round his neck. Out into plain sight came the key.

"That's what opens it, is it?" said Thomas. "Better put it away."

"Right you are," said Jean Pichon. He dropped the key back inside his shirt. "You put our box back under the counter and I'll go unbolt the door."

Thomas did as he was told and neither he nor his father said any more about the strongbox the rest of that day or the next. Nor did Thomas give it any further thought. It had made for an interesting few minutes on an otherwise dull day, that was all.

Two nights later, however, Thomas woke abruptly in the darkest hour. He sat up straight in his bed and recalled a time when he was young and at the oceanside. He didn't know exactly where he was or how old he was, but his father was with him. They were walking along a shore. What he remembered was the seabirds wheeling in the air. Gulls and terns. A few of the birds went to the shoreline and picked up something in their bills. They climbed to a great height then dropped what they had picked up. Down the birds would swoop to peck at what they'd just dropped.

"What're they doing?" Thomas remembered asking.

"Mussels," was the reply. "They're cracking them. Once the shell gives way, they eat the meat that's opened up inside."

"Oh," Thomas had said at the time.

He lay back down in his bed, mulling the memory, rolling his head from side to side. He wondered why such a long-ago day was coming to him now. Odd, to be sure. Wouldn't it be better to get some sleep? Tomorrow was another day in the shop, and after that another two full weeks.

And that was when it came to him. It arrived in a rush that was so sharp and clear that he couldn't get back to sleep at all. He could only think about it over and over, step by step.

"Pretty easy," he said out loud at last, rolling over onto his side. He fixed his eyes on the moonlit rectangle of a window across the room and marvelled at what man could learn from nature if only he opened his eyes.

—

The question Thomas wonders about over the next few days is the matter of what is right and what is wrong. Is it as simple as the priests and the courts say? Is it really all laid down, on pages in this or that book? Well, who is the author of those books? Might their rules not be in their own unnatural favour?

The conclusion Thomas comes to on one of his early morning walks, approaching the fountain of Esmangard on his way to a quick tour of the inside of the church of Saint-Thomas – he no longer worships on his knees in front of the Blessed Virgin, but he does still like to walk past the painted statue and give her a knowing nod – is that the mighty lawmakers don't know the particulars of his situation. If they were in his shoes, they'd see it the way he does. Is not justice supposed to be blind? Exactly. And if it's blind, it means that no justice officer nor any pope in Rome for that matter, can grasp what Thomas grasps. And that is that little, maybe nothing, is as simple as white or as black. No one but Thomas knows about the obligation his parents are supposed to have. If the two of them, or even one to start, would only think about what really matters they would come to the same conclusion that he has. Reason, simple reason, is his one and only guide.

Thomas stops at the fountain, puts a hand in the water and stirs it around. He supposes he'll miss the fountain a bit, though he knows there are bigger and better in some other towns.

Yes, it's clear. If his parents really want him to show backbone and be a man, they'd want him to carry out the plan that's in his head. One could almost say they owe it to him. That's right. But he's going to save them the trouble of figuring it out for themselves. His father and mother are the parents of an aspiring and capable son. He should not be held back by their non-recognition of a solution for Thomas's situation that is right before their eyes.

More than a few times at night in his bed, Thomas rolls over on to his back and focuses his gaze on the little window across the room that looks out on the world. Starry sky, cloudy night, the milk-white of the moon. It doesn't matter. Each time he comes to the same conclusion. It's not his fault, it's theirs. His parents owe him a choice, something other than what they know he doesn't want. If there be selfishness or stubbornness anywhere in this scheme, it's on their part not his. He wants only what nature intends, that he live up to his talent and aspiration. He'll follow the seabirds' example and peck his way to meat.

—

For two more nervous weeks Thomas works out what he hopes are all the necessary details. First, there is the question of the diligences to Paris. Twice a week there is one that rolls through Vire in the early morning. It arrives around seven a.m. en route for Lisieux. From Lisieux another carriage takes travellers on to Paris. Two nights at inns along the way, then the coach pulls into the great city. Thomas has heard that it has a thousand spires and domes and that there are maybe half a million people living there. It's hard to imagine. Thomas can hardly wait. He has picked his time, the last week of May, when servant Servanne is supposed to be away, back home visiting her mother in Condé-sur-Noireau. Next, he selects what he'll take with him. Not much, for little does he own. Just a satchel. In it he'll put the necessary bread and cheese, the book Jean-Chrys loaned him that he is going to keep (Ovid's *Metamorphoses*), a change of breeches, chemise and socks, and the sheets of paper with his verses between board covers. That's all he needs. For now. The future when it comes will be when he'll acquire lots more things.

"Something wrong?" Thomas's mother asked a couple of times.

"No, why?" he'd reply, with as much nonchalance as he could muster.

And so the calendar advances, onward to the night that Thomas has picked. All that is left is that which is hardest of all, the doing of the imagined deed.

—

Thomas goes toward the corner counter, hands spreading the dark air. The plan calls for him to light no candle. He'll just have to work in the dark. He does not want to give any clue to someone who might be walking by on the street and see a glow. His blind right hand makes contact with the counter ledge first, the left clutching on quickly after. He slides sideways and bends down to where the strongbox is kept. If it's not there, if his father somehow divined what kind of plan was forming in his son's mind, then it will be all right. Thomas can still go back to bed. This is a point of easy return.

The strongbox, however, is there. All right. The plan can move ahead. Thomas is to drag it out to where he can lift it and move it to an open place.

The sound of scraping on the floor makes him shudder. He pauses to listen if it has brought someone running. He could just take off and no one would know who brought it out from under the counter. No, Thomas doesn't hear a thing. So lift the box he does, though it's heavier than he recalls. Is that because of the dark or does it contain more than it did that day his father let him hold it? Let it be the latter. Thomas struggles to swing the weight past the counter, and strikes his hip on the counter edge as he goes by. The hip flashes pain and Thomas clamps his lips tight shut. He staggers with the box to the open area of the dark shop he has come to know well. This is where he'll have the room that he needs. He puts the strongbox down and listens once more. He counts to five and hears not a thing. All right, on to the next step.

He feels his way over to the display shelves where this month's selected fabric bolts are on show. They run from cheap to fine, beginning at the bottom. Just like in society, Thomas often thinks. No cloth of gold and silver in his father's shop, but he does have some satins, taffetas, moirés and corded silk. Then the different wools, linens and cottons. Thomas bends down to the lowest display, the green serge he hates so much. This is what he decided a few days ago to use. Anything better would be a waste. Waste not, want not is one of his father's credos.

Thomas unrolls the bolt, spilling unseen ells to the floor. Down he lays what's left of the bundle of unfurled fabric, beside the bunched-up spill. It must wait its turn.

He stands above what he can but only dimly see. His eyes have adjusted a bit to the dark so the shop is coming to him a little clearer than before. It occurs to him that it's still not too late to put things back. He's left himself this additional point of possible return. Yes, he could tidy up and go back to bed.

But no, Thomas shakes his head. He's doing this not just for himself but for everyone involved. He has reasoned it for two weeks, and the conclusion was exactly this. He has to follow nature's call. He has to become what he is capable of and not wear the cassock for which he has no call.

He bends to lift the strongbox one more time. "Rest in peace," he whispers, and beams at his wit. As he wiggles his fingers beneath the shaky old wooden box he extends the thought. What he is doing, moving the box from its hiding place to the centre of the floor, it is a sort of funeral procession. Not just for the strongbox but also for him. By following through he will be burying a life that was never for him.

Thomas gets the box in the air, and labours with his legs to carry it a few steps. He comes to feel the spread-out serge beneath his shoes and he sets the thing down. He can't help but issue a delayed grunt and a gasp. Another listen, just in case. Still nothing.

Thomas reaches out with his shaking hands to grasp the wooden box. He feels the strong iron bands and he tugs at his father's new lock. He cannot but smile. He rolls the box upon its side then completely upside down. "Weakest side up," he mouths to himself. He cups a hand to his ear. There's nothing amiss. A cat somewhere out in the street or in a nearby yard is merely yowling some complaint.

He grabs the rest of the bolt of serge and places it as thick as he can on top of what is now an upside-down box. He bunches the fabric thick and thicker still, enough to do the job.

Still not too late, he thinks again, though his head shakes a different answer. No, it has now come too far. With a sigh and the sense of a rope tightening round his chest, Thomas listens once more. This time it's a count to a mere three. His racing pulse won't let him go on. No, no one's coming. Yes, it is time.

"So be it," he says, softly like in church. An intake of breath and he moves swiftly toward the door he came through only moments ago, though it feels to him like an hour. The eyes are seeing better now, the adjustment to the dark fully made. And his heart is beating like it's in a race.

He goes into the kitchen and over to the stack of split wood piled beside the hearth. The tip of a wooden handle is sticking above the top layer of wood. "There," he says in a voice that is near normal. The word is out before he can stop it. He freezes on the spot, his left hand across the offending mouth. The house is quiet except for the racing of his breath.

No, what's that? Something is moving, a rolling sound. Thomas's heart stops its race for a moment, till the sound comes clear in his ears. Someone down the street is moving a wheeled cart on the cobbled stones. The sound is coming this way.

Thomas forces his feet to lift and steps long across the darkened kitchen floor. He grasps the contoured handle of the axe hiding behind the pile of wood. The handle is surprisingly smooth and accommodating to the touch. He lifts the axe up and away, and takes it back into the shop.

Isn't it a lot brighter now? Why it's almost like day. Oh my God, am I taking too long? What if Mother, or worse still Father, wakes early and comes down to the shop? Thomas stops and stares at the mound of piled serge on the floor, visible now in the rising light of an approaching dawn. It's a dark lumpy shape with something hidden underneath. Ah yes, that's his future under there.

The cart's rumbling wheels on the cobbled street are just outside the shop, but they sound like they're inside his head.

Feet planted and axe on high, Thomas hesitates. Then he whispers to himself: "In remembrance of me." He winces at the blasphemy but sucks in a shallow intake of air and completes the arc of his swing. The unstoppable weight of the blunt end of the axe comes down.

The crash is muted, the green serge having done its job. It is only a thud, less than he feared. The splay of wood, the crack and splinter, sound good to the ears of a son turned thief. He closes his eyes to take in the delayed tinkling of a hundred pounded coins. The rumble of the cart wheels out on the street is beginning to subside. It is moving safely away.

Thomas stands over top of what he's done. He almost tosses the axe away but hold on, he may need it yet. As a weapon. He swivels at his hips to stare at the doorway that connects the shop to the house. He sees that he left it open in his haste. He listens for footsteps, intending to count to twenty to be safe. But he stops at nine. The throbbing in his chest he has to control. He must exhale. He has to slow his heart's pace.

I could still put it all back, he tells himself. Then he looks down at the splintered box and scattered coins at his feet. No, it's too late for that. Unfold the fabric and scoop the coins, he urges his hands to begin. He needs enough, just enough to get away. To start his life anew. Cannot be caught. I'm past the point of return.

From his knees, with cupped hands, Thomas dips and delves a dozen times. He nods a silent count, depositing the handfuls into his satchel. Yet there's still so much left, so he scoops on past the number twelve. It's a change of plan he cannot resist. At sixteen he stops. There, that's enough. Then he scoops two more into the satchel. Let them keep what's left. They, his parents, they'll need something too. The breathing settles. The heart finds a slower pace.

Up Thomas stands. He grabs the green serge by its scruff and drags it and its lightened load, the smashed strongbox and remaining smatter of coins, over to where it is routinely kept. He shoves it with his foot under the corner counter. There, it won't be seen until someone goes and looks. By then it will be too late. He goes back to get his satchel, to test its weight. It's heavy, yes, but not too heavy to carry down the street. Its uncounted treasure rests atop what clothes he put in first. He puts the satchel back on the floor. Down there underneath his future is all he owns in the world. Two pairs of socks, two chemises, an extra pair of pants, half of yesterday's baguette, a block of cheese wrapped in its linen cloth, and some pages with his verses kept between the two board covers and Jean-Chrys's Ovid.

Oh, and a small square of blue silk. Thomas doesn't expect to need it anymore, not in Paris, but he brought it along rather than leave it behind.

Thomas slides an arm through the handles of the satchel and swings it on his back. He can tell right away that the weight is going to leave a red mark on his shoulder. No doubt about that. So be it. A small price to pay to purchase a life that he wants, not the one his parents wanted to impose.

Thomas sweeps to the door then descends from the shop down to the cobbles of the street. The cart he'd heard before is nowhere to be seen. There's not a soul, and the only sound is the creak and whine of his father's shop sign. Oh, he was wrong, he sees. There's that old yellow mangy dog curled up on the steps of Monsieur Carré's house. The dog raises his head to study Thomas then lowers it again. Down the street Thomas pads.

So far, so good. Every few steps he shifts the weight of the satchel from one shoulder to the other. It is much, much heavier than he thought, and it's getting worse with every step. The strap is burning into his shoulder, but he staggers on.

—

Thomas peeks round the corner to check the time. It's a little after half past six according to the clock on the tower gate. Worry darkens his face. The diligence should have already arrived. More importantly, it should have already set off again, with him safely aboard and cleanly away.

Is this not the day? And the hour? Thomas was sure that it was, but now … What if his father is up and in the shop? What if something is bothering him, and he decides to check it out? He will know something has happened. He will go right to the corner counter and look underneath. Thomas's head swivels between where the diligence will board its passengers and the street that leads back up to his house. What if the diligence doesn't come at all? It could be held up by highwaymen, Cartouche or some other. Or maybe a wheel came off outside of town. An axle broken en route.

Thomas looks down at the satchel, pinned between his two feet, his knees touching above it like crossed swords. All he's done so far is touch the top of the jumble of coins. He pulled out as many as he needed to cover the fare for the three-day diligence ride to Paris, no more. Yet what he glimpsed of the rest is more than enough. Four or five *écus* and even one *Louis d'or,* along with the expected mix of coins of lesser denominations, a hundred or more *sols* and *deniers*. His father has done well, done well to rebuild the business after the setback at the hands of La Motte. The man should be pleased with what he's accomplished, his father should. He is good at what he does, being a cloth merchant. The portion Thomas is taking – an anonymous gift of sorts from unknowing parents – will not hurt them too much. No, he's pretty sure about that. They're meant to run the shop they own. It's just that Thomas's future is different from theirs. In time they'll come to understand that.

What exactly Thomas's taking will all add up to he won't know until he's somewhere safe and settled. Then he'll do a full count. That won't happen on a street corner in Vire or anywhere else where there could be prying eyes. Thomas can't be too cautious about that. There are thieves all around. His father taught him that.

Thomas tips his head so his tricorn touches the stone wall beside him. It is as close as he's had to a moment's respite since the morning in full darkness began. He allows his lids to cover his eyes for just a moment. Much as he'd like to sleep, he knows he cannot. Not yet. He'll just rest his warm eyes until he's on his way. He allows his hands to dangle by his sides and they come in eager contact with the stones and mortar valleys of the wall. His fingers find the grooves and trace their curving path. He tells himself that once inside the diligence, once the departure is complete, why then he'll…

"Thomas? Thomas! What? Why are you…"

Thomas's eyes fly open. The hands jerk to come up as fists. It's Jean-Chrysostome, whom Thomas has not seen in weeks, not since he began to work each day in his father's shop. And there beside Jean-Chrys – Thomas feels his face pinch at the recognition – is Vinaigre. Thomas feels his chest contract and his whole body dips. His knees bang together in a ridiculous attempt to hide the satchel that is clearly visible and wedged between his feet. Thomas glances down and sees how stupidly he's reacted. He fights to stand erect and nonchalant. It's an awkward, failing attempt.

"Up early you are, Jean-Chrys." Thomas begins. His smile is as false as it is fleeting. He gestures at Vinaigre, "and with … a friend." Thomas doesn't recall Vinaigre's real name and he doesn't want to say Vinaigre. "Didn't know you two…" He leaves the rest unsaid.

"Bet not," says Vinaigre with a sneer. "C'mon, Jean, let's get going. Better get there early rather than late."

"A minute," says Jean-Chrysostome, hand upraised. "Tell you what, Nic, you head on. Catch you up in a bit, all right?"

"All right," says Vinaigre.

It comes to Thomas that Vinaigre's Christian name is Nicolas.

Vinaigre starts to walk away, but turns round over his shoulder and nods at Jean-Chrysostome. It looks to Thomas like Vinaigre is sending some kind of warning. "Till later, Jean-Chrys."

"Understood." Jean-Chrys touches his tricorn with the tip of his finger as a goodbye to Vinaigre. He swings round to Thomas, whose eyes are burning into the one walking away.

"Nic? You call him Nic?" parrots Thomas in a mocking tone. "What are you doing with that one? He smells like piss."

"He does not. And me, what am *I* doing?" Jean-Chrys's voice rises in incredulity. "Haven't seen you in weeks and when I do, here you are hunched over hiding round a corner, crouched like a wastrel looking like you haven't slept. Is there somebody after you or something? And what's that you're trying to hide in the satchel? What's going on?"

"Nothing. Just…" Thomas tries to manufacture a grin. He reaches out to tug on Jean-Chrys's sleeve, "…just waiting for the diligence, that's all. And I got up up too early, I guess. Worried I'd be late. That's it. Off to visit … an uncle."

"An uncle? You don't have any uncle. Your mother's only brother died last year and your father doesn't have a brother."

"There's one you didn't know about, all right? He's on my father's side. In Vitré. That's where I'm going, Vitré."

Jean-Chrys steps back. The expression on his face says he doesn't believe a word of it.

"Oh yeah? Well, the diligence on this day doesn't go toward Brittany. It goes to Paris." Jean-Chrys's face is pained. He shakes his head. "I've got to go. When you want to tell me what's really going on, you come see me. Understood?"

"Understood." Thomas issues a slight exhale.

Jean-Chrys turns and trudges away, looking back twice at Thomas before he turns the corner. With a final shake of the head he disappears from Thomas's sight.

Thomas exhales long and deep, ridding himself of all the air that wasn't any good to him over the past few minutes. That was stupid. Careless. And what are those two doing together anyway? They can't be friends. Though what if they are? He's leaving Vire. Jean-Chrys and everybody else in this little town can have any friend they want. He doesn't care anymore.

The thrum and clop of horses turns Thomas's head sharply to the right. Into the open area in front of the clock-tower gate come four chestnut horses kicking up clouds of dust. The diligence on its flexible frame bobs in behind. The coach rolls to a stop. All of a sudden the previously empty square becomes a tiny hub. When Thomas arrived he was by himself, not counting the water carrier who was seated, back against the gate, repairing some part of his equipment. Now, in an instant, there are a half dozen people gathered beside and around the coach. One fellow is bringing the horses their water and oats; the rest look to be either there to meet someone arriving or, like Thomas, about to board the diligence on its way out of town. Thomas scans the baggage pile. No one else is carrying what he is, just a satchel. Everyone else has something more substantial. There are two wooden trunks, a large wicker basket filled with something cloth-wrapped, an empty birdcage, a large canvas- and rope-wrapped shape as big as a giant dog, if dogs were square.

Thomas looks up to the tower clock. Ten minutes of seven. With any luck at all, he'll be away in a few minutes. He picks up his satchel and its awkward weight, somehow even heavier than before. His shoulder feels like it's on fire. He hurries as best he can toward the coach, straightaway to the driver who has just jumped down from his seat. The man is stroking the closest of his four horses. For what seems like forever, Thomas stands behind the man and waits for him to notice him standing there. Unable to wait any longer, Thomas taps the driver on the shoulder.

"Monsieur." Thomas lowers the satchel to the ground.

The driver swings about. "Young pup. What is it?"

"Oh," says Thomas, recoiling at the man's onion breath and the gaps between his teeth, "just thought I'd let you know I'm ready." Thomas unrolls his fingers to show the man his coins.

The driver sizes Thomas up, beginning with the well-worn satchel on the ground and the dust-covered shoes. He continues all the way up the tan socks, navy breeches and sand-coloured *justaucorps*, up to his plain collar and unwigged dark brown hair tied in a loose queue.

"Ready are you, pup? Well, youse be ready all you like. It's when *I'm* ready that counts. Understood?" The driver curls his lips and arches back his head. Thomas can see up his nose. It's not a pretty sight.

Thomas acknowledges the driver's words with a nod. He steps back to wait for an announcement or some other sign that the diligence is boarding. The clock tower says it's now a minute of seven. All the passengers who were aboard the diligence when it rolled into the square appear to have descended. The coach is still more than half full. Thomas wonders if all the baggage that's to come down has been removed from up top. His head is on a swivel, eyes left to the diligence, right upon the clock face on the gate and then up the street that leads to where he lives. Used to live. Thomas feels a steady trickle in each armpit.

"Passengers! All passengers!" shouts the driver. He is standing beside the fold-down step that leads up and into the middle passenger compartment.

Thomas grabs his satchel and lifts it with scuffling feet over to the driver. He plops the satchel down at the man's feet.

"Still ready, are you, pup?"

"Yes, sir."

"Sir, is it? We likes that."

Thomas can think of nothing further to say so he blinks his eyes at the man. The driver allows a hint of a smile.

"Ready to go?"

"Yes I am."

"To Saint-Malo it is then?"

"Saint-Malo? No. But, but," stutters Thomas. His face is that of someone being punched. "Isn't this coach for Paris?"

"Oh no, is it Paris you're wanting?"

"It is."

The driver smacks his own forehead with the two palms of his hands. His expression of comic stupidity is profound.

Thomas doesn't know what to say or think. Everything was planned around this being the day for the diligence to Paris. It has to be Paris. Thomas looks around, and especially up the street where he expects his father to come running any moment now. Thomas picks up his bag. He'll have to go hide somewhere outside of town, maybe down in the subterrane. That'll buy him a day or two, until …

"Oh yeah," says the driver at last, bored with his game. "It is Paris."

"It is?"

"Aye, it is. You'll be in the back compartment, pup. Put the satchel up top first, then find a seat inside."

Thomas goes pale.

"No, the bag, the bag has to stay with me."

The driver arches an eye and tips his head back. Thomas looks away, not wanting to see up his nose again. His feet pinch tight upon the satchel between his legs.

"Does it now?" says the driver. "I think I said on top." He scratches his head. "Yes, yes I did. And I'm the driver, right? Youse agree? Good. Well the rule is up top."

"But—"

"Too crowded for a large satchel inside. It's up top with your bag or it's wait another day. Youse can hope for the best."

"But—"

"The compartments, pup, the compartments. People don't want to be tripping over bags. Next passenger," the driver shouts, looking past Thomas.

Thomas turns to see a large man behind him, as pudgy as prosperity can make a man. He has ruddy cheeks and is breathing heavily. The pudgy fellow is digging inside his *veston* for something. A pocket watch comes out.

"Please, sir," says Thomas to the pudgy man, "just a moment more."

Thomas holds up a single finger to demonstrate that his word is good. It will just be a single minute. Pudgy makes a face. Without waiting for anything more than that Thomas steps closer to the driver, into where the man's onion aura is strong. Thomas whispers in the man's ear.

"How much to keep the satchel? With me, I mean? There's … family heirlooms in the bag. Can't lose them. How much to keep it with me?"

"Ah," says the driver, wrinkles appearing at the edges of his eyes, "that's different, isn't it? Family looms. How nice. Another fi- ten *sols* is what that'll be. Yes, ten's the rule if I remember right. Then youse can keep the bag. On the lap though, young pup, on the lap. Crowded it is, understand."

Thomas nods that he does. He crouches down and undoes the ties to the satchel. He opens it as little as he possibly can, just enough to allow his hand to squeeze through. He digs around inside, coming up with a few coins. It adds up to seven *sols*, not enough. Thomas thrusts the hand back in. He pulls out an *écu* this time and drops it like it's on fire. He glances up at the driver to see if he has noticed. Caught showing too much interest, the driver looks away. Thomas retrieves just the right amount the third time.

"Next passenger," the driver calls gruffly. The portly man who is that next passenger needs no such shout. He's not even an arm's length away. He recoils at the driver's loud call.

"There," says Thomas with a whisper, straightening up. He's made sure his satchel is re-tied. "There's the ten."

"That's the way," says the driver in a low voice, a hand closing over the coins. He sees how Thomas treats his satchel like it contains his very life itself. "Keep your family looms close, pup. And be careful who you trust. The road has its thieves. Away youse goes. Up and in now."

Thomas twists away from any further conversation. He is angry at himself. He said and showed too much. But what choice did he have? He couldn't put the satchel on top.

Up the fold-down step Thomas climbs. At the top step he sees at once why the driver didn't want any baggage inside. All three compartments are filled, or near enough. Thomas turns around and looks at the pudgy fellow who'll be the next one up the steps, and behind him there's a Capuchin monk who has a hood covering his head. Thomas takes a deep breath.

"Oh well," he says softly, and turns sideways to step inside the coach. The compartment with the best chance for a seat is the one in the rear. There is also a pretty girl. Thomas sees that she is dressed in shades of blue. It looks like taffeta but he's too far away to tell. The girl is seated beside a matronly looking woman he surmises is an aunt or a governess. As Thomas squeezes past those already seated he makes his excuses, especially when the coin-laden satchel strikes people as he goes by. Each person, without fail, tells him the bag has to go outside and on top. He gives an uncomprehending shrug to one and all, and clasps what he is carrying ever closer to the left side of his chest.

"Anyone sitting there?" he asks the girl in shades of blue.

The girl, whose name Thomas will later learn is Marielle, looks at him blankly. She shifts her gaze to the empty bench opposite her, suggesting with her eyes that this young man with the satchel clutched to his chest sit there. She does not say a word.

"I will leave that side for those coming next," says Thomas. He inclines his head at the portly fellow who is now filling the doorway of the diligence. The Capuchin is almost certainly right behind.

The girl rolls her eyes but nonetheless does what he implies. She shifts over on the seat to make a bit of extra room for the young man. Thomas plunks down next to her. Their hips make full contact, though both keep frozen faces to pretend they don't feel a thing. Thomas brings the satchel to rest upon his lap. Its heaviness is at this point a comfort, a reminder of what he'll have to make a fresh start. He supposes he'll feel differently about the weight later on. The journey to Paris will take three days, with overnight stays at two inns along the way.

"Shouldn't be in here with that," says the pudgy fellow to Thomas as he sits down directly opposite the girl in shades of blue. He introduces himself to anyone listening. His name is Georges Strombeau, a wine merchant from Bordeaux. He's pointing at Thomas's satchel and pointing upward to the roof of the diligence to show where it's supposed to go.

"So I hear," says Thomas. "Thank you." He nods at the big fellow while covering his satchel with both hands and holding fast. He'll not let his satchel go anywhere he cannot see.

You've done well, my fat friend, Thomas thinks, looking across at Strombeau. The merchant has a bulging waist, an outfit of matching reds, and a grey wig that doesn't hide a few tufts of reddish-looking hair peeking out from beneath. He also has a pocket watch that must be new, judging from the way the fellow checks it every other minute.

"We're late, don't you think?" Thomas asks of Strombeau. Of course he knows the answer, but cannot help voicing his worry. Any minute now he half expects his father to run out from under the clock-tower gate with his fists upraised.

"More than a quarter hour," says Strombeau. The smile on the merchant's face says that he is pleased there's someone who shares his disapproval of the diligence not running on time. Nonetheless, he eyeballs the satchel in Thomas's lap and gestures to the lad that it could and should go up top.

The Capuchin is the next to find a seat, directly opposite Thomas. Père Athanase is the name that he mutters to no one in particular at all. Now inside the coach his hood is down his back, exposing his tonsured head. He's dressed in the homespun brown, with the standard rope cord around his waist and with sandals on his feet. He's thin with dark, sunken eyes and a pointy nose. The chin and cheeks have a thin, almost non-existent beard. His is the kind of face and frame, Thomas decides, a man of God should truly have. He's gaunt enough to show that he's suffered already and there's more to come.

There's a shout from above. Then comes the sound of a cracking whip. The diligence lurches forward and after a few jerks starts to roll. The coach and its passengers are on their way. Lisieux tonight after a full day's ride. Évreux tomorrow after yet another long day. Then it's the arrival in Paris and the future begins.

"About time." Strombeau looks at Thomas as a kindred spirit on the matter of timeliness.

"Indeed." Thomas leans back with a tiny smile he simply cannot hold back. He's startled by the relief he is feeling. It's as if his body knows what's happening and what it is he has in the satchel. He feels muscles he didn't even know he had suddenly let go. He closes his eyes to savour the sensation. Yes, he could use a good sleep.

"Why, look at that fellow." There is laughter in Strombeau's voice. "How vexed is he? My, my. Missed the diligence is my guess. Tough luck, I say, because they'd better not stop now. Not since we're late and only finally on our way."

Thomas opens his eyes. He presses his face to the glass. He sees his father running hard, face fierce and fists upraised. Jean Pichon is through the opening under the clock-tower gate and heading for the moving coach. Right behind comes Jean-Chrys, then it's Vinaigre. The two boys are pointing at the diligence and yelling at his father. Thomas cannot hear what the boys are saying, but Jean Pichon's voice rings out loud and clear.

"Thomas," his father shouts above his panting, "stop. Thomas, it's all we have."

Jean Pichon narrows the gap, arms outstretched. He's closing in on the back of the diligence.

Thomas takes his face from the window. He thrusts his shoulder blades against the back of the seat, eyes straight front. His hands clutch the satchel like he's at sea and the bag is jetsam keeping him afloat. If he lets it go, he'll sink and drown.

"How red is that face! I tell you." Strombeau gestures toward Thomas, urging him to look out the window. "Better watch it, I'd say. Looks like the fellow could explode."

"Can't see," says the matronly woman on the other side of the girl in blue. She is Madame Soule, a woman of inescapable size, a monument of inquisitiveness. "What is it? I cannot see."

"Running fellow," replies Strombeau. "Chasing someone named Thomas." He glances across at Thomas and cocks an eyebrow. "You're from this town. That anyone known to you, some Thomas?"

Thomas's shrug comes with a wince. His face is the colour of cheese.

"And what's your name? You didn't say." Strombeau's eyes do not match the light-hearted smile on his face. The eyes are narrowed and calculating.

"Jean," says Thomas, borrowing the Christian name of his father and of his friend Jean-Chrys. "Jean Tyrell," Thomas adds, lifting the family name of a girl he sometimes adores in church.

"Tyrell? Sounds English," says Strombeau.

"Long ago." Thomas tries to take a breath. He feels like he's going to be sick.

"It's theft, Thomas, it's theft." It is his father's voice. It's coming loud and clear from alongside the moving diligence. Right alongside. "Can you hear me, boy? It's theft."

A swirling feeling fills Thomas. He takes a quick glance and sees the top of his father's head and a hand reaching out. He cannot look, he cannot do a thing. He turns to the Capuchin, who is staring back at him. Père Athanase shakes his head slowly. There is disapproval or is it disgust on his gaunt face.

"Oops," sings out Strombeau.

"What is it? I still can't see," says Madame Soule with a deeply furrowed brow.

"Well, that's that." Strombeau sits back in his seat.

The diligence rolls on, faster than before. Its bobbing becomes a steady rhythm of the horses' clips and clops.

"What happened?" asks Thomas. His voice is a croak.

"The running man bit the dust," says Strombeau, sounding disappointed. "Just like that." He'd been enjoying the spectacle.

"Bit the dust. Whatever does that mean?" asks Madame Soule, the crimson on her cheeks enflamed.

"Just that," says Strombeau. He uses his hand and fingers to make a running man then collapses it into his other hand.

Madame Soule shakes her head. She does not understand.

"For God's sake, the yelling man grabbed at his chest just as he was coming alongside. Then just like that he fell to the ground. He had an awful look on his face I do say. A couple of young ones running behind came to his aid."

"And?" asks Madame Soule, a hand outstretched in Strombeau's direction.

"Don't know. The road turned. Fellow's out of sight." Strombeau looks at Thomas, whose pale, pained face gives him a start. "What's wrong with you? The fellow will be all right. Don't take it so."

Thomas shakes his head. "Sorry," he says, and closes his eyes. He squeezes back what feels like tears, but his stomach won't quit. It's churning acids and there's a surge in his chest.

"Couldn't see a thing," says Madame Soule. "I missed it."

"Half an hour late," Strombeau announces to the compartment. "Not so bad. The driver can make it up by nightfall if he pushes the horses."

Thomas doesn't even hear the banter. There is too much going on in his stomach. He thinks of his father running and shouting and falling to his face. His stomach is on fire. There comes a heave and then one more. Then it's a series of burning pulses. Thomas brings his eyes back to open. He's no longer in control of his body. The compartment and people of the diligence are a blurry view. Thomas grabs the window handle and down slides the glass. He sticks his head out to suck a bit of air. There is a pause. Then the entire diligence hears the young man at the rear window spurt and retch.

—

The smell of smoke is strong. Thomas wakes with a start.

"What is it?" he asks, blinking, straightening in his seat. He shifts the satchel in his lap. It makes no difference. The weight of the thing has long since numbed his whole groin. He hates to think how he might have ruined his poor thing. "Is something burning?" he asks.

"A fire in the forest. That's my guess." Strombeau is the only one to respond. "First noticed it a ways back. You've had a long sleep, after your … well, you know, your…" Strombeau points at the window.

Thomas acknowledges with a wince the reference to his vomiting. He looks around to see if anyone else wants to remind him as well. No? No, they're all asleep, like he was until a moment ago. The Capuchin, Père Athanase, has an unopened book clutched to his chest. He sits slumped beside Strombeau with his mouth wide open. Madame Soule, the matron accompanying pretty Marielle, she has a pinched look to her large sleeping face. It looks to Thomas as if in a dream Madame Soule is smelling something bad. And Marielle, well, Marielle has her head on Thomas's shoulder. So he tilts his head back and takes a good look. Hmm, she smells like some kind of perfume. Flowers and something like ginger. He follows the rise and fall of Marielle's stomacher and the bare movement of the rounded tops of her breasts. Her cheeks are flush with heat. You are blessed young woman, thinks Thomas, with your particular beauty. Your face is pretty, but of a kind normally seen in mourning. The underlying sadness, for Thomas, doubles the appeal of the girl.

Visage de tristesse
Amour de justesse.

Hmm, thinks Thomas, that's not bad. He'd write that down if he could. There is paper in the satchel, but he has no quill, no ink and no room on his lap. The lines might be there later, though more likely they will not. Whatever the case, it's good to have some rhymes coming to him at all. It's been a while since he's written any little thing, not since … well, not since he started to work in the damned clothier shop. That's behind him now.

"Lovely, isn't she?" says Strombeau in a loud whisper. He waves a hand in Marielle's direction. Thomas looks to the window rather than acknowledge the comment. It's inappropriate, coming from someone as old as Strombeau.

"Won't see a thing out there, my boy," continues Strombeau, eager to have someone to talk with about the smoke and the fire. "Holding us back, it is, the fire and its smoke. No doubt about it. We'll not make up the lost time. The driver will soon have to stop. The horses can't go on much longer."

Thomas nods half-heartedly and turns back to the window. Oh yes, now he sees what is happening outside. Beyond the diligence is a thick haze, like a shroud as seen from the inside. It's a blanket of smoke and the coach is barely moving. No wonder. Neither the horses nor the driver will be able to see a thing. Now that he listens, Thomas can even hear the horses snort and wheeze at the dirty air.

"See what you're saying." Thomas is again looking at Strombeau. The portly merchant has his watch out again. "The thick smoke is holding us back."

"Exactly. Can't make Lisieux before dark, not at this pace."

"Suppose not."

Marielle stirs on Thomas's shoulder. She opens her grey eyes and sees Thomas's brown ones mere inches away. She springs back.

"What're you doing?"

Marielle's sudden words wake her lady companion, Madame Soule. The Capuchin comes to life as well. Thomas raises his hands to show his innocence, to any who would think he's done something he has not. "You fell asleep on my shoulder. That's it. I swear."

Marielle studies Thomas with great doubt. She is now as erect as a nun.

"Can't be too careful," says Madame Soule knowingly. She squeezes the slender fingers of her young companion's hand, pulling her away from Thomas.

Père Athanase curls his thin lips at the young man. He says, "You shouldn't, you know. Swear, that is." And with that, he shifts his gaze slowly away, toward the book he begins to pretend to read. Only Strombeau is amused at the confusion. That's because he actually saw what happened: nothing. He catches Thomas's gaze with a wink to let him know that he's on his side.

The diligence comes to a halt. The coach sways forwards and back. The sound of horses stomping and pawing the ground fills the compartment. Thomas imagines what he hears is the horses rearing and kicking to get away from the dirt and grit in the air.

"Can't go on, we can't," shouts the driver. He's come down from on top of the coach and climbed part way up the passenger's pull-down step to make his announcement. "Horses can't breathe in the smoke. Can't see myself. Hands in front of me, no not even. Darkness'll come quickly. That it will. So we stops while we can. Inn's right there." He points through the diligence to what lies on the opposite side.

A dozen heads turn to where the driver is pointing. Sure enough, through the thick smoke each can just make out a sprawling half-timbered building. It has a sign and a sprout of greenery to show it's a drinking establishment and an inn.

"Down youse gets, one and all. Lucky you're with me. Lookin' out for youse, I am." The driver stands at the ready as each passenger comes down the steps. His left hand provides a helping hand to their elbows while the right is cupped and out where all can see, as though he's hoping for a little recognition of his attention to their care, a coin or two as the passengers descend and file by. The first three to descend choose not to notice the driver's cupped hand. The fourth looks right at it and makes a snort. The driver curls up his fingers and puts his request away.

—

The inn is crowded, with all three upstairs rooms already taken by other travellers. So the passengers and the driver from the diligence are told they will have to bed down where they can, the men in the main room on rolled out *paillasses* and the women in a storage room out back. The improvised sleeping arrangements are not particularly comfortable, yet no one complains. Well, no one except Madame Soule, but that is expected. Complaining is part of who she seems to be. She says she's never ever stayed anywhere near so rough, and if she had known she would … but no one hears the end of her rant. Oddly enough, Monsieur Strombeau, the wealthiest in the group if one can judge by the cost of his clothes, has lots of words to share with anyone who will listen, and not one is a complaint. In fact, he tells everyone who will listen that the rough accommodation reminds him of his youth. He's stayed in many worse places he announces time and again.

After a night of drinking to excess, the driver beds down beside Thomas, their straw mattresses an inch apart. He reaches over and gives the "young pup" a push as he leans in close to the his ear.

"Psst."

"Huh?" says Thomas, opening his eyes.

"Tired?"

"Guess so."

Thomas is curled up on his thin mattress, the satchel tucked in tight against his mid-section. He's been going over the events of the day, especially the reports Strombeau gave him of his father running and falling as he chased the diligence. Many was the time he wished some ill upon his father or that he'd just go away, but it pained him to picture the scene that Strombeau described. His stomach did the rest. Thomas doesn't wish him dead, not cold as a stone in the ground. The man provided for Thomas and the family and never got cross with him or whacked his ass when he didn't deserve it. As for his mother, back in Vire probably wringing her hands worried about her vanished would-be priest, she'd eventually come to understand. Not now, but someday, she'd see why he had to go and take some coins to help him start out. That's true, isn't it? He chose a different future, that's all. It wasn't to harm anyone or because he gave in to some dark desire. Was it? Thomas tossed and rolled on the straw mattress thinking about such things. The end result: he decided with a clench of his hands that one day he'd go back to Vire. He would tell everyone what he'd done and seen, and how high he had climbed. He'd share stories of his adventures and successes. Then his parents would be glad their boy did what he did. They would clasp him to their chests. He would be a prodigal son all their own. It was at that point that the driver gave him a push and whispered, with a bit of spit, in Thomas's ear.

"Sorry, pup." The driver is leaning on his elbow, his head and his shoulders swaying like he's had too much rum. His hot breath, a mix of alcohol and onions, is invading Thomas's face. "Thought you'd like to know. Make up some time. Tomorrow we will. To Évreux before dark or God take me he will."

"Good." Thomas rolls over to face the other way. "Thanks." He adds over his shoulder as an afterthought.

"Yeah, good."

The driver lies down, but only for a count of four. Up he gets, back on his elbow. Since Thomas is showing him his back the driver has to crawl around the top of the boy's mattress. Thomas hears the commotion but keeps his eyes closed hoping it will go away. The driver puts two firm hands down on the mat. And lowers his face so his mouth is near enough to touch Thomas's ear.

"Knows a place in Évreux you'll like. Sets up the pup, we will."

Thomas does not say a word. Nor does he move. But the eyes are as wide open as two eyes can be. The driver's hot breath and wet spray is filling his ear. Thomas is ready to strike out to defend himself against the man if he must, if the driver tries to put his hand down his pants. Jean-Chrys told him that once in the sacristy of Saint-Thomas one of the priests tried to fondle his rear. Thomas readies his elbow. It will lead the way if he has to strike out. But then he hears the driver scuff away on his knees. The driver has retreated to his own mattress, the one right beside, taking his odours and hot breath with him.

"That's right, pup," Thomas hears the driver say. The man's voice is slurred like he's giving in to his liquor and dropping off to sleep. "Set youse up. Knows what I mean?" An instant later the driver's snoring begins.

No, I don't know what you mean, Thomas says to himself. He rolls over to stare straight up at the rafters overhead. And I don't want to know. Whoever you are, driver man, you have nothing to do with me. Thomas pushes himself to the far edge of his *paillasse*, as far from the driver as he can get. It takes him quite a while to close his eyes and allow himself a bit of sleep.

—

Off and on throughout the next day, as the diligence bobs and rolls along its route toward Évreux, Thomas goes over what the driver said to him the night before. Yes, it was dark and Thomas was tumbling asleep, and yes, the driver was drunk, but whatever did he mean about setting someone up? Thomas purses his lips and decides that the driver should have kept his drunken talk to himself.

At the inn with the green drum on its sign, where the diligence stops at midday to change horses, the driver reminds passengers that it's quite a ways to the next stop. They might want to relieve themselves and to get something for lunch. Thomas decides not to spend any of his money on food – he still has a bit of bread and cheese – but it comes into his head that yes, he could do something else when he goes to take his piss. He could lighten the satchel a little and at the same time spread around a bit of what's hidden within the bag. He heads for the little room where travellers are told to do their necessities. As always, he carries the satchel. Once in the room, with the door closed and locked, Thomas opens the satchel before he lowers his breeches. He scoops out a handful of coins. He comes up with a mix of all sorts, even a couple of *écus* and one *Louis d'or*. Into each shoe he places a sprinkling of the coins, just enough so he can still squeeze in his feet. Then he scoops some more and wraps them in two *mouchoirs*, one for each pocket of his *justaucorps*. He walks a bit to see how it feels to the soles of his feet, and to make sure there's no telltale jingle. He's thinking of highwaymen, the thieves of the road. Cartouche is said to be anywhere, so one never knows. If he or some other thief stops the diligence and takes away everyone's bags, at least they won't get all of Thomas's money. He'll have out-thought the thieves on that.

"Much longer?" an unknown voice calls out, rapping on the door of the little room. "Can't wait much more."

"Almost done," Thomas yells back. He repacks his satchel and lowers his pants to perform the other thing he came to do.

—

"Hurt your leg back there?" asks Strombeau of Thomas when everyone is back in the diligence.

"No." Thomas studies his seatmate. "Why?"

They're side by side now, after a switch of seats Thomas has made. He wants to have a better look at Marielle, and that's accomplished across from her rather than right beside.

"Oh, I don't know. I thought you were walking a little funny coming back to the coach, that's all. Like you have a sore foot or bad leg."

"Oh that." Thomas scrunches the bottoms of his feet to feel the circular shapes of the coins underfoot. "Yes, you're right. I twisted my ankle. It'll be all right." Thomas cannot help but smile. A secret is not an easy thing to keep.

"Maybe if you didn't always carry that satchel everywhere." Strombeau hunches his shoulders in a quizzical way.

"You could be right. But it's not for too much longer. The ride'll soon be over."

"What's that got to do with it? Put the damn thing up on top right now."

"Sure," says Thomas, seeming to agree yet going his own way with the rest of his remark. "One more night and we'll be in Paris."

Strombeau blinks at the lad's resistance to do what he suggests. In the silence that ensues, Madame Soule leans forward to start what a conversation of her own. She directs her words at Père Athanase, but she speaks so loudly that the entire compartment has no choice but to hear what she has to say.

"You've been to the Mont, I assume."

"The Mont?" the monk replies, looking up from his book. "Which mount is that, Madame? There are many, you know."

"Saint-Michel of course. Honestly. We are still in Normandy, are we not? Really. When I say the Mont, I mean Mont Saint-Michel."

"I see." Athanase goes back to reading his book.

"Well?" says Madame Soule, taken aback that the Capuchin is not delighted to engage. "I would value your opinion, Father, I would. I was at the Mont a month ago. Most disappointing, more than a little. It struck me – and this is why I ask you, you wear the Capuchin habit after all – it struck me that no one goes there for salvation anymore. It's to brave the tides, risk the quicksand, touch the effigy, buy a souvenir and fill their faces. Am I wrong? Am I not right? You must have an opinion. You're a monk."

Père Athanase puts a finger to mark his place in the book then pauses to consider his reply. That reply, when it comes, is delivered with a slowly turning head like he is speaking to a raptly listening crowd. "Well, it is my experience, and I speak to you as a fellow Christian traveller on the road of life, that…" Père Athanase clearly enjoys the sound of his own voice. "… so yes, Madame, your observations about today's pilgrims are mostly apt. Yet on the other hand…"

Thomas does not follow the monk's talk as it goes on and on. He is able to block out Athanase's drone as well as the occasional interjection of Madame Soule's counterpoints. Instead, the sound of horses' hooves on the road swells in Thomas's ears. From time to time he glances at Marielle, whose attention is on the embroidery in her busy hands. Her long delicate fingers move surely and silently. Thomas is drawn to the way she barely moves and rarely speaks. Her only movement seems to be the motion of the coach itself. She reminds him of long grass in the wind, swaying slightly. Marielle's neck is slender, the colour of cream, so lovely to look at with her blue velvet choker and tiny pearl. He's sure that she comes from money, from a family at ease. How nice that must be. Not to have coins in your shoes and a satchel on your lap, but rather lots of money safe at some grand home. He and Marielle would make a good couple, would they not? She would be his devoted wife and they'd live on her parents' large estate. He'd write verse as they came to him and maybe a play or a book. Perhaps a history of something or a novel about an adventurous young man. Thomas imagines he's cradling Marielle's face, placing a hand upon her pale pink cheek. She is warm to his touch, soft as new wool. At once, words come to him, words he dares to mumble barely aloud.

Adrift in the dark,
No wind in the sail.

Closer, my beauty,
I'll tell you a tale.

Marielle looks up. Her grey eyes meet those of her admirer. She gives Thomas a change of expression. It's not quite a smile, but it comes close. Her lips part for an instant. Down goes the embroidery to her lap. She inclines to one side, crossing her ankles. The movement shifts the folds of the fabric covering her knees. Thomas recites what lines come to him next. He speaks them loud enough for Marielle to just hear.

Bend
Bend in the breeze.

Willow!
How you sway
and you tease.

"The emptiest vessel," says Madame Soule in a voice intended to command the entire diligence. She looks right at Thomas. "It makes the loudest noise." Madame sends a nod as if that drives home her point.

Thomas raises his eyebrows at the irony of what Madame has said, and he sees and hears Strombeau chuckle out loud. Thomas sends Madame Soule a smiling wink. That causes a flutter of Madame's lashes. She reaches out and forcibly turns Marielle's face away from the disreputable young man and points at the embroidery she should be doing.

There is no further conversation for a while. Père Athanase goes back to his book, Strombeau to reading a letter he's unfolded from a pocket and the young woman and her older companion to busy needlework in their laps. Thomas hears no more lines of poetry coming his way. The clop of hooves and the sway induced by the horses' steadily tugging pull bring an afternoon of drowsiness to him, and indeed to all passengers along for the ride.

—

It turns out that the inn the diligence stops at for Évreux is not in the town but on the outskirts. As inns go, this one does not look promising. Even Thomas, who hasn't travelled much up to this point in his life, is disappointed. This is his new life, and it's supposed to be a promising start. He expected some comfort, a level or two above what he knew back in Vire. What he sees is nothing of the kind. The place where the coach has stopped looks more like a rundown farmhouse than an inn. Though it does, it is true, boast a pole and a sign. There are no words on the sign, but there is a peeling paint image of a boar's head. It looks like the sign was painted a generation ago and has not been touched up since. Some of the timbers of the main building are sagging. There is what appears to be rotten fill here and there, with sprouts of vegetation. As for the roof, its thatch has not been attended to in quite a while. Instead of seamless and smooth, the thatch is tufted and uneven with some thin, sunken patches. Thomas is not the only passenger to check the sky when he steps down off the diligence. Nearly everyone is checking for any sign of rain. They can see from the outside that the roof of this inn may well leak. Loose grey clouds are blowing swiftly over head. There's a hint of blue in the distance, so the travellers just might be all right for the one night they have to pass in the boar-sign inn.

Chickens scatter and cluck to get out of the driver's way when he descends from up top. He lowers the walk-down steps for the passengers to get out for the night, then whistles at the inn. A child in oversized clothes, a boy of seven or eight but wearing the hand-me-downs from someone nine or ten, comes out of the main building at a run. From what Thomas can make out from the gestures, the driver wants the boy to help him unload the diligence. He holds up a coin for the lad if he will climb up top and toss down all the bags and sacks. The boy comes closer, checks out the denomination of the coin then nods and goes about his task.

One after the other all ten passengers in the three compartments step out and come down. Each stretches and shakes his or her legs once they get to the ground. Thomas is the last to descend. He had stalled, hoping to help Marielle make her descent, his hand in hers and maybe a touch to her waist. Alas, Madame Soule was too smart for that. She batted away Thomas's hand when he tried to make his gentlemanly move.

"If you please," was all Madame Soule said. Marielle, however, acknowledged his attempted assistance with a shy smile.

By the time Thomas is to the ground everyone is well into the swap of stories about how unbearably long the journey was and how ravished and parched he or she is. Thomas resists the urge to join in. Instead, with his satchel of coins and clothes clutched to his mid-section in his two arms, he heads for the open doorway of the inn. A large man, balding in the centre of an unruly mass of hair, steps into the frame. Behind him, in the shadow of the interior, is a skinny serving girl with a low-scooped chemise revealing ample breasts. The serving girl adjusts her bonnet as she looks out to see how many there will be for the evening meal. Thomas nods at the girl and she curtseys him back.

"Welcome all." The innkeeper's voice is loud. "Everything you need is right this way. Food, drink, a place to sleep. It's all yours." He pauses for effect. "All yours for the paying, that is." The line is practiced, just like the smile. Sadly, this time, with these tired travellers, the response is nil, not even a smile.

Disappointed by the reaction, but still with a grin on his face, the innkeeper steps along the path toward the road. With a bow and a sweeping arm gesture worthy of a Turkish sultan's ambassador, he encourages each and every passenger to step inside his shabby inn.

"Pup," says the driver, grabbing Thomas by the elbow and pulling him off the path. He directs him over to where no one else will hear what he's about to say.

"What is it?" says Thomas, letting his fatigue and boredom show. He's paid the man both the regular fare and the additional bit to keep his satchel with him inside the coach. What else can the fellow want?

"Not forgotten," says the driver in a hushed voice. "Set youse up tonight like we said. It's all agreed. Send a signal sly like. Let youse know when the time is right."

The driver winks and Thomas blinks. He hasn't a clue what the driver is talking about. If it's a trick to get more money, Thomas will be on his guard.

"Look, I don't know what exactly you want." Thomas frowns as he hoped to put it more nicely than that. He does still need this man to get him to Paris in the morning.

"What we wants? It's what you wants."

"I don't want anything."

"Yes, youse do."

"You don't know me."

"Thinks we do."

"I have to go. Inside." Thomas keeps his voice down, but this driver is starting to make him angry. The man is a dolt.

"Half the fun, pup, half the fun," the driver calls out as Thomas walks away.

Thomas stops and turns round to face the man.

"Not knowing," says the driver with a wink. "Not knowing. Youse wait and watch. Be a sign there will."

With that, the driver gives Thomas a double wink, then beckons Thomas to return to hear what he can only whisper. Thomas glances about. He doesn't want to be seen with this man. Half of a person's rank comes from who you are seen with. Should he do as the driver asks or turn his back and get inside the inn as quickly as he can? Thomas sees there is no one else about. He decides to take the few steps, to give the driver a last chance to make sense.

"The little one," whispers the driver close to Thomas's ear. Thomas cringes and wipes off what he is sure is spit. "The little one," the driver repeats.

And with that the driver is gone, back to the diligence to oversee the work of the lad he's hired to unload the bags up top.

With his satchel cradled in his arms like a baby, Thomas shakes his head at the conversation he's just had. The driver is crazy, or near enough. Thomas steps over to the threshold of the disappointingly rustic inn where he has to spend the night. "The little one," he mutters under his breath. What on God's green earth is that about?

—

The evening drags on for everyone, perhaps for Thomas more than the rest. He is the youngest of the passengers and as such takes to waiting the least. He dearly wishes the diligence ride were over so his life in Paris could begin. With what he's brought away in the satchel, his parents' unknown parting gift, he can start to become who he was meant to be. That means medicine, or maybe some other worthy field.

As he waits for the drinking and eating to end and the candles and lamps to be put out, it occurs to Thomas that maybe just maybe the driver is hinting about sex. The very possibility sends a message to his loins. The man said something like "set youse up" and later mentioned "the little one." Fifteen and not yet with a girl, Thomas wonders if maybe the driver's muddled words might mean just that. Wouldn't that be a fine surprise? Though what a place for it to happen. A run-down farm inn that smells of smoke and onions and cider and wine. Worse still, a dampness that suggests a pile of wet blankets and socks.

"Oh my," says Strombeau, giving Thomas a gentle shoulder push. "Such a faraway face."

The two of them are sitting side by side waiting for the platter to arrive that will hold their supper meal. Old enough to be his father, the merchant Strombeau, with no children of his own, is taking a shine to the lad. Thomas can see it in the man's eyes, and he's not sure he likes it. He's just got rid of one family and doesn't feel the need of another. At least not yet.

"Wistful? Sorry to see our little journey come to its end?" Strombeau laughs. "Tell me, Jean Tyrell, do you so hate to say goodbye? Is it that?"

Thomas gives a diffident shrug and a raised-cheek smile. Why won't this evening just end and the next day begin?

"I'm just tired," he says, and is relieved to not have to say any more. The serving girl who had curtseyed to Thomas earlier at the inn's entrance brings the long-awaited meal. It comes not on a platter as expected but in a large crock. When she returns she spins across the table the required number of bent pewter spoons and a trencher for each one.

"What's this?" asks Strombeau. His face is sour for the first time Thomas has seen. "We are supposed to have a ragoût. And with ceramic dishes at least."

The girl shrugs. "I'm not the cook. I'll be back with your bread."

"I'm from Bordeaux," Strombeau starts to explain, but the serving girl has turned and is rapidly moving away. Strombeau lifts two uncomprehending hands to his tablemate, a laughing Thomas. "All right, Jean Tyrell, our conversation is on hold until later on." The pudgy merchant lifts the lid of the crock and sniffs and peers in at what wafts below. He spies white beans and sausage bits. "That's not bad, but it's no ragoût. That's cassoulet. Cook must be from down south."

"I suppose. After you," offers Thomas.

"As you wish." And Strombeau ladles a hefty three spoonfuls into his nearly overflowing wooden bowl.

The night proceeds from there, with the merchant from Bordeaux savouring every drop. His mood is helped along by what Thomas counts as four – until there comes a fifth – tumblers of wine. Thomas is still nursing his first, not wanting to spend any more money than he absolutely must. Also, he cannot risk having his caution and judgement impaired. He needs his wits to keep his future safe, and that future is at his feet between two close-pressed shoes. Strombeau, clearly, has no such worries. He's drinking heavily and is making jolly with all, even the serving girl each time she brings him another glass of wine. The merchant makes an increasingly funny picture to Thomas as the big man's wig gets more and more askew.

With his belly filled, Thomas takes a quick scan of the rest of the inn. The driver of the diligence is over by the fireplace. He's winking and drinking with some man Thomas does not recognize. They are taking turns slapping each other on the back. Continuing his tour of the inn, Thomas sees the Capuchin and Madame Soule two tables over, deep in yet another animated conversation. Thomas is glad he's not seated over there. The ever-uninvolved Marielle sits quietly nearby. She chances to look Thomas's way just as his gaze happens to come to her. Their sightlines joined, Thomas stands and sends her a courtly bow. He sees her laugh and is elated. He cannot help but wonder if somehow it could be Marielle the diligence driver described as the "little one" and that somehow the crazed driver really could set them up. No, he doesn't think the real world works like that.

"Smitten, you are smitten," Strombeau says to Thomas. "Ah, to be so young again. I can almost recall." The merchant laughs. "Not lugging your satchel around tonight? That's a change." Strombeau leans back in his seat.

"Ah yes, it's between my feet," says Thomas. "Safer there."

"Ah, very wise. One never knows." Strombeau makes a face. "Who to trust, I mean."

"No, I think you're right." But what is Strombeau saying? Has the Bordeaux merchant figured out what it is that Thomas guards so close? Is he hinting that he wants some of it for himself or else? Thomas feels his body go rigid.

"Oh relax." Strombeau's voice is not much more than a whisper. "I'm not after what you've got down there, my young friend. Whatever it is, my guess is it's got something to do with the running man we saw chasing our diligence back in Vire."

Thomas cannot help his eyes darting round the room to see who else is listening. No one is as far as he can see. Thomas comes back to face Strombeau.

"I don't know what you're saying."

"Oh, I think you likely do. The man was calling for a *Thomas* to come back as I recall." Strombeau gives his tense tablemate a quizzical look.

Thomas does another rapid swivel of the room. Everyone is either locked into their food and drink or in conversations.

"Aha," says Strombeau, "that answers that. No denial or defence means that I'm right."

Thomas opens his mouth to protest but before he can say a word Strombeau leans over and whispers as low as he can. "Not that it's any business of mine, is it now?"

Thomas's face is cold and blank.

"No, that's fine. I even admire your pluck. Can't have been easy, making off with whatever it is in your heavy sack. Money, I suppose, though there's other things even better than coins."

The merchant takes a sip of wine then puts the tumbler down. He offers an understanding expression on his face.

"Must be something to have everything you own in one small bag. So simple it is to be young and starting out."

There's more than a little nostalgia in Strombeau's voice. Thomas remains speechless.

"Well," says Strombeau, rising from the table, "time to drain the lizard. Back in a bit."

Thomas follows Strombeau with his eyes as the merchant weaves his way through the half dozen tables of the inn toward the door that leads to the back room where the necessary is located. As soon as that door is closed, Thomas assesses his situation. Should he take Strombeau at his word – that it's none of his business – or should he get out of there? But out into the night with the heavy satchel and on foot? No, definitely not. He wouldn't get far. He doesn't know the country around Évreux at all. There could be thieves. Might be wolves as well.

Thomas's worried eyes search for the only person he thinks might be able to help. That's the crazed driver of the diligence. He finds the man chatting up the serving girl across the room. The driver already knows there are coins in the satchel. Not how many, but he did see a few back in Vire. And yes, the man says incomprehensible nothings but he has offered several times to help. Maybe Thomas can ask him to hide the satchel somewhere that Strombeau will not find. Thomas stands and thinks to gesture the driver to come over and have a talk before Strombeau returns. But the driver is not seeing Thomas. He's wagging his tongue at the serving girl. The moment the girl turns round to speak with someone else he's pinching her shapely ass. The serving girl bats his hand away without even looking or turning around. Thomas figures she gets a lot of that from lowly men who come to this kind of place.

"Oh, oh. Down in the dumps again I see."

Strombeau is back, smiling at Thomas like they're fast friends. Thomas knows not what to say. Strombeau takes his seat then across the table. He gives Thomas's shoulder a friendly push. Thomas glares at him as if to say: do that again and I'll knock you off your chair.

"Whoa, sorry there. Didn't know you didn't like to be touched."

"Well, I don't."

Thomas releases a long breath and swivels slowly in his seat. He wants to see if he can get the driver's attention this time. No, the man is up on his feet filling his tankard from the inn's barrel while the serving girl has her back to it. He helps himself to a long pull on the tap. Seated again, the driver laughs uproariously. Thomas can't tell if it's because he stole his drink from the barrel or because of some joke. Not once does the driver turn in Thomas's direction.

"Think I'll turn in," he says, swivelling back to Strombeau. "It's getting late."

Strombeau smiles at him like there's nothing amiss, yet Thomas senses the merchant knows everything about him – the departure from his parents and maybe even about the theft.

"So it is. Early to bed, early to rise, the theory goes. I understand. And I'm tired too. Let's say we go together."

Strombeau gets up and heads for the area over near the fireplace where the innkeeper is spreading out the straw mattresses and a couple of the overnight male guests have already bedded down. Thomas stays put, seated at the table, head in his hands. He doesn't know who to trust. The driver? Strombeau? Or only himself? Thomas walks over to see what Strombeau is doing. He lay down as soon as he got there and hasn't moved since. The man has his eyes closed and is snoring like a dog in front of a fire.

Thomas studies the open spaces on the *pailleasses.* Which area, and beside whom, should he choose? He takes off his greatcoat and drops it to his sleeping space and kicks off his shoes. He'll sleep just as he is, in his chemise and breeches and with his socks left on. Though he'll need a blanket as a cover.

He hears footsteps and turns around. It's the driver of the diligence.

"There you are, pup," comes the man's gravelly voice.

He is speaking, for the first time Thomas has seen, through a hand covering his mouth. Thomas squints to understand. Is this the dolt's way of being quiet, to pass on a secret?

"Didn't forget now, did youse?"

"No. Yes. I don't know."

"Late's better than never, is it not?"

Thomas nods that it is.

"Right youse are."

Thomas is perplexed. He glances at the large form of Strombeau snoring deeply on his straw mattress. He seems harmless enough. Should Thomas still tell the driver that maybe Strombeau has eyes for the satchel, with the family heirlooms?

"This is the way, pup."

Thomas looks in the direction the driver is pointing. It's toward the white-painted door that leads to what seems to be the inn's storage area. Throughout the evening Thomas noticed the innkeeper and the serving girl go there from time to time, returning with small casks of wine, bowls and plates, fresh tablecloths and the like. Why would the driver want to take him there? Has he found a place for Thomas to sleep where he'll be safe all by himself? Thomas nods sagely. The dolt of a driver is maybe not such a dolt after all.

"No satchel?" the driver asks. "Thought youse kept it pretty close. The looms and all."

"Oh my god." Thomas rushes back to the table where before he was seated, along with Strombeau. Sure enough, the sack is still there. It's underneath where his tired feet in his battered leather shoes had been standing guard. He drags the heavy cloth bag out with a foot then picks it up and clasps it to his chest. "That was close," he says to the driver. "Thank you so much. I don't know how I could have left this behind."

"Sure, pup. Understands." The driver steps quickly over to the white-painted door. A flick of the latch and it opens.

The room they enter is dim and dark. The dominant smell is of canvas and wood. Thomas can make out wooden racks to the left and right, with different size barrels and casks in one area and stacks of dishes and clean linen in other spots. There are some wine- and food-stained tablecloths in a large wicker basket. The only light in the room is a candle flickering against the far wall. Behind the rack of barrels the candle is out of sight on entering.

The driver closes the door behind them and puts a finger to his lips. Thomas nods automatically, though he doesn't know why he has to be quiet. Isn't it a storage room? Then he hears something. It sounds like someone stirring up ahead.

"Here she is. The little one. Like promised." The driver steps past the barrel rack and makes a grand gesture with his arm.

Thomas steps forward to see. He is completely taken aback. There on a rolled-out *pailleasse* on a corner of the floor, kneeling with her hands on her hips and a smile upon her face, is the inn's serving girl. She's wearing the skimpiest of chemises. Through the thinness of the cloth Thomas can see nearly all there is, including most of her breasts up top and the triangle of a shadow down below.

"Well?" the driver says.

"Well … well," is all Thomas can mumble. There is confusion on his face.

The girl covers her chest with crossed arms. She is glaring at Thomas and the stunned look on his face. "No one's forcing you," she says, curling her lips.

"Shush," says the driver to the girl. "Youse looked after." His tone is sharp. Turning back to Thomas, in a softer voice, the driver says, "Give it a try. Go on. Here. Puts that satchel here."

Thomas does as he is told. He takes his eyes off the girl and hands the man his satchel. He keeps his gaze focussed on the heavy bag, as the driver places it in an open space between two barrels on the wooden rack. It's safe there, Thomas decides, right in his sight line. And with a nod he sends the driver his appreciation. He notices an odd little smile on the man's face, which Thomas understands to be a reference to the waiting girl. He will recall that smile later on and think differently about it then. The driver makes a fist to say that his work is done. He quickly turns and is gone, round the barrel rack and into the darkness that lies behind. That's kind, thinks Thomas. He appreciates the privacy for what he thinks he and the girl are about to do.

"Well," says the serving girl, moving on her knees closer to Thomas. He is still standing where he was. "What do you say now? Interested after all?" She reaches up and touches him lightly on his chest.

Thomas does not answer, but his body responds. His heart is off and running. The thing between his legs is pressing against his pants. The serving girl notices the bulge and smiles.

"The little soldier wants to stand and fight."

"Soldier? You call it a soldier too?"

"Among other things. Let's see if he is ready to salute."

She reaches out and unbuttons Thomas's breeches. As soon as the pants tumble down, leaving him naked except for the cover of his chemise, Thomas falls to his knees beside the girl. He reaches underneath her chemise. He can't believe what he finds. How could anything be so slippery to the touch?

"Whoa," she says, "go easy. That's not dough you're working there. That's better. Now, let's see what you can do." She grabs hold of his chemise and pulls it up and over his head. She leaves her own shirt on. She scans him up and down. There comes a tiny smile. "Best to take off those socks, don't you think?"

Thomas rolls to put his legs in the air, and pulls off the offending socks.

"That's better," the girl says.

It turns out it's over pretty quick. Her hand no sooner guides Thomas's soldier to the spot than he is off, a-trembling with the relief. The girl gives a little laugh.

"Your first, am I?"

"I'll be better next time, I will."

"Next time? Pretty cocky. What makes you think …"

"Can we? Once more at least?"

"Think you can?"

"In a minute. It'll come back. What's your name anyway?"

"Hélène."

"Thomas."

"All right then, Thomas."

Hélène sits up on the mattress and pulls off her chemise. Thomas tries not to stare at and repeatedly scan this entire landscape of skin that Hélène presents, but he can't control his eyes. He barely hears her tell him about how her parents died long ago in an accident and how ever since she's been looked after by her mother's brother, Uncle François, the keeper of the inn, and his mean-mouthed second wife, Isabelle. The couple have always kept her fed and clothed in return for Hélène working in the inn. They even let her go to a parish school for a few years, long enough to learn the morality the church taught and how to sign her name. She can even read a bit. But once Hélène reached thirteen and began sprouting tits, aunt and uncle started hinting there were other ways for a pretty girl to bring in some money, besides helping out with the cleaning and serving in the inn. Hélène resisted for a while, but her complete dependency took its toll. She agreed to take a paying customer once in a while. One price for a fondle; three times that for a fifteen-minute ride. For every amount put in her uncle's hand, Hélène was to receive a fifth. Thomas barely hears a word she says. His wide eyes override his ears. His gaze keeps going to her belly and down to her loins.

"You're not listening, are you?" Hélène picks up Thomas's hands and places them lightly beneath her breasts. "How 'bout you be nice to these girls first?" He does as he is told, but then takes the hands away. He places them on her face, one on each cheek. He leans forward and gently kisses her on the lips. Then he descends to ravish her neck and throat.

"That's good," she says.

Thomas stops kissing her throat and places his cheek to hers. They rub their cheeks, soft on soft for what feels like a long while.

"All right," Hélène breathes in Thomas's ear, "let me see what I can do with your little corporal. Maybe I can make him a sergeant now." She starts to caress his thing with her two hands.

It takes a few minutes, not that anyone is keeping track or cares. The two young people focus only on helping each other enjoy the gentle friction of their lips and their hands. Neither sees or hears a thing, other than the things that are his and hers. For Thomas it's an entry into a world he's long yearned to explore. As soon as his soldier is back to standing at attention they begin the second time. And sure enough, this time it's better for them both. Thomas gets to feel like a man and not a boy.

"How come he did this for you, anyway?" Hélène asks Thomas after they are done. They are still intertwined.

"What?" Thomas laughs. He walks his fingers across the top half of her naked body to tweak a nipple small and brown. She removes his thumb and finger and sends him a pretend frown. He reaches to the bottom of the mattress and finds his chemise. "What was that?" he asks, the eyebrows arching up. "Who did what?"

"I don't know," says Hélène covering her breasts with her hands. "It's just a little odd. Unless you're his younger brother or nephew, I suppose. I'm no whore, but from what I've seen, them that pay are them to get the ride. But you don't look like that fellow at all."

Thomas sits up. "Who are you talking about? Who's *he*?" His face is serious now.

"Antoine," says Hélène.

Thomas gives a confused face, the eyes blinking. "Antoine? Who's that?"

"You know. The driver of the diligence. Antoine. Guess he's not your brother or uncle if you don't know his name."

Hélène pulls on her chemise. The fun is over, she can see.

Thomas reaches out and grabs her hard by the wrist. "What are you saying? The driver? He paid you for … for this?"

"He gave my uncle the money and my uncle told me to keep you busy for a while. Doing this."

Thomas gets up off the straw mattress in a hurry. He clambers over to the barrel rack.

"You did get two for one. There's that."

Her words might be the hum of bees. Thomas doesn't hear a thing. He's grasping the wooden barrel rack like it's a ship's ladder to pull himself out of the sea. Where he had seen his satchel on the rack is now an empty space. The satchel with his money, his future, it's not there.

Thomas pulls his breeches on in a rush and searches the storage room in a panic.

"It's not here," he says.

"What?" Hélène asks twice, then gives up.

Out the door and into the big room Thomas goes. He's not yelling at first but his muttering and the shifting of objects creates a stir. The sleeping guests have no choice but to be disturbed. Uncle François and Aunt Isabelle descend from their little room upstairs and light some lamps. Looking round, and round again, and finding not what he seeks, Thomas begins to yell and punch the air. He shouts that he has been deceived. The driver of the diligence – Antoine is his name – he's gone. Thomas lays out the blame. He doesn't at first say what the blackguard has taken, but he uses the word, he calls the man a thief.

"What's he taken?" asks a sleep-disturbed Strombeau, a hand placed on Thomas's outstretched arm.

"The satchel, my satchel."

"Oh," mutters the Capuchin.

"That," says a scornful Madame Soule.

The other travellers turn away, wanting to go back to sleep. No one, it is made clear to Thomas, sees that he has lost a thing. It was just a baggy sack. Only Strombeau, with a muffled "Oh" shares the lad's concern. The merchant had already deduced that the young man had all he owned, and something valuable at that, in his traveller's bag.

"That's too bad, young Jean."

"It's worse than that," says Thomas, relieved that one person at least is a little aware of his loss. Thank God he is not completely lost, thanks to his foresight in stuffing as many coins as he could into the bottoms of his shoes.

Thomas has a thought and runs to the front door of the inn. "Good," he mutters to the darkness and immediately returns back inside. He notices Hélène has disappeared from the big room. He goes to Strombeau.

"The diligence is still there. All the horses too. So maybe the driver is still around. Do you think he'll realize the crime he's committed and come back?"

"No, lad, I think not," says Strombeau. "Stealing a coach and its horses would be far more serious than lifting that satchel with your clothes."

"But it wasn't just—" Thomas almost speaks about all the coins.

"Wasn't just?"

"Nothing." Thomas is not going to speak about how he got the stash of coins in the first place. Though they were his birthright, they were. "Nothing. I'd better get some sleep."

Of course, there is no sleep for Thomas as the inn goes back to dark and all the travellers to their straw mattresses and the innkeepers to their beds. The young man's mind spins like a child's pinwheel in the wind. He keeps going over the past few day, and what the driver said and did. He must have planned the theft two days in advance, beginning when he glimpsed a few coins back in Vire and heard Thomas insist that it had to stay with him. And pay extra to do so. He would have seen how heavy the satchel was to carry and figured out the rest. Then there was the final touch, the set-up with little Hélène. Now, the bastard has vanished in the night, taking what he really wanted while Thomas was distracted by his loins. He sits up on his portion of the mattress and puts his head in his hands. The driver must have stayed in the ill-lit storage room and while the serving girl kept Thomas distracted, took the satchel and off he went. "A hard cock is a terrible stupid thing," Thomas mutters under his breath.

When morning comes at last, the various fellow passengers again offer their condolences to the exhausted-looking young man. Thomas varies his thanks for their thoughts, but to each he feels compelled to say that the driver tricked him with an unkind ruse. No one asks what ruse that was because the truth is no one much cares. The worry among the passengers is rather about the trip to Paris for which they have paid. With no driver to control the horses, will they have to stay in the lowly farmhouse inn another day and night?

"A thief! Honestly. I think there's nothing worse," offers Madame Soule, before she sidles off with relief to oversee her charge, the vulnerable Marielle.

"Indeed," says Père Athanase, breaking off a chunk of baguette to go along with his morning chocolate, "I did wonder if he was of that type. You can never be too sure about people. He didn't look like a worthy type."

The Capuchin flinches when he realizes he's saying this to Thomas, whom the monk also thinks is hiding something from the world. Thomas takes a deep breath and moves over to the table where the pretty Marielle is seated. Madame Soule has just gone to the little necessary room to do what must be done.

"He took all your clothes?" she asks. "Oh my."

"Yes. I lost it all." Thomas samples his morning chocolate with a sour expression on his face. It's not the chocolate; it's the continuing anger about being duped. He's down to only the coins stuffed in his shoes and socks. "Not a penny left," Thomas says with a moon face directed Marielle's way, "not a one."

"But what then …" Marielle looks like she's about to cry.

"He'll be all right," interrupts Strombeau.

Thomas plunks himself down. It appears there's nothing he can do. He's stuck with his sorry fate, and with only the coins he has stuffed in his pockets and hidden in his shoes. He burned the bridge with his parents. He can't simply go back to Vire and make this move to Paris some other time.

"That bag of yours, it was a ratty old thing in any case." Strombeau sits down at the table alongside the downcast young man. Thomas glances up. The merchant from Bordeaux is not wearing his wig at all this morning. With all his red hair fully showing his face looks particularly ruddy. "You're better off without it. That's what I predict. It means you have to make a complete fresh start. What do you say to that?"

"Nothing. I don't know what to say. I had things in the satchel I could have used. Simple as that."

Thomas reaches for one of the portions of the two baguettes on the table, just dropped there by the innkeeper. The bread is not only cold, it's hard as wood. It must be a day, maybe two days old. Thomas tosses the bread back onto the tabletop.

"Just the same," says Strombeau, "it's a chance to show what you're made of."

The merchant grabs one of the bread portions and breaks off a tiny dry bit. He pops the fragment into his mouth. When his mouth is empty again he says to Thomas, "Time to grow up."

Thomas's eyes go wide then narrow to near slits. The expressions on the faces of Marielle and Madame Soule say they cannot believe what they just heard.

"All right," says Thomas straightening in his chair.

Strombeau checks the hour on his pocket watch. He scowls and clicks the cover shut then puts it away. "That innkeeper's not going to do a thing until he's fleeced our pockets the best that he can. Everyone's out for himself, mark my word. Except for certain ones." Strombeau waves vaguely in the direction of Père Athanase. "And I'm not so sure about them." The merchant exhales loudly and breaks off another morsel of dry bread. "What do you say do that, young Tyrell? Do I have things about right?"

Thomas leans in closer toward the man. He's liking him more and more. He's not just a pudgy merchant with a watch. He sounds like he's been out in the world. Strombeau puts a hand near his mouth to shield what he is about to say in a loud whisper from Madame Soule and Marielle.

"No one gives you anything, Jean. If you don't take it, rest assured someone else will. Understand?"

"Yes, I think I do."

"Hey," calls out the inn's serving girl, Hélène, from across the room. "Hey, you."

The entire table where Thomas is seated looks up. One by one they realize that the servant with the low-cut chemise, half of her bosom showing, is beckoning none other than the young man in their midst, the one victimized by last night's theft, the downcast Jean Tyrell.

"Hey!" The servant girl is wiggling a finger for him to come hither. She adds a toss of her head, a length of hair showing out the back of her bonnet. "I need some help. To *lift* something in the storage room. You coming, Thomas?"

"Thomas?" says Strombeau, clapping his hands and allowing a grin to fill his face. "I thought so," he says pointing at Thomas. "You're not a Jean after all."

Thomas gives a sheepish look. He darts a glance at Marielle. Her eyes are those of a jeweller examining a stone that is proving to be fake.

"It's all right," he explains to her with a shrug. He continues the explanation in a low voice he does not want the waiting Hélène to hear. "I just told her my name was Thomas."

Too late he realizes that does not sound so good. He hunches his shoulders at Marielle. Oh well, the shoulders say, I guess now you know. And then to only Strombeau, with a whisper in the merchant's ear, "Had to give her some name, didn't I? Didn't want to use my own." Thomas pulls back and winks at the merchant's smiling face. The man from Bordeaux beams back.

And with that, Thomas avoids any more eye contact. He pushes back from the table. The others' eyes follow him intently as he crosses the room and catches up with Hélène. She leans in and up. She bestows a kiss on his delighted cheek. The young couple goes immediately into the storage room, where she is about to tell Thomas her whole life story, and this time he will be all ears. He will hear about the heavy downpour that caused a flash flood of the Seine when Hélène was five. It overturned the rickety ferry at Les Andelys just when her parents were crossing with a wagon of hay. They could likely see the Château Gaillard as they were drowning – Hélène for some reason will throw this in. And so with their deaths she will explain she was raised by her Uncle François, the keeper of this inn. He isn't mean to her, though he and his wife, her Aunt Isabelle, do allow fondlers and fucksters to have fun with her in the storage room. Thomas's whole face and body will react to the story that she for the second time shares. It arouses more lust than sympathy, he's not proud to say. In return, Thomas will recount the entire tale of his own thwarted life. It comes down to how he was misunderstood and nearly forced into the Church, which is why he's fleeing for Paris to begin his life anew. He will acknowledge that his life story is not nearly as tragic as what Hélène endured. She will nod that he is right. Oh, and he will leave out mention of any strongbox under any counter. Those breathless explanations, accompanied by busy hands, lie moments ahead. As the door is closing to the storage room, before the young people are completely out of sight, the watchers see the serving girl tug at Thomas's chemise, pulling it out of his pants.

III

Arrival

Paris

June 1715

The city makes its first appearance from well away, before its surrounding walls are glimpsed and long before its west gate will be passed. Paris comes in the form of spires and towers, cupolas and domes. There are only a few at first but as the diligence draws closer along its twisting route there are too many to count, and there is one spire that is larger than the rest. Does the city have a hundred spires and domes or is it that what a thousand looks like? Thomas doesn't know and supposes it doesn't matter. What does matter is that it's Paris, the centre of a world that he wants to know. With each turn of the four wheels, Thomas is farther and farther from Normandy and the town of his birth. He feels like he's rolling headlong into the future. Never before, that he can remember, has his chest felt so light.

Thomas twists in his seat to look at the other faces in his compartment. Most of them are new. That is, he has sat with them only since leaving the inn near Évreux. Before that prolonged stop Thomas was in a different compartment. He thought it best to sit somewhere else, away from those who knew too much about him from the earlier stage. He has moved away from Strombeau, the Capuchin, Marielle and Madame Soule and has new seatmates in a different part of the diligence. He knows not a single one of their names, nor does he care. To him they are simply the man in grey with a face that's grim; the man with too-large hands and a wig long out of fashion; the thin woman with pock-marked complexion who prefers to stare at the yellow shoes on her feet; and of course the young woman beside him. All but the last are strangers. Thomas figures the ride will soon be over with everyone going separate ways, never to see each other again, so why should he introduce himself to them or even speak. He likes the anonymity of this kind of travel. It's so unlike growing up in Vire, where he knew near everyone and everyone knew him. He imagines that this silent nameless life will be what it's like in Paris. It's a new kind of living he's certain he will enjoy.

"Is that Notre-Dame? The big spire?" whispers Thomas's seatmate. Her breath is hot in his ear.

"Yes, I think so," he replies quietly to Hélène, gazing into her playful eyes. He wants to pat her knee but decides he'd better not. It might lead to something else, and they're not alone for that.

Hélène, the serving girl from the inn, has come along with Thomas. It was a last-minute dash when her innkeeper uncle went back inside the inn as the diligence was rolling away. The last time they were alone in the back room together Hélène told Thomas that she envied him and wished she could do the same.

"Why don't you? I could find enough to pay your way."

"I wish, but I can't. They need me here."

"To fuck on their behalf?"

"I just can't."

And Thomas thought that was it. But no, there she was, a small sack clutched in her hand, sprinting across the inn's yard the moment Uncle François stepped back inside. It was a sight that made Thomas beam, his lover coming after him as if in a dream. Though a muddy dream it was, he admits. Hélène came from around the far side of the inn, splashing through the puddles in the yard. She muddied her skirt as she ran. Luckily, there was room enough right beside him for her to squeeze upon the upholstered bench in the compartment he had chosen.

"You've not been there before, have you?" Hélène whispers in his ear.

"To Paris? No, this is it. First time. Looks good, doesn't it?"

His face is so earnest that Hélène takes both her hands and exerts a squeeze. First on Thomas's elbow then on his cheeks.

"How big is it anyway?" she asks.

Thomas's eyes grow distant while he thinks about it. "I've heard half a million, but how can anyone know? Really? I mean, it's not like you could ever go around and count everyone, up all the streets and into all the buildings. There are too many, that's for sure. And there will be beggars and vagabonds too. I doubt anyone would include them in a count. How could they? They're always moving about. So I'm thinking that there is no precise figure. Half a million? Maybe. That's what I say. Half a million it has to be, don't you think?"

"Sure," says Hélène, bringing up a hand to hide a grin.

The diligence rolls and bounces on, its creak of wood and leather a comfort to those who have an inclination to doze. For those awake and eager to see what lies ahead, and that includes Thomas and Hélène, they get to see the spires of Paris grow slowly but steadily large. Their wide eyes and keen attentions are drawn out the bouncing windows whenever there's a glimpse of the city through branch and bush and twist of the road.

"What are we going to do?" says Hélène in a sudden rush. "I mean *there*." She gestures with her thumb at the latest Paris vista.

Thomas turns to his lovemaking friend of the past two nights. He takes in her pretty face. Her eyes are dark brown, even darker than his own, and her hair colour is not far off from his as well. It occurs to him that they could be mistaken for a brother and a sister though he thanks the saints above that they are not. He and Anne never got along. Instead, Thomas takes the physical similarities with Hélène as a sign that the two of them are meant to be together. Maybe, if there's a need some day, they could pass as siblings. That is, if there were some reason to keep the nature of their real relationship away from prying eyes. He likes it especially when he feels the warmth of her whispers near his ear, like he has just done.

"My thoughts were elsewhere just then," he says. "What did you ask?"

"I asked what we are to do. For money. To have good shelter. Something to eat."

Thomas takes in a breath. Oh yes, the details of being on one's own.

"Well, I *was* going to go into medicine," Thomas whispers in her ear, unable yet to pass over that now vanished part of his dream. “”Now I don’t know. Not after all I’ve lost. But I’ll think of something.”

A shadow passes over his face as he wonders about how long the thirty or so coins in his pockets, socks and shoes will hold up. He has no idea what rent in Paris will be or how much it costs to dress and eat. He’s never lived anywhere but under his parents’ roof. He sucks in as deep a breath as he can. “Be all right. Not to worry. Not yet anyway.” Thomas pats Hélène’s knee.

“Not exactly worried,” she says. “It’s only I don’t know what’s ahead. I’ve never been anywhere but around Évreux.”

Hélène tilts her head to rest upon his shoulder. Thomas holds still then looks down at her chest, at the tops of the breasts he’s come to know quite well. He can’t wait to get back at them and the rest of Hélène once they’re in Paris. Yet maybe, he thinks, maybe those delightful pleasures of hers are a little too visible in the coach. They are after all nearly spilling out of her low-cut chemise. Thomas reaches out and with a careful thumb and forefinger he lifts up the front line of her chemise. Hélène opens her eyes and smiles.

Thomas straightens in his seat and looks around. The passengers directly across from him and Hélène – grey grim face, big hands and downward-looking lady – all saw what he has just done to Hélène’s chemise. Each averts his or her eyes with speed. Thomas gives a vengeful glare, having caught them in their voyeurism. A distant cough – the kind one fakes to get attention – turns Thomas’s attention toward the back. Sure enough, in his old compartment at the rear, there’s Monsieur Strombeau wanting to make eye contact. He gives Thomas a wave and a wink. Then he holds up what appears to be a sheet of paper folded over. Thomas nods as if he understands, though he has not a clue what the merchant from Bordeaux is trying to communicate. Strombeau winks again, like Thomas has understood, and makes sure Thomas sees him put the paper safely back inside his coat.

—

Paris makes its presence heard and felt well before its walls and gates, along the very road itself. All of sudden the surface beneath the hooves of the horses and the wheels of the diligence switches from beaten dirt road to cobbled way. The change makes all the first-time travellers look out the nearest window to see what has happened to the sound they had lived with for hours, and in some cases days. They are all impressed. Where they come from, Vire, Évreux and other small towns, the cobbles don't begin until the very gates. Thomas nods his appreciation: Paris is not just any town.

Another change the travellers notice is that the diligence is now rolling not through untamed forest but a kind of parkland, with planted trees in neat rows. Thomas stands up for just a moment as the diligence rolls on to peer through the window on the other side. The grim-faced man in grey, whose knee he nearly touched when he stood up, radiates an annoyed look. Yet Thomas sees what he came to see. There are fortifications and a huge chevron-shaped gate up ahead.

"What's that one's name?" Thomas asks the man in grey. "The gate? Its name?"

"No idea. Sit down," the man replies and looks away.

"The gates in Paris are often named after saints," Thomas whispers to Hélène when he's back into his seat. "Saint-Louis, Saint-Antoine, Saint-Martin. Don't know which one this might be. Could be something else."

"Maybe Saint-Thomas?" Hélène touches a finger to her lips. It's a pretend pensive gesture, meant to be a joke. Thomas gets the joke and smiles. He guesses Hélène doesn't much care what things like gates are called.

The replacement diligence driver is slow to rein in the horses and there's a jerk to a sudden halt before the lead pair and then those following clatter to a full stop. They've nearly struck the toll man standing in the middle of the gate. Shouted insults and a general dressing down for the driver begin at once. The "idiot" – as the offending driver is labelled by the toll man – is ordered to the ground. He dutifully stands and takes the tongue-lashing for a while. But then he explains that he's new and inexperienced because the regular driver, a thief it turned out, fled in the dark two nights ago. The official who was yelling uncurls his sneer. The volume of the voices climbs down. The passengers cannot hear the rest, but they see the six summoned soldiers put their muskets back on their shoulders and march back to what seems to be their guardhouse. The toll is paid, and the new driver is back up top. He cracks the whip and makes sure that his devil horses continue on at a walking pace. Clip and clop, slow and steady, they're on the streets of Paris now.

"It's June first," Thomas says to Hélène. He says it as if it were a date she should write down. He's not sure which saint day it is on the calendar of the Church. Whatever it is, it feels like it's an advent of sorts. For him and Hélène if for no one else in the Christian world.

—

The advance is worse than slow. It's barely a crawl up streets as narrow as those Thomas knew back in Vire. Thomas is surprised. He was sure the city would be more open everywhere he looked. Another surprise is the stink. Paris is worse than ever little Vire had been. The smell is a mix of things Thomas cannot easily separate out. There's the horse dung of course, but there's also the human night soil flowing with the yellow piss in the centre of the streets. And then there's the sweat and covering perfumes of all the many classes of people he sees in the streets. Thomas inhales deeply, thinking he has to, to become a part of this place. Hélène chooses not to. She covers her mouth and nose with a *mouchoir* she pulls out of her sleeve.

As the diligence rolls slowly on, Thomas concentrates on the buildings of Paris rather than the congestion on the streets. Some are a marvel to his young rural Normandy eyes. They can reach up twice as high as the buildings in Vire and Évreux. And the people! Why, there are more people on the streets in front of and alongside the diligence than Thomas and Hélène have ever seen in one place before. It's as if there is some big event, an execution or a *Fête Dieu*. Yet it's obvious from the way people are walking by, in all directions, that there is no single big event this way or that. It's just how Paris is. Men with an assertiveness in their strides. They display their importance through the eagerness of their hurry. And the women, such prudence and elegance! There is a previous unseen finery about their clothes. Of course there are humbler sort who are dressed like back in any town or village, but Thomas's gaze passes over them.

The number of children is surprising. Their little hands, legs and mouths are never not in motion. Does Paris not have any parish schools? How can there be so many brats and urchins on the street?

Everywhere Thomas and Hélène look are bustling bodies of all the hundred ranks of society. The cries and calls and taunts of the pedlars make a veritable hum. Each one with his or her patter competes to rise above the rest. Thomas stares open-faced to drink it all in, trying to absorb one tableau before moving on to the next. Hélène, on the other hand, shifts from scene to scene quickly. It's like she's almost peeking at this and that.

Gentlemen and ladies strolling, beggars and wastrels pleading. Pedlars with trays of hotcakes, fish, ribbons or oil. Men with water containers strapped on their backs or fagots for fireplaces carried about in their wooden backpacks. Congestion is the only rule. The diligence cannot advance except at a crawl. The streets are clogged not just with people but with other carriages and coaches. Some are large, some very small. The wheeled conveyances come in a dozen shapes and sizes. A few are like nothing Thomas has ever seen. Those ones are low in the front and angle up. It must be to make the corners on the busy and narrow streets. There is confusion at every intersection. Thomas can't imagine that it can be like this everywhere in the city, yet everywhere the diligence goes that's exactly how it is. Thomas and Hélène stare out at what they see, then check back in with each other with large eyes and gently shaking heads.

—

The diligence comes to a halt.

"Hôtel de Ville." It's a shout from outside the compartment, a deep voice from the spread of cobbles below.

"You have to descend here," says the grim-faced man. His expression says that he's had just about enough of Thomas and Hélène and their wide-eyed talk and stares about Paris.

"Descend? Yes, of course." Thomas tries to pretend he knew that all along.

The descent from the diligence takes time. Thomas exhales loudly while he waits, until Hélène elbows the impatience out of him and whispers in his ear, "We have to wait our turn." He seeks to slow his breathing down. But I can't help it, he thinks, I want to be in the swirl on the streets and squares. Yet bide his time Thomas must. Hélène's warm hand clasps his. She presses to his side. "Where do we go? When we get out of the coach, I mean?" Her eyes are filled with faith and trust.

Thomas wrinkles his brow. He is sorry to disappoint such an expectant face. "Not a clue," he whispers then kisses her brow. "We have to find some place we can afford. That's first." He reaches to caress her ass. "Then maybe we can take off our things and … you know."

"But," Hélène says, and only that.

Down at last on the ground, Thomas catches a look of something sour on Hélène's face. "You all right? You look … a little sad."

Hélène summons a facsimile of a smile. "How's this?"

"I, I don't know." Thomas tilts his head. Oh my. Other people do have their ways. "All right then, where are we?" he says, really only to himself.

He scans the Hôtel de Ville right to left then up and down. He knows already that it is one of the two buildings from which Paris is partially administered. The other centre of power as far as buildings go, is the Châtelet. That's where the royal authority is based. He's read, or maybe heard, that Paris is like a coin. It's circular in shape and divided into different zones spiralling out from along the Seine. The river divides the city in half. Thomas gives his head a little shake to put such thoughts away for a while. He turns back to Hélène. The quick, fake smile is gone. She's back to that strange sour look. Maybe she's feeling queasy after the long ride.

Thomas takes a deep breath and admires one more time the slate-roofed structure of the Hôtel de Ville. The building is tall and elegant. It looks light on its feet, if only it had feet. He smiles at his little joke. The structure is basking in the deepening light of late afternoon. He wonders if Hélène would like to hear what he has to say about the beauty of the building. But he sees that she's wandered off. It appears that she's admiring the square in her own way. She has her arms outstretched, face up to the sky, and is turning slowly around.

Thomas feels a firm hand on his shoulder. He is surprised to see Strombeau. The merchant's wig could not be more tightly fitted. Now that he's in Paris there's not a hint of red hair sprouting anywhere. The cravat is in place, and nicely tied, and at the cuffs of the deep red coat are billowing spiffy trims of lace. Aha, observes Thomas, arrival in Paris has turned the previously unkempt merchant from Bordeaux into someone else. Thomas is impressed. So that's how it's done. He files the thought away. He has now learned from Strombeau something he can use. One must dress for the part one wants to play.

"I'm off, young friend. Jean or Thomas or whatever your name really is." Strombeau chuckles and shows not a hint of ill will. "Business to attend and already a day late." Strombeau holds out, between thumb and forefinger, a neatly folded-over sheet of paper. "Here. For you. My guess is that you might find it useful."

Thomas's eyes narrow as he takes the paper in hand. He unfolds it and reads what's written inside. "But it's a name and an address."

"Ah, so young." Strombeau glances skyward then back to Thomas. "Certain names and certain addresses are what this city is all about."

Thomas flinches then nods that he can grasp that.

"This is one of those names, and he is found at that address." Strombeau removes the smile from his face and adopts a serious look. "Not everything comes clear all at once. You'll come to see that's true if you don't know it already. Trust me on this, though I know it goes against your grain." Strombeau claps Thomas on the shoulder. He lowers his voice for what comes next. "Seriously. Go see this man once you're settled. I'm doing you a favour here. That's all. Let's leave it at that."

Strombeau swings away, clearly disappointed that the kindness he's showing to a possible protégé is only being considered not embraced. Thomas reaches out to grab the merchant by the forearm. The young man's expression has shifted from puzzled to apologetic.

"You have to admit. It's not much to go on."

"I don't have to admit anything." The smile is back on Strombeau's face. He's almost laughing. "Least of all to you, you sweet-faced lying bastard. If you want to light your fire with this piece of paper, you go right ahead."

Thomas blinks at Strombeau. He is trying to understand how a sheet of paper can be as important as all that.

Strombeau exhales. He leans in close so no one else but Thomas can hear.

"Look, skepticism is a good quality. I offer my applause. But this name and that address," Strombeau jabs at the paper with a finger, "they're a gift. Believe me that. The world doesn't owe us a thing. Either we earn it or we take it. That's how it is. And if you don't take it, someone else will in your place. The man whose name I've given you, he has a position, a certain role. I leave it at that. If you're as quick-witted and capable as I think you are, you'll do all right by him. And him by you, make no mistake."

"But why me?"

Strombeau brings out his pocket watch before replying. "Why you? Because you remind me a bit of myself, back when I was … well, when I was young and half the size I am now. I didn't have anything in the beginning but what I had stuffed in my shoes. Yes, I walked with a little limp back then, much like I see you do. But I was smart. And not afraid to be resourceful. And ambitious. I wanted to rise above the crowd, far beyond where I was born. Does that sound like anyone you know?"

Thomas tenders a cautious nod.

"Well then." Strombeau whacks the paper in Thomas's hand. "There it is. A start."

"All right," mumbles Thomas. "Thanks."

"I should say some thanks are due." Strombeau winks at the lad then turns and strides away.

"What'd he want, that fat coot?" Hélène sidles over to Thomas after Strombeau is ten feet gone.

"Not exactly sure." Thomas turns to face Hélène. "He gave me a name and an address. Some kind of job, I guess."

"Well, that's good, isn't it?" Hélène's spirits rise. Thomas can see it on her face.

"Yeah. I'll find out, I guess. C'mon, let's find a place to live before it gets dark."

—

The room is far from the best, but it's the best Thomas and Hélène can find in two hours of looking. It's also the best they can do with the amount of money Thomas has hidden in his shoes and socks and Hélène can contribute from the small pouch inside her sack.

"I didn't know you had anything," he said when she held open the pouch and he looked in.

"Well, I do, and this is it."

Thomas was about to ask where she got it, but he remembered the story she had told him about her aunt and uncle and decided he'd better not. Hélène, however, saw the thought cross his face.

"That's right, the fondle and fuck."

"I didn't say anything." His hands go up. "My money comes from somewhere too. Maybe just as bad."

"Oh, what's that?"

"I… I… I borrowed it from an uncle. With a bit of a lie."

Hélène's eyebrows arch. "That's it?"

"Well, I'm not paying him back."

"No." She shakes her head. "I win."

That was an hour ago. Now the two newcomers to Paris stand gazing at the floor of the third room they've looked at since descending from the diligence. The concierge, a woman who acts as the watchtower for the building, talks, is pointing out all there is to see in the room. It's not much. By her accent, the concierge is not from France. The accent is not of any region Thomas or Hélène has ever heard. Their guess, whispered one to the other, is that she is from Poland. The woman waves her arms as she speaks in staccato.

"Fine room, yes. Fine. And dry. Clean too."

In fact, the room is not at all fine and not particularly clean, but the couple does not contradict her. Their spirits are sinking fast. They are running out of time to find a place to call their own. A few minutes ago, when they entered the building, it looked fine and respectable on the ground floor. Also, it was in a fine part of the city, not far from the Louvre. The name of the street is what spurred Thomas on: rue Saint-Thomas-du-Louvre. He took it as a sign and said as much to Hélène as they entered. "Many a great one began in just such a spot," he said. Hélène rolled her eyes.

With each set of stairs they climbed, getting narrower and steeper as they went up, to this attic space at the top on the sixth floor, the rent progressively went down, as did the quality of the rooms.

"It's only until we get some money coming in," Thomas said through clenched teeth on the stairwell as they climbed higher still. After that, Hélène kept any objections of her own completely to herself.

"Happy here. Know that. Know that for you. So happy."

The concierge curls her upper lip and taps a foot. She is waiting for an answer.

"Normandy, from. Good. Normandy-ers like it here." She takes a step closer and repeats the last words, only this time as a question. "Like it here, yes?"

Thomas and Hélène look at each other, exchanging shared disappointments. Each can smell the mildew that pervades the room. What they had imagined and wanted was something larger and in a better building on a lower floor. And there was to be more and finer furniture. Instead, they're standing in a pitch-roofed attic whose floorboards have curled and lifted and whose plaster has dark spots that look like they come from dampness having its effect over time. There is but a single beat-up table, four damaged chairs, and a country cupboard. They both had just as good, or better, back in their earlier homes. As for a bed, there is none. Where they will sleep is on a rolled-up straw mattress on the floor. Beside it is what looks like an ancient chamber pot. It is cracked, with a wire repair job holding it together. Hélène looks at it with a long face. Thomas looks at the same pot and the wash basin in the corner and he thinks of the long hike it is going to be up and down the six flights of stairs whenever they need to get water to wash their hands, faces and other places, and to carry out the chamber pot with all its swirling and floating charms.

As they climbed the stairs up to see this attic space, Thomas like Hélène was dismayed by all the people they glimpsed on the upper floors. On the upper floors the building is a human anthill. This level and the next one down are filled with tradespeople and hawkers, people prone to yelling even when not out in the streets. Down below, where the fuller pocketbooks live, the people stay out of sight. The smell of laundry, damp and heavy, and who knows what else, is everywhere on the top two floors.

"What say? Take room or not? Must know."

Thomas and Hélène take turns nodding inconclusively, she with closed eyes. Thomas sighs deeply. The hesitation draws a frown from the concierge.

"Window," she says, pointing to make sure the two young people understand that the room has a window.

Thomas and Hélène do as they are bid. They drag their feet for a second time to the window. Its glass is covered with smudges of grime. Yet even through the grit the two young renters can see enough to know there will never be a view, unless the courtyard six stories below might be considered a view. Thomas goes up on tiptoes and makes out a tiny man gesticulating wildly at two miniscule boys. He strikes first one then the other. A master with apprentices, Thomas concludes. That's the same everywhere, he knows, but he had hoped for better in the part of Paris where he is to live.

Thomas turns back to Hélène. He wants from her some sign of consent. Otherwise … well, he doesn't know. It's obvious that the decision as to where they live matters more to her than to him. His big worry is the money: how to make it last. There's an unmistakeable disappointment on her face. For the first time since he saw her smiling face run across the yard of the inn, Thomas wonders if Hélène is now having second thoughts about having left Évreux.

"Are we close to anything here?" Thomas blurts out. He's desperate to find something, anything to cling to. He has forgotten that they are near the Louvre, the Tuileries and Palais Royal and not far from the Seine. But then, nothing in Paris is far from the river, on one side or the other. As for the Louvre and Palais Royal, since he's not staying at either the one or the other, what does it matter how close to them he might be? Yet it does matter, to be close. Proximity is important. It will allow him to forget from time to time that he's going to be living in a sixth-floor *grenier* upon which the young king's lackeys would look down.

"Is perfect," smiles the concierge. "Close very close. Everything. Close."

"All right, we'll take it," says Thomas, making a silent vow to find some place better as soon as he can.

He looks to Hélène, to see that she supports his decision. But she has swiftly turned away. It's her back alone that greets him. He can see the rigidity of her muscles through her clothes.

"One month. Advance," says the concierge. "Bring me now."

—

Thomas is the first to wake, or so he thinks. He stands and stretches, slipping on the clothes he wore yesterday. It is also what he wore the day before that. He has no choice. The few other garments he possessed were in the stolen satchel, and there were not many of those when he set out from Vire. So buying some clothes is the first thing Thomas has to do this day. There will undoubtedly be used clothing shops or stands somewhere nearby. He needs things that will present him in a suitable light. He must dress for the position, any position that matches his talent, his ambition. He knows now exactly how much money he has. He did a count after Hélène tumbled off to sleep. It's enough to pay three months lodging and food as well as the purchase of some clothes. If Hélène throws in her money as well, they have an extra month, maybe two. But that's not forever, so they both need to find work.

Thomas thinks there's probably enough to buy a few books. He has nothing to read, no books to inspire his own muse and quill. Well, he has no quill either since the theft, but that's a need that's easy to fill. He trusts that his muse is still well. He's never gone long without some lines running through his head. And this is Paris after all. He can't wait to see what they have in their bookstalls. He expects to make an entry in the writers' world sooner or later. The republic he's heard it's called. That entry will have to wait until after he's found something that will give him a wage on a regular basis.

All dressed and with his shoes on, Thomas relieves himself in the chamber pot. The pot is halfway full after the two of them last night and now this contribution. Thomas puts the lid on the cracked ceramic container, making sure it's on tight. He glances over at Hélène's sleeping form. It comes to him that he should take the pot down the stairs and dump it in the stinky gutter in the middle of the street then bring it back up and put it in inside the door while Hélène sleeps on. She would appreciate him for doing that, no doubt. She's not fond of the room they have chosen to live in nor of the building itself, and any little thing he could do to make her happy will count. However, he also knows that he needs to find some kind of paying work, and find it fast. The chamber pot is not full to the top. He'll empty it later on, when he comes back in a few hours.

Hand on the door handle and ready to leave, Thomas looks Hélène's way once more. She's still coiled in a sleeping ball upon the *pailleasse* and breathing deeply. He recalls that last night was the first time they'd lain together and not touched each other's tender parts. They were simply too tired, and Hélène seemed distant. So they just closed their eyes and went right to sleep. We'll get back to it later on, he thinks.

As he descends the stairs, running his fingers along the railing all the way down like he's exploring every contour and crack, Thomas has a worrying thought. Whatever is it that Hélène is going to do in Paris? This is not her uncle's inn in Évreux. Well, thank god for that. But can she pay her own way? She's really good at one thing – he smiles reaching the ground level and going out the door – but she can't be doing that except with him. They are together now. Still, she does have to find something that brings in coins. It's a troubling thought.

—

The used clothes Thomas has purchased feel both too large and too small. That's because they are. The hat is so loose that it slides upon his head as he walks. The *veston* and the *justaucorps,* on the other hand, they are more than a little too tight. The breeches, only the breeches are just right. As for the chemise, it'll do. It's nothing fancy but at least it's not stained anywhere that anyone will see, just faintly under the arms and down low on the back where it will be tucked away. Despite the poor fits, Thomas decided after an hour of trying on that it was better to purchase things suitable to a middling level than what was closer to his size and shape but made him look like he's in the working poor. The prices were a bit of a shock, twice what he'd have paid if he bought them back in Vire. If things continue in this way, he'll have to recalculate how long the money will hold out.

As the newly attired Thomas climbs the stairs heading back up to his and Hélène's attic room – to drop off his old clothes and empty the chamber pot – he takes out and looks once again at what is written on the sheet of paper Strombeau gave him when they got off the diligence. That person and that address are next on his list.

Odd, thinks Thomas as he unlocks and opens the door to the tiny room on the attic level, it looks like Hélène is not there. Nor has she left him any sign of a note. Nothing. Oh well, he concludes, she's likely out getting something to eat, or better still maybe looking for work. He does not think to check to see if her sack is anywhere in the room. If he did, he would find that it too is gone. He misses that detail because he has his own immediate future on his mind. He says aloud three times what is written on Strombeau's sheet, to commit it to memory. It's the name of a marquis and the name of a street. He doesn't want to take the paper with him and look like a stranger as he moves about in the city. Directions for the street he may have to ask as he goes along because Paris is for him still a maze, and a vast maze at that. Yet he does not want anything to give away that he's someone new in town. He wants to blend in and be a part of this Paris, the city where he is determined to compose the as yet unwritten pages of his life.

Thomas puts down Strombeau's paper. He stoops to pick up the chamber pot, carefully grasping it with both hands. He'll empty it then come back up and get ready to go find the marquis at his address.

—

What Thomas missed while picking out his new used clothes was this: Hélène tosses off the cover as soon as he left. She squats over the only chamber pot there is, near stinking full, then freshens her face and hands as best she can. The water in the chipped blue basin is not just cold but has an oily skim from all the dips from Thomas's and her hands the night before. She changes into the clean chemise she brought with her in her sack but the socks, skirt and jacket are the same she wore the day before. She'll have to see if she can find something better in a used clothing shop. She'd like to look more like the ladies she sees in the streets, with their *robes volantes* and air of ease and grace. She is only sixteen and a country girl, but she knows already that it is with the right clothes that that attitude begins.

Hélène can also see that she is going to miss having nearby the little outdoor laundry she had back at the inn. It was hard work, but at least it was convenient, to wash clothes and keep clean. There is not even a mirror in this attic room, no matter where she looks. So she squints at herself in the window reflection and first brushes her hair then bundles it up in her little white cap as best she can. She does everything in a rush. Hélène doesn't know why, but she feels it important to get up and on her feet before Thomas comes back and catches her still around. They'll speak later on, but first she wants to see a bit more of the city on her own. With luck, she'll find work and he'll stop worrying about that. It's clear that Thomas's pockets are not as flush with money as she once thought. She thought she'd be more than a servant in Paris.

At the last moment, in a second thought before she leaves the attic room, Hélène decides to take along her sack with all her possessions. She is going to lock the door but who knows if that is going to keep thieves out of this room. Better safe than sorry, her aunt often said. Though she was talking about what Hélène should and should not do when the fertile days of her cycle come around.

Out on the streets below, Hélène wanders wherever her gaze chooses. She is not ten minutes gone from the attic room when she stops to look through the window of a bookshop. She's not read a book in her life, but she would like to someday. She knows all the letters and has read a few prayers under the sisters' instruction. But she likes the look of books, especially the ones in this bookshop window. The golden leather covers tinged with a bit of red look particularly important. She imagines they contain the histories of great kings or maybe the poetry of love songs from far away and long ago.

Does she stay too long gazing through the bookshop window? Maybe. A skinny fellow with a long wig and a perpetual grin comes to stand on the other side of the glass. He too is drawn to the window display, though in his case he wants to see if any of the books might happen to bear his name. He glances up to see a pretty country girl gazing in. He likes the way she looks, not the slightest style at all, a farm girl in the city, yet with a pretty face. He beckons her to stay right where she is. Hélène smiles back, quite charmed. She noticed the man before he saw her. Fine clothes, an impressive wig, a wrinkled smile, and posture like a noble. Everything about the young man suggests confidence. And with confidence, as far as Hélène knows the world, comes comfort and standing.

The young man comes outside the shop. He invites her to come with him for a stroll. She sees no harm in that. He asks if he might carry her sack. She smiles and holds it up. He tosses its weight over his shoulder, letting it dangle down his back.

"Would you like to dine together one day?"

"If you mean right now, I'd say yes to that." She is so hungry and tired of the stale bread and wooden cheese she took in a rush from her uncle's inn.

"Well," he says, charmed by the directness of a girl and the mischievous twinkle in her eyes, "it would not be called dining at this hour, would it?"

Hélène touches a finger to her chin. "Well, no, I suppose not."

"My name is François."

"Oh," Hélène makes a face, "my uncle has that name. He's not the best man there is."

"Ah. Well then, I have other names. François Marie Arouet." He bows, as if she were a lady at a ball.

"And I'm Hélène." She curtsies in return.

—

The streets twist and turn endlessly. Almost all are cobbled though there are still a few of packed earth. When it rains, Thomas can imagine, they must turn to mud. Which, added to the horse paddies and stream of human excrement in the gutter that runs down the middle of each street, will make things pretty rich.

There is hardly a street name posted anywhere that Thomas can see. That was all right back in Vire because there were only a few streets and he knew them all by heart. But in Paris it's an impossible task. He tries to note landmarks as he goes past them – the facades and spires of striking churches and some unusual signs for fish shops, butcheries and jewellery stores – but after a while it all becomes too much. He wonders more than once if he'll ever find his way back to the building with the attic where he and Hélène are lodged. Of course he will, he concludes, because he can always ask for the Hôtel de Ville and find his way back to their *grenier* from there.

As he wanders, Thomas notices that the signs of the inns and other businesses hang higher up than back in Vire. There must be some regulation at work. He approves. An ordered world is better than one that is not. He also observes that all the houses, regardless of their size or design, have bars in their ground-floor windows. This confirms what he has heard: that Paris has lots of thieves about. His meandering path takes him by several great houses, each with a *porte-cochère*. Those wide gate openings make a statement about wealth and standing. As he admires a particular opening just off the rue des Rosiers, he hears the clattering rumble of a carriage coming fast. He steps aside before the coachman's horses run him down. The coach goes underneath the arch, into the courtyard within. He cannot help but wonder why he didn't come into the world in one of those families of style and ease instead of to the one he did.

"Born wrong," he mumbles to himself.

After an hour of exploring this way and that, through rivers of people streaming by, and finding no sign for the street Strombeau wrote down, Thomas decides it's time to speak to someone. The first passerby that deigns to stop and answer his raised hand and mumbled query is an old lady with a limp to her stride. He sees in her expression that she takes pity on his plight. Better still, she is able to point him on his way. After that it's a bit of a loop and backtrack, no doubt about it, but it's an exploration he mostly enjoys. The city is becoming his Paris with every step. His feet have to learn it sooner or later, so it might as well be now.

Most streets have iron lanterns hanging down in the middle of the way. There seems to be one every twenty paces, with a box of glass and metal that looks to be twenty feet above the centre of the street. The coaches, even the high ones, all pass safely beneath, though some not by much. The rope that's used to let the lanterns down when it's time to light them is fastened to the closest building, secured with an iron funnel and a lock. Thomas will come back out on the streets at night to see how the lamplighters bring them down and go about their business. He also wants see how much the lamps glow when they are lit. He's heard they put four big candles inside each night. He's curious how long they last. Can they burn all through the dark or only until midnight, maybe a little past? And at what cost? If in truth there are four candles in each and every one, multiplied by however many lanterns there be and that number by the whole year long, why that's no small cost. "City of lights," Thomas murmurs, a phrase he often heard before he arrived in Paris. Now that he's a resident it's a boast he's entitled to repeat.

City of Lights, yes, but a city of stink as well. It's not just the horse droppings, though thanks to all the coaches, there are more plops in Paris than Thomas has ever seen before. Worse than the horse shit is that which comes out of all the people. Who knows how many thousand chamber pots are overturned each day and night? Or how many are too lazy to make a descent and simply throw the reeking contents of their pots from windows out to the streets? Thomas picks a careful path wherever he goes, though twice already a carriage rolling past has splashed bits of spray his way. His breeches take a few squirts and his shoes are soon a mess.

It takes the better part of two hours for Thomas to find the street Strombeau wrote upon the sheet. He wants to confirm that he's arrived where he is supposed to be by asking a passing water carrier, a man with a long scar upon his cheek.

"The Marquis d'Argenson, is he to be found in there?"

The water carrier does not answer. He breaks eye contact and swiftly moves away, spilling some of his wet cargo as he goes. It looks to Thomas as if there's suddenly someone after the man.

Thomas looks again at the stone building with ornate columns and pediment. He notices for the first time that chiselled upon a stone plaque on the surrounding wall are the words Police de Paris.

"Oh," Thomas mutters for no one but himself. All he knows about the Police de Paris is that the city is the only place in France with such a force. Everywhere else it's a garrison of soldiers or musketeers or nothing at all. The force is supposed to keep the city safe from cut-throats and footpads. But why would Strombeau send him here? His idea of a joke?

—

The atmosphere inside is quiet, reminding Thomas of the entrance to a church. Is this, the Police de Paris, yet another secret world? Two men dressed in drab middling coats and breeches, both dark in colour but not quite a uniform, come out a door down the hall to the right. Their conversation is hushed. Each man seems to be given to making sudden gestures and shooting fervent looks. Another man, a tricorn tucked under one arm and a sheaf of papers in the other hand, is coming down the grand staircase in a hurry. No one gives Thomas the slightest regard.

From a door to the right emerges someone else. This someone's appearance and stately posture make Thomas stand up straight. The man's coat is the colour of a ripe plum, highlighted with silver embroidered brocade. Each sleeve has an elaborate cuff, and the man is wearing a lace neck-cloth. There is a knot of white ribbon at the shoulder, which matches the white silk of the stockings below. The shoes are square-toed with jewelled buckles and low red heels. Thomas's eyes widen as he appreciates the full ensemble, the like of which he's never seen before. The man's wig consists of long grey curls that sweep off his shoulders and tumble down his back.

"Excuse me, sir," Thomas ventures, "can you tell me if a Marquis d'Argenson should reside in here?"

The well-dressed gentleman touches the brim of his plumed hat as he purses his lips. His expression is as if Thomas had not been speaking French, or if it was French it was with an accent the man could not quite comprehend. The man's eyes go up and down the lad's clothes, which are both too large and too small. After a slight shake of the head the eyes come back up to the young man's face. He pulls a *mouchoir* from a pocket of his *justaucorps.* He covers his mouth and nose.

"Resides? Here? The marquis?" Each syllable comes out of the mouth well rounded, as if there is some hidden joke. Thomas hears mockery, mockery at his expense. "*You* are asking for the marquis?"

Thomas's eyes go down to his own shoes and breeches. He sees how mud- and shit-splattered they are, and realizes how he must look and smell. This gentleman, on the other hand, is giving off a scent of a sweet perfume. Orange water or something better is Thomas's guess. For an instant, the young man's gaze flicks past the gentleman to the framed engravings on the closest wall – fortress towns and battle scenes. Farther on there is a large painting of justice – a blindfolded woman holding a scale – and there at the end of the hall, in the place of honour, hangs a full-length portrait of the king. Thomas has heard that Louis XIV has not been well of late, though since he has been on the throne forever it's unlikely any malady could ever kill him off. He's outlived his children and grandchildren too.

"Someone gave me the marquis's name. A Monsieur Strombeau. We met on a coach."

The eyes of the gentleman facing Thomas briefly light up. He lowers his *mouchoir.* But if he was fleetingly tempted to say something, that thought does not stay. He recovers his mouth and nose and looks away. Thomas takes the expression to mean that the gentleman has nothing further to say.

"My mistake," Thomas says after a long delay. "Must have the wrong name or the wrong place. I'll be on my way." He spins to head for the door through which he'd entered barely a minute before.

"No," comes the voice of the well-dressed gentleman. It's the voice of someone who is used to being obeyed. "You'll wait where you are."

Thomas does as he is told. Maybe Strombeau's direction to come here was not in vain after all.

The gentleman in the plum-coloured coat lifts a hand in the direction of the two men in dark clothes in conversation at the base of the staircase. The raised hand all by itself interrupts their talk. It beckons them to come closer with a motion of the tips of his fingers as slight as slight can be. One of the beckoned men, tall, thin, with neither hat nor wig, responds to the gesture. He wears what looks to be his natural hair in a queue. His face has barely any features, no eyebrows that Thomas can see. The faceless man strides forward to where the gentleman stands waiting patiently, but patiently as if he were a king or pope, who will not wait for long. Thomas can just barely make out the following bits of their exchange.

"Collier," says the man with the *mouchoir,* looking into the distance not at the man himself. The expressionless man comes to a deferential stance a few feet away.

So that's the faceless man's name, is it, Thomas surmises. Collier.

Snippets from the distinguished one: "…young fellow asked … the marquis … paper from … Strombeau."

"Ah, Strombeau," is all Collier says, Thomas is pretty sure.

"…too young of course … but speak … what he is about…"

"Yes, Monsieur le Marquis," says the one named Collier, louder than before. His heels come together to make a tiny click.

Thomas's eyes swing from the man he'd first approached, whom he now hears is the Marquis, down to stare at Collier's just-clicked shoes. Collier waves a hand to break Thomas's gaze.

"This way please."

Intrigued by the curious world of the Police de Paris that Strombeau's note has brought him to, Thomas follows in the direction Collier directs. The two of them, Collier nearing forty and Thomas a mere fifteen, walk down the corridor until they reach the third door on the left. The Paris police official turns the handle and gestures for Thomas to go in first. Inside, Thomas finds a table with three simple wooden chairs. There are two on one side and one on the opposite side, with four more chairs, of superior craftsmanship, around the perimeter of the room. That is all there is: not a thing on the walls and no windows either. It suggests to Thomas a room for interrogations. Odd, he thinks, but he steps in just the same.

"Any seat." Collier speaks softly, as if he might have bad news he is reluctant to share. "You select."

Thomas's gaze goes to the door Collier has just closed behind the two of them. Thomas stands behind a chair but is now uncertain about pulling it out to sit.

"I ... I don't need to sit. I was only looking for a name. Well, a man with a name. Given to me by a friend. Well, an acquaintance I suppose. A Monsieur Strombeau. I gather that you know his name."

Collier's face is a blank. Just as it has no features so it has no indication of interest at all. He says nothing. Thomas feels it's up to him to continue to make sense of the morning by himself.

"I, I don't know who he is, the Marquis d'Argenson. Strombeau wrote his name and that of the street outside. He said I should look him up. More than that, I don't know. It's all a big mistake."

"What's a mistake?" says Collier, pointing for Thomas to indeed have a seat.

"This." Thomas waves round the room they're standing in, the one with no windows, only a table and a few chairs and the door that Collier has just closed.

"Oh this is no mistake. Please take a seat."

Thomas hesitates then does as he is told. He gives a faint protest with a loud exhale. He moves from where he is standing over to the side where there is but a single chair. If he must sit, he'll take that one, the one all by itself.

He thinks he sees Collier smile, but when he looks again there is no smile on the man's face. There is nothing there. No smile, no expression, no features at all.

Collier sits directly across from Thomas, pushing the second chair away so that the table now has but two chairs, the one facing the other.

"Please start over. I've not heard your story."

"Story? It's not a story." Thomas feels the top of his head getting light and tingly, like it might float away. If only this Collier's face would give him some kind of clue. Not knowing what else to do, he does start to tell his story. "Well, I arrived in Paris yesterday and…"

"No, that's not how it's done. You start with your name and your profession."

Thomas makes a face. What is this? A court of law? An inquisition? His raised eyebrows and imploring eyes have no impact on the man across the way, so Thomas thinks he has to go along. "It's Thomas." He blows a stream of air through his lips.

"Is there not a family name with that?"

"Of course." Thomas's mind races. Something tells him not to give out any more than he must. He's already told Strombeau and the others on the way to Paris that he was not Pichon but Tyrell so he'd better stick with that.

"Tyrell. Yes, Tyrell. Thomas Tyrell."

Collier's face offers a hint of upturned lips. "You're sure? You sound a little … dubious."

"Of course I'm sure. It's my name."

"And how old are you, Thomas Tyrell?"

"Twenty, well, nineteen, nearly twenty." Thomas straightens his shoulders and stretches up tall.

This time Collier allows a highly visible and obviously doubting smile.

"Maybe try that again?"

Thomas looks into Collier's eyes. They're grey if they're anything. The man's face is a mask, with next to nothing revealed. And yes he does have eyebrows, but they so pale and thin that they almost can't be seen.

"No, that's good as it is. Nineteen."

"Where do you live, Thomas? And your occupation as well."

"To start, I'm on Saint-Thomas-du-Louvre. And my profession," Thomas hesitates and glances fleetingly at the ceiling, "I've not yet completely worked that out. Some details still need to be … sorted. You understand. I'd say it's unclear. At this point." Thomas raises his eyebrows like they might be a punctuation mark. But then he looks away from his questioner in a hurry. He glances down at the tabletop then quickly around the room. When his gaze comes back to Collier he adds: "I'm thinking of medicine. But it's too early to tell."

"I see. So, to put it bluntly, you have no means of support?"

Thomas stiffens. The mask that is Collier's face is too carefully arranged. Is he joking? Thomas is so young and he's only just arrived. There must be hundreds, likely thousands, just like him.

"I have means, some means. I'll be all right for a while." Something comes to mind. He hesitates to say it, then he does. "Is it *Monsieur* Collier? Is that it, or is there a first name that goes along with that?" Thomas smiles in triumph. He's just turned the tables on the man across the way.

Collier does not reply, nor does he give any more facial reaction than that which might come from a statue. Thomas shakes his head in defeat. He wonders how a person gets to hide his thoughts and feelings like that. It must be handy to be so in control. So much practice it must take. But then, judging by the colour of this Collier, who is as pale as a corpse, the man must never get out in the daylight. Perhaps all he does all day is practice how to be a mask.

"Yes, I have *means*," Thomas says, breaking the silence. "Though it's true I need to look for a position appropriate to my … my aspirations." As soon as the word is out of Thomas's mouth he regrets it. He sees Collier's eyes pinch to a closer focus.

"And these aspirations, what might they be?"

"I … I'm not sure. At this time. Not right now. What I need is to find something. Some work. A position. Later on …" Thomas halts, not knowing what to say next. He doesn't have a clue what might come later on. All he has is an aspiration to be and to possess more than he is and has.

"Could you say a little more?" Collier adds a slow, deliberate blink of both eyes. Thomas begins to spill what's going through his mind as if the cork has just been removed from his bottle.

"This … coming here … with the name Strombeau gave me on that piece of paper, folded over. He made it sound like it might be a job. He did. Or that's what I wanted to hear, I suppose. I don't know. But he did suggest that I need to start somewhere. Leading to a position. I have much to offer. Yet you're grilling me like I'm a criminal. I'm not a saint, but I … I come from Vire. That's in Normandy. My father is a clothier...." Thomas waves a hand to dismiss the last remark. He doesn't know why he's told Collier so much. "Sorry."

"What are you sorry about?"

"Nothing." Thomas shifts in his seat. "Look, I need to go. It's getting late."

"Thomas, do you know that the name on your piece of paper, the one Monsieur Strombeau gave you, that of the Marquis d'Argenson, that he is the Inspector-General of the police of Paris?"

Thomas's eyes widen, yet he makes himself hold his tongue.

"And do you also know – I think you suspect – that it was the marquis himself you were speaking with near the entrance to this building. After you wandered in."

"I had deduced that."

Collier says no more. He simply sits there staring at Thomas. After a count of four, Thomas feels forced to speak. "I see," is what he says.

"Exactly. You see." Collier's hands slide across the tabletop to clasp together. "And what do you see?"

"I see, well, I see." Thomas rolls his head as he waves at the walls and the ceiling of the room.

There begins a silence that stretches as taut as a rope before it is forced to snap. With Collier's eyes on him, Thomas shifts his away to burn at only one thing. The closed door and how he'd like to go out. Now. Thomas pushes back his chair, hands on the table's edge, but with his ass still planted firmly on the seat. He thinks: this man, this Collier, he has no right to keep me here. I've done nothing wrong. I have rights in this kingdom as an innocent man.

"Do you know what we do here, Thomas? Here in this part of the police of Paris?"

Thomas relaxes a little, though he keeps his hands on the table's edge, ready to propel his body to a standing position.

"Catch thieves, I suppose. And vagabonds. Murderers too. People like that."

Collier exhales.

"Very good. But those are only some of the useless people we put away. Sometimes before we punish all we do is anticipate. That's right, anticipate."

Collier lifts both hands and spreads them in the air in front of him as if he has been asked to conjure a globular shape. His eyes stay fixed on Thomas's eyes as his hands hold the shape and his explanation rolls on.

"Paris is an apple. That's right. And sometimes there are worms and rotted spots. By anticipating, we can cut out those worms and spots. Before they spoil the rest of the fruit."

Thomas blows out his mouth like a silent whistle. This man is crazy, as baffling as a mystical monk. Thomas has heard enough. He cannot fathom how any of this relates to him.

"Can I leave now?" Thomas tilts his head toward the closed door.

Collier asks, "Are you afraid?"

"Afraid? Afraid. Why would I be afraid?" Bewilderment fills Thomas's face and his voice. He feels a trickle of sweat under his arms. "I've done nothing wrong."

For the first time, Collier allows his face an expression. It's a smile. Well, a smile of sorts. "Your friend Strombeau, he was once associated with this force, the Police de Paris. Did you know that?"

Thomas starts to nod like he agrees, but then he shifts his motion. His head sways side to side.

"He started out around the same age as you are now. Young and recently arrived. He too had ... what did you call them? Oh yes, *aspirations*. He too had aspirations. That was long before he began to make money in *other* ways. When that happened Strombeau moved on. Man of business instead. Relocated to Bordeaux. But Strombeau started here. And, as you see by the note he gave you, he still takes an interest in what we do. And occasionally, every year or so, he sends us someone, someone like you."

"How?" Thomas's hands are off the table edge. They're clasped in his lap. His body is leaning back trying to grasp what Collier is saying.

"How does Strombeau do it?"

"No, how does this affect me?"

"Do you know what flies are?"

Thomas shakes his head. He doesn't want to say small flying bugs. He wishes now he hadn't said his name was Tyrell or that he was nineteen. His heart is knocking against his chest. His hands and armpits are all wet. Why didn't he just say that he's Thomas Pichon, barely past fifteen? His face feels so very flushed. It comes to him that it's maybe not too late. He should set the record straight with this pale-faced man. He wants to have the success of Strombeau. Prosperity, a puffy waistline, people to know his name.

"I … my … I'm not really Tyrell and I'm not really nineteen."

"In a moment." Collier holds up a hand to stop Thomas before he can say more. "We'll get to all that. First, let me tell you what you would have to do as one of our flies."

—

It is late afternoon when Thomas gets back to the attic room. He heard church bells tolling somewhere in the distance as he was approaching the building. He wasn't sure if it was for *nones* or vespers, and didn't care. It is late and he is tired. His head is spinning with all he's heard from Collier. There's no obligation, said Collier at the end, no compulsion. It's merely an opportunity, an opportunity for Thomas and for the kingdom too. Yes,

Thomas could see all that clearly enough while they were speaking face to face and he had said as much. Yet after the shake of hands and with Thomas retracing a weaving path through the warren of streets back to the building with his attic room on Saint-Thomas-du-Louvre, he began to have second thoughts. Is this why he left Vire? Is this really what he is destined for, what he wants to do in Paris after all it took to get him here? The answer might be no. There is a choice here. He doesn't have to do what Collier suggests. Still, there is the matter of an opportunity, an opportunity he might not get again. Should he not take something certain, something that will pay him a not half bad sum, until something better comes along? The answer to the question put that way is yes. Of course the bird in the hand is worth more than two in the bush. His father liked to say that. He also said he never looked the other way when an opportunity – a pretty term for a customer – walked into the shop. "A sale has to be made when one can be made, because it may be a while before there's another." Funny how his father's words come back to him. He thought he'd left the man and his advice behind.

Too fatigued to think about it anymore, Thomas empties his bladder in the chamber pot. He notices that there has not been any additional contributions since he left hours before. Hélène must have been out all day. He goes to the *pailleasse* and tumbles down. He grabs at the blanket and pulls it up over him as his cover.

Hélène, he thinks, but where's Hélène?

He gets up on one elbow and looks around the room. No sign of her or, what is stranger, her things. He recalls that she had a sack that contained all her clothes. He stands to take a better look. He scans under the table and moves the few chairs. Nothing. Over to the rickety standing cupboard. Again not a thing. There's no sign Hélène was ever in this room.

"Where's she gone?" Thomas asks the table and its chairs. If she were just out – getting something to eat or looking for work or something else, would she have taken her sack? Maybe. After all the talk he heard from Collier about foists, nips, whipjacks, cutthroats and footpads, Hélène may have been wise to take her things with her, just so she could be sure her stuff was safe. But then again, could she not have been attacked? Is she lying in an alley somewhere?

Thomas sucks in a deep breath. Hélène, where are you? The eyes narrow. There comes a different thought. Much as they have enjoyed their few days together, the kiss and touch and the slap of belly on belly, how much does he really know about his Hélène? She's pretty and fun loving, but what else can he say? That she used to do what she does with Thomas with other paying men at her aunt and uncle's inn. Could she have so despaired of this disappointing attic room – he knows she didn't like it, she made that clear – that she's gone off on her own to find some better space?

Thomas stands and finds his key. He will lock the door and head out onto the streets. He has to find Hélène before something happens to her.

IV

Positions

Paris

December 1719

It's long since dark when Thomas leaves the building. The man he and everyone else calls Rooster, the red-haired office clerk who rents one of the other attic spaces in the building, stopped him on the stairs and asked him where he was going. Thomas was evasive. "Stretch my legs. Back in a bit."

It was true enough, just not the whole truth. The last thing Thomas wanted was for Rooster to tag along. It is one thing to spend a few minutes chatting with the man on the stairs of the building or even occasionally going inside his room. It would be quite another for Rooster to come along to meet the group Thomas regards as his true friends. Well, true acquaintances, because Thomas is not quite sure what it is that distinguishes a friend from an acquaintance. Some people are smarter and better looking than others; some have more money and talent; and some are more or less useful depending on the situation. All that is clear enough. But what should he call the fellows he's hurrying to meet? Like-minded acquaintances, though that's too long a name, is it not? Good sources. True, but that sounds like he's using them. Which maybe he is, but he likes them too so that has to count for something. Besides, it's not entirely correct to suggest any kind of exploitation. Some of his friends, or acquaintances, would be flattered if they knew that Thomas sometimes repeats one of their stories, maybe even two. He often has to embellish their tales, to be sure, but he does give attribution where attribution is due. So he doesn't think it's wrong to bandy about their names when the occasion arises. They should likely thank him for that. Give them a bit of a reputation among those who care. How rare it is, they would have to admit, that something they said turned out to be of consequence to anyone but themselves. But since Thomas's friends don't know a thing about his life as a fly and the tales that he passes on to Collier, his contact in the police, it's best to keep it that way.

Thomas could see from Rooster's eyes – real name Pierre Charpentier, but no one uses that name because the nickname fits so much better, what with the reddish hair and the way his upper body jerks when he walks – he could see from Rooster's eyes that he suspected Thomas was not just stretching his legs but heading out to meet someone. Yet he didn't say so nor did he did press to come along. All Rooster said was: "Maybe I'll see you later then, my friend."

"All right," said Thomas with the smile he uses when he knows there isn't the slightest chance of his doing whatever the asker has asked.

Out front of the building, having shed Rooster and believing he has also evaded the eyes and ears of the concierge, whom he calls La Sentinelle, Thomas quick-steps from the entrance. He does not slow until he knows he's safely away, out on the rue du Louvre. He's relieved that there is not a soul close by. The dark months are upon Paris and there's a special chill in the air. The latest cold snap is keeping people off the streets unless they absolutely need to be out, which is how Thomas feels about his own outing. He has his needs, three in fact this evening. First, there will be the enjoyment of his circle of friends. Second, he must come up with a report of some sort for Collier. And third, best for last as the saying goes, he will satisfy his soldier. Since Hélène left him that first day in Paris four years ago, without so much as a trace, he has had to find his body's pleasure with someone else, someone in the plural and as often as he can afford. It's a secret he keeps to himself, which only adds to the satisfaction he feels.

He turns one corner then another, hurrying on, hoping to make the first rendezvous with time to spare. That way, the second meeting and especially the third will unfold as they should, the third at a sweet pleasured pace. Thomas wonders what might come up this evening with his writer friends. Of course, there will be the usual complaints and ambitions. There always are. It's a sacrament to be observed, about how unappreciated they are.

In Thomas's case, the litany of gripes is fodder to be chewed on and noted for later recall to Collier's ears.

There is also the matter of the Mississippi Company. Thomas wants to talk to the group about it. By all reports, no joke, everyone is getting rich, or will be soon enough. Too good to be true, yet so it is. That's why the company headquarters on the rue Quincampoix now has soldiers guarding it, to hold off the frenzied would-be investors. The shares have taken off and there's no limit to how high they'll go. From five hundred *livres* a share they've gone to ten thousand. That's what Thomas is hearing. A genius, that canny Scot John Law, everyone is saying so. Thomas wants to be a part of it and will say so this night. Some instant wealth would give him rank and position right away. How much better than waiting years and years. Yet Thomas wants to know first, before he sinks in his teeth, his hard-earned money, what the others think, these grumbling scriveners he meets with at Le Procope. Are they in already? Would they be willing to go in with him and buy some shares together? They could all begin to live lives they've only dreamed of, instead of watching others do so from the downcast sides.

With the river twenty paces ahead, Thomas puts his imaginary future wealth out of mind. He has to have his wits about him going over the bridge. He has chosen the Pont Neuf because it's the only one that does not have buildings on it. That gives good visibility in all directions, especially at night after the daytime spectacle has come and gone. Gone are the pedlars and jugglers and charlatans and booksellers, and the hundreds of gawkers and buyers and the pickpockets too. Nonetheless, there are always dangerous types lurking about and more in the dark than in the light. Once Thomas gets to the other side, over to the left bank and on to rue Dauphine, he'll be back in an area with street lamps and feel better. A father's warnings and a mother's worries come back to him. How often they warned him back in sleepy Vire about the darkness and its perils. How much greater the dangers are in this city than in Vire. Fingerers and rogues, cozeners and lunatics, they're all about. Thomas sees them in the streets day and night and has so far been spared their impact. But he hears tales of the criminals' wrongdoing every day. That

Paris has lamps is good, yet it is no cure-all, he knows that. The large lanterns, once lowered and lit and hoisted back up by the ropes, don't give off so much light as one would hope. Paris at night is a city of lights, but those lights are dim, a mere smoky glow. And the large candles don't last much past midnight. So if Thomas is out really late, there'll be no glow at all. After four years of living in the city, he knows the nighttime is to be feared. Anything is possible, oh mother of surprise.

Thomas pauses midway on the Pont Neuf. He stands beside where the statue of the equestrian king, Henri IV, rides his horse of bronze. He takes a deep breath. Were it still daylight, there'd be beggars round about, huddled near the long-dead king, hoping for the chicken Henri promised for each of their pots. By day, those beggars use outstretched arms or religious appeals, and sometimes a threat of damnation, to win a coin or two. By night, they need no such ruse. In the darkness, they simply take what they want. The parapet railing on the bridge is low all the way across, so Thomas does not get too close to the edge. One push and he'd be over. It was only a few days ago that some poor soul, drunk perhaps or more likely shoved, fell off. No one knew until the next morning, when someone spotted the body in the water down below. Of course, every day someone's found dead somewhere in Paris, usually in an alley, of one unnatural cause or another. If the city were to mourn them all, the citizens would be swimming in tears.

Thomas takes a deep breath. The Seine smells different in the dark than it does during the day. He prefers the pungency of the nighttime to the choke of day. He inhales its aroma. The vapour is cleaner, almost vinegary, which Thomas supposes must keep away the foul evils and frenzies that afflict so many in the city. He has been lucky in that regard, though in this world luck lasts only so long. One must enjoy good fortune while one has it, because once it's gone, it's gone. He takes the wafting smell of the Seine as an omen that the evening ahead holds promise.

A chill wind rises from the river. Thomas rubs his hands and shakes his arms. He fastens the top button on his greatcoat. He may soon need a warmer coat. Paris is already cold and this only the beginning of the winter. Of snow there's a hint, but the rain when it comes is stingingly cold. Already he has burned through nearly a quarter of a cord of firewood to keep his room warm. The unexpected cost is another reason why in winter he doesn't stay in any more than he has to. It's cheaper to go to inns and taverns and have a long, slow drink, where someone other than Thomas pays for the heat.

He is still living in the same room atop the building on Saint-Thomas-du-Louvre where he and Hélène first landed after the diligence came in from Évreux. He could afford better now, but he is attached to the dump of a place and the oddball characters in the building. He really does like Bazoches, the failed lawyer who lives on the second floor. The man is often drunk and to see him stagger up or down the stairs is quite a sight. With each intoxicated step Bazoches writes a drama to those standing nearby. Thomas missed the time the lawyer fell, but he heard about it from Rooster. The "flight of angels" is what Rooster called it. Rooster himself can be funny that way. Back Bazoches went all the way down, ass and legs in a whirl, amazingly unhurt when he came to a heap at the bottom.

Another character who intrigues Thomas in his building is the Polish count. Like Bazoches, he too is on the second floor. The count never misses an opportunity to tell Thomas why he's in Paris. "I went into exile with my king, as duty and honour dictate. Not one regret." If you have no regrets, Thomas often muses silently when they speak, why do you talk of nothing else?

And there's the widow Auger on the fifth floor. Pressed to make ends meet, she takes paying customers in her bed several times a week. Yet she never entertains anyone from the building, Thomas notes. He admires the widow for the restrictions she has set.

And then there's the cabinetmaker with fingers as slender as a pianist's. He lives on the fourth floor. Actually it's not him but his young wife who draws Thomas's interest. He loves her scent. She has the smell of roses when the two of them pass on the stairs. Perhaps he has looked too often or too long, because lately she averts her eyes from Thomas when they meet.

As he stands on the bridge a little longer in the chill night, Thomas notices a few stars push through the cover of clouds that broods above the statue of Henri IV. He recognizes his own sign, the Scorpion, just above a roofline in the sky to the south. The zodiac sign sends him a message that it's time to move on. His friends at the Le Procope will be awaiting his arrival.

Striding off the Pont Neuf, beginning to head up rue Dauphine, a warm aroma captures Thomas's attention. He recognizes the scent of roasting turkeys, a scent as a boy he loved to catch when he was out late in the right part of town. Here on this Paris night the scent is coming from a poultry shop where the rotisserie men cook until dawn to be ready for the morning trade. Thomas always makes a point to stop in front of their shop when he's near here at night. He imagines the sizzling fat dripping into the pan beneath the turnspit, pooling in a golden greasy bath. It makes him hungry just to think of it. He'll get something to eat at the Procope when he gets there.

—

At Le Café Procope Thomas's friends are just where he hoped they'd be, filling a table as close to the fireplace as they can get. That's smart on a night like this. They must have got here early. He's eager to warm up his chilled frame. However, he sees from a distance that there's not a seat left for him. Didn't they know to expect him?

Thomas asks at a table near the front where there's a spare chair if he might take it away. The two men at the table, two actors is his guess judging by their stage-managed postures and elaborate gestures, and the fact that he knows the Comédie Française is nearby, indicate with a flourish that he may indeed have the chair he wants. Thomas carries the chair above his head as he makes his way through the café. He taps the broad-backed Caylus on the shoulder when he gets there to let him know that he wants in. Caylus and Tinville say nothing, but they exchange understanding glances as they shift apart. Each slides his drink and his respective bundle of papers as they move left and right. They create just enough room for Thomas to insert his chair and sit down between them. It's warm in the café and he sheds his greatcoat and puts it on the back of the chair.

"Aha," says Fougre, known lovingly to his friends as Bougre. Well, Bougre is the nickname used most often. There is one other that Fougre does not like to hear. The bookseller Jean Gallatin, seated at the far end of the table this night, sometimes calls him Pokus. It's a Latin affectation Gallatin often adopts, since he's a devoted reader of Roman history. His use of Pokus – the long version of the nickname is Pokus Inter Anus – is Gallatin's way of pointing out Fougre's preference for men over women.

Fougre takes a drag on the stem of his clay pipe then gives a long plume of exhale. He sends a wink toward the long-faced La Coste, who is seated beside Gallatin. La Coste shrugs off the wink prefering to study the pipe in his hands. Fougre turns to Thomas instead.

"Halt, dear colleagues, our Norman friend, sweet Thomas, has arrived. If you would …" Fougre offers an outstretched arm in Thomas's direction, pretending to welcome him in.

Fougre is a sometime essayist who alas is rarely published anywhere that anyone at this table ever sees. But he tells them that he is being published and no one ever demands the proof. More typically Fougre is a writer of pornographic tales. He writes for the yellow press, an occupation that brings in enough money for food and rent. He always gives Thomas a warm greeting when he shows up. If Thomas didn't know better, he'd say the older man is in love with Thomas's brown Norman eyes. So Thomas plays it up to make Fougre happy. More than that, Fougre occasionally buys him a drink. On this particular evening, as if he were a nobleman or knight, Thomas offers Fougre a half bow from the waist and a sweep of one arm. No one other than Fougre laughs or even smiles. Dear Fougre, however, is attentive and all smiles.

"Speak, friend," says Fougre, who at nearly forty is twice Thomas's age. "What torrid scene makes you come so late to our gathering? A little lovemaking on a cold night? Ah, why not? The Venus chamber has its charms, so I've heard. But do give us details, because it's details I need. Grist for the mill, as we say. It's been a while since I've been with a lady friend so I'm eager to hear that which I have forgotten. The lumps, the humps, the little Venus cleft and … is there anything else? Do tell, Thomas. Any tale you can share is surely better than what has been said so far around the table this night."

Thomas glances around to see if that's everyone's assessment. But no one is paying the least attention to what Fougre has been saying.

"Bougre," says Thomas loud enough for the whole table to hear, "let me buy you a drink for a change."

"What's this?" Caylus slaps the tabletop. "The Norman opening up his purse for a friend? My oh my. News for the *Nouvelles à la main* is it not?"

"Indeed it is," chimes in the bookseller Gallatin, much louder than his normal voice. "Be wary there, Pokus. The innocent Norman lad may not be so innocent after all. Plying you with a free drink."

Thomas tenders a tired look. There's truth in what they say. He is frugal because frugal is the way to be – waste not, want not – but can this crowd not overlook the slightest chink in anyone's armour?

"Don't mind them," says Fougre. "I'll take your drink and give you no guff."

Thomas stands to go get something to drink for Fougre and for himself. As he walks over to the counter he wonders where he'll get the best tidbits tonight. He has to have something for Collier later on. He has a recipe he aims to follow when he comes to be with his friends. Three quarters of an evening's talk is for his own pleasure; the remaining quarter he shares with Collier. He figures it's a fair enough deal. Life's an exchange, a choosing of choices, the good with the bad. It's important to have a moral compass. That's what he has.

Walking back toward his friends Thomas sees that he may have picked the wrong end of the table this night. The two writers he is sitting between, Caylus and Tinville, look particularly silent and glum. Caylus, the toad-faced poet, appears already drunk while La Coste is puffing on a pipe and staring with intent focus into a mug of something clasped between his hands. If only, thinks Thomas, I'd picked up their moods earlier, I'd have tried to squeeze in at the other end.

Down at the other end of the table Jean Gallatin is holding forth in a way that Thomas does not often see. The bastard usually keeps to himself, except when he is being pithy and sarcastic. But tonight the bookseller's jaw wags up and down and his hands are gesturing this way and that. Thomas comes in late, but it's a tale about some *curé* in Provence. The priest has lately run amok in his parish. None of Gallatin's tablemates are paying more than half-hearted attention to the story, but Thomas's interest is piqued. The tale is clearly one Gallatin wants to tell, and to provide every sordid detail. Anything to besmirch the Church and its clergy is Gallatin's rule. The whole table knows that, and Thomas doesn't complain. And judging by the volume of Gallatin's voice and the motion of his hands, he's determined to lay this particular story out in all of its sad details. No one interrupts or asks the bookseller to stop. In other words, Gallatin has a completely free hand. Interesting as a debauched priest may be, there's nothing in the story that Collier will want to hear. His focus is on only one thing: Paris and the threats to the powers that be.

Thomas turns back to those at his end. Maybe he can get something out of the glum Tinville. The fellow has his pencil out and is scribbling something in his notebook at a feverish pace.

"What's wrong, my friend? Such a long face and the evening still so young."

"Nothing a little grease on the pole couldn't fix."

Tinville glances up from what he's writing. He wants to see if his crude line might have won some kind of reaction. There is none, but he doesn't give up. "It's a cure, you know, sex is, for near everything." Blank faces all round, and back to his notebook Tinville goes.

Delayed by his own drunken state, Caylus reacts to what Tinville said a few moments earlier. "Fuck and be fucked, that's what you're saying?" Caylus reaches out and pokes Tinville's right hand, the one with the pencil.

"Hey!" Tinville scowls.

"Oh sorry," the drunken Caylus says, "but that's the crux. Of what you're saying? It's all about the cock?"

Thomas gives Caylus a wary look, but he's the only one. Everyone else looks at Caylus with understanding and sympathy.

"What, what's going on?" Thomas asks.

Fougre is the one to reply. He jerks a thumb toward Caylus. "He says he's lost it all. He has nothing left."

"It's true," the poet Caylus says with a slur, and he takes another swig.

"Lost all of what? What's true?" Thomas senses that maybe there's something here after all he'll be able to share later on with Collier.

"The Mississippi," the poet replies, his voice thick with emotion. "It's smoke. On a mirror."

"Oh, John Law," says Thomas. "But no, that's not what I hear."

Caylus's head is looking wobbly on its neck, yet he is keeping Thomas fixed in his gaze.

"Three days ago I sunk a thousand. All I have. Correct me: all that I had. Now, it's lost." Caylus waves a hand at the far end of the table. "It's lost. I'm lost. Me. Nothing left."

Tinville looks up from his notebook. He nods to Thomas that it's true.

"But why? The Mississippi is golden everyone says. A way to get rich." Thomas searches the table of sad faces with his wide eyes.

"Past tense, dear boy, past tense." Fougre scratches the back of his neck. "Ask the bookseller. Right, Gallatin?"

Unable to get the attention of Jean Gallatin, who is in conversation with a nearby table, Fougre thumps the tabletop with both hands.

"Here, over here. Bookseller! Gallatin! Stop your rants about our blessed Church and its priests. Tell Thomas what you've heard. About the Mississippi and John Law."

Gallatin presents a stern face, chin upraised, not happy about Fougre telling him what he should do. "The Norman is no dummy. He can read and see for himself."

"Yes, but he's obviously not seen what you have on the rue Quincampoix. Tell him."

"Oh that," says Thomas in a quiet voice, reluctant to admit it. "No, I've not yet been over to the street. But I hear the place is a madhouse. Doesn't that mean the business opportunity is good?"

"Well, you go and see for yourself." Gallatin rolls his eyes. "Know this, Thomas, and the rest of you for that matter. Whenever everyone wants in on something, that means it's time to get out. It's a bubble, that's the new saying. A bubble. That's your John Law and his Mississippi scheme."

There is a silence around the table, with all eyes focused on the bookseller. Gallatin cannot resist taking advantage of the stage they are giving him, so he continues on.

"Our government, our people of rank, they are supposed to look out for us, are they not? Yet what are they doing? I ask you that: what are they doing about this ruinous scheme?"

Caylus glances down and examines his fingernails. La Coste issues a burp. The rest keep their eyes on Gallatin, including Thomas, whose expression says he is the most taken aback. He's absorbing what the bookseller just said. Does the man realize he is speaking in a public café, where anyone could overhear?

"Nothing, that's what." Gallatin looks even more smug than usual. "Not a thing. The regent is a fool. Or else he's bewitched by John Law. I'm not sure which is worse. Either way, it's a crime. We're led by a fool, the regent, I say. That's all there is to say. And it's suckers like Caylus who eventually pay. The Mississippi is a scandal and the regent a dupe."

Thomas feels his eyes pop. He looks at Caylus, who is burying his head in his hands. Gallatin is calling the man a dummy and a sucker too. And what he has said about the regent is even worse, because words like that bring trouble deep. Thomas will be able to use some of Gallatin's rant with Collier, but he'll have to temper it a bit. Or else, pity the loudmouth Gallatin.

"So, there you are," sings out Fougre, trying to lift the mood of the table. "And with that little lecture by our bookselling friend, I say we forget our cares by getting drunk. Thomas, may I return the favour? A brandy, perhaps?"

"Brandy it is," says Thomas. "Thank you, kind sir."

"Hey," says Tinville, turned around in his chair. He's staring at the door to the street. "Look who's here. Who would have guessed that *he* comes here too, just like us?"

Everyone at the table turns toward the entrance to Le Procope. A man and a woman have just come through the door. They are the centre of attention down at that end of the café. Half a dozen people are milling around them, shaking hands, kissing cheeks and exchanging greetings.

Thomas can hardly believe his eyes. It's Hélène, *his* Hélène from Évreux. It's the first time he's seen her since she was curled in their bed asleep in their attic room four years ago. He worried for weeks she'd been raped and murdered, but when he neither heard nor saw a thing about her she'd gradually vanished from his thoughts. But here she is, right here at Le Procope.

She looks a little older, and with much finer clothes than what she had to her name back then. Now she's dressed like a well-to-do lady. She has a fancy brocade dress and nothing less than the latest headdress, the commode. Despite the change of fortune, it's her, there is no doubt. As slim as ever and still not shy about showing off her charms. The top halves of her breasts are well exposed after the domino cloak is cast off. From what Thomas can see, Hélène is enjoying the attention of those gathered round her table. The pretty face Thomas knew four years earlier has if anything grown prettier still.

"He's got a new name, have you heard?" Tinville is speaking in a hushed voice.

Thomas turns Tinville's way. "Who are you talking about? Who has a new name?" Thomas notices for the first time that there is a man beside Hélène. He is skinny, with an amused grin stuck on his face.

"That, my friend, is Arouet. Well, he's calling himself Voltaire now. It's a pseudonym he's picked. Bit pretentious, I'd say." Tinville makes a sour face.

"Envy's a terrible thing," says Caylus, relieved to be able to pick on someone away from their table for a moment.

"I suppose it is," says Tinville, propping up his chin, "but what can I do? Envy might be my middle name. Arouet, Voltaire, whatever he wants to call himself. He's not even thirty and he's, well he's all cleverness and wit. If you like that kind of thing. Did I mention readers? Yes, well, he has those too. Why wouldn't I be envious? Which of us at this table is not?" Tinville looks around, pointing his right hand at his tablemates like it's a pistol. "Do any among have as many readers as Voltaire?"

"I might," says Fougre, head held high and slightly back.

There's a groan from the rest of the table. Though Fougre's yellow press pornographic tales are indeed well read, his name is not attached to them nor does he want it to be.

"Quite enough, Pokus," calls out Gallatin.

The table goes briefly silent. It's Caylus who breaks it.

"The Voltaire name is an anagram of some sort. Heard that from someone somewhere. Not sure exactly how, but then who cares? It works. You remember it. Voltaire." Caylus sends a hand into the air like he's a conductor without a baton. "Voltaire."

A fresh silence covers the group, this time of failure and disappointment. They are a group of either little-known or completely unknown writers. And one bookseller, the ardent Jean Gallatin. Voltaire's arrival serves only to remind them of their obscure place in the literary world of Paris. Unable to help themselves, all eyes except Thomas's follow Voltaire as he takes his seat. The young hero brushes back his long wig over his shoulders and sits up straight as an arrow. He displays his smiling monkey face the whole time. He knows eyes are upon him and he looks to be as pleased about it as a man could be.

Only Thomas is focusing not on Voltaire but on the person the writer is with. He cannot get over the smug look on the lips of the woman who once was his girl Hélène.

"You all right, my friend?" Fougre asks Thomas with worry on his face.

"Nothing."

"Nothing? What kind of answer is that? Whatever your 'nothing' is, it sure looks like something. Is it Voltaire? Has the bastard written something to burn you? You're not alone, you know."

Thomas does not reply. He stands, seems to think about something, then heads off toward the entrance to the café.

"What's he doing?" comes from Jean Gallatin down at the far end of the table, arms upraised to emphasize his disbelief.

"No, Thomas." Fougre rises from his seat. "Just leave the man. Not here."

The warning comes too late. Thomas is gone, heading for the couple's table. He has a hand on each hip, a swagger that turns a few heads at different tables as he goes along. He comes to a halt facing Hélène. She looks up puzzled to see someone, and not the server, standing as stiff as a sentry a mere body length away. Then she recognizes the face.

"You!" Hélène turns an initially startled look into a welcoming smile. "It's Thomas, isn't it?" She quickly looks across the table at Voltaire. "François Marie, this is an old acquaintance. He's from Évreux. We shared a diligence ride into Paris way back when." She turns back to Thomas. "The diligence. Yes, Thomas, I remember that."

Thomas makes a face. As if she has to make an effort to recall who he is. "Yes, Mademoiselle. Only I think we shared more than just one ride."

Hélène throws a searching look at Voltaire. The renowned writer casts back at her much the same look. It's as if he is her mirror. Then he rediscovers his more usual grin.

"Well," Hélène continues, "that *was* way back when, wasn't it? You had a little friend with you as I recall."

Thomas tilts his head until he catches her drift.

"That's right. A soldier."

Hélène's lips half pucker in amusement such that Thomas can see the humour in the whole thing. But Thomas cannot leave it at that. Something within him makes him say more.

"Strong little guy, wasn't he? He could go on for a while as I recall."

Voltaire tilts his head at a quizzical angle, recognizing the innuendo.

"Well anyway, Thomas, how wonderful of you to come say hello." Hélène has picked up Voltaire's suspicion and she wants to turn the conversation in a different direction. "Perhaps we will see you again sometime. We are just about to order. You understand."

Thomas feels his shoulders slip. The country girl he once knew has evidently become someone else.

"Pichon, Thomas Pichon," says Thomas, not moving away. He is speaking now exclusively to Voltaire. There is a fierceness in his voice that wasn't there before. Hélène cannot just dismiss him like that. Thomas gives a quick stiff half bow. "It's Voltaire, is it not? Hélène did not properly introduce us to each other, did she now? Foolish girl. And you're a writer too, I understand?"

Voltaire rests his chin in his hand. The grin on his face tells Thomas the man is thoroughly pleased. "Why, yes I am. Are you as well, Thomas Pichon?"

"From Vire in Normandy, not Évreux. And yes, a writer like you." Thomas bites his lower lip for what he has just said. He has written much but not yet published a thing.

Voltaire rises from his seat, amusement in the eyes as well as forming on his lips. He extends a hand.

"Pleased to meet you, I am, good friend of Hélène that you are. From Normandy and a writer like me. My goodness."

The two young men shake hands like each is trying to damage what the other writes with, if Voltaire is right-handed, which Thomas does not know.

"The same," says Thomas, "just the same. Pleased, that is."

The mutual grips come apart slowly. Each man wants to wipe off his now sticky hand on his pants but neither does. To do so would be beyond impolite. So the two of them stand where they are, feet nailed to the floor, doing nothing but staring at each other with pretend grins locked on their faces. Hélène brings a hand to her mouth to hide her smile.

"So," begins Voltaire, the grin finally gone, "what have you published, Thomas Pichon? I have to confess I don't recognize the name. But you will forgive me, I'm sure. No one could read everything. There is so much out there, is there not? And I don't often see what comes out Normandy. No, I don't. What does come out of Normandy anyway?"

"Calvados and cider," says Hélène. Her lips are now shaped into their own version of Voltaire's usual tiny grin. "And some cheeses, of course."

Thomas glares at her before returning his attention to Voltaire. "Normandy?" he says, putting a hand to his chin, somewhat like he saw Voltaire do when seated moments ago. "Hmm, I don't know what comes out of Normandy."

Thomas glances around the café. To his surprise he sees that nearly everyone in Le Procope has their eyes turned toward him and Voltaire. And that but for his own table of friends, where everyone appears to be in deep gloom, everyone else has a laughing grin on his face. That's when Thomas realizes that he is an object of ridicule, nothing else. Heat rising with the blood to his head, Thomas turns back to the standing Voltaire. The supposedly great writer, the man who is intimate with the woman who was once his Hélène, appears to be studying Thomas like he's an insect whose wings he has just plucked. Is that right? Well, Thomas could change that by punching this Voltaire right through his smiling mouth. That would be one thing that comes out of Normandy, would it not?

A numbing sensation lodges in Thomas's forehead. He can't think of anything further to do or to say. Why, for god's sake, did he tell this man standing across from him that he is from Normandy and a writer just like him? Bits and pieces of incomplete essays in his room. Verses once, and only back in Vire when he was a boy. The lines of poetry don't descend on him like they did before.

Thomas glances down. His two legs are twitching like they want to go somewhere else. Sudden words echo in his head: "Failure is mine, saith the lord, no one else's." The words bring a sad smile to his face. It's funny, it is. A clever twist on the line from the Bible. If only he could share it with Hélène and maybe even her Voltaire.

"Have to go," says Thomas at last. Voltaire and Hélène exchange baffled looks. "Yes, I have to go," says Thomas beginning to twitch his arms. "Busy. Busy, you know."

"Well said," offers Voltaire, retaking his seat. "That more or less sums it up, doesn't it? Busy. Yes, it does. Well said."

Thomas feels his eyes narrow. He is uncertain whether Voltaire is genuinely agreeing with him or just making fun. Thomas judges that the absence of a grin on the man's face means that for a moment the bastard is serious. Satisfied, Thomas continues in a rapid mumble as his feet start to shift.

"They're manuscripts. Not ready yet."

"Ah," says Voltaire, smiling benignly. He might be a surgeon telling you he's sorry, but your leg, it will have to come off. "But of course. That's the trick, is it not?"

Thomas says nothing in reply. It's simply time to go.

"Hélène," says Thomas bowing curtly before his former lover. "Monsieur," he offers to Voltaire.

And with that, he's off. He's out the door of the Le Procope and into the street. It is not until he has gone a dozen paces, and starting to feel a growing chill, that he realizes that he was wearing a coat when he went into the café. He slaps at his upper arms and his chest as he recalls that he put the coat on the back of his chair when he first came in. That was down at the table with his friends. Well, there's no going back now, not so Hélène and Voltaire can laugh at his mistake. Instead, Thomas heads home in a rush. His scheduled rendezvous with Collier and his desire for a tumble and thrust with one of the women he pays for the privilege are not going to happen this night.

As he steps onto the Pont Neuf Thomas feels a need, despite the cold, to reach out and touch the stone rail. He wants to make contact with the world through which he passes. He stops for a moment in front of the statue of Henri IV. He does not glance the ancient king's greenish way but rather vows he'll not be going back to Le Procope any time soon. There are hundreds of other places for him to gather with his friends and obtain their information, or simply to drink and despair. The Café de la Régence, for example. He'll not risk a second encounter with Hélène and Voltaire. There are enough disappointments in his life. He does not need any more. He doesn't want to see Hélène again, not so long as she's with someone else. Least of all a writer who is the talk of the town.

As he starts to move again, tapping here and there the stone parapet along the bridge, Thomas comes to a decision: he has to move out of his pitiful attic room. A better address he must find, rooms suited to the position and life to which he aspires. It may not win Hélène back. Well, likely not, but he has to start living like he is more of a success than he really is.

—

Thomas is at work, in the law office where he toils as a junior clerk. He pauses in his copying work. He lifts the quill and looks to the window, its panes spotted with tiny drops. He imagines a great, dark cloud is advancing toward Paris. It's coming to unleash a downpour, like piss from an unseen cow. It will bring another day of wintry rain. When it begins, the rainfall drumming on the cobbles and those streets that are still of packed earth, people will scatter and scurry. They will run for cover as best they can, hoping to get out of the downpour before it's made their garment colours run and takes the starch out of their stiff-pressed ruffles. Splattered and soaked, they'll hurry this way and that along the streets.

Is it really wrong to smile at the thought of other's misfortunes? Thomas muses. He remembers his mother's remark to that effect. Right and wrong, so simple then. But to be thankful that he's dry when others are not, there's nothing wrong with that. We all get our share of troubles, do we not? So why not rejoice in being safe and dry when it's others' turn to be wet?

He glances at the quill in his hand. He supposes there is no need to think about things like that. Life is complicated enough without bringing morality into it. That brings a grudging frown. His indoor work this afternoon is not what he would choose to do if the world gave him a choice. However, the world does not often work like that. Choices are few and far between. So he is by day a copy clerk in the law offices of the great Pontécoulant. The man who hired him, Monsieur Deauville, Pontécoulant's *premier commis*, said he was impressed that little Vire could produce such a well-educated lad. Thomas's level of French and Latin was "strong," or so pronounced Deauville. And Thomas's knowledge of the classics was regarded as "not so bad." So Deauville offered him a copyist job, which in truth required not much knowledge of anything at all, but only a good and steady hand. Thomas gladly took the position four years ago, yet how differently he feels about it all now. Four years of copy quillwork six days a week has long since become drudgery. It has driven the poetic muse and every other muse far, far away. Or at least that's where Thomas lays the blame. Moreover, the low salary of the position does not allow him to eat, drink, dress and generally live as he would like to. That is where the other source of income comes in, that which he receives from Collier in return for stories about fellow writers passed on. And all that involves is for Thomas to listen carefully and retell a few highlights to the man of the Paris police. That particular job could be described, this is what Collier claims, as helping to keep the realm safe. Thomas cannot but smile at that. Safe for whom, and at whose cost? Thomas does not really care about the boy king or his realm. But he does want and need the extra coins. More than that, his involvement with Collier gives him something the lowly clerk's job beneath Deauville and Pontécoulant does not. That's the satisfaction of being part of something bigger than just himself.

Thomas glances down at the work before him. He is halfway through his latest set of documents. He is to copy all the paperwork relating to a case in which reimbursement is being sought for expenditures made in the service of the king. The claim is on behalf of the widow of a certain Pastour de Costebelle. The man was a naval officer and governor, originally from Languedoc where he was born a younger son in a family of lesser nobility. He apparently served and died overseas. Thomas looks again to see where the death occurred. It was in some colony called Louisbourg, the capital of a colony called Isle Royale, also called Cap Breton. Thomas is not sure exactly where it is, but he thinks it's near Terre Neuve. Whatever the particulars, it's across the Atlantic and far away. Thomas thinks perhaps he should purchase a map of France's holdings across the sea.

Why anyone would venture across any ocean is beyond him, though he supposes it has to do with either duty or advancement, or maybe both. In any case, it's Costebelle's young widow, an Anne Mius d'Entremont, who is asking for compensation. Thomas does not always pay attention to the details, but this case sounds sad. The aforementioned Governor Costebelle fulfilled his duties in the colony of Isle Royale but in so doing went deep into debt. That was the thanks he got for establishing the settlement and keeping up the king's honour and good name. The widow is now in France and reduced to penury. At least that is what she claims. There are lessons in this, thinks Thomas. The first would seem to be not to get caught in an overseas colony, where out of sight is out of mind. The second lesson is this: do not go too far out on any branch on behalf of any king. Branches break and no one catches you when they do.

Thomas puts the content of the widow's case out of mind. Instead, he takes pride in the form and shape of his script as he writes. It is as fine as he can make it, all that he can claim as his own in this office. He sighs that his aspiration to be a writer is reduced to this. He turns to see what Rooster might be up to down at the far end of the suite of rooms. At the moment, his red-haired sometime stairwell friend and fellow office clerk is listening with rapt attention to everyone's master, Monsieur Deauville. It looks from Thomas's distance as if Deauville has yet another new vest-coat. By Thomas's calculation, that's at least the eighth the man has in his circulation. Thomas has but two and Rooster three.

Thomas takes a shallow breath and returns his gaze to his quill. A gift from a goose, he thinks, and smiles at the thought. Some gift, plucked out of the goose's body after his neck is wrung. He turns his attention back to what it is he is working on atop his writing table. Thomas's loops and links are well constructed, with the flowery esses at the end of lines as good as any. The quill moves surely and swiftly under his control, with nary a sign of where he's lifted the nib and gone to dip for ink. He takes the blotter paper and lays it gently on top of his first copied page.

Thomas straightens and stretches to begin a yawn. The skies outside are darker still. It truly is almost like night. The rain has picked up, driving against the panes. He turns back to his task, and before he dips his quill again into the ink he examines the nib. It is truly and finely cut. He dips the quill into the well and writes a while then dips again and adds words to the second page. The first paragraph is done. The letters are well shaped, the words well spaced and the sentences are holding the imagined line. He moves on. He begins to copy the part that is the conclusion to the widow's appeal for compensation when a roll of thunder rumbles through the office. Thomas turns back to the window. The rain is pounding now, angry fists thumping on the glass. Unbidden, the nib of the quill in his holding hand touches the paper without him feeling the contact. Black ink spills from the carefully cut tip, spreading to form a tiny pool. The ink spreads to swallow nearly an entire word. Thomas turns back to his work and notices too late. He sighs out loud. He'll have to start the page over again. It is an effort lost, but then every hour he spends in the law office as a lowly clerk is time lost.

He reaches for a fresh sheet of paper, straightening the alignment of the paper on the table. The lines of everything – chair, paper, body posture, arm and hand – have to be right, just right. Quill in hand, Thomas hesitates to dip the nib. He gently shakes his forearms, as if there were some bit of dust to remove. To the inkwell at last he goes, a ceramic container from Moustiers in the south of France in its distinctive blue and white. The quill is loaded with ink, so to· speak, yet Thomas does not take it to the paper. Instead, one more time, it is to the window that his face turns. The panes are a-blur with winter's rain driving hard. A shudder courses through the young man's body, a chill he cannot shake. Thomas's face is that of someone sad and lost, someone meant for more than this, a copyist in a lonely office of the law.

—

The smell in these places is never pleasant. Sometimes a stall partitioned off with canvas from two others busy doing the same thing, sometimes a room with an actual door that closes and gives a semblance of privacy. It doesn't really matter much. These places always reek of sweat and spills. And vinegary from the attempts to clean things up after the business is done. It doesn't seem to matter to which place Thomas goes. His least preferred are in certain cabarets where it's just a wooden partition between Thomas and his fifteen-minute friend and everyone else in the place. At first he used to wonder if everyone else was listening to his sounds, like he was to theirs, but he doesn't give it a thought anymore. Now he doesn't hear a thing while he waits his turn, so why should anyone else listen to him when he's the one? Outdoors in the backyard gardens, in those establishments that have such a fenced-off zone, that can be exciting for a change. But the weather is not always the best. So it's usually to a place in the Saint-Germain area that he goes. The women who work there, they're good at what they do. They occasionally make a joke – "wow, that's some weapon, quite the gun" – but usually they do not. Ultimately, it's about the exchange. Money to the handler on the way in, then a rub and a poke and a spill once there. It's pretty simple and doesn't take too long. No gentle caresses when it's over. It's just a business. Each customer gets his time then makes room for whoever is next. It is, he sometimes thinks, really not so different from being in his old *grenier* with a strip of silk.

Of late Thomas has been coming to the stalls at least once and sometimes twice a week. The position he has come to prefer is the bent-over way. It's an anonymous position like a dog in a rut. Ass and chink are toward him. With hands on shoulders or her hips, away the soldier goes. The result's the same, a fleeting excitation and spilling reward. Thomas sometimes wonders why he prefers it that way. He has decided it's because it does not claim to be about more than what it is: a wetted friction and an inevitable release. It might be different if he ever got to know one of his confidantes in the stinking stalls, yet he never has and cannot imagine that he ever will. He figures that's for the best because he doubts they want to know him anymore or any better than he does them. It's a business: in and out and on one's way. The satisfaction, such as it momentarily is, has but one merit. It clears Thomas's head for what he next has to do.

—

The message, received two days ago, was to meet in the little church on the left bank, the one across from the abbey of Saint-Germain-des-Près. The particular name of the church escapes Thomas as he makes his way toward the rendezvous, but he knows the building well enough. He often notices it on his way to and from the prostitutes in the stalls. It is an uninspiring structure with a short steeple and a poor excuse for stained glass windows. For an instant, when he read where the meeting was to be, he wondered if Collier had selected that particular little church precisely because it's close to the stalls of Saint-Germain. It would not surprise Thomas if Collier knows about the visits to the trollops. Does not Collier know every little thing that goes on in Paris? Is that not precisely why Thomas finds himself part-time in the man's employ? To give his pale-faced friend the few remaining tidbits of information that had escaped him in his quest to know it all.

Collier tells Thomas that he is a "tell-tale," a term the young informant does not mind. It is better than "fly," the word that Collier uses to describe the dozens if not hundreds of other informers in his pay. Compared with fly, tell-tale is not half bad. It has a harmless ring, and besides it tells the truth. Telling a few tales is exactly what he does.

Every two weeks or so, usually a Thursday evening, Collier has Thomas come to one or another of Paris's dark corners to talk awhile. The police agent prefers the back of a church. The hush and gloom of those buildings are a comfort to them both. Thomas never knows which church Collier will select, but of late they have met in Saint-Nicolas-du-Chardonnet, where in daylight hours there's some sort of construction under way, and Saint-Julien-le-Pauvre. Before that they met at Saint-Séverin, which Thomas likes for the long, skinny gargoyles that extend out over the street, and Saint-Étienne-du-Mont, which has a magnificent pulpit and a fine set of stained glass windows. The church atmosphere, no matter which church Collier picks, encourages the passing on of information. Thomas regards his passing on of his writer friends' stories as small confessions of a worldly sort. Collier says that Thomas is helping to keep king and country safe from dangerous thoughts and deeds. Thomas does not disagree. He's content to play his part as long as something comes his way in return. That something – coins – is helping him get ahead. It will allow him to move into a new apartment next month on the rue Saint-Roch. Two rooms he'll have, and he'll no longer be up in the lofty heights of a *grenier*. Plus it's a better address, better to impress. Though *whom* he's going to impress, Thomas has not yet thought to ask.

Thomas enters the little church. Its silence, lit candles and smell of cold stone are familiar and a comfort. Memories of his childhood in Vire and the church of Saint-Thomas come swirling back. There's no sign of Collier yet, which is no surprise. Monsieur likes to arrive last and leave first. Thomas takes a seat in the second last row. That's because Collier will, as always, take the row just behind.

Thomas sees no one else anywhere in the nave, though he does hear someone stirring in the side chapel hidden by a pillar. Even when there are others around, Collier never seems to mind. The comings and goings of worshippers does not bother the man, as long as their own hushed exchanges are kept too low for anyone to hear. In fact, Thomas speculates, Collier likely figures that having a few people around gives a cover to their own murmurings in the back two rows.

The rendezvous is a game Collier and Thomas both enjoy. Collier's the one on top, of that position there can be no mistake. The man of the police sometimes gets mildly annoyed – revealed by an edge to the voice – when Thomas hesitates to tell the required tales. Thomas does it on purpose from time to time, thinking it is more satisfying when he plays the mouse to Collier's cat. Of late, that's become the usual approach. Thomas starts off by saying there's not much to report. His friends are lukewarm in their attachments to the regent, the child king and the Church, but that's nothing new. Sometimes he yawns to show that everything is old hat. That's when Collier gets to coax more information out of his man, wanting specifics and not idle chit and chat. That's when Thomas gives the man a little more, bit by bit. Full true, half true or pure inventions, it doesn't appear to greatly matter. It's the plausibility of the stories that counts. In fact, the less truthful the story Thomas has found, the greater likelihood Collier will want to hear more. Like the one he spun about Caylus harbouring hatred for the wife of the Marquis d'Argenson because of something he'd heard she'd done. It was a complete lie, inspired by a satirical poem he'd heard about the woman on his way across the Pont Neuf en route to the rendezvous. It had nothing to do with poor Caylus at all. Yet Thomas had to hang it somewhere, and he picked Caylus. Collier was all ears. He wanted every little bit, down to the pathetic little rhyme. Sad, really. It strikes Thomas that reality is no longer good enough. Everything has to be enlarged.

Thomas nods at a woman entering the church. She doesn't nod back but looks away, a little offended. She goes directly to where she gets a small candle off a tabletop then pads out of sight to the side altar where Thomas expects she'll light it and say a prayer for some departed soul. An instant after the woman disappears behind a pillar, a man Thomas decides is the sacristan comes out of the same area. He squints at Thomas, who takes it as an admonition to get down on his knees or at least have his hands clasped in prayer. Thomas flashes the man a little smile, and leans back and spreads his arms to rest them on the top of the adjacent bench. The sacristan shakes his head then strides off out of Thomas's sight. The door to the sacristy closes with a bang.

As his wait continues, Thomas has a fresh thought. What if Tinville or Gallatin or some other from Thomas's group is also on Collier's payroll? What if they are also telling a jumble of stories, tall or true, including ones about Thomas himself? How then would Collier figure fact from fiction?

A sudden slide and slap of footsteps on the stone floor behind interrupts Thomas's thought. He twists to see that it is Collier. As usual the expressionless man is dressed in drab, though with an addition for this cold Paris night. He has a cloak round his shoulders with the hood pulled up and over his head. He lowers the hood as he nears where Thomas is seated. As expected, Collier selects a bench in the last row, directly behind Thomas. He waits a moment, a prudent pause, before he leans forward. It is the usual delay before he begins the hushed back and forth of questions and replies.

"Your evening so far?"

It is not the usual beginning, so the question makes Thomas blanch. Does Collier really know that Thomas has just come from the stalls? He must. Why else would he ask such a question and in such a way? Thomas will have to find a new place to satisfy his urge, one that monsieur of the police cannot track.

"Nothing special. How is yours?"

"You didn't show up last time."

"I am sorry." Thomas turns all the way around to look the man in the face, to make amends with puppy eyes. He cannot tell Collier that he forgot about the rendezvous because he was upset and angry about a girl called Hélène and her being with the writer who calls himself Voltaire.

"Will it happen again?"

"No."

"Because if it does…"

"It will not."

Thomas swings back around to face frontward. It occurs to him that he *could* mention Voltaire's name and make up some story that will blacken the grinning bastard's reputation. That might be fun, and serve him right besides.

"Something came up," says Thomas over his shoulder. "At the Procope. Do you know the Café Procope?"

"Everyone knows the Procope. What was the something?"

"It involved Voltaire."

"I'm listening."

Yes, you are, Thomas says to himself. This is a good idea. There's a note in your voice, dear pasty Collier, that's not usually there. It's an eagerness you don't show when I talk of ordinary me and my ordinary friends.

"He says some surprising things, Voltaire that is."

"Don't try and write a play, Thomas. I don't have all night. Just give me what you have."

"Of course." Thomas turns back to face the front of the church. He cannot speak fast because he doesn't yet know what he will say. Also, it amuses him to make Collier stare at the back of his head, at the queue and its black ribbon tied in a bow. Thomas mulls the matter a little longer, wondering what might meet the police agent's expectations. Ah yes. He swings his head just enough to speak over the other shoulder.

"He's partial to the English, Voltaire."

"Go on."

Thomas swivels his head the other way, and decides there is no one else in the church that matters so he can turn full round.

"Says the English system of government, with their king more as a figurehead than ruler, is superior, superior to our own."

Collier hunches his shoulders. "That's it?"

Thomas blinks his surprise. The police agent thinks it's nothing that Voltaire speaks of treason? Thomas does not know what to say.

"I do read, Thomas," says Collier. Unusually, his face is not a mask. For once it shows exasperation. "Did you not know that he spent nearly a year in prison, eleven months, if memory serves? Imprisoned in the Bastille for satirizing *our* government. That was only a few years back."

"Voltaire? Arouet by birth?"

"The same."

"Oh." Thomas is lost as to what to say next. His usefulness as a tell-tale is in serious doubt.

"Move on. Since you don't have anything new about Voltaire, is there nothing else?"

Collier's face and tone of voice tell Thomas that the man is about to stand and go.

"Well, with my usual crowd, the ones I tell you about all the time, there continues to be lots of sour talk. It's just who they are. Theirs is a complainers' world after all."

"Yes it is." Collier brightens. He appears to like the phrase Thomas has used. "And what is the latest in that complainers' world?"

It clicks for Thomas that the renowned writers of the Parisian world, Voltaire and a few more, are of relatively little interest to Collier precisely because their views are known. The man does not need Thomas to give him information he already has. It's the opinions and actions of the unknown and unsuccessful, the scribblers living in garrets and hovels, that Collier seeks. They are the real threat. Unlike fashions, which descend from high on down, discontent and rebellion come from the bottom up. If the writers in Thomas's world were all Voltaire, as good as they imagine and able to make a decent living, they'd be happier with their lot. It's not the favoured and fortunate Collier worries about. It's the malcontents and hacks who lurk below. The mediocre and the talentless are the greatest threat. There are not cells enough for Collier and the marquis to lock all aspirants away, so information is how the police play the game. As long as they keep track of the discontented via a tell-tale's wagging tongue, why, that's enough. They don't necessarily need to imprison every one. Thomas brings his hand up to cup his chin while he seeks to prime his memory for some recollection he can use.

"Let me help," presses Collier. "Tell me, for instance, what is your circle is saying about John Law and the Mississippi Company."

"Ah. That it's a bubble and cannot last?"

"Yes, well everyone is saying that. But *who* are they blaming? That's the important part."

Thomas turns halfway round, far enough to make eye contact once again. Collier's impassive face and cold grey eyes give him a chill.

"I'm not sure they blame anyone. In particular, I mean."

"Oh, of course they do." Collier rolls his eyes. "Blame is the currency of the world. Do they mention the regent or is it only John Law?"

Oh, that's right. A candle lights the memory of that night a week ago. Thomas's reply, his longest yet, names every writer in his crowd, and provides a detailed recollection about what he heard each say about the Mississippi craze and John Law. More than half of it is true, as accurate as he can recall. Thomas tells Collier about how worried sick Caylus is about the amount that he invested and now seems to have lost and then he moves on to what Jean Gallatin said and how much impact it had around the table.

"And this Gallatin, he's a bookseller you say?"

"Yes. Left bank, Latin Quarter. His father was a lawyer apparently."

"A lawyer. Really? You've not mentioned a Gallatin before."

"Maybe not. He's a sour one. Sarcastic mouth. Anyway, yes, I think he's from some small town in the Pyrenees. I don't recall the name."

"And this Jean Gallatin said the regent is a fool." Collier's voice and eyes are asking for precision. "And that the government's inaction was a crime?"

"Something like that."

"He did or he did not?"

"He did. That was exactly what he said."

Thomas does not recall Collier ever having such an intense reaction to one of his tales. He wonders too late if perhaps he should not have said quite so much about poor Gallatin. He wasn't trying to get the man in trouble, was he? Well, in fact, he admits to himself, that was exactly his intent. It's sink or swim, and he wanted to swim. Who would not? Then again, how could he know how Collier would react? He never knows what will or will not intrigue his pale-faced friend. "Yes, that's what the bookseller said. But, he did go on to say that maybe the regent was bewitched by the Scot. That it is the foreigner John Law who is the one really at fault."

Collier gives Thomas a wistful look. "Oh my, you do give your friend a praiseworthy defence. Good for you, but it's too late. Are you worried I'm going to have this bookseller Gallatin rounded up and put away in the Bastille? For an idle remark one drunken evening made? I'm touched, Thomas." For the first time, Collier gives Thomas a wink followed by a smile.

"It was a passing comment, that's all." Thomas adds a shrug to reinforce the trivial nature of Gallatin's remark.

"We'll have to see, won't we?" Collier stands and straightens his outer clothes. "And that's why I have you, is it not?"

Collier leans forward to whisper what else he has to say close to Thomas's ear. There is practically no one else in the church and no one anywhere nearby, but still he will take no chance.

"Find out more for me about Gallatin." Collier leans back so they are a normal distance apart. "Remember the apple? That Paris has its bruises and rotted spots?"

Thomas nods that he does.

"Well, that's all. We want to know is if this is rot or just a little bruise. That clear?"

Thomas scrambles to his feet. He has never seen Collier quite so pleased.

"Take that worried look off your face, will you, Thomas. It doesn't suit you. No one's hurt in this. All you're doing is listening and telling me what you hear. That's all. Now, if you will excuse me." Collier turns to go. He adjusts the hood of his cape to get it ready. He wants to cover his head the moment he leaves the church.

"But—" Thomas hates to hold out his hand. He is no mendicant. Yet it seems he has no other choice. He turns the palm of his right hand upward though he keeps it low, down by his hip. Collier glances down.

"Oh, that's right. Almost forgot." Collier leans in close once more to Thomas's ear.

"We don't want to wait until the next time you meet up with your whole crowd as a group. Drop by the man's bookshop. We need a little more on just him and his views."

"All right."

"That's the attitude." Collier reaches into the pocket of his *veston* and retrieves the coins he has there for Thomas. How many he passes on depends on what information the tell-tale gives to him. Collier extends a hand. He places not the usual three or four but six coins onto the waiting palm. Thomas closes his hand over what he's been given. Without looking at exactly how much it adds up to, he knows that his little tale of Gallatin has been rewarded.

"Take some time, if you must," says Collier just before the double doors that are the entrance and the exit from the church. "We don't want to scare the poor man with our haste, we just want the truth. But no later than early January, right after the Feast of the Kings. Understood?"

"Yes, of course."

The cloak goes up and with his head covered Collier is out the door. Thomas does as he's supposed to do. He counts to thirty before he takes his own turn and steps out into the night. He opens his hand and in the dim light of the nearest hanging lamp he looks at what is warming in his hand. It is indeed the most yet that Collier has passed on. Thomas has done something right. Gallatin's loss is someone else's gain.

January 1720

The Feast of the Kings passes throughout France as it always does, with many special cakes baked containing hidden beans. As a child, Thomas twice was the one to get the special slice with the lucky bean. For children and older loved ones it is also, sometimes, a time to give small gifts on the twelfth day of the Christmas season.

Thomas tells himself that he does not miss receiving his own piece of special cake because that would mean he was still back in Vire. When Rooster asks him if he misses his childhood town, Thomas insists that he does not. He says he is relieved to be in Paris and on his own. He does not mention how and why he left and that he cannot go back until he is able to prove he did the right thing, leaving how he did. It'll all work out in the end, he likes to think. The problem is, he's gradually realizing that the end is no closer now than it was five years ago. As for the gifts associated with the Feast of the Kings, a custom inspired by the three wise men who made their way to Bethlehem, Thomas knows that that part of his life is long gone. He'll soon be twenty. Childhood is far behind. He supposes it doesn't matter, seeing as how there is no one in Paris who holds him dear enough to bake him a cake or send him a gift. A little sad, perhaps, but he would not have it any other way. The price of doing business, his father used to say. Well, that's sort of how it is with Thomas in his own way. He honours the Feast of the Kings by heading to the stews and stalls. It's in a sweat-smelling room in the Saint-Germain that he gives and receives a different kind of gift.

As for the assignment Collier gave him, he has put it off time and then time again. He's not sure how to proceed or, once having obtained something from the bookseller, if it's as incriminating as Thomas believes, what to tell Collier he has found out. The tell-tale business is more difficult than he was once wont to believe. Nonetheless, until Thomas has a higher position in the world, Collier must be served. So the day after the Feast of the Kings, as soon as he's finished at Pontécoulant's law office for the day, Thomas sets off.

He's been past Jean Gallatin's bookstore several times in the past two weeks. He's just not found the nerve to go in. The shop is located near the Sorbonne, a half-hour walk from the law office. It closes two hours later than his own office so he knows he has the time to get there and at last obtain the information Collier wants. The problem is not getting there but how to put the questions once he opens his mouth.

Believing he needs a cover for a visit, Thomas has settled on inquiring about Ovid's *Metamorphoses.* It's a book title that always springs to his mind, though more for the erotic woodcut images that stirred his boyish loins than for the verses. *Metamorphoses* is to serve as a cover, an excuse. Gallatin need not know the details, how Thomas once possessed the book, that it belonged to Jean-Chrys and that Thomas took it away in his flight. It should be enough to tell the bookseller that it was a gift of sorts from a boyhood friend back in Vire. Thomas will explain to Gallatin that he would like another copy for his collection. That should establish why he's dropping by. After that, Thomas has no idea how the conversation will go, though he expects it will be tricky. Gallatin is no fool nor is he prone to confidences as far as Thomas has ever seen.

It's rare for the two of them to sit side by side at the weekly gatherings of the would-be writers. Even when they do, there often seems to be some kind of barrier between them. Oil and water, or something like that. Unlike Thomas, so Thomas thinks, Jean Gallatin is a doubter and a skeptic. And it's not just the Church and clerics he's against. He distrusts nearly everything. Thomas can't remember a time when Serious Jean, as Caylus calls him, took the time to joke or to laugh. He always has some gripe or weighty matter to discuss. And the bookseller's face, long and thin as a face can be, is not an easy face to relax around. Some people have faces that make you smile and feel at ease. It's the opposite with Gallatin. The knitted brow and narrowed eyes: they always put Thomas on guard. It's like the bookseller has seen it all and is irritated by more than half. His expression gives off a warning that you better not come too close. In other words, Thomas is not looking forward to obtaining the information Collier has instructed him to collect. But tomorrow night is his next rendezvous with Collier, and Thomas has only one last chance to get what Collier wants.

—

The walk across the Pont Neuf in the dying hours of the day casts a fleeting spell on Thomas, as it always does. It slows his hurried pace. He goes close enough to the parapet wall to tap it lightly as he goes along. A few of the sellers are already starting to pack up, though Thomas can see that the main show is still going strong. A namesake, so to speak, Le Grand Thomas, continues to hold court. Dressed as always in his scarlet coat with a tricorn hat decked out in peacock feathers, and a string of human teeth around his neck, the giant is holding spellbound what must be the last dozen or so of his daylong crowd. Stopping to listen for a moment, Thomas hears the giant boast, as usual, that he is both the "honour of the universe" and the "terror of the jaw." No one would ever dispute the latter claim. More than a few times Thomas has seen the show. It never disappoints. Le Grand Thomas has all the tools and what's more the stature of a seven-foot giant to pull teeth out of afflicted mouths right there on the spot. If necessary, he lifts the poor souls right off the ground. Till the tooth gives way and the patient tumbles down. It's like an execution, except in reverse. The blood gushes out to help the person and not to end his life. It's a remarkable scene. First, the cries of the patient then the bright red spout from the mouth. Meanwhile Le Grand Thomas's booming voice echoes along the river. Between extractions the giant sells his famous elixir. It's a stinking concoction he calls a "solar balm." It's always fun for Thomas to see the suckers getting duped to buy one or another of big Thomas's services. Poor and rich, titled and unknown, all of Paris comes to the Pont Neuf to catch the giant's show.

To the left and right of Le Grand Thomas, spreading across the bridge, Thomas sees what's left of the other daytime attractions. Charlatans and quacks are the most common. Their positions change from day to day, depending on who gets there first and claims the spaces closest to the terror of the jaw. This evening there is still one of the poet-singers. He smiles at his admirers as he recites the nasty rhymes. He draws hoots from the shocked yet appreciative crowd, rhyming as he does about the court at Versailles. True or false, it hardly matters. It's the mockery of the people high above that makes for the fun. Sure enough, there are a number of people of high rank and position in the crowd. They are the ones laughing the hardest, likely because they know that the scandalous verses are half true.

Off to the left there are a couple of fortune tellers with their final customers of the day. They slowly turn their tarot cards or read their clients' palms. Baffling people with prognostications is how they earn their daily bread.

Today it looks to Thomas like there are an unusual number of sellers of tinctures and ointments, unguents and elixirs on the bridge. It must be the time of year. It's cold and damp, and people want to believe that their chills and shivers can be relieved by some drink or balm. Thomas walks past portable shelves of bottles and flasks that their sellers guarantee will settle the stomach, thin the blood, disperse the vapours, roll back the wrinkles and lengthen what every man wants lengthened. Thomas cannot help but wonder if that last one really works. Of course it doesn't. Yet what if it did? Meanwhile, the carters are starting to pack it in, and those selling something to eat are making their last rounds with their wicker trays. One has oranges from Portugal while others have pies and breads they claim are still hot, though everyone knows that it's all long gone cold.

Thomas comes to a halt to watch two tumbling midgets. They are attired in stripes like clowns. Suddenly, as part of their act, a third midget springs from the inside of a wooden trunk, its lid having popped off. The new midget begins to juggle three wooden pins. That lasts a minute and then down he tosses the pins and gets up on stilts. The midget hops and caroms here and there, nearly losing his balance, or is that part of the show? He's dressed like Harlequin. The act attracts a small but delighted crowd.

Thomas moves along the stone railing of the bridge, his hands caressing the grooves and fissures of the stone. He hears something going on down below, either in the water or on the sand spits. He can't see a thing. So he crosses to the other side to have a better look. He knows that in summer boys swim in the river, using one or the other of the two sandy beaches as their base. On this January day, however, there can be none of that. So he's curious what the commotion is about. At last he spies half a dozen boys down on the beach called the Sands. They are putting something in the cracks of the rocks. Whatever it is, they don't announce. Yet the boys prance around in anticipation. Bursts of smoke issue from the rocks followed by the sound of the pops of the explosions that produced them. The onlookers applaud. The boys are setting off firecrackers. Another round of pops goes off, much louder than before. But something's gone wrong. One of the boys is holding his face. There is blood on his hands.

"Blown off his nose," Thomas hears a boy shout from down below. "Help! Help!"

Thomas shakes his head and pushes off the stone parapet to the middle of the bridge. There's nothing he can do to help anyone down there.

He's jostled a few steps farther on, and he swings round with his elbows out. He is ready to defend his purse from any pickpocket. It turns out it's only a couple of ladies. Well, maybe ladies they are not. They are old as he remembers his mother. Their faces are over painted and the necklines of their blouses are low, exposing over half of their sagging chests.

"Ever had it, dearie?" says one.

"Care to give it a lift?" adds the other. "Two for one. Just for you."

Thomas's elbows and hands come down. He smiles at the prostitutes, hoping he's never been with either one. Yet he really doesn't know. It's possible in some of the dark spots he's been. Maybe he should reconsider his preference for taking them from behind. That way he might remember the faces better than he does. Thomas finds a faint smile for these particular prostitutes and adds a gentleman's uncoiling of the hand.

"In a bit of a hurry, Mesdames."

"We'll do all the work, dearie," says one with a wink.

"I do not doubt it a bit, but you see—"

"Hey," shouts a man's voice behind Thomas's back. Thomas doesn't think the yell is for him. He doesn't even glance around.

"Hey," comes the voice again. Then a forceful hand grabs Thomas on the left shoulder. "Hey, stop, Thomas!"

Thomas swings round. The hands go up, ready to defend himself. He finds a young man his own age facing him. The fellow has bright eyes and an eager, smiling face. It takes Thomas an instant to realize that he's staring at a face from his past, from his boyhood days in Vire.

"Jean-Chrys?"

"Yes, it is."

Jean-Chrysostome claps his former friend with two hands, one on the upper arm and the other on the shoulder. Both hands stay where they are put, clasping Thomas so as not to let him get away. For a long moment the two check each other out. Each wants to see how the other is dressed and how he has changed, filled out, grown taller and thicker. Smiles, shy boy smiles, creep onto each face.

"You don't look too bad … for a Parisian." Jean-Chrys's hands finally unclasp Thomas's clothes.

"Nor you, for a bumpkin."

Thomas reaches out as if he is going to pat Jean-Chrys on the cheek. Instead, he flicks Jean-Chrys's tricorn right off his head. His friend catches it and laughs.

"Good to see you again, Thomas, I can't begin to tell you."

"The same. The very same. So good to see you here. On the Pont Neuf no less."

"Even if…" the smile fades from Jean-Chrys's face.

The contented look on Thomas's face disappears. The reminder casts a blanket over the two young men, taking away the mirth of their reunion.

"No choice, I had." Thomas's whole body has gone as taut as the rigid line across his lips. "I couldn't, Jean-Chrys, I couldn't stay. I had to get away."

"I suppose." Jean-Chrys's eyes show his friend that he wants to understand, even if he can't. "Your parents, well, they're still trying to understand. Even after all these years. I see them from time to time."

"He's all right then? My father? He fell that morning as the diligence left. Or so I heard."

"You heard?" Jean-Chrys is bewildered by the word choice. Thomas makes it sound like he wasn't there. Jean-Chrys lets it go without any further comment. "Yes, he's all right. He just lost his … his breath."

They both glance away, down to the ground then up to the sky.

"And mother? And Anne?"

"Both well. Your mother, she misses you of course and regularly asks me if I've heard. A letter from you. But no, as you know. You don't write. And Anne, why, she's married now."

"Not serious."

"Yes." Jean-Chrys's smile is back. "A small merchant in Condé-sur-Noireau."

"Small in stature or small in rank?"

"Both, I suppose." Jean-Chrys laughs at the question. Thomas never did have much good to say about Anne. The good mood of their reunion is briefly back. "But I meant his height. He's not even as tall as she is."

Thomas beams at the news. "Serves her right," he says, though he doesn't know why he is feeling so mean. He has hardly thought of his father's precious Anne since he left Vire years ago. Why should he? He's the one in Paris, while she's in sleepy Condé, with a man smaller than herself.

For a moment there is no further conversation. The two young men stand easy, relaxed. It is the way it used to be, except that it's not.

"Listen." Jean-Chrys raises both hands in front of him. He appears to want to wring something from the air. "It was wrong to take their money, Thomas, it was. It was nearly everything they had."

"Is that it then?" Thomas turns away and shakes his head. "This, this chance meeting is not chance at all? You're on a mission to take me back?"

Jean-Chys reaches out to his boyhood friend, to grab his shoulder. Thomas shrugs it away.

"You go back to Vire. You tell them you couldn't find me. Do you hear?"

Thomas turns and walks away. Jean-Chrys follows after, calling his name, asking him to stop. They are soon completely off the Pont Neuf, with Thomas striding away quickly along the left bank. The teasing smell of roasting chestnuts, coming from a stand not ten feet away, causes Thomas to slow down. Then he stops.

"So they sent you here, my parents, to get me home?"

"They're in trouble, Thomas. Deep trouble. You won't be surprised; it's La Motte again."

"What this time?" Thomas's chin is jutting out.

"An appeal. A process in Rouen. They're sure they can win this time, but they want … they need your help." Jean-Chrys's voice starts to trail off as he continues. "They've heard you're a lawyer. It's why I'm here. Looking for you. Been in Paris a week already. I've roved this damned bridge every day looking for you."

With the slightest of nods, Thomas takes it in, word by word. He says nothing in return. But the chin does come down and the face is no longer fierce. Should he explain that he's no lawyer, merely a copyist? No, Jean-Chrys doesn't need to know that. If the word back in Vire is that he's a lawyer, there's some good in that.

So Thomas begins to talk. He explains how the money that went with him from his parents is all gone. Taken from him soon after he left Vire. He never got to use it at all for … for its intended purpose to get him into a medical school. As for right now, Thomas has only what he requires. Requires to live in Paris. He sees doubt then deep disappointment spread across Jean-Chrys's face.

"But your parents, they still need your help."

"So what can I do?"

"Well, you're a lawyer and it's the law that's got them…"

"I'm not, Jean-Chrys. I'm not. I work as a copyist in a law office. Though maybe I could…"

Just then, Thomas glances over Jean-Chrys's left shoulder. He sees that Le Grand Thomas is all packed up and his watchers are heading home. The fortune tellers and ointment sellers have already folded their tables and the jugglers are gone as well. Thomas turns his face to the sky. It's gone close to dark. The only light is from the overhanging lamps now lit. He's supposed to be at the bookseller Jean Gallatin's by now.

"What time is it?" Thomas almost shouts.

"I … I don't know." Jean-Chrys is startled by the question and the volume at which it's hurled at him.

"Have to go." Thomas fears he'll be late for the very reason he's come across the river and over to its left side. "I have somewhere … something … I have to do."

"But …" tries Jean-Chrys.

Thomas holds up. "I must."

"Your parents," cries out Jean-Chrys as Thomas widens the gap between them.

Thomas's momentum does slow. "Where are you staying?" he shouts. "I'll come by later this evening. We can talk some more."

"Rue des Aveugles. Right across from the church. Third floor."

Thomas repeats the address twice as he begins to run. Rue des Aveugles. It should be easy to recall. Then it's back to business. Thomas has to have his wits about him for the conversation at Gallatin's bookshop. Collier wants something, and what Collier wants is for Thomas to provide.

—

It has descended to near black. The flickering glow from the streetlamp near the small bookstore is just enough for Thomas to see that the possibility of satisfying Collier is still there. Thirty paces ahead he makes out the lean frame of Jean Gallatin standing outside his shop. He is putting on the padlock.

"Jean!" The name comes out garbled. Thomas is breathless from having run for three blocks. He didn't think he'd make it. With his destination in sight, he starts to slow down. "Jean. Jean Gallatin."

"Pichon? Thomas? Is that you?"

"It is." Thomas comes to a full stop beside the bookseller. He folds over to allow his lungs to catch up. He hears Gallatin laugh, a snicker of sorts.

"Who could have guessed? The quiet Pichon, the observant one, inclined to run like a … like a thief, I suppose."

"You're right." Thomas is gradually regaining his breath. The words come between gulps of air. "I'm not. Just. Had to. See you. Before you closed."

"Too late for that, I'm afraid."

"Oh no, I want to buy a book."

"So badly that you ran? Must be some book." Gallatin digs in his pocket to grab hold of his key.

"Ovid," says Thomas with a satisfied expression. His self-satisfied smile suggests that the mere mention of that particular author is answer enough.

Gallatin's eyes go wide. He shakes his head and looks dubious. "Ovid? The Roman poet?"

"Yes."

"The erotic verses?"

"No, the *Metamorphoses.* I used to have a copy but it was stolen. A gift from a friend, it was. I'd like to get another so I could give it back. He's from my hometown but in Paris this week. I just saw him this evening. I could give it back."

"If it was a gift, why then are you giving it back?"

"That's right." Thomas's expression deflates. "I thought I'd return the favour, that's all."

Jean Gallatin shakes his head. "To give your friend back the same book that he gave you?"

Gallatin makes a show that he has changed his mind. He's putting the key to the padlock back into his pocket. He will not re-open the shop after all. "Come on, Thomas, you have to do better than that. I have somewhere else to go."

"I'll take the other book then. The erotic verses." The words jump from Thomas's mouth. He doesn't want to show panic, but he has to report back to Collier tomorrow on a conversation with Gallatin that he is yet to have.

Gallatin starts to walk away then comes back to make his point. "Look, you've never before come to my store. Not once. Yet tonight you run here as I'm closing to purchase Ovid. Who has been dead, I don't know, maybe seventeen hundred years. And if it's not one book you want then it's another. I'm not opening up the shop for some bizarre little joke."

Thomas is lost for words. He's embarrassed by the idiocy of his poorly thought out pretence.

"What's the real reason you're here?" Gallatin gives Thomas a searching look. His dark eyes and arched brows pinch even more than usual. Thomas opens his mouth to explain, but before he can say a word Jean Gallatin jumps back in. "Someone told you, didn't they?" He waves a finger accusingly.

Thomas hasn't a clue what Gallatin is referring to but he's more than willing to play along. It might be a way out of his stupid Ovid request and into further conversation. He smiles coyly. "I'm not supposed to say."

"La Coste. It was La Coste, wasn't it?" Gallatin runs a hand over his eyebrows. "La Coste or Tinville, it doesn't matter. Neither could keep a secret if his life depended on it."

Thomas shrugs. If the bookseller wants to blame La Coste or Tinville, why should he argue with that? Means to an end, he thinks, means to an end.

"All right," says Jean Gallatin, out-shrugging Thomas, "you can come along. You didn't need to pretend you were looking for Ovid." He studies Thomas's reaction. "That is why you're here, right? To see for yourself?"

"I was hoping." Thomas tries not to wrinkle his brow. He has not the slightest inkling what it is that Gallatin is talking about. When the bookseller says "see for yourself" and "come along," what is he referring to? Are they going somewhere?

"One thing, Thomas." Gallatin holds his index finger skyward. "You have to do what I say. Follow my lead. Understood?"

"Understood." Yes, but no.

Gallatin nods. A twist of the shoulders and a roll of the head tells Thomas they are to get going. The bookseller wheels and sets off down the street. Thomas hurries to keep up and walk alongside. Literally and figuratively in the dark, Thomas is nonetheless pleased. He might still get what he wants, additional information out of Gallatin for Collier. Nighttime is indeed the mother of surprises and this time, for once, for something good.

—

The conversation is limited. How cold it's been, how much wood each has to burn and what it costs. Thomas waits five minutes before attempting to steer things toward a way that might bear more fruit.

"So, Jean, what do you think now of the Mississippi Company and John Law?"

Gallatin blows air out his lips then mutters: "Made Controller General, can you believe it?"

Thomas waits half a block then tries again. Not knowing where they're going or what will happen there and then, he realizes that he'd better get to the subject of Collier's interest before it's too late. "That night at the Procope, a while ago, did you mean what you said about the Duc d'Orléans?"

"And what was that?" Gallatin's voice is as ordinary as it can be.

"About him being no better than a fool."

"Do you really have to ask?"

On they go, another block; Thomas ventures once again.

"I've been thinking, Jean. The English have a superior system of government, don't you think? Their checkered monarchy, I mean."

Gallatin puts a hand on Thomas's shoulder. He brings the two of them to a halt.

"What's with you? We're out for a bit of fun and you're running the inquisition. If you want to talk politics and government, wait till later. After we're done. I've most of a bottle of wine back in my rooms. All right? Now, that's it. No more talk. We're coming up to the alley just ahead."

"Right." Thomas nods acquiescence. He'll be able to get back to what Collier wants in a little while. The alley is just ahead. What alley is that? And why would Gallatin take him to an alley?

"It's *checked.* The English government. You said 'checkered.' That doesn't make sense. Checkers is a game, nothing to do with government. Checked means it's balanced or restricted."

"I see."

Gallatin keys an imaginary lock on his lips in pantomime. Thomas does the same. It feels like a game, whatever it is they are about to do. Together, they enter the alley, which is complete blackness compared to the dimly lantern-lit street.

From what Thomas knows of this part of Paris on the left bank, he guesses that the alley might twist and turn all the way through the block over to rue Mazarine. That is, if it goes that far. It could just as easily and maybe more likely be a cul-de-sac. Why are they going into a cul-de-sac?

Thomas feels his body temperature rising as he goes. He doesn't enter alleys for a reason. The streets of Paris are dangerous enough; the alleys are worse, worlds unto themselves. They're unlit, dark even at midday, and this one is like going down into a mine at night. Anything could be lurking in here. If Thomas had known Gallatin was taking him into an alley on this walk, he might have declined. Then he remembers why he's here. He has to satisfy Collier's curiosity and keep earning extra coins. Thomas tries to take a deep breath. It does not want to come.

Not three steps into the alley the smell becomes strong, very strong. Urine, shit and rot. Whether it comes from men or animals Thomas cannot say. Nor does it matter. He steals a shallow breath and blows out the vapour in tiny puffs as he goes on.

There are puddles where they step. How is that? It hasn't rained all day yet there is standing water here and there. Or are they pools of piss? Thomas recalls a cave he was once in as a boy and all the blood and guts. His heart begins to thump so he tries to relax by making a little joke. The voice that comes out is nearly as high-pitched as a girl's.

"No minotaur at least."

Gallatin grabs Thomas's arm and gives it a pinch. With the other hand the bookseller places a single finger in front of pursed lips.

"Forgot," Thomas whispers back.

Jean Gallatin mimes the act of cutting a throat.

A dozen carefully raised and lowered paces into the darkness, that's when there comes a noise. It sounds to Thomas like a whir, maybe a bird in flight. No, that's not right. It's more likely a pack of rats. Yes, there goes a rat. The long tail trailing behind the large thick body that climbs up and over what remains of a broken-up wooden crate. The two men jump back.

"All right," Jean Gallatin whispers. He gestures that it's safe to continue on.

Thomas glances back to see how far they've come, wondering about a retreat. He vowed long ago to never go anywhere without the possibility of an out. Gallatin notices the regard. With a waving hand and a shake of his head he warns off Thomas of any thought of turning back. Thomas tries to exhale his worried breath.

The two young men creep forward into the darkness. They advance like they are boys again, testing a winter river's first ice. From who knows where, Thomas hears two lines in his head.

Something here, something to fear.
Eye can't see and ear can't hear.

He turns to Gallatin. His gaze asks the bookseller if he too hears the verse. Apparently not. Gallatin stares uncomprehendingly back. Thomas treads on. This is the first time in five years, not since he moved away from Vire and the childhood he had there, that verses unbidden have come Thomas's way. There comes one more.

Bravura, brave boy

Thomas recognizes that one. He'd heard it in the subterrane on the outskirts of Vire. It makes him shudder. What's going on? Are darkness and fear the missing muse? Must he put himself at risk to have poetry come his way?

Advance soft shadow
Down the dark wind

Deepen the twilight
Dust of the sinned

He opens his ears very wide. He recalls them from on high, overlooking Vire's river outside its walls. He would dearly love to hear them again, and this time come to their natural end. Thomas stops and stands and closes his eyes.

"Hey." Gallatin spits the word.

He grabs the laggard by the wrist. The bookseller is pointing at a squint of light coming from the building up ahead to the left. Thomas stumbles forward, the lines of verse jarred and scrambled. He looks skyward, into the dark. There's nothing there. The words are gone.

Forlorn, Thomas steps to where Jean Gallatin is jerking with his thumb. With a scowl on his face Thomas turns to see why Gallatin is so excited about this escape of slender light from the building in the alley. It looks to him like a shutter has slightly spread. It must be a broken latch or maybe a warped frame. He turns to Gallatin to ask with only the expression on his face: is this is it, is this the destination for our jaunt? He shakes his head as if to say, surely not.

Gallatin ignores Thomas's inquiring look. With an odd grin on his face he climbs up on an abandoned crate to put himself at the same level as the sliver of light emanating from the shuttered window. The bookseller presses one eye cautiously to the glowing chink. He seems to settle in. Thomas is drawn to see for himself. He pulls himself atop the same crate. Gallatin elbows him to wait. It is a minute, maybe more, before Gallatin steps back. He gestures Thomas to put his eyes where his have just been.

Through the chink of the broken shutter Thomas sees into a dining room with four people at table, two men and two women. It is an evening gathering, a dinner of some sort, in a very fine home. The walls are painted a pale green with decorative pastel-coloured flowers emerging from carved wood trim along the spaced vertical lines. But he ignores what's on the walls and takes in instead that there are cabriolet chairs along one wall and an impressive secretary in the middle of another wall with a delicate-looking clock directly above. As for the four diners, their eyes are wide, their gestures animated as they move in and out of conversation. Thomas recoils. He turns to Jean Gallatin.

"You brought me to peep?" It's an angry whispered complaint. Jean Gallatin's eyes blink in surprise. He beckons Thomas to come close.

"Aristocrats. They don't even know we're here. I thought La Coste told you."

Thomas is lost for words. The expression on his face gives him away.

"He didn't, did he?"

Thomas shakes his head.

"Then what—?" Gallatin grabs Thomas's coat and bunches it at his throat. "We'll talk later, you understand?" Thomas raises his eyebrows and makes big eyes. Gallatin lets go of his coat.

The bookseller turns back to his peep while Thomas finds his face forming a gradual grin. He has to admit that peeping in on the diners at table does feel pretty good, fascinating in a taboo way. He taps Gallatin on the shoulder and asks with curling fingers only if he can have another turn.

"Not so opposed to this pleasure after all?"

Thomas blinks. "Guess not," he whispers back.

"The English," says Gallatin in Thomas's ear, "they call it keeking. To steal a look, to spy on private scenes one doesn't normally see."

"That makes it all right? As long as we name it, as long as we give it a word then it's all right?"

"Correct."

Thomas settles in a second time at the chink of light. Left and right as far as he can see. There are a couple of good-sized tapestries on one end wall. Hunting scenes they are, with a stag taking his last breath in one and a party of high-born riders in the foreground of the other. On the other end wall there are three framed prints, hung side by side. Engravings of a single battle scene. That means this is a man's house or at least a man's favourite room. That same end of the room has a long buffet of dark wood. Toward the corner there hangs a portrait of some notable from at least a century ago. The time period is revealed, more or less, by the man's suit of armour and that he's sporting a now passé long curly wig. An ancestor of the host no doubt. All the trappings around the room are furnishings that only money, lots of money not good intentions, can acquire. Whoever owns this place has inherited well over several generations.

Thomas steps back, gesturing like a gentleman to Gallatin. Gallatin waves him back, and holds up two fingers, which Thomas takes to mean two more minutes.

He obliges the bookseller and again puts his face to the chink. This time, he focuses on the four diners. All, he notices right away, have the posture, facial expressions and gestures of those born to comfort and grace. He wonders how it is that the well-born can do things so differently from everyone else. It's as if there is an imaginary artist in the corner giving the diners instructions on how they should lean this way and that, turn their profiles just so. Or how to hold out their hands and wrists with purpose and subtly curl their full lips. Is it learned or does it come to them from birth? Of course, it's but an accident of birth that they are in there at table and he is out in the cold. Yet how he wishes it were the other way around.

Thomas watches as a dark-skinned servant boy, trafficked out of Africa or the Islands, no doubt, enters the room. He looks to be not more than eight or nine, and he stumbles with the tray of opened oysters he's labouring not to spill. The host of the dinner, or at least the man Thomas thinks is the host because he's the oldest in the room, stands and lends a steadying hand. Then he points the servant boy over to where he is to set the tray down. The host is wearing a salmon-coloured coat. What ease he shows in retaking his seat. He is directing the proceedings from his spot at the table head. A roll of the wrist seems to bring forward another domestic. This time it's an older man. His posture is upright stiff with an almost arched back.

Thomas feels Gallatin tug at his shoulder, but he does not yet yield his place at the broken shutter. The stiff-backed older servant is busy. He has two fresh carafes of wine, red in one hand and white in the other. Thomas imagines the man a dispossessed Polish count who has somehow lost all his family wealth in some war and now finds himself service bound. Back to the host goes Thomas's gaze, to the ruddy-faced older man. The fellow pauses in mid-sentence and rests an elbow on the table. Everyone in the room, the diners and the servants, wait for his cue. Thomas shifts his gaze to the lady on the right. She's turned in her chair now, facing the window. Her taffeta dress shimmers in precious hues of silver and gold. There's a bow of muslin clinging to where the cleavage begins. Dark eyes, dark hair and pearls round her neck, with one hand just off her lips.

Thomas stiffens to recall that Hélène, judging by her dress at Le Procope, has now entered this world.

The woman at the table is now touching the fabric that rounds her waist, surreptitiously pushing up the unseen inner shields that lift up her breasts. Thomas feels in his loins a longing to be by her side.

The host is speaking again, pointing to the tapestry on the end wall. All eyes that way turn. Then the host lifts the carafe of red and stands to offer a few words. The toast completed, he tips the carafe and pours a burgundy arc into a lady's glass and then a second arc into his own. There are splashes – it cannot be helped – but the host he does not seem to mind. The white linen tablecloth is there to absorb what misses the mark.

"Hey." Gallatin nearly spits in Thomas's ear.

"Sorry." Thomas steps back. "That's enough for me. My feet are getting cold. You stay and see how it comes out, this little play of yours."

Gallatin adjusts the shutter so it is more closed and steps over to where Thomas has moved. "Joke all you want," he whispers, chin sticking out. "It *is* a play, a play of our so-called betters. Don't forget that if we were in there, we'd be servants at their table."

Thomas holds up his hands, as if in protest. Gallatin continues: "For a few people to live like that, the rest of us have to suffer. That's how it is, don't you agree?"

Thomas supposes that might be true, but he takes exception to the thought that if he were inside this house he would be a servant. He doesn't think that has to be true. There might be ways for him to rise. However, he is not going to argue atop a crate in the dark of an alley outside a house. If they were caught where they are, they'd be thrown in prison and it wouldn't be easy to get out. Thomas goes to the edge of the crate and starts to climb down. This little adventure has gone on long enough. He'll just tell Collier the truth: that a report on the bookseller Jean Gallatin will have to wait. He will not mention anything about this alley at all.

Down at the level of the ground, Thomas starts to trudge away.

"Hey," calls out Gallatin, "wait up. I want some answers."

—

"So, what's this all about?" Jean Gallatin has lit a small fire in the grate of his room. "And don't say Ovid, all right?"

He passes his guest a brown cup whose handle is broken off. Thomas takes hold of the cup. Gallatin splashes a generous portion of red wine, filling the cup to near its brim. Thomas takes a sip. The wine is strong, not diluted with water the way it often is in the cabarets. It tastes of the earth. It's as if there are granules of the soil in which the grape vines were grown.

"It's good. Where's it from?"

"Saint-Emilion. Inland from Bordeaux. Are you stalling?"

"I suppose I am."

Thomas looks around the main room of Gallatin's apartment. He sees and smells that the bookseller burns tallow candles: the dark yellow ones made from animal fat not wax. They give off a stink when lit. So Thomas is ahead of Gallatin in that regard. He now burns beeswax candles in his rooms.

There are a half dozen rush-seated chairs and two tables – the small one they are both sitting at and the larger one that appears to function as a desk. It's piled high with a couple of stacks of books and a bundle of loose paper tied with a black ribbon. Along two of the walls are piles of books, more books than Thomas has ever seen before in someone's living space. It is almost like a bookshop. The room itself is about the same size as the one Thomas lived in when he first came to Paris and stayed in for far too long. If Gallatin is still living in a place like this then Thomas is also ahead of him in that regard. Yet Thomas doesn't see a *pailleasse* or any bed or mattress anywhere. So where does the bookseller sleep?

"You're wondering about the bed?" Gallatin is smiling. He appears to be amused at Thomas's not-so-secret survey of his room.

"None of my business, I suppose."

"That's right. But because you do not ask, I shall explain. Who knows, my example might even serve to inspire you to change your ways. From what I hear, you need it."

Thomas sits up straight, his brow wrinkling. Gallatin laughs at the bewildered reaction. He rises to put another stick of split wood on the fire. Next, he goes to the chamber pot and takes off the lid and unbuttons his breeches. "You don't mind?" he says over his shoulder, his back facing Thomas. Thomas shrugs. He barely hears the sound of Gallatin's piss hitting the pot above the crackle and spit of the fire. But the smell of urine does waft around the room. It puts a little bite into the air. To change the scent in his nostrils Thomas sniffs the wine. He glances over at Gallatin who is now finished. The lid is back on the chamber pot and Gallatin is splashing his hands in the water in a basin. Thomas wonders if that is something the bookseller does each time after he performs his necessaries or if it's a show just for him.

"Neither bed nor mattress," says Gallatin, coming back to sit once more across from Thomas, "because I don't sleep here. I live with a widow in an apartment across the hall."

Gallatin pauses to see how Thomas reacts.

"Ah, look at that. A little smile from a man who lives alone but spends many an hour poking whores."

The bookseller waits again, but Thomas does not say a thing, though his eyes narrow slightly.

"Let me tell you this, Pichon, she's a good woman, she is, my Marie. And good for more than you're thinking. Women, if you don't know this already, they're different."

Thomas raises his eyebrows. He speaks at last. "I did notice that, Jean. A couple of differences I can think of. They're built for us, for instance. To receive us. To give us pleasure."

"No." Gallatin waves his hand dismissively. "No, I used to think that as well. But it's wrong. Women are not built for us. They're built for children. That's not the same thing. They think differently than us, Thomas, they do. And sometimes, not always but sometimes, they come up with better than we would on our own."

Thomas leans back in his seat. He tries not to smirk. This is good, really good. Here is Jean Gallatin, cynic, skeptic, he who makes caustic pronouncements and instant dismissals when the writers gather, the man is a femme-o-phile. Thomas is not sure this is a word, yet it fits nonetheless. Here, in his rooms, Jean Gallatin is a domesticated cat whose claws are trimmed.

"And do you have children with this Marie?" Thomas strokes his chin to help keep a straight face.

"No, Marie is past it now. She bore three with her husband but they had all died when they were young. Before I met her. So no, alas. That husband fled, disappeared up north somewhere. Calais, I think."

Thomas feels his eyes flutter. Gallatin's widow woman is old enough to be his mother. "I see," is all Thomas says.

Gallatin's face registers disappointment. He turns to studying the fingernails on an outstretched hand.

"It's important to keep yourself clean, do you know that, Thomas?" Gallatin says without looking over at his guest.

Thomas does not reply. He doesn't know what to say. Perhaps it's time to go.

But Gallatin is not finished with the topic. "It is, Thomas. Hands, face, the whole body."

"The whole body?" Thomas's face wavers between bewilderment and amusement. He takes a sip of wine. "Everywhere?"

"Especially everywhere." Gallatin gives Thomas a knowing look. "The arsewipes people use, they're not enough. And instead of covering our stink with musk and ambergris and other scents, we should all be washing. Cocks and asses too. And women, they need to clean their furrow with water. Did you know that?"

Thomas is incredulous. He is thinking of the risks there are to putting one's body in water. The chills and the risk of vapours.

"Look to the ancients, Thomas, the ancients. The Romans sat in baths for hours. Your precious Ovid too, I'm sure he bathed long and often."

Thomas looks away. The reference to Ovid makes him livid. So stupid of him. He takes a longer sip of the wine. Sit in water and wash every part! Whatever is the bookseller talking about?

The conversation staggers along awkwardly. A polite inquiry from Thomas about Gallatin's Marie, which leads to a long answer Thomas barely hears. Then an insincere remark by Thomas that yes, he should find himself a good woman and stay out of the stalls. Gallatin jumps on that one with warnings about how if Thomas picks up a malady the mercury treatment might make him drool and burn his thing right off. That thought makes Thomas and Gallatin both take a long drink. Thomas is the first to leave the thought of venereal diseases and their treatment behind. He finds himself again wondering about Gallatin's widow across the hall. Just how old is she and is there anything left of her looks? He'd be curious to meet her and see for himself.

"Your Marie," begins Thomas, not knowing exactly how to proceed, except cautiously, "she lost her children you say? How did you meet?"

"Look, you don't care about that, so don't pretend that you do." Gallatin's face is gone stern and serious. "I've not forgotten about your earlier deception, Thomas. You running to my shop. That had nothing to do with any book, did it?"

Thomas's mind races to find a way through the maze he created for himself with that fake cover story. Why not take the safest path? Start with the truth, or at least a portion thereof, and see where it leads.

"You're right, Jean. Ovid was just an excuse. I came to the shop …" he hesitates for effect, "because I wanted to see you. I wanted to hear your views on … on politics and forms of government. I've realized lately I'm not well informed."

Jean Gallatin is silent, yet Thomas can see that the man's eyes are busy trying to determine how much of what Thomas has just said he accepts. Thomas pretends to relax as he waits.

"You've never shown any interest in my views before. Not at all." Gallatin raises his chin as he speaks. "Or not that much. In fact, we hardly know each other, Thomas Pichon. The only thing I can say for sure about you is that you don't like Voltaire."

"Voltaire! I've nothing against the man at all." Thomas's voice and hands go up in protest. "That time at Le Procope, it was all about something else. It was the girl with Voltaire, if you must know."

"Really? The girl? She was pretty as I recall."

Thomas shrugs.

"In any case," says Jean Gallatin, "you and I have never been close. So why are you here tonight?"

"Exactly," says Thomas, trying a new tack. He retrieves the cup of wine and this time he does take a sip. He likes the musky swirl in his mouth and then the warm line of descent it makes as it trickles down his throat. "It's time to change that. You sometimes say interesting things, you do. About events and people. About the regent, for instance. And other things I don't know. I'd like to hear more. If you would." Thomas delays then adds in a softer voice, like he has the remains of a sweet pastry in his mouth: "Like what you think of the regent and the council, for example?"

Gallatin gives Thomas a long look over the top of his cup of wine, which is cradled in both hands in front of his mouth. The intensity of his stare forces Thomas to glance away.

"Sounds false." Gallatin puts down his cup on the tabletop with a bang, spilling a few drops. "Made up. Puffery."

"It's not rehearsed, if that's what you mean. I can tell you that," says Thomas in complete honesty.

"You know what, Pichon, you're trying to butter me like a piece of bread." Gallatin snorts the air. "If I didn't know better, and I don't say this lightly, if I didn't know better I'd say you were one of the Marquis d'Argenson's flies."

Thomas's eyes go wide then dart away. His mouth opens yet no words come. He makes no reply.

"Thomas?" presses Gallatin, leaning forward. The eyes wait for an answer, some form of denial. Thomas shifts in his seat. "Thomas? Look at me, will you?" Thomas comes close to eye contact but cannot quite do what Gallatin commands. "Oh my God, you're not! Don't tell me that." Gallatin claps a hand across his mouth and nose.

Thomas's head is spinning, everything awhirl. He wants to come back with a denial, he wants to say oh no, it's just a joke. I was just teasing, that's all. But Thomas cannot find any such words to send past his lips. Instead, he feels a gush of air issue from his mouth. He's suddenly chilled, and it's a chill that spreads. There's a knot in the back of his neck.

Gallatin's hands spread wide on the tabletop as he waits. The opened-up hands want a reply. The only sound is the crackle from the fire. The taste of twin silences is bitter and dry.

Thomas licks his lips. He switches from one gaze to nowhere to another stare to another nowhere somewhere else. His left hand rises as if it might scratch the side of his head, but then Thomas notices it and wills the errant hand back down.

"Thomas?"

Thomas tries to meet the speaker's gaze but he cannot. He continues to make silence his only reply.

Gallatin leans back in his chair, his right hand scratching his chin. Thomas knows he is being studied, but there is nothing he can do. His eyes choose to focus nowhere. He hears the bookseller take a shallow breath.

"Oh my, oh my, Thomas. Thomas, Thomas, Thomas."

"I know." Thomas looks up at Gallatin, with a hint of watery eyes.

"For how long?"

"Does it matter?"

"Suppose not."

The admission on the table and confirmed, the two men sit in silence. They communicate with furtive glances and equally furtive sips of wine. In both cases the taste in the mouth is not what it was only a moment ago. It's gone sour and flat. The wine has turned to vinegar in the last minute or two.

Thomas brings both elbows to rest on the table. He starts to put his hands up to cover the front of his troubled face. But he resists the urge and sends the cowardly hands back down where they belong, flat on the table. He thinks it important that Gallatin sees his face just as it is. More than that, he wants to know what the bookseller thinks of what he has just found out.

"Is it wrong? I mean, have I really done anything so very wrong?"

"Only you know that." Gallatin's face is glum, resigned.

Abruptly, Gallatin stands. Thomas flinches yet Jean Gallatin is not making a move at him. Instead, the bookseller leaves the table and goes across the room to pick up a piece of wood, which he tosses on the fire. There is a burst of sudden sparks. Gallatin returns to the table and retakes his seat.

Thomas does not look his way. He is going over what the bookseller just said: "Only you know that." Is Gallatin saying that God and a king's justice do not count? That everlasting hell and the punishments of the body it will bring are of no consequence? That Thomas should not be troubled by what he has done, the insignificant confidences he might have betrayed? Does that not mean that Thomas is his own judge, the one and only who matters? His head is swirling. Why does he not just stand and run? He could make good an escape and never see the bookseller or any of the others ever again. Paris is a big city. Or he could leave Paris and start again somewhere else. There are other lands than France.

"Gone sour hasn't it?" asks Gallatin. He holds up his cup.

Thomas makes eye contact. He nods that yes, the taste of the wine has gone bad.

"Want something different?"

"Sure," says Thomas, astonished that Gallatin is still playing the host.

The bookseller is up and away, out of the room. This is the perfect time for Thomas to bolt. He sees that right away. Yet he stays where he is, nailed to his chair. A face comes back to him.

The visage of a man running after the diligence leaving Vire. The face is red, cheeks huffing out and sucking in. The wheels make a grinding sound, churning crushed stones, as they roll away.

"You all right?" Gallatin has returned. He is startled by how pale Thomas looks.

"Yes."

"This should be better. From the Rhône valley." Gallatin is holding a bottle and two fresh cups.

A bit of colour comes back into Thomas's cheeks. Gallatin pulls a small knife out of his pocket and cuts through the wax covering, then removes the cork. He pours two long splashes, the first for his guest and the other in his own cup. He picks up his and extends his arm forward. He waits for Thomas to clink cups with him, which Thomas does.

"To your health."

"And to yours." Thomas cannot remove the puzzled expression blanketing his face.

Gallatin smiles smugly.

Rolling a gulp of wine round his mouth and across his tongue, Thomas wonders if he's just been duped. Did Gallatin make a show of opening the bottle in front of him because he had already put poison in it? Perhaps after they clinked their cups Gallatin only pretended to sip. Maybe he spit back in his cup the small amount that he took? No, Thomas thinks that's unlikely. An overactive imagination. He swallows the wine he has held too long in his mouth.

"So?" Thomas asks at length, brow wrinkled.

"So what?"

"So … what you were saying earlier." Thomas's voice becomes suddenly sharp. "That it's my opinion and mine alone as to the rightness of what I do."

Gallatin cocks his head at an angle. He says nothing.

"Whether it's good or bad, right or wrong," Thomas continues, getting insistent. "Our morality, in other words. It's not up to the Church or the King or for that matter the Marquis and his police. No one decides morality but us. It's peculiar to each one. Is that not it? Do I have you right?"

Thomas puts down his cup of wine. He wants Gallatin to say something back. The bookseller has a distant, unfocused expression. In his own way, though not for the same purpose, the bookseller's unreadable face reminds Thomas of Collier's mask.

"No," says Gallatin at last, as though he's made a difficult decision, "no, I didn't say that. I was referring only to your apparent betrayal of us, your supposed friends. We thought we were your companions, equal at table. And that the confidences we shared were for our ears alone. But we were mistaken. You were playing us for dupes. When I said 'only you know that' I meant only you know what and how much you have passed on about us."

Thomas opens his mouth to explain that he's never told Collier much at all, yet he doesn't get a chance. Gallatin's hand goes up, commanding the air above the table.

"But what you just said, Thomas, it's interesting. It is. About each of us being responsible for ourselves. For our own morality. Not the business of the Church or of the king's officials. It's a thought worth discussing." Gallatin looks pensive, then continues. "But some behaviour, some urges of men, they cannot be allowed. They must be condemned."

Thomas exhales and nods that it's true. Paris has many dark corners and they have witnessed some terrible things.

"But tell me now," says Gallatin, with a light in his eyes, "just what have you already told the Marquis about me and my friends? Is someone on his way to lock me up in the Bastille?" Gallatin makes a caricature of a smile.

"Oh, you're safe," says Thomas, and wonders if that's true.

"You look troubled, my friend. Guilty about doing me in, or scheming to find some fresh way to do just that?" Gallatin laughs, but it's a nervous laugh. "Well, here, I have a cure for your ailment." He makes a swirling motion with his hands, like a magician about to show the audience his reveal. He pulls from the inside pocket of his coat a small silver flask. "Calva," he says, smile on his face.

"Wonderful," Thomas says. He forces a smile.

The feeling in Thomas's chest, however, is anything but wonderful. It's a strap that is tightening fast. The need to betray friends and acquaintances is no easy game.

Gallatin unstoppers the flask and tips it twice, dribbles of gold into two tumblers of clear glass. He hands one to Thomas and takes the other for himself. "Tell me what you think."

Thomas has only sipped calvados once before. He was only a boy. His father was out of the house one evening and he dared himself to steal a nip. It burned his tongue and throat. Thomas clasps the glass with both hands and sniffs above the rim of the glass.

"It's an orchard, it really is." Thomas's smile is broad. The scent of the apple liqueur pushes away the thought of passing on secrets to Collier. "Who said we are never as happy or unhappy as we imagine? Because I'm imagining I'm pretty happy right now."

"La Rochefoucauld," says Gallatin. He pours himself a little top-up, having quickly downed the first. "That's who said that. Or wrote it rather. It's much easier to be clever with a quill than with our mouths."

"Isn't that the truth?" says Thomas. "If only we could talk like we write. Well, like we sometimes write."

Gallatin takes a long sip. He closes his eyes in appreciation. "This comes from Marie's father. He put it down the year she was born, or so the story goes."

"And how long ago was that?"

"Dying to know my woman's age, aren't you, Thomas?"

"No, not at all. Just wondered about the age of the calvados is all."

"It's all right, but you're not fooling anyone. Marie is thirty-eight."

Thomas gulps and the calva burns. Gallatin's widow really is nearly twice his age. Thomas stares at the bookseller like he's never seen him before. The ears are a little large, the complexion a bit ruddy, the eyebrows close together, and the hair a tad straw-like, but what a remarkable man and fine host he is. This is a man whom Thomas is supposed tell tales about, in Collier's ear, with who knows what consequences. Yet, here he is, earnest and good, serving Thomas whatever it is he has to offer. Like this golden, delicious liqueur.

"Thank you, Jean. Seriously, I want to give thanks."

"Give thanks. You make it sound like a prayer."

"Sorry. I'm sorry. Just thanks is all I meant."

The two men make eye contact in a way they until now have not. Both know that Thomas is thanking Gallatin for much more than the calvados and before that for the wine. He is also thanking the man for not casting him out when he learned that Thomas works for the police as a fly.

"Ever consider turning it the other way?" Gallatin puts his head at a quizzical angle.

"Pardon me?"

"The police. Your contact man. What's his name?"

"Collier."

"How appropriate is that? He's a collar you wear. No, what I mean is, do you ever think of playing him instead of him playing you?"

"I'm not following." Thomas holds the calvados away from his nose so he can concentrate.

Gallatin takes a sip from his tumbler. "I'm referring to your *friendship* with the police, your role as their fly."

"Yes, I know. What about it?"

"Well, I'm suggesting you keep on with it as you have, only you start feeding *them* instead of them feeding off you." Thomas's face remains blank, though his eyes eventually blink. Gallatin continues: "Fill *their* heads with nonsense, Thomas. Make things up to lead them astray."

Thomas leans back in his chair. He lifts the tumbler to his nose, sniffs, lowers it to his lip and tips in a swirl. As the liquid heats its way down his throat he looks at Gallatin with yet another fresh regard.

"You mean all the time, not just now and then? That the truth be no obstruction?"

Gallatin nods. That's exactly what he means.

"To what end?"

"To the end of having a bit of fun. To confuse and waste their time. To continue to get your coins. That's three good reasons, is it not?"

Thomas sips and sends a golden charge round his teeth and onto his tongue. He recalls liking honey this way, but this is even better. Yes, fiction could be his friend. How much better that sounds than lying.

"Yes," Thomas says out loud. And to himself: I like this man, this Jean Gallatin. He is a friend to me.

"All right then, more of our Normandy nectar?" Jean holds up the little flask.

"Good old Normandy. We have orchards near Vire, you know. Oh my god," Thomas shouts. Gallatin's head snaps back. "I … I … I'm supposed to go."

Thomas has recalled that he was to meet Jean-Chrys that very night. He stands up and puts both hands to his head. He searches his memory for what they'd said as they left the Pont Neuf. There was a street and a building Jean-Chrys yelled out. Something about the crippled or the deaf. The name just doesn't come. It will not come. Thomas regains his seat. "I was to meet someone," he says in a defeated voice. "An old friend. From Vire he was. Well, he still is I suppose. The one who once loaned me Ovid."

"Tomorrow perhaps?"

"I don't know. The name of the street that he gave me will surely come. Once I'm sober and out for a walk."

"There you have it." Gallatin holds the silver flask high in the air. "You'll see to your other friend tomorrow. Why don't you stay and we'll finish this? It's a pretty cure for things gone wrong."

Thomas tilts his head to one side to acknowledge that yes maybe he would like another drink. The sweet-tasting calva is starting to make his hair lift. It's a sensation that he likes. The complications with his parents and with Jean-Chrys can wait, can they not? Why, yes. The pleasures of the present moment always trump any unknown.

—

Thomas will spend the night at Jean Gallatin's. He will sleep in the room where he and the bookseller are drinking too much. After another hour of talk and more raised glasses and cups, Thomas near passes out. It seems some pleasures, after all, can be too much. Gallatin steadies his friend as he pisses in the pot then goes to wake up the widow Marie to help him drag over to that room a not too badly stained *pailleasse.* That's where Jean insists Thomas will sleep. Thomas mumbles his thanks to them both, and that they're probably right: it is too late. He's in no shape to go out safely into the night. Just before he closes his eyes, Thomas has a muddled vision of Marie as she brings a basin with water into the room and then bends to place a blanket on his curled-up frame. The bookseller's widow is not too bad looking for her age. He goes to sleep hoping he didn't say that aloud.

—

Thomas wakes as the sky starts to lighten. His mouth is filled with parched wood. His scalp is in the grip of a giant like Le Grand Thomas. He pulls out the little watch from the pocket of his breeches. He's supposed to be at Pontécoulant's office in less than an hour.

He has to get up on all fours. That's the only way there is off the straw mattress. I'm an invalid, he thinks. But he rights himself and gets to his feet. That's when it comes to him, what he tried to remember the night before. Jean-Chrys said he was staying on the rue des Aveugles. Across from some church. A room on the third floor. Thomas is pleased with himself. He'll go there in the evening, right after work. It's the least he can do for an old friend.

He does his necessaries in the chamber pot. He covers what he's done with the lid then takes a corner of a small linen cloth and wets it in the basin. He dabs his face then rubs at his hands. What's that Gallatin said? He should wash everything. He'll have to think about that. That would require a bathtub and there's nothing like that here. In the meantime, he uses the linen cloth to dabs around his eyes, which he sees in the mirror are bloodshot, and then his throat and behind his neck and ears. He puts on the rest of his clothes.

When he leaves Thomas closes the door as quietly as he can. He slips down the stairs like a cat. As awful as he felt up in Gallatin's room, he gets a small burst of life coming out the ground floor door onto the street. It's not what anyone would call warm, but it's not as cold as it's been. It's a good sign. As is the mist he spies rising off the Seine. Yes, things will work out. They always do. He'll start handing Collier a new kind of tale. Instead of being the bait on the hook, Thomas will try to cast the line. Gallatin is right. Thomas will have to make sure that his future tales to Collier don't do the bookseller any more harm.

The building where Thomas toils in Pontécoulant's office comes into sight. The thought of the great lawyer and the other aspiring lawyers prancing in the suite of rooms on the second floor brings a shift in his mood. No matter how good a clerk he is, he'll never be able to join their club. Thomas glances up at the grey sky overhead, churning with dark clouds. There descends a thought, like he once received verses from the muse. It concerns the matter Jean-Chrys spoke about, the ongoing dispute his parents have with La Motte. Yes, the clouds are right. He knows what he can do. When he sees Jean-Chrys later in the day – he will not forget, to the clouds he makes a vow – Thomas will tell his old friend that to Rouen he will go. He'll help out his parents, yes he will. And he'll go as the lawyer they need, just like they expect. No harm done, some good in fact. It's the career his parents have heard he has. It'll be a bit of a bluff but not all that much. He's kept his eyes and ears open in the office. He reads and in fact copies nearly everything. He's learned enough to pass muster in Rouen. It's not like it's Paris. He'll tell Jean-Chrys this evening, but he'll make him swear not to reveal the truth. It'll be their shared secret, one that helps his poor parents out. Filial assistance in name and deed.

Thomas enters the building considering the trip to Rouen and the reunion with his parents almost as good as done. He trusts it will make amends for that early-morning departure he was forced to make those years ago.

March 1720

Thomas has to walk. He has to clear his head. The coach ride back from Rouen was long and slow, the other passengers a mostly tiring lot. There were those who slept and those who talked a bit and those who simply would not shut up. The worst were those who had never been outside their little Norman villages before, so excited were they to be coming to Paris. Thomas recognized that he and Hélène were once a bit like that, but not so irritating, he's sure. There were stretches when Thomas thought the trip would never end. Now that he's back in the city and dropped his small trunk in his rooms, he wants to stretch his legs. Over to the Saint-Médard parish area near the mount Sainte-Geneviève and the counterscarp. It's usually a lively spot and it's been a while since he was that way. Gallatin tells him that the Roman roots run especially deep in that part of the city. And nowhere more so than on the narrow street Thomas likes to wander up and down. Winding rue Mouffetard with all its market stalls and shouting voices will sooth his disappointed mood. Then a ride upon a whore in a stall, though in truth he doesn't really feel like that.

Rouen was not the reunion with his parents he'd imagined it would be. Thomas was not the prodigal son. His parents did not trumpet his return nor tell him how proud they were. Nor how they understood he'd made a difficult but correct choice. They begrudged his assistance though they'd requested it through Jean-Chrys and though they benefitted in Rouen from his pretend lawyer's advice. They wanted more. They wanted their money back. And they did not believe him when he told them about the theft. Or if they finally did accept it as the truth, the expression on Father's face was as clear as it could be: serves you right. Jean-Chrys tried to help out, but there was little he could do. Thomas got on the coach back to Paris without having seen much of Rouen. Except to note how the Seine twists in that city, the giant clock and the square where the authorities allowed the burning of Jeanne d'Arc. Yet another object lesson to keep your life and your views to yourself.

A file of three women market-goers, their baskets filled with their purchases from the stalls along the street, come toward Thomas as he reaches the top of rue Mouffetard. He flattens against the stone wall and lets them past. They are talking about an ascetic priest who lives somewhere nearby. A churchman whose sacrificing example they admire. Their chatter tweaks Thomas's ears. He decides to turn and follow behind the women and listen in.

The women spread out side by side as they walk through the square. Thomas gets as close as he can without giving himself away.

The priest in question seems to have the last name Paris. Thomas shrugs. It could be, some people do. He comes from a wealthy family, the women say, and gives away his family pension to the poor. He is a follower of the Jansenists, that bunch. Wears a hair shirt and walks on the cobbles in his bare feet, says another, and pays the price. He flagellates himself with a whip, the lashes tipped with iron, adds the third woman. Probably for things he's done. Serves him right, comes off the lips of one.

"He's a hermit. Lives not far away," says the first woman. She's nearly as wide as she is tall.

"I know, I know," says the woman in the middle, the tallest of the three. Thomas is close enough now to see she has a couple of cabbages and a whole fish wrapped in paper in her basket.

"Hey," says the tall woman in the middle, turning round. She puts a hand on her hip and challenges Thomas with her stern face. "Get away from here. Go follow someone else."

"I was only…" Thomas begins but doesn't bother to finish. He waves a hand at the women and turns around. He goes back the way he has just come. He was only curious about any priest who lives the way the women say. He'd like to see the fellow and judge for himself if self-punishment really does make one more worthy and holier than everybody else.

Back on rue Mouffetard Thomas buys two golden apples from a stand. They are *reinettes* from Normandy. Their dry tart taste he has loved since he was a boy. He'll savour the first one bite by bite as he wanders around and save the other for later on. He stuffs it in a pocket of his *justaucorps.*

With a few minutes of rambling this way and that, the first apple is consumed and its core tossed to the street. Not long after Thomas wonders if that's not a familiar figure coming across a tree-shaded churchyard. He's headed for the church. Yes, it's Collier, of that Thomas has no doubt. But he does not have his cloak upon his head the way he always does when they meet at night. He's just gone into the church. It's little Saint-Julien le Pauvre. Is he going in to worship or is this a rendezvous with someone special? A tell-tale like himself? It's a temptation he cannot resist. This is an opportunity he never imagined he'd have. If he's careful and soft afoot he'll be able to spy on Collier while he's meeting with another fly. Odd that it's daytime, but maybe Collier makes exceptions for certain bits of news. That makes sense. Not everything can wait for night.

Thomas is more than eager to see how the pale-faced one works with someone else. And who that tell-tale might be. He waits barely a count of five then crosses to the church. He knows that meetings can sometimes be short so he is quick to step inside. He'll have to be careful from here on in. Yet no sooner is he in the gloom of the entryway than he hears Collier's voice. The voice is loud and getting louder. It's coming Thomas's way. The police agent is not whispering, not whispering at all. He's starting to say goodbye. He's speaking to the curé. The conversation is about money, how Collier as a parishioner promises soon to make his annual contribution to the maintenance of the church.

The door swings outward into the entry space where Thomas is now trapped. He turns up the collar of his greatcoat and tugs the tricorn down hard to cover what he can. In desperation Thomas turns to face the wall. His nose is a mere six inches from the stones. With his back to the two moving voices sweeping through the entry Thomas nods his head back and forth, repeating a prayer that his mother used to say every night. He's pretending to be a crazed woshipper who has chosen the entryway of Saint-Julien to pray.

The final words of Collier's parting are said. Thomas hears the priest pad back into the church. There comes the noise of the slow closing of the door that leads outside. Thomas peeks around. Collier is gone. Should Thomas wait? No, he should not. He edges out the door. Collier is sauntering through the yard with his back to the church heading slowly toward the fountain. He is taking his time. He is at most thirty paces away from Thomas, completely unaware.

An idea arrives, come from who knows where. Thomas touches the second *reinette* in his pocket. Its familiar shape brings a smile. Will not Gallatin have a good laugh? Sure, why not? As a boy he had quite an arm for throwing rocks.

Out the apple comes, a hard little golden orb into his hand. Thomas stands where he'll be able to quickly run and hide. He fixes his gaze, cocks his arm and lets the *reinette* fly. Sure enough his aim is true. The apple strikes its mark some thirty paces away. The apple explodes into pain, pulp and juice upon the stroller's head. An instant too late, Collier glares in anger at the porch of the church from which the apple came. He spies no one at all.

V

Advancement

Paris

October 1726 – February 1727

"Oh my God," issues from Thomas's mouth, words that match the startled look on his face and the queasy feeling now pulsing through his body. He is just through the doorway and at once he is face to face, literally, with the head of a dead body lying on the table. He cannot help his reaction. He turns his gaze away as quickly as he can. Too late. His stomach is heaving, wanting to be sick.

"But I thought you knew." Monsieur Verney, the surgeon acting as a tour guide, looks to be more amused than concerned. He shows Thomas a gloating smile. "What else did you think the study of anatomy would entail?"

He places a hand on Thomas's back as the young man bends over. He can feel Thomas's body convulse as he struggles not to vomit.

"How could we study the body without having bodies before us? But of course we have to take them apart."

Verney has given enough comfort to bent-over Thomas. He turns to the other visitor, the elderly Monsieur Salles, and sends him a half-amused look. Verney knows Salles well. The gentleman who has brought Thomas along today is a frequent visitor to the dissecting room. It is a place where one dissects. Bodies, of the human kind. And where inquiring scientists figure out what makes them work. Verney sees Salles every few months, when the elderly fellow comes to the Royal Physick-Garden to see what might be new. Monsieur Salles has not been disappointed yet. There's always some heretofore unknown or rarely studied wrinkle about this or that body part. Though not a surgeon, an aging financier in fact, Salles takes great interest in the anatomical field. He finds the body a fascinating study and has brought along his prospective son-in-law, Thomas Pichon, to see if he has a similar scientific bent. Apparently not, it would seem, at least not for the dissecting domain.

"Didn't know," comes from Thomas, barely audible, speaking to the floor. He is seated on a hall bench now, facing away from the horror, both arms wrapped tight around his stomach. He gasps for air and takes relief in being so far successful in keeping the stomach down. He pinches his forearms to make them hurt. He hopes the pain will drive away what he just saw: a head separated from its torso. "Bit of a surprise, that's all," he says with a weak voice, still not looking up.

"As I was saying, Monsieur Salles," says Verney, turning to face a guest whose keen interest in anatomy the surgeon respects, "we've been fortunate of late. More than the usual number have come our way. Vagabonds and criminals of course, as usual, those found or executed, but there are some fascinating specimens among them. Here, follow me."

Though he remains seated in the hall Thomas can hear the two men carry on their conversation inside the dissecting room. He wishes he could not.

"Take this fellow. Look here. See the arm Henri just removed. Not half an hour before you arrived. Do you see how the veins and nerves run parallel? And how the muscles have come asunder? A marvellous example, is it not?"

"It is, it is," chirps Monsieur Salles in return. "Though quite a lot of goo."

Thomas puts his hands over his ears to not hear any more. To be sure, Verney said it was a dissecting room as they were coming down the hall, but Thomas had no idea. He thought dissections were for amphibians and cats. That's what he'd seen and done as a lad in Vire. Frogs were easily cut and separated and even kind of fun, though the smell of their dead and wrinkled skin could make one's nose curl. He had no idea that the anatomy studied in the Physick-Garden was of men. Yet there they were on the long table as he came through the door, that head with a face, a man's face with bushy eyebrows and eyes staring wild, watching him step in. And beyond that head there was the torso, cut completely open at breast and belly.

Thomas wants to wash away the recollections of what he saw, yet he cannot. There were two surgeons beyond Verney's outstretched arm. They were working on the torso, one on each side, instruments in their hands. There were cords seeming to tie the cadaver down. Averting his gaze as quickly as he could, Thomas nonetheless glimpsed a skeleton on a distant T-frame along one wall and racks with cutting tools of some sort. There were cabinets along another wall, he now recalls, and benches and stools beside the main table. A man behind Verney was wielding a long knife, or maybe it was a saw. As Thomas spun round to escape he looked down. Within a basket on the floor there were other types and sizes of cutting instruments. What a frightful sight. When at last he glanced back up, past the staring body-less face, he saw the torso one last time and farther on an arm and a leg. A tray of some sort lay between them, full of what looked like bits of flesh.

"Good thing you're not in the army," says Monsieur Salles with a chuckle in his voice as he comes back out into the hall. He gives Thomas a pat on the back. "Or a butcher for that matter." Salles gives Thomas's arm a tug, wanting to hoist him up. "Come on. Nothing sharper than a quill for you, I wager. Just the way it is, I suppose. Oh well, straighten up, young man. Let's go. If you're not going to look at the dissections, there's not much sense in staying around."

Thomas is not inclined to answer but he does get up, weak and wobbly though he feels. He does not see Monsieur Verney or his assistants again, to thank them for the tour, but he hears them roar with laughter as he walks away, assisted by good old Monsieur Salles. Their laughter does not sting. He accepts that he's not cut out for the science of the body, as Verney and Salles are wont to call it. Funny, he once imagined that a career in medicine was for him. It appears it was a foolish thought.

"Thank you, sir," Thomas says to Monsieur Salles as he starts to get his legs back at the end of the corridor. "I'm fine, I really am."

"You're still pale, but maybe walking by yourself will do you good."

Thomas's thoughts are no longer on whether or not he is going to vomit. He is over that. The question now is the more important one: will his squeamish reaction to seeing bloody body parts have an impact on Monsieur Salles's acceptance of his pending marriage to his daughter, Marguerite?

—

"Oh my," says Jean Gallatin on hearing Thomas's tale of queasiness in front of Monsieur Salles retold. "Oh well," he adds, above the squeaking sounds of the horse-drawn coach, "I guess it could have been worse."

"How so?" Thomas leans in to hear.

"Not sure." Gallatin glances out the window at the Paris street scene rolling by. A beggar who had been pretending to be a blind cripple is up and running, chasing away two boys who have taken coins from the hat on the street in front of him. "It's just what I'm supposed to say, I think."

"Thanks for that."

Thomas turns away, over to the window on his side. A well-dressed couple is strolling along, their heads swivelling ever so slightly to see if anyone else is noticing how elegant they are. Thomas grimaces in contempt.

The coach is one Thomas and Gallatin have hired to take them to the outskirts of the city. It's rolling at quite a clip. It seems that November first, the Feast of All Souls, is a time of relative quiet on the streets of Paris. The pedestrian and coach traffic will pick up later on – it is a feast day after all – but at the moment, early afternoon, there are not many other wheeled vehicles or walkers clogging up the streets.

Gallatin reaches over and taps Thomas on the shoulder. "The butcher crack was especially bad. I mean, after all, he is to be your father-in-law. You don't expect that from family."

"I know." Thomas shakes his head. "The old bugger thought because I showed an interest in his cabinet of curiosities – he has a very nice collection of rocks and minerals, by the way, and a jawbone of a shark and Indian things from the Americas – he thought that since I was showing an interest in those things, well then I must be a closet scientist at heart. That's how he fancies himself, as a man of science even though he makes his money in business and finance."

Gallatin nods, taking it in. He always likes to hear about how the people above him live and think. He wants to be ready for the day when he gets there himself.

"'Anatomy in action,' said Monsieur Salles." Thomas holds out his hand as if the rest is obvious. "And naive fool that I was, I agreed to go along."

"What 'Indian' things does he have? You said they were from the Americas. From Brazil?"

"No, mostly from Cap Breton, if you know that colony. It's one of ours, renamed Isle Royale. Louisbourg is its port. Up north somewhere, if I'm not mistaken. Anyway, Salles has a box made out of the hair of some kind of animal, only that hair is really prickles. He called them quills. Oh, and a pair of baskets the Indians strap to their feet."

"Baskets? On their feet? Why would they do that?"

"Maybe not baskets. No, they look more like the rackets of the *jeu de paume*. You know those?"

Gallatin nods that he does.

"Well, the rackets allow the Indians to walk on deep snow, according to old Salles." Thomas hunches his shoulders, not about to argue with what he was told by the wealthy father of the woman he's soon to marry.

"I wonder if he has that right. The rackets are probably just to play some Indian game. Maybe they too have the *jeu de paume*?"

Thomas shrugs. He doesn't know, nor much care.

"You know, I sell a travel account about that part of the world. Should you want to broaden your reading. I could give you a special price." Gallatin holds out his hand.

"Thanks, but no thanks, Jean. The last thing I want to do is cross the ocean. Just imagine tramping around some wilderness. I used to have dreams about that. Running wolves and things.

They weren't good. Anyway, I'm off the point. The point is that my intended's father thought took me to see anatomy up close. Anatomy, for god's sake!"

"Don't slight anatomy." Jean Gallatin winks at his friend. "You still have an interest in that subject if I'm not mistaken. Albeit to only the outside parts it seems. The pudding, as some like to call it. Speaking of which, how goes it with the widow?"

Thomas gives a reluctant smile. He recalls what happened two nights before. He and Marguerite were having a quiet evening at her apartment, sitting in the salon and reading their individual books. Hers was a recent novel of romance and his a tome on the natural history of the Antilles. From time to time one would ask the other if he or she could read aloud certain parts, which they did to good effect. It passed the time and was pleasant enough. No, that's not saying enough. It was much better by far than the many evenings the two of them otherwise spend alone and apart, Thomas in his apartment and Marguerite in the suite of rooms she inherited from her late husband.

When Thomas met Marguerite at a dinner party six months ago, she was a widow of two and a half years. The word was she was comfortably well off, which piqued Thomas's interest right away. He'd taken Jean Gallatin at his word, and had been hoping to find a widow, one with money, if he only could. Though at forty-five Marguerite is now near twice his age, he likes her lively eyes, her sometimes coy gaze, and what he takes to be her steady, quiet ways. Following weeks of Sunday afternoon promenades and other hours of keeping company, he has finally convinced her that they might be right for each other, no matter the difference in age. During their courtship, twice he'd had her upper garments undone, to cup and kiss her breasts. But for the longest time he was not allowed the ultimate touch and then the ride. Biding his time as he was, Thomas still gave his soldier an exercise in the stalls about twice a week. But what a surprise two nights ago when after a long period of silence, each deep into their books and the only sounds a crackling fire, Marguerite suddenly closed her book with a slap and up she stood. Without a word she went and got the screen, the one with oriental designs and black enamel trim. She unfolded it to partition off a portion of the room. Then she went behind the screen and Thomas couldn't see what she was about. He put down his book and stared at the screen. There was a sound of fabric being pulled.

"Everything all right?" Thomas inquired at length.

"Not yet." Thomas was sure he heard laughter in Marguerite's voice. "All right, I'm ready."

Up Thomas got in a hurry, rounding the screen. Oh my, it was quite the sight, one he'd seen many times before though not quite as Marguerite was presenting it now.

"Well now," was all he said, and unbuttoned his breeches as quickly as he could. They went at it right there on the red divan with Marguerite the one in charge. She told him where and how. It only lasted a few minutes but it was a coupling Thomas will long remember nonetheless.

"Thomas?" asks Gallatin, waving a hand in front of his seatmate's eyes.

"Sorry, what?"

"I was asking how things are going with the widow, your prospective bride. You went into a trance."

"I did, didn't I? Well, it's going well. We sign the marriage contract in a little over three weeks."

"That's it? Things are going well?" Gallatin sucks in a deep breath. "A model of discretion, you are, my friend. I applaud you. My question was but a test. Will you at least admit to me that I was right? That widows are the best? I was the one who first told you that, if you'll recall."

"Yes, I do recall, and I thank you for that."

Thomas is relishing his tight-lipped replies about his pleasuring with Marguerite. There really are, he decides, few things more satisfying than a secret well kept. If the world wants to call such discretion a virtue, then so be it. In that regard, he is as virtuous as any man could be.

—

It's the first time either Thomas or Gallatin has been to a *guinguette*, one of the unlicenced drinking places just beyond the Paris city limits. They've chosen to go to the largest of them, and the most renowned. It's the Au Tambour Royal, though it is more often simply identified by its owner's name, Ramponeau. The *guinguettes* are the talk of the city, places where anything can happen and usually does. They are really just cabarets, but being outside the city they are unregulated. That means there are no taxes on the drinks. Wine and other alcohol are one-half or one-third the cost they are in Paris proper. So instead of being called cabarets, they are known as *guinguettes*. Customers drink more than usual, then often dance and maybe do things they might not otherwise get away with. The rumour Thomas and Gallatin have heard is that some customers even fornicate while others watch.

That there is cheap liquor available in the Ramponeau is obvious to Thomas and Gallatin well before they get to the door. The volume of the voices coming out of the building is loud. The two young men look at each other as they step down from their coach. The ruckus coming from the Au Tambour Royal makes Thomas think of the cheers one hears at public executions. For Gallatin the association is a happier one, of a crowd roaring at the fireworks on the Fête de Saint-Louis.

Three artisans stagger out the door as Thomas and Jean approach. The artisans are bellowing a rude song that apparently gives them great joy. They refuse to give as much as an inch as they come roaring out through the doorway. Thomas and Gallatin move over to let the singing drunkards stagger past. Right behind them is another group, this time of five people. Among them Thomas recognizes a familiar face. In the lead, stepping over the threshold of the *guinguette* like he is prancing, comes Voltaire. Thomas sees the famous writer around Paris from time to time, but the two of them have not spoken since that night a few years ago when Voltaire was with Hélène at Le Café Procope. Thomas has not seen Hélène since, not with Voltaire or anyone else. Recently, a few months back, Thomas and Voltaire were both at the same gathering for the release of some dismal poet's book of disappointing verse. They didn't speak or rub elbows at all. But Thomas did take note that when Voltaire arrived at the event the sun stopped shining on the author whose night it was supposed to be and shifted over to the grinning, witty one. Thomas thought it rude of Voltaire to have shown up at all, eclipsing the unfortunate poet like that. Nonetheless, Thomas flashes a smile and extends his hand at the entrance to the *guinguette*.

"Ah, Voltaire, we meet again."

"Oh, hello."

Voltaire sports the usual bemused look. He passes quickly on, no notice at all taken of Thomas's outstretched hand. Four others, two men and two women, neither of which is Hélène, brush past Thomas and Gallatin. They are in a rush to catch up with the rapidly moving Voltaire.

"Didn't recognize you, I guess," says Jean Gallatin. He is doing a poor job of trying not to laugh.

"Really?" says Thomas sarcastically. His face is momentarily long and sour. Much as he dislikes and envies Voltaire his talent and his fame, he finds himself wondering more about Hélène. He supposes the witty one has cast her off. But where might she have gone? Back to Évreux and its rustic life, or somewhere in Paris with another man?

Thomas and Gallatin step inside the *guinguette*. What was a hubbub when they were outside is now a roar. Despite the departure of the singing artisans and the group with Voltaire, the place is packed. There's not an empty table in sight, though that doesn't much matter to the clientele that Thomas and Gallatin see. Half the place is standing, everyone with a glass or tumbler in hand. Most of the customers are men, but there are a few women. Everyone is shouting just to be heard.

The walls are whitewashed and filled with large sketches, giant cartoons of people and animals. On one wall it's a soldier brandishing a halberd. On another it's a lady with a wide skirt. There are also drawings of a minstrel, a duck, a crowing cock, and a naked Bacchus astride a barrel. The last-named has a grapevine sprouting between his legs to hide what he has there. Gallatin points at it and nudges Thomas in the ribs. Thomas has already seen it, but he smiles back as if it's funnier than it really is. The largest of the many sketches is on the chimney above the hearth that faces customers where they come in. It's a charcoal drawing like the others, only done with more care. There's shading and details to make it look like someone real. The caption tells Thomas and Gallatin who it is. It's Ramponeau himself. His watchful image gazes down on the buxom wench at the counter just inside the door. She's taking money and pouring drinks for customers as they come in. Thomas and Jean give her the money for their first glass of wine. They make their way through the tumult to find a place to stand.

"Quite the spot," shouts Thomas near Gallatin's ear, a worried look upon his face. It was his idea to come, but he's not sure yet if it's safe. Neither he nor his friend is ready for a fight, unless it were a debate. Still, he hopes the bookseller is not disappointed with what he sees.

"Every bit of it," Jean yells back. "Better really." His expression says he's delighted that he came.

Thomas hunches his shoulders to show that he too is pleased. It had not taken a lot of convincing to get Jean Gallatin to take the trip. With all the hours the bookseller spends in his shop, reading the books he has in stock and sometimes even making a few sales, he's ready for an outing once in a while. Even for Gallatin, there is only so much one can say about John Locke, the idea of a *tabula rasa*, and the superiority of the English government in comparison with absolutist France. As for his hobby of peeping on people above him on the Parisian social ladder, the bookseller is open to diversifying his pastime a little. He accepts as an article of faith Locke's idea that there is an implied bond or contract between those who govern and those who are governed. He told Thomas on the ride out that this trip to the *guinguette* is an opportunity for him to learn more about the people on the ladder's lowest rungs. According to what he's heard, or so Gallatin told Thomas, aristocrats often go to the Ramponeau just for fun. To mingle with the little people.

"Hey, look." Thomas gives Gallatin's sleeve a tug. At the far end of the room two drunken fools are dancing some peasant twirl, bumping into those standing nearby. Oddly, no blows rain down when they do. There is just an exchange of laughter. Thomas and Gallatin do not watch the scene for long. They know that to show too much curiosity might bring a punch to the face. Closer to where they're standing is a man with a demonic grin and only one good eye. He has a patch on the other.

He's trying to reach up beneath the dark red skirt of a serving girl. The girl, carrying meat pie pastries on a wicker tray, swings round and kicks the one-eyed bloke. She sends him crashing against the wall.

"Not a place for the weak of heart," observes Gallatin.

"Come on." Thomas has spied a party of four men getting up from a table. Their early afternoon of drinking is apparently done. Thomas races to stake his claim, Gallatin following after. Another man – the one with the eye patch – arrives at the same table an instant after Thomas. The stranger slaps his hand down on the table whereas Thomas had merely touched the back of one of the chairs.

"Well done, my friend, well done," says Gallatin, coming to stand behind Thomas to reinforce their claim. He claps Thomas on the shoulder and stares at the third fellow's one exposed eye. Gallatin thinks his hearty words and gesture of congratulations are demonstrating to the little fellow that he staked his claim but a moment too late. "The table is ours," Gallatin announces. "Even you can see that for yourself."

The man with the eye patch barks a noise in Gallatin's face, a sort of laugh perhaps. At least that's what Thomas and Gallatin hope the noise means. He gives a wink and a crook of his head, first to Gallatin and then to Thomas. Out of nowhere he brings up a truncheon and slams it on the tabletop. He must have been holding the baton down by his leg, out of sight. Everyone nearby, the standing and the seated, goes silent. The sound of the wooden stick whacking the table for an instant commands the room.

The one-eyed man acknowledges the attention by bowing to his onlookers. He picks up the truncheon and dangles it like it's a sword and he is a knight twirling it in a strange salute. Next comes a version of a lady's curtsey, his face bearing a broad smile. There is laughter all round. An instant later, the noise in the Au Tambour Royal goes back to what it was before the slamming on the tabletop. Thomas and Gallatin look at each other then round the *guinguette*. They appear to be on their own with this one-eyed man.

"You're sayin'?" says the stranger. His focus is entirely on Gallatin, at whom he points the truncheon. "*Even* me can see for myself. Was that it?"

The stranger brings the truncheon up to touch his cheek and circle round his one good eye.

"Not mockin' me, you?" He shifts the truncheon and taps the patch over the hidden eye. "Don't know how I lost it, you? Been a war? Maybe. Could be a hero. Yes I could. Don't know, you? Fighting *for* and not against the old king. Good story that. War 'gainst Spain it coulda been. What say you to that? To the one good eye? Respect, my friend, respect. Not callin' you tiny cocked am I?" The stranger scrunches up his cheeks and puckers like he's sucking an invisible lemon.

Thomas cannot stifle a laugh. When this little man speaks he's an actor on a stage. A ragged ruffian in some comic part. The stranger hears Thomas's snort of laughter and looks his way. He uses a hand to shield his face so Gallatin can't see. With his eye he gives Thomas a conspiratorial wink.

"Look," Gallatin replies, keeping his voice low, "I only meant that my friend Thomas got here first. To the table. You have to admit it. That's all I want to say."

"You sure that all you got?" The stranger tilts his head to one side and rubs his chin with the end of the truncheon. "Not a preacher maybe? 'Cause preachers don't ever shut their gobs."

Thomas laughs out loud. It's a bark. "How about," he says, venturing one hand to tug on Gallatin's sleeve and the other, palm up, extending out over the table. The open hand beckons the man with the truncheon to lean in closer than he is. "How 'bout we share the table? There are chairs enough. Indeed, there's one to spare. How would that be?"

"Preacher and peacemaker. Well, I'll be."

The one-eyed man sends Jean Gallatin a crook of the head before he lays the truncheon on the table. Next, he places one hand across his waist and the other out of sight behind his back. He gives a jerky version of a courtly bow. The gesture completed, the man holds out his right hand to shake with his newfound tablemates. Thomas is the first to accept the offered hand. Gallatin grimaces but follows suit.

"Jacques, that's me," the one-eyed man says as he takes his seat. "Though more just call me Prêt à Boire. 'Cause I am." Jacques taps the tabletop with a small empty tankard he's just pulled from somewhere. He must have had it in a pocket of his greatcoat. "Don't often mix with your sort, but it's All Souls, so why not? End up in the same place so might as well start now. What say you to that?"

"A very Christian sentiment in its way. My name is Thomas."

"Ah, the doubter, no doubt," Jacques interjects.

"And I'm Jean," says Gallatin, reluctance in his voice and on his face. "By the way," he adds, unable to stop himself, "I don't hold to what you just said. That we go to the same place in the end. I don't think we go anywhere after death but into the ground. To the worms is what I say."

"Eh?" Jacques is squinting at Gallatin.

"Heaven and hell, they're fabrications of the Church. All that hierarchy, the teachings, all of it. It's made up, I say."

Jacques' jaw twists as Gallatin pauses. The eyes are angered, or are they bewildered, by Gallatin's little rant. And the bookseller will not leave it at that.

"A sop. A story. A complicated story, to be sure, but still just a story. To confuse us and keep your likes down. If you don't mind me saying so."

"My likes? What's my likes?"

"I didn't mean anything by that." Gallatin waves both hands in front of him to erase the words from the air. "I'm sorry. I meant all of us."

"Got a poker up your back end?" Jacques asks Gallatin.

Thomas explodes with a harsh laugh. "He can't help it," he explains, clapping Gallatin on the shoulder. He gets a glare in return. "He doesn't get out often enough. Works in a bookshop, you know."

"That'd do it." Jacques makes a face at Gallatin. "Bend over, preacher, I'll take it out. Seen worse than the darkness of your ass, I'm sure."

Gallatin shakes his head in disgust. He looks down at the tabletop. Thomas is smiling broadly at the crudity of this one-eyed stranger: "A joke, it's a joke, Jean. Our friend Jacques is being funny."

What Thomas doesn't say but is thinking is that Gallatin, who has so much to say about governments and the relationship between the higher-born and their obligations to the little people down below, is not doing well with this one-eyed member of that group. Gallatin is face to face with a man of the trades, and he doesn't know what to say or do.

"So," says Jacques, grabbing hold of his truncheon once again. He lifts it off the table. "So what brings two *gentlemen*, oh yes gentlemen, out of the city? And to dear old Ramponeau? See the other half – hell, the other nine of ten – how we riff-raff live? Study trip, is it?"

As if they are attached, Thomas and Gallatin stiffen like someone has indeed just shoved twin pokers up their asses. Jacques puts down the truncheon. He winks at Thomas and unleashes an ungodly bark of a laugh.

"Good to relax." Jacques holds out his empty tankard in Gallatin's direction. "Likes rum from the Islands, don't we now? Off with you, young cock. Don't forget the name now." He mouths "Prêt à Boire." "Got that?" He mouths it one more time. "Fill 'er up, tiny cock."

Gallatin reluctantly takes the tankard from Jacques' hand.

While Gallatin is over at the counter paying for Prêt à Boire's rum and red wines for Thomas and himself, Jacques turns to Thomas.

"A good bunch, you two. I'm looking out for you in here, count on that. It can be dangerous, if you don't know. But I'm here. You can relax."

"You're kind," says Thomas. "We'll be fine."

"'Course. Never mind."

Over the next few minutes, before and after Gallatin returns to the table with the newly purchased drinks, Jacques launches into an uninterrupted string of tales about a lifetime of adventures travelling around France. The stories come one after the other, like a river over rapids, with no comments sought or questions allowed. Thomas tries a couple of times to get in a word or two, but Jacques waves him off like he's a gnat. The one-eyed man's speech reminds Thomas of a clock that's just been wound. Once it starts ticking, it goes until its time runs out. The one and only pause in the telling of Jacques' stories comes when the man drains his tankard in a single swallow. That accomplished, he holds it out for Thomas to do the honour of filling the mug the second time around. To Thomas's own eye-blinking surprise, he does exactly what Jacques bids. He brings out his little leather pouch from its hiding place and selects the required coins. Walking over to the counter to buy the drinks he does a calculation and decides that this set of drinks for the table will be his last. He has to have enough left to pay for the coach ride back into the city and something besides saved for who knows what. He will not turn his hard-earned money into nothing more than another man's piss.

Thomas listens to more tales from Jacques with wide-eyed fascination. Gallatin does the same, but with a pinched and doubting face. More than a few times Jacques swears that what he's about to say is the honest to God truth, may he be struck by lightning if it's not. He tells his tablemates that he's a glazier by occupation, a Parisian by birth and upbringing. He's just back from an eighteen-month tour of France where he earned his master's status in his trade. Along the way, in a dozen towns and cities, beginning north and circling west and south, then east and north again advancing alongside and up the Rhône, he's worked on a dozen jobs. He's been in and out of money more times than he can count. And that's all right by Jacques because coins are made for spending, so spend them fast he does. As he travelled, or so he claims with many a wink, he found women willing to lift their skirts wherever he went. Thomas lifts his head at such a claim while Gallatin looks away. Can it be true? This Jacques, so short and homely with scars and pocks upon his dirty face, the scruffy hair tied back and a patch upon his eye, can he have delved as often as he claims? His clothes are not so bad, yet they are a mixed sort to say the least. To Thomas they appear to have come from here and there, likely auctions or thefts in every town he's been to. Can this man really get sex for free, that for which Thomas until recently has had to pay? Of special note, Jacques says, were the bosses' wives. He had them now and then and once even their daughters too. More commonly, the tale goes on, he favoured farmers' wives. Even a gypsy woman in the woods. Only once, he says, the voice going deep and filled with pretend regret, did he bed a fellow glazier's betrothed. He wishes now that he had not. "Brothers in trade, you know," he explains with a downcast face. He stops and looks away as if his storytelling just might be through. "Still, it was in the two of us, her as much as me. So we, well...." Jacques holds out an open palm, smacks it with a fist and makes a rolled-eye face.

Thomas and Gallatin turn to face each other. The same thought is in both their gazes. Is this finally it? Can they at last say good day to little comic Jacques and slip away?

"Enough 'bout me, thank you much," says Jacques. "Your turn it is. Where you two been and what you two done?"

Thomas's and Gallatin's eyebrows arch up in unison, but they resist exchanging glances this time. Instead, each one looks over at the door of the *guinguette*. It's time to leave.

"Nothing, eh?" says Jacques. "So sad."

"It's not really any of your…" mutters Gallatin, but then shuts his lips.

"No business?" Jacques reaches for the truncheon. "Try this. Try speaking to the stick."

Thomas's and Gallatin's heads recoil.

"Joke, a joke," says Jacques. He drops the truncheon on the tabletop. "Relax. Just making conversation."

Thomas and Gallatin each slowly finds his feet. Jacques makes a face as they rise, but it's a grimace that says he's trying to understand. He too stands and holds out his hand for his tablemates to pump. The shaking over, the glazier gives them a trademark tilt of the head along with one more wink.

"Paths could cross again. Think on that."

"Of course," says Thomas, lingering. Gallatin gives him an elbow in the ribs and the two are off.

Neither Thomas nor Jean hears Jacques' footsteps following them as they wend their way through the crowd and its din. As they emerge from the Au Tambour Royal, out where a quilted blanket of grey cloud cover is darkening overhead, they think their *guinguette* adventure is done. They've had some laughs and seen the place. Now they need to locate a coach to carry them back into the city.

—

Marguerite Salles stands by the freshly upholstered bright green chair as her visitor scurries into the room. The ruffling sound of her cousin's full silk dress fills the salon as the aging woman shimmers past. Marguerite silently mouths "Hail Mary full of grace" three times before she moves at all. With her cousin seated on the matching green chaise longue, Marguerite reaches out to close the door. An instant later, she hears the footfalls of Simone, the diminutive servant originally from Le Puy, down the hall. The seated cousin, the widowed Madame Dufour, nods approvingly. She knows from sorry experience how servants love to listen in and then exaggerate with each telling what they think they've heard. Her cousin, the even longer widowed Marguerite Salles, is wise to take precautions. Whatever she and Marguerite will say during the visit is none of Simone's or any other servant's business.

Madame Dufour still wears the mourning ring and black veil to honour the custom of marking the memory of a late husband. The ring and veil are the last of her widow's apparel. She can't wait to shed them as she has shed the black dresses. A few more weeks she tells herself, only a few more weeks. Monsieur Dufour was a large, wheezing man who paid little attention to her when he was alive. His preference was to see her at table and almost nowhere else. More to his liking were the women he met outside the marital state. Monsieur engaged in as many affairs as his pocketbook and libido could stand. It was a reality Madame Dufour put up with for over twenty-two years. Relief came six months ago when a tumour in his throat took Monsieur away in a matter of weeks. "Poor soul," she said when the doctor told her the news at the end. That was the full extent of her expression of sorrow. The man's passing meant only that she had to alter her attire for six months. The ring was handed down to her from her mother. Soon enough, she'll put it back into its box for safekeeping. She's not likely to ever wear it again, unless she is to remarry and outlive the next one as well.

For the six months of her public mourning Madame Dufour has made it a point to call upon dear cousin Marguerite Salles once a week. It is her preferred way to catch up on all the latest news, big and little, as she waits out her widow's relative isolation. What she longs to hear, and tries to follow at her imposed distance, are the stories coming out of the court at Versailles and the highest levels of Paris society. It both piques and satisfies her to hear what's going on. First, however, before she can taste the main course, she must get through the appetizer. That is cousin Marguerite's own situation, the pending marriage to what's his name, the young one Marguerite is so fixed on. Madame Dufour doubts she'll hear anything today she hasn't heard before, but one has to go through the motions nonetheless.

"Well," says Madame Dufour when Marguerite finally sits in the chair closest to the chaise longue where Madame has struck a regal pose, "and so, how does it feel to be so close to signing the contract? All set to marry once again. Anxious, I'm sure."

"It is wonderful, yes," says Marguerite, smiling as if she means it with all her heart, "that it is."

Madame Dufour is taken aback. Her cousin's smile is simply too robust. Like she might still be a girl and the upcoming marriage her first. Instead of a mature woman who should know better than she apparently does.

As if she can read Madame Dufour's mind, Marguerite's smile slowly wilts. It disappears completely as she recalls what her father told her when she asked about her betrothed's visit to the anatomy class. All he said was: "He could never be a doctor, your young man. Let's just leave it at that."

"To speak with complete candour," says Marguerite to her glum-looking cousin, "I am a little anxious. Nervous, I guess."

"His age, is it?" says Madame Dufour. She presents an understanding and forgiving face. For weeks she has disapproved of the age difference between her cousin and her intended groom-to-be yet not said a thing. Why, Marguerite is nearly twice the young man's twenty-six years. Moreover, she has a life of comfort and elevated position whereas the intended has neither. Real life is not a story, Madame Dufour has wanted to say, but she has kept her wisdom to herself. She simply nods sagely at

Marguerite. They have each finished reading the same novel in the past month in which true love wins out in the end. Yes, they both cried their separate tears when it ended, but Madame Dufour understands, as Marguerite apparently does not, that the reason one reads such things is precisely because they're not real. A book about real life would be boring and without end.

"His age? No, why? Do *you* think that Thomas is too young? For me, I mean."

"Me? Heavens. He's fine, isn't he, your Thomas? Husbands have to be younger or older, don't they? So one might as well have a young one, I suppose."

Marguerite's eyebrows twitch. Why can't her cousin just come out and say what she really means: that Thomas is too young and possesses insufficient rank?

The room is silent except for the tapping of Marguerite's foot on the parquet floor. Madame Dufour smiles as she waits, hands clasped in her lap. She's said enough. She did her duty and gave her cousin all the warning that she could.

Marguerite's brow furrows. She did not think her cousin disapproved so strongly of the match. But so what if she does? Cousin is only jealous, there's no mistaking that. You would think that at nearly sixty and beyond plump, Madame might call it quits. Yet that is not the case. She clearly resents the happiness Marguerite has found.

Marguerite casts her glance down to the floor. For a dozen years she was happily married to her first husband before he went to Marseilles on a business matter and didn't return. Smallpox, the letter said. Marguerite never even got to see the body. He was buried down there, in some improvised graveyard away from everything, the letter said. She resigned herself to being a widow for the rest of her life. She was comfortable enough with the estate he left behind, so she did not fret about marrying again. For three and a half years she was content, when, out of nowhere, at an evening salon near the Place des Vosges she ended up standing beside a young man who said something funny. The renowned Voltaire was making a toast to the author of some new book, going on gushingly about it and its author. In a whisper, the warmth of his breath stirring her ear and neck, the young man said: "You could spread that on your strawberries, could you not?" She laughed out loud, like the call of a bird, and everyone looked her way. Yet the whispered words were true. Voltaire's outpouring of words was mere cream, too sweet and thick by far. When the official talk was over the young man introduced himself as an aspiring man of the law. That was her first introduction to her intended, Thomas Pichon. She liked his brown eyes and the smooth look of his skin. More than that, she liked how he listened to her every word. She caught a vanilla scent on his breath and a different tang from his clothes. The latter was a sort of burned chocolate smell. She imagined he spent his evenings alone in dark cabarets. Until that moment Marguerite had not known that she still wanted a man in her life. With him so close to her ear and neck it seemed that maybe she did.

"Are you all right, Marguerite?" Madame Dufour is leaning forward.

"Yes, yes," says Marguerite, her focus coming back to the salon. "Distracted is all."

"So it seems."

A fresh silence blankets the room. Each lady ponders what to say next. Madame Dufour wonders if it's not finally time to switch the topic of conversation away from Marguerite's upcoming marriage and over to the latest rumours swirling from Versailles. She's heard that the young king's marriage to the older Polish princess is not a completely happy one, though perhaps they shouldn't speak of that. Too tender a topic no doubt, given that Marguerite's situation is nearly the same. Madame Dufour gestures with her hand, a sign of impatience cousin Marguerite knows all too well.

"He's bound to rise higher," Marguerite says in a rush. "Eventually of course. Don't you think so? That Thomas too will advance? In law and its positions, I mean."

"But of course, my dear cousin, of course. Of course he will advance." Madame Dufour smiles like a piece of sugary candy is melting in her mouth. "Why would he not? Is there some reason why not? No, of course. Don't you worry about that. Your Thomas has lots of time. He's very young after all."

Madame Dufour pushes her fixed smile higher still. She recalls how the snippy young man virtually snubbed her on the one and only occasion they met. She mentioned that she'd been reading and enjoying Montesquieu's *Persian Letters*, thinking they could speak of it while Marguerite was out of the room. Thomas, however, her cousin's chosen one, replied: "Oh, Madame, are people still reading that?"

"I see," Marguerite says to her cousin. Her shoulders have slumped.

Madame Dufour continues: "Oh yes, you see when you speak with him that he has a, well, a *particular* intelligence." She pauses to glance over at the little doll on the ottoman, the one she and Marguerite examined last time she was here. It's the way to see the latest fashions and make the choices that must be made. She returns her gaze to Marguerite. "The young all have a bright future ahead of them. That's their main virtue. They can still get better while we, well, we're stuck with who we are."

Marguerite wants not to glare at her cousin for her words, so she sends a rapid glance around the room. The drapes briefly catch her eyes, especially the panels that have faded badly in the sun. When she comes back to Madame Dufour she finds she cannot rein in her words.

"Thomas has already overcome a great deal, if you must know. He was to have a career in medicine and was considered promising in the field. But there was a problem in his family back in Normandy. No fault of his own. Filial duty, is all he says. He does not complain, but I suspect it was his parents who let him down."

"Surely," says Madame Dufour.

"So he's chosen law instead. He began as a clerk and has risen steadily. I forget how many posts and offices he's been in, but he's in demand."

"Of course."

"In fact, he's on the inside track for a post as a secretary to a magistrate. Yes, one of the first magistrates of the Parlement of Paris and a councillor of the state. That will advance him nicely."

"Doing well then."

"Yes." Marguerite pauses to allow a tiny smile. She recalls what she and Thomas did on the divan two nights earlier, behind a closed screen. She raises her eyebrows to go back to the subject at hand. "On those evenings when he's not here with me, why, he writes at his place. He's working on a treatise of some sort. Philosophical precepts. And in Latin, I think. His Latin is that good. Quite the writer, my Thomas."

"I'm not surprised."

"He'll do well, he will."

"Yes, well, you know what is said. Marriage is a great adventure."

Marguerite's eyes blink. She had not thought of it quite like that. Her cousin just might be right.

"Speaking of which," Madame Dufour continues, desirous of completing the shift, "what news this week about the older Polish princess and our young king? Have you heard anything delicious? I'm curious to know."

Marguerite Salles sighs as she gives her dear cousin what she wants. She turns to the gossip that her cousin's visits are really about. "Have I told you what the duc de Saint-Simon said the other day, regarding the Polish queen?"

"You certainly did not."

"Only hearsay of course, but apparently...." And so begins nearly an hour of obligation for Marguerite Salles and a much appreciated entertainment for Madame Dufour.

—

It's going to be a long walk; Thomas and Gallatin both know that. And it's not just the distance. It's also the aches and pains each is feeling thanks to the whacks their one-eyed attacker, Jacques the glazier, gave them the moment they stepped outside the *guinguette*. With Gallatin it took only one blow from behind. He was down like an animal shot between the eyes. Thomas was not so lucky. He heard the truncheon strike Gallatin's head and turned to glimpse a fierce-faced Jacques pulling back his bat to wield it once more, this time at him. Thomas raised his arms to protect himself, but that likely made it worse. Unlike Gallatin, Thomas saw all too clearly what was coming. Jacques rained down blow after blow to beat Thomas to his knees. Hands and arms, shoulders, back and chest: each part had its turn. It was only when Thomas pulled out his money pouch and tossed it at his attacker that the beating stopped. Jacques took the pouch and bent down to get the other one he wanted from the inside pocket of the knocked-out Gallatin as well. And with a jingle of the pouches' contents, a crook of the head followed by a smile and a wink, Jacques was off.

"It's going to take us a couple of hours." Jean is rubbing his shoulder, which hurts as much as his head. He figures he hurt the shoulder when he tumbled unconscious to the ground.

"If not more," says Thomas, resigned to his fate.

"I didn't like him, not one bit. Didn't trust him from the start."

"I know."

"You thought he was amusing. You thought we should sit and listen to his tales. They were all lies, by the way, in case you didn't know."

"You want me to say it was my fault? Is that it?"

"No," mutters Gallatin. "Well, yes, maybe I do."

"All right. It was my fault."

With that out of the way, the two friends walk along in silence marked by the occasional moan as one or the other feels the need to let his companion know how he sore he's feeling as they trudge along.

Thomas's thoughts are no longer about the struggle with the glazier and the few coins the man took from each of them. Thomas figures the beating was likely overdue. The city is filled with brigands and pickpockets, mountebanks and robbers, footpads and foisters. Considering how many late nights and dark places he's been in and out of over the past decade, he's almost thankful that the beating and the robbery weren't worse. He can still walk, well, with a limp. Besides, he didn't have that much money in his pouch to lose. He makes sure he never does when he goes out. Instead, he keeps what he has saved hidden in his room. It's in the hollowed-out centre of the big book on the bottom of the stack of books behind the door. No one will ever find his money there.

Though he may have been due for a thrashing, he hopes that's it for a while. Next time it could be worse. Thomas didn't have a hint it was on its way, not until he heard the whack on Gallatin's head. Is he losing his edge, his awareness of risk and of danger? Has he become just another Paris stooge waiting to be taken? He hopes not. If he has to make a choice, he'd much prefer to be one of life's predators than its little prey. Whatever else happens, he never wants to be prey.

Thomas looks over at Gallatin. His friend appears to be still locked in a funk. His eyes are fierce yet unseeing. Thomas cannot but smile. The older he gets the harder he finds it to keep any emotion around for long. As soon as one comes along it's soon gone, as if evaporating in the air. He's aware that it makes him a little distant from his life as he goes through it, but what's wrong with that? The very thought makes Thomas go and touch the wooden piquet fence bordering a likely garden on the other side. Such touches reassure him now, as they did when he was a boy, that he is very much in this world.

Thomas understands that Gallatin is different. The bookseller has attachments and passions. Thomas almost envies him for that. But *almost* is as close as it gets. Thomas will stay who he is, thank you very much, not that there's any choice in that. He's advancing at a not bad rate. The upcoming marriage to Marguerite will surely help him out in that. The moment the knot is legally tied it moves him up a tier or maybe two. Mediocrity is an ugly word. The marriage to Marguerite will speed his climb.

"I've been thinking," says Gallatin as the two young men go past the windmill at the corner of rue du bas Pincourt and turn left on to the rue du Menil-Montant. He says no more, distracted by the large wooden arms of yet another windmill up ahead on the left. Neither of them especially likes being in this largely uninhabited part on the far left bank of Paris. If they wanted to live in the country or in some small town with lots of gardens, then that's where they'd choose to live.

"Yes, all right," says Thomas, "so you've been thinking. I always thought you might. Eventually."

"Funny. Look, I wasn't sure I should say it out loud or not. But here goes: I've been thinking, thinking I might move away."

"Away? What's away? Away from what?"

"Out of Paris. Over to London."

"London? Seriously?" says Thomas, reaching out to halt his friend. They both come to a stop.

"Yes." Gallatin glances down at the cobbled street and then back up to look Thomas in the eyes. "Maybe it sounds foolish, but it's a thought I've had off and on ever since I started reading John Locke."

"John Locke?"

"I thought you'd laugh."

"Do I look like I'm laughing?"

"No, but. It's just that the more I read about politics and government the more I'm drawn to England. Well, to London."

Thomas says nothing. He's blinking at his friend.

"Do you read their newspapers, Thomas? The English ones, I mean."

Thomas gives his head a shake. Ever since Gallatin's lady friend, the widow Marie, died of the bloody flux a few months ago, Jean Gallatin has become increasingly oblique in the things he says. It's like he's lost his compass bearings the last while.

"Well, I do." Gallatin continues. "And I'm convinced their system of government is much superior to ours." He looks at Thomas like he's expecting some sort of challenge.

Thomas merely shrugs. "By 'their,' you mean the English?"

"But of course."

"Real life is not in the newspapers, Gallatin. You know that, right?"

"I didn't think you'd understand."

Gallatin begins walking again, at a faster pace than before. Thomas quickly catches up. The bruises and limps from the beating they took are no longer in either man's mind.

"The Church is not a factor over there," says Gallatin. "Well, they have a Church of course, their own not ours. Their king is its head, not the pope."

"That's better? Aren't they godless heretics? That's what I've always heard." Thomas is smiling. He knows he's pushing the right lever to get Gallatin going some more.

"That's just it. With the king at the top of their church it doesn't matter. It's clever, it is. Because their king is checked by their parliament. Religion doesn't come into it."

"I somehow doubt it, my friend. Religion always comes into it. There's no other way."

"You're right, but not into their government. In England religion remains what it should be. A story for the gullible. The English leave it at that. It's so much better than a faith that blinds you to other truths."

"If you say so." Thomas makes a waving gesture, showing his weariness of hearing Gallatin sing the praises of England. The man is an Anglophile as well as a Femme-ophile.

"Brush me off all you like, but it's true. The English model of government is perfect."

"Perfect?"

"All right, nothing's perfect except in our imaginations. But there's better and there's worse. And I say England is better and France is a lot worse."

"Good thing I don't report back to the police anymore. Or my old friend Collier would have you locked up. And throw away the key."

"You did it long enough. You were smart to call it to a halt, though I know you hated losing the coins. But that last year, you only passed on lies, did you not?"

"More or less, and he began to figure me out. When I told him I'd done it enough, he didn't object. However, your ravings about England a moment ago are too good not to use. I think I'll get in touch with my man again."

"I assume you're joking." Gallatin has an uncertain smile.

"You'll know by sundown," says Thomas, deadpan. "When they come to take you to the Bastille." The face allows a slow smile. "If I were really going to betray you, do you think I'd tell you in advance?"

Gallatin acknowledges with his face that's likely true. He halts his walking pace and reaches out to grasp Thomas's shoulder. "If you'd do some serious reading, my friend, you'd come round to my way of thinking, you would. England is the place for all rational men."

"They don't have vineyards over there, do they. Or cheese or bread."

"They do so. Well, cheese and bread at least. And they import our wines."

"But nothing else. They don't have anything we Frenchman eat. We have cuisine. Their food is only grub."

"Thomas! It's only across the water, for God's sake. Pardon the expression. For reason's sake."

Thomas doffs his hat to his friend as they begin to walk again. "Will you be able to move back to France if England isn't what you think it is?"

"It will be, mark my words. But, if God forbid, it were not how could anyone stop me? I could almost swim."

"Do you swim?"

"No, but I could hire a boat."

Thomas shrugs. He's never left France. He has no idea if it's easy or difficult to go from one kingdom to another or for that matter, from one loyalty to another. Can it be as simple as changing shoes, or simpler still, changing shirts? Thomas takes a breath. He keeps that question to himself.

"Anyway," says Jean Gallatin, "It's time I put my ass where my mouth is."

Thomas winces. Gallatin does the same an instant later. "Sorry," the bookseller says. "It's time to practice what I preach."

"You'll sell the bookshop?"

Gallatin nods.

"But then how will you make a living? Over there, I mean. You don't *speak* English, do you?"

"No, but I read it. A lot. So how hard can it be to speak? The English speak it, after all. I'm the match of any of them."

Thomas supposes that's true enough. He remembers a teacher priest once telling the entire class that English was a little language. Little and with none of the complexity, beauty or subtlety of French. He suspects the priest was exaggerating but that there was more than a kernel of truth. Thomas imagines English is like the French that the peasants speak. It will have a small vocabulary, nothing polished and refined. Gallatin's right. Learning that little foreign language should not be too hard.

Once again Gallatin places a firm hand on his friend's shoulder. They come to a full stop. "You have to keep everything I've just told you in confidence. You know that, don't you, Thomas?"

"I do."

Thomas adds a firm nod to show just how well and deeply he understands. He appreciates that Gallatin has just made this conversation a confidence matter. There are not many things he likes more than having a secret, especially one as potentially dangerous as this one. That his best friend is leaning toward a kingdom other than the one in which he is living and in which he was born. They begin walking again, Gallatin visibly relieved and Thomas very pleased.

"There's more," says Gallatin. "I in fact have already found a position. It's not official yet, but it soon will be. A distinguished customer came in the shop a few weeks ago, and it seems I impressed him with my knowledge."

"If you do say so yourself."

"Yes, I do. Well, it turns out that he is an ambassador from Holland." Gallatin's face shines as if he were basking in warm summer sunshine though it is a chill November afternoon. "It seems he's been appointed to England. Yes. Well, he was looking for a suitable tutor for his children. Wants a Frenchman, of course. So right there and then, after we'd spoken about authors and books for half an hour, he asked me if I'd consider the post."

"And you said … ?"

"I said I'd think about it, but that was only for show. I decided the moment he asked me. I should be gone before the end of the year or not long after. Once he's settled in as the ambassador he will write to me and I'll be away."

"Well, congratulations, I guess." Thomas's words, however, sound like he's disappointed.

To the slap and tap of their shoes as they make their way along the cobbles Thomas urges his downcast mood to lift. He wants to let Gallatin know he's happy his friend is getting something he wants, even though he feels left out. No, it's more than that. It's that Gallatin is doing something Thomas has never once even considered. The bookseller is selling his occupation and starting over as something else in another land.

"That's great, Jean. I'm happy for you." Thomas's lips and eyes offer a reasonable facsimile of a smile.

"Thanks. Maybe you'll come and visit sometime. To London. See for yourself."

Thomas nods. "Sure, that would be … amusing."

"Amusing? Yes, I suppose it might. We'd be Londoners together. How about that?"

"No, how about this?" Thomas crooks his arms on high and tight upon his chest while his legs kick stiffly out from side to side.

Gallatin instantly does the same. For a full minute the two young Parisians forget all about their aches and pains. And about Gallatin's imminent move. Instead they strut down the street like marionettes.

"Londoners, we're Londoners." Thomas speaks through a grin, his arms beating the air and flailing about.

"Londoners!" shouts Gallatin, doing exactly the same.

When they tire of their prank and return their arms and legs to a normal walk, Gallatin is the first to speak: "And Madame? What about Madame?"

"What?" says Thomas through a happy uncomprehending smile. "What's that? Who's Madame?"

"Marguerite. Marguerite Salles, the widow. Your bride to be. Will she come along to London as well?"

Thomas's eyes close in recognition. He'd completely forgotten about Marguerite. The mirth of the moment disappears. "Oh yes. I'd forgotten I'm soon to be wed."

"Aha. Best you keep that to yourself."

"Yes, indeed. To myself."

—

The coupling ends as it began, as a passionless and tedious exchange. Each takes turns providing the required stimulus and response, but with no great result for either sprawled atop the bed. When it's finally over it's a relief to both. Neither has much to say. What communication there is comes with furtive glances and averted eyes. The wedding ceremony is only a day behind them and already it feels far, far away. Something elusive has begun to rear its head.

Marguerite wonders if the problem might be the bed. It's a four-poster with a bright yellow hanging overhead. It's only the second time she has had Thomas join her there, on the very same mattress she used to share with her late husband. On the other hand, the yellow hanging is new, so it's not exactly the same. The colour brightens the room considerably she thinks, especially as it's reflected in the mirror above the dresser across the way. It fills the room with a lovely glow. Yet if the bed *is* the problem, well then they'll have to move it out and bring in something new. She wants their life together to be what she imagined it would be.

Marguerite supposes Thomas might be a little put off to have to perform in the same bed as his predecessor, who was much richer and higher ranked than he. Truth be told, however, the first husband never did some of the things Thomas does to her, nor nearly half so well. Yet something's not right, just the same. And what if that something turns out not to be the bed? Marguerite turns onto her side.

Thomas too is puzzling over what went wrong. His soldier was almost limp when they began, not something that has happened before. Therefore, he decides, Marguerite has to be the source. Marguerite is a little older and heavier than he might prefer, with a few folds he'd rather she didn't have, but that's hardly a surprise. Is it that he's missing his visits to the stalls? It brought a variety, it did. But, no, his last visit was only four days ago. No, Thomas thinks it's more likely that his mood of disappointment has to do with the realization that his marriage to a well-off widow may not be all he needs. It's a definite advancement to be sure, but look at Gallatin, for god's sake. He changed kingdoms to get ahead. Now tied to Marguerite, Thomas can do no such thing.

Thomas rolls onto his back. He stares at the yellow hanging overhead. Its bright colour is an indictment of a glow he does not feel.

Luckily, thinks Thomas, Gallatin wasn't at the marriage ceremony. Safely in England, the former bookseller did not have to block his ears or look away when the priest made bride and groom repeat their vows and take part in the mass that followed. Gallatin would have smirked at the talk, the idea of a sacrament and how a man marrying a woman was akin to Christ and the Church. Of course, Thomas repeated the words the priest had him say. Why would he not? If such words help him get ahead, what's the harm in that? Marrying Marguerite makes good sense. About that, Gallatin always agreed. Nonetheless, while his head counts up the advantages, Mister Dangle – which is what Marguerite calls the thing with a mind of its own between his legs – is not inspired.

The newlyweds roll back toward each other. It's a half-hearted act. Each would prefer to get up and wipe off their sticky parts, but it's too soon for that. So each stays put. Marguerite speaks first. She pushes back from her husband and pulls the sheet up to cover herself up to her neck.

"Does this…" Marguerite makes a sweeping motion with her hands, "does it mean anything to you?"

She rolls her head to take in Thomas's reaction. He stares back as if she is some sort of puzzle. Marguerite squints at the blank expression on her husband's face.

"Making love with me, I mean. Is that how you see it too? As lovemaking? Or just as something to satisfy an urge? A duty with someone twice your age?"

Thomas gets up on an elbow. He looks at his bedmate and bride from above.

"Marguerite, it's a pleasure not a duty. And of course it means something."

Her furrowed brow tells him that what he's said is not enough.

"It's an expression of love. Between man and wife. It's what we are pleased to do. It pleases the senses and it's a sacrament to the Church."

The brow is smoothing out. Thomas thinks he can detect a hint of a smile.

"We do this to be close, as close as two can get." Thomas reaches over and pulls down the sheet that is covering his bride. His thumb and pointer finger want to tweak the closer of Marguerite's nipples. She bats the hand away and re-covers her chest with the sheet.

"Sometimes when you speak, Thomas, it sounds, I don't know, a little contrived."

Thomas lets his upper body come down to the flatness of the bed. He gives a loud exhale.

"No, Marguerite, I speak from the heart. But sometimes, sometimes, a man is not his normal self. He can be tired, I guess."

Marguerite's expression shifts. She allows that what her husband says might be true. Maybe men's little pistols can't always shoot.

"You need to tell me such things, my husband." Marguerite cups a hand to Thomas's groin. "Maybe I can help."

Thomas gently removes her hand and covers himself with a portion of the bed cover. "Maybe I need a nap?"

"It's my bed, but yes, of course, you do that."

Thomas keeps his eyes closed until Marguerite has left the room. Once she has gone, the door pulled softly shut, he takes in the *chinoiserie* clock on the mantle. He listens to its ticking. He sighs deeply and decides that maybe a nap is not what he needs after all. He throws back the cover and gets out of bed. As he dresses, he hears some lines.

Fruit to stem, so very bound
Fearing the flight
The waiting ground.
A heaviness, a weariness?
Yes
A love unripe.

Thomas doesn't much care for the verses. Then he allows a smile. Maybe they still deserve to be written down. His paper, ink and quill, however, are over in his own room, not here in Marguerite's. Since the insufferable Madame Dufour is coming for dinner in a couple of hours, he'd better record them while they are still in his head. Any conversation with dear cousin drives his muse far away.

—

"Entwined," Thomas says aloud.

He reaches out to touch one of the buildings along the Quai des Augustins as he goes by. He likes to see if the mortar between the stones if smooth or rough. He notices the glare from two men approaching in the opposite direction. They clearly don't like anyone talking to himself or touching walls.

"Sorry," says Thomas with a laugh, tipping his tricorn in their direction. They both look away. "But yes," Thomas mutters softly to himself, "the entwining is the best part."

For the past few minutes, as he weaves his way through the streets on the right bank of the city in the last light of the day, Thomas has been mulling over what exactly it is that keeps him going once a week to the prostitutes despite his recent marriage to Marguerite. He's decided that it's less the culminations, the little deaths as some would have it, than the tentative beginnings. No longer is Thomas merely about the in and out, over as fast as he can be and do. Now he wants the touch of limb and torso, the tentative explore and fondle, each time different. It's the expectation of unexpected nuances, of being with someone he's never met before, that keeps him going back for more. He gets enough ordinary sex with Marguerite. With unfamiliar women he gets what she can't give, the unknown.

It comes to him that he must soon write Gallatin back. In the last letter from London, Jean opined that England was way ahead of France in denying the existence of any god. Thomas doubts that this is in fact the case. Moreover, he does not like the topic at all. It makes him nervous because he half expects the sky to open up and lightning to strike him down. But he thinks he can have some fun with the subject of God in his own way. He will write to his friend telling him the best argument for God is the existence of women. Gallatin will widen his eyes at that. Yet Thomas is serious. How could there be such a wondrous creature without some kind of intervention from above? Thomas beams at the idea. Will Gallatin scoff or might he for once be forced to agree? Ah my, Thomas misses having Gallatin around for the stupid banter they used to have.

Thomas again runs a finger along a line of mortar that separates two courses of the nearest stone wall. He likes the way the hardened mix feels on his fingertips. It's both rough and smooth, and it reminds him of Vire. He would walk the streets in the early morning hours and touch masonry walls here and there. One particular morning comes back to him. Hot it was already. The air thick with moisture and nowhere for it to escape. Along one wall, the one that defined the west side of the Ursulines' if his memory serves, his nostrils were teased by a damp, rich perfume of blossoms unseen. It was a heavenly scent. The blossoms he imagined were a deep red. Their scent was coming from the other side of the stone wall, from the sisters' unseen world. He imagined that there was a stream of water running through the grounds. And a square of grass with nearby flowering shrubs. It struck him then as it strikes him now, that such unseen gardens and hidden scents are best. Those who give their lives over to an unseen god deserve to have pleasures that go to them alone and no one else.

Thomas blinks at the memory. He wonders why it comes to him now. What is the link? Oh yes, the wall. The tips of his fingers on rough mortar. The same sensation, then and now.

His thoughts stay with recollections of Vire. He recalls that as a boy, expectation was his abiding faith. So much lay in the future. The unknown could be anything, which made it the best. Grow up, move away, rise high, be something his father was not. The expectations were multiple. How he almost wishes he were back in that state, able to look expectantly ahead.

It occurs to him that it is much the same with the loins. Nothing seems to heighten pleasure so much as a longing not instantly satisfied. The wanting of what you do not have. He wonders if he should write to Gallatin about this. About the pleasures of delay. Like the chocolate warming in the pot before it swims upon the palate. Pastries stared at in windows but not yet put in the mouth. Hot loaves of bread resting on their peel. The glance exchanged by two first-time lovers about to go somewhere they've not been before. The brush of skin on skin, an accidental touch.

Thomas grins at the absurdity of the argument taking shape in his head. If what he has just said is true then would we not all be happier if we never acted on urges and desires? If instead of us giving in we left our pleasures always unfulfilled? The greatest pleasure would be a never-ending anticipation. Clearly, that will never happen, for the species insists on having what it wants. Still, Thomas concludes as he crosses over the Pont Neuf, it is better to draw things out, to delay then delay some more. He will demonstrate the theory, if only for himself. He will not go straight to the rooms where his new unknown pleasure waits. He will follow a more circuitous route, a long way round, which starts by strolling first along the Seine.

In the added minutes of peregrination Thomas's thoughts turn to his wife. He is fond of her, he admits, biting his lip. Moreover, he is pleased that the marriage brings him a definite advance in rank. Yet she does not stir up anticipation. No, alas, when he goes home each evening he does not look forward to seeing her there. Still, he respects the vow that he took. He now uses something to prove just how much he respects the union he has joined. Assurance caps they are called, though he prefers the word "safes." It's not so much making a trollop pregnant that he fears, but rather the blisters and sores that could later show up. It would be wrong, a failing on his part, a disloyalty of the lowest sort, for him to bring anything so vile back to his dear wife. So he makes a point to put on a safe just before it's time to dip and delve. The linen ones have some chemical imbued into them and he doesn't like them much. The smell is off-putting and the feel of the stiffened glove around his soldier not pleasant at all. So this evening he will try a different type. It's a little more expensive because it's made of animal intestine stretched fine and thin. An acquaintance told him it's like wearing a second skin. That sounds better. He is pleased to try it for the sake of Marguerite. It'll be as if the soldier has not been anywhere it shouldn't. Instead, uncovered, it'll be fresh and ready for her advances when they come. It would not do to disappoint her in bed. Most nights she likes a tumble before sleep.

Thomas glances toward the river. Two barges carrying stacks of firewood are slowly making their way toward the mooring point alongside where he is walking. In winter, the number of cords of wood that make their way into the city, from up and down river, is phenomenal. But then, there are a lot of cold rooms and shivering people the firewood strives to keep warm. Now that he's living in Marguerite's apartment Thomas doesn't give the cost of the wood even the slightest thought. It's one of the many ways in which his life has improved. He watches approvingly as the scrawny little man in charge of one of the barges makes an angry face. The man shouts and waves his pole menacingly. The other barge man yields the day. It's the little guy who first poles his cargo to the docking spot.

Thomas strides on, adjusting the black ribbon that keeps his hair tied in a queue. He's been thinking lately that maybe it's time to get a wig. In certain mirrors, in an unflattering light, it looks as if his boyish brown hair is starting to thin and lose its sheen. Sooner or later it happens to every man, but he was surprised to see it happen to him and so soon. At least it's not the same as what happened to his father, whose hair thinned on top in an oval shape like he was tonsured. Which was quite a laugh considering his father's views on the idleness of the religious orders. Well, Thomas won't be caught with a thinning hairline as he gets older. With his marriage and his position in the magistrate's office, he has to look the part. It is only correct for him to start wearing a wig, and one that suits the level he is now at. He'll not be taken for a fop or a sword-dragger, with a *perruque* overdone. He'll ask Marguerite when he gets home this evening as to which type and colour he should choose. She will have good advice. She's been in these circles far longer than he.

There's a shout from behind, a yell from the river. Thomas turns. He sees that the scrawny little fellow on the firewood barge has knocked the other bargeman he was yelling at into the water with his pole. The victor is waving the instrument of his triumph above his head. The loser, a foul-mouthed lout, is splashing about in the Seine.

"Well done," shouts Thomas toward the river. His encouragement brings a victor's wave and an upraised chin. "Enough of that," mutters Thomas under his breath. His delay has gone on long enough. The temperature is dipping. He now wants to be inside where it'll be warm, and someone will make him feel right.

Thomas turns the corner onto rue des Augustins. It will take him over to the rue Saint-André des Arts which leads down to the rue de l'Eperon and finally on to the rue du Paon. That's the street where his evening's expectation awaits. He picks up his pace.

He's surprised to see a new bookshop up ahead on the rue des Augustins. He doesn't remember one there at all. Was it not a tailor's shop a month before? Funny, he thinks, there are so many books for sale all over Paris. It's as if all the world wants to read. Yet if that's how it is, how come authors find it so hard to make a living from what they write? Thomas blows out a stream of breath. Yes, he would prefer if he could to make a living from his imagination and his quill, but unpublished manuscripts don't pay any bills. Thank goodness he now has Marguerite. As well as his clerk's toil for the magistrate, short and bushy-browed Sieur de Karsozy. But how much better if someday he were independent of all that.

Thomas strides on. There is a rise in his groin. The expectation of an evening of pleasure is making its presence felt.

On the rue Saint-André des Arts Thomas's thoughts turn to Jean Gallatin, who has crossed over the Manche and is now in London. The former bookseller has already sent Thomas two enthusiastic letters. He is working as a tutor to the Dutch ambassador's children, children who are not too bratty, it seems. He doesn't mention a new woman, but then Gallatin is always so discreet. Thomas wonders if his friend will again search for an older woman like he had in the late Marie.

What Gallatin does tell him is that in the evenings he gets about with London's scribbling crowd, much like he did in Paris with Thomas and the rest. Every so often he runs into Voltaire in this or that café. The wit has been in England since he insulted the Rohan family and chose exile over incarceration in the Bastille. A wise choice that. Though Voltaire was never the least bit interested in Gallatin when they were both in Paris, Gallatin reports the fellow is friendly to him now. Both being Frenchmen out of France has given them a fleeting bond. Gallatin writes that Voltaire's English is very good, much better than his own. Though Jean says his English is coming along.

In the second letter Gallatin wrote that he's mostly chumming around with a young writer called Henry Fielding. They went downriver together to a place called Greenwich and had a splendid time. They climbed its hill and tried to get into the observatory but were denied. Fielding told the sentry that he knew where to look in the sky to find a seventh planet if only the soldier would let them in. The guard was not amused, seeing as how the noonday sun was right overhead. Gallatin and his friend then spent the afternoon eating bread, meat and cheese and drinking far too much in an establishment at the water's edge. On the return trip they both felt the effects of too much alcohol imbibed. As the boat bucked and tossed, Fielding was the first to retch his lunch over the side of the boat. Gallatin did the same soon after. Thomas wishes he'd been there. He misses Gallatin. He is sure that he'd like this Fielding as well.

Of most interest to Thomas in the letters received so far is the news that Gallatin has spoken with the great Daniel Defoe. Yes, the writer of the marvellous Crusoe tale. Defoe is apparently a crusty type, as well he might be given his accomplishments and great age. Nonetheless, he agreed to have a glass of wine with Gallatin, provided the latter did the buying. Jean also reports that he has seen at a distance Isaac Newton. The old man was holding himself erect without a cane walking around some park or other. "At least," Thomas mumbles to himself, "he does not claim to have seen or met his dead hero John Locke." Thomas allows himself a grin.

Thomas comes onto the rue du Paon, the street that is his destination. He pulls out the folded over piece of paper he was given. He reads it one last time. It is the house on the corner, the one with the turret covered in slates. There, in that very room with the turret is a woman he is looking forward to meeting. She plies her trade on her own without a handler, no pimp or abbess at all. Odd to be sure, as is the neighbourhood in which she does her business. This part of Paris is not one Thomas associates with this sort of thing.

Thomas reaches out for the handle at the street-level door. The sheet in his pocket says to climb up two flights then knock on the second door on the right, the one with fading blue paint. His arrival is anticipated. He is impressed with the quality of the stairwell. This building is as respectable inside as it looks to be on the outside. Pity, he thinks, he didn't know about such discreet places before. He's sorely tired of the dreary places he's had to go in the stalls. Well, "had to" might be a bit strong. Nobody was forcing him.

Two knocks delivered, Thomas waits to hear something from the other side of the door. He is excited. It's true what he was thinking before: anticipation is everything. How much better this evening is going to be than when he was first in Paris. Slipping off into a back room of a cabaret or lowering his breeches in a stall that reeked and resounded with the moans and shouts of others in their own nearby stalls. Oh, what we do for sex.

Out of the blue Thomas recalls Gallatin once telling him that the reason the Church makes people abstain from eating meat each week and for all of Lent is because those animals fornicate. That's right, they fuck. Fish, on the other hand, they do not. The male fish spill their seed on eggs laid by the females so there is never any rutting involved. Gallatin assured Thomas with upraised hand that that was the Church's reasoning for the meatless days.

Thomas hears a scuffle of feet on the other side of the door. He takes a shallow breath. The door swings open. He sees a woman dressed in a watery-looking silk dress, vertical shades of delicate blue and white. Her gaze is averted. She does not look directly at him. It's as if she's being modest. Thomas likes that touch. He also likes that she looks like a real lady with a lace cap atop her well-coiffed hair. Thomas inhales deeply. He's made the right decision coming here. This evening's adventure is with no trollop. She pushes the door a little wider, wide enough for him to step right inside her rooms. It is only then, when she has given the door a shove behind him and they are standing face to face, when she turns her eyes for the first time fully on her client, that there comes the moment of recognition. She sees it first. An instant later he sees it too. There are two gasps.

"Hé … lène, Hé … lène," Thomas stutters. He shakes his head. "Hélène?"

Hélène it is, and she's as shocked as Thomas. This is the room where she lives and where she receives her clients. But this is the first time a client has been someone she knows from her life before she started doing what she now does.

"What?" says Thomas before his confusion gives way to anger. "Why?"

"Shit," is all Hélène replies. She reaches out and pulls Thomas by the hand over to the other side of the room, away from the door where anyone walking by might hear a scene. She sits him down on the dark blue divan. They spend the next few minutes catching up. He begins by asking about Voltaire. She replies that the skinny imp left her for another woman a couple of years ago. No, she corrects herself and says in an artificially articulated voice: "It is time for me to think about my advancement. It is time for me to move on. It will be for the best." She recites it like she might be on a stage, nose lifted up. She finishes by saying she's heard that Voltaire has gone to England. Thomas nods that it is so.

"Well, after we parted it wasn't easy to make ends meet. So I took a job in a cabaret. It was just like I was back in my uncle's place in Évreux. So many men tugged at my skirt and ogled my tits that, well, one evening I decided to give them what they wanted."

Thomas makes a face of disapproval. Hélène scowls. She reaches out to grab him by the chin.

"And you, why are you here, if not to do me the same?"

Thomas's eyes admit that is true. She releases his chin.

So, Hélène continues, she started to "see company," but only on her terms. She became a courtesan. No, not a whore. She runs her own business with no one else taking a share. She demands enough so that she only has to see about one visitor a day. She takes days of abstinence off. She observes the Church's rule about that. It's been enough to buy herself some finery. She points at her dress and the rest of her ensemble. Thomas nods that she is indeed dressed very well.

As for the encounters, they happen where and when she selects, of late in this very place. The more she charges the clients the more they like it and the greater the demand. It allows her to move in the lower circles of high society. Hélène waves a hand in the direction of the turret that overlooks the busy street below. "Not bad, don't you agree?"

Thomas glances around the room where they are seated and what he can glimpse of what lies beyond. It's true: Hélène's rooms are well appointed. Maybe not as expensively furnished as the large apartment he shares with Marguerite, but much better than what he had when he was living on his own. The candles are beeswax, the chairs and divan are upholstered with the same dark blue fabric, suggesting Hélène bought them together as a set. Thomas brings his gaze back to the woman he has come to … well, the idea was to ride. He has something to tell her about himself.

"I'm married."

Hélène's eyebrows arch. "Well now."

"A widow. She's rather well set up." Thomas cannot help but give a self-satisfied smile.

"I see." Hélène leans away. "And yet...." She unfurls the fingers of one hand, gesturing around the room. "And yet, here you are, not with your widow, your well-set-up wife, but with me."

She recoils the fingers of her open hand and brings the formed fist back to press against her chest. Her raised eyebrows ask Thomas to explain.

"Ah, well." Thomas shrugs his shoulders and pouts. "She's much older and she's...." His voice trails off.

"Ah." Hélène's voice is low, not quite a whisper but not much more. Most of her clients have stories like Thomas's. Their wives or women friends are too old or too young, too skinny or too fat, too this or too that. She never asks like she has with Thomas, but sooner or later they tell her why they are there. Why they have come with a bulge in their pants, looking for an hour's escape. An escape from something they cannot face or wish briefly to forget. Too bad, Hélène often thinks with narrowing eyes as she hears variations of such tales, too bad that their wives can't do the same thing for themselves. Such is the world as it is, a world made by men for men, with the women doing the best they can in between the cracks. Or *with* their cracks, she thinks with a little smile.

"What's that about," asks Thomas, "that tiny smile?"

Hélène answers with a shake of her head then stands. She leaves Thomas seated on the divan and walks over into the circular space that is the inside of the turret. She puts her hands on the back of the big wooden chair she keeps there. From time to time, when she is by herself and feels like it, she sits in the chair. She likes having an undetected regard on the city as it moves past, from one window to another of the turret. Right now there is not much daylight left in the sky. The hanging lamps are just starting to be lit and raised back up with the ropes. In the dusky glow she can make out an old man pushing a squeaking cart filled with barrels. Coming the other way are three young men, arm in arm and already wobbly drunk. They are singing a tavern song.

Hélène turns round, not to face Thomas but at least more or less look his way. She wishes she did not know him from an earlier time and place. Though he's just another man with a need, he's one she's been with a few times before; it's just not as easy as with a stranger. She and Thomas were both younger at the time and it was just for fun. Now she doesn't do that for free. So Thomas has to pay and she must insist he does so before she gives him what he came to get.

Thomas remains seated on the divan. He is unaware of it, but his hands are clasped like he's a lad in parish school. It makes him look younger than he really is. Like he doesn't know what is going to come next. He studies her in profile where she stands, from the lace-capped dark hair down her shoulders to where her waist narrows just before her hips. The gaze continues down all the way to the tiny greyish blue leather shoes. He cannot explain it, but he likes what he sees very much. He wonders why. Why are we drawn to those to whom we are drawn? Whatever it is, he wants to be with Hélène, in the same way as when they were young. But this is awkward. It would be easier if they didn't know each other at all.

Hélène shifts her gaze to focus on her client. The sight of Thomas seated on her divan, hands clasped as if in prayer, makes her laugh.

"Going to church? To little boy's school?" There's a broad smile on her face.

Thomas looks to his lap, where his hands are clasped. He sees what she finds so funny and unclasps his hands. He stands and strides toward her. He grasps her by the elbows.

"So," she says.

"So," he replies.

"Just you and me."

"Exactly."

"Well, not exactly. You have to pay me now."

Thomas shakes his head. Hélène is not sure what it means. Does she have to spell it out? "You … have … to pay," she insists, shaking off his grasp. "It's how I…"

"Not that. It vexed me to see you with Voltaire that time at Le Procope. You should not have run away from me before that. It was our very first morning in the city and I had to find work. You didn't give it a chance. You just took off."

"Enough," says Hélène, arms extended. "I know."

She walks back into the turret and grabs hold of the back of the wooden chair. She sees no point in arguing over what's past. What's done is done; it's good and gone. Maybe, she thinks, maybe she should just ask Thomas to go. An evening's lost wage, but that's likely better than dealing with a sulking man.

Thomas grimaces at Hélène. Fine, he concludes in a hurry, maybe this whole visit was a mistake. If he'd known it was her, would he still have come? It's hard to say.... No, of course, he would.

"Look," he says, moving closer to where she stands, holding onto the chair and staring out into the darkening night, "I know there's no going back."

"That's right."

"So?"

"So."

"So maybe I should go?"

"Maybe you should."

Thomas turns and takes the first step toward the door. But then he hears Hélène exhale, as deep a sigh as he has ever heard. It makes him turn around. There's a look on her face that he's never seen before. It's the face of someone fighting disappointment yet who is clearly on the edge of tears.

"What is it? What's wrong, Hélène?"

"Wrong?" Hélène's voice is sharp. The tone is angry but the eyes have a skim of wet. "What's wrong?" she repeats.

Her hands flash in the air, like she's chopping something only she can see.

Thomas bites his lower lip and stays where he is. He crosses his arms on his chest. He has no idea what to do next. Is she angry or sad? Whatever is it she wants him to do?

The two of them stand in silence, the eyes of one locked onto the eyes of the other.

All at once, in a burst of hurried shallow breaths, it is Hélène who gives way. Her shoulders slump and her eyelids close over eyes gone so very hot. They shut out a client of a man and the world of purchased lust to which he belongs. A single tear issues from the corner of one eye. It makes its way down her cheek beside her nose. Thomas closes the distance. He takes her hands off her hips where they seem frozen and he holds them in his own.

"I don't feel good," she says.

"I see that. Do you want me to go or to stay?"

Hélène recoils in surprise. Her head swivels left and right until she catches herself and nods that yes he should.

"Which? Stay or go?"

Her face pinches and scrunches. Full watery eyes are on the brink. Thomas encircles Hélène in his arms. He presses hard upon her back. That action brings from Hélène a sob unleashed.

"Not what I wanted," Hélène gasps into Thomas's shoulder.

"I know. I know."

Hélène buries her wet salty face, tears streaming hot, into his throat and neck.

VI

Conundrum

Paris

March–April 1727

The solution does not come to Thomas all at once. It takes shape in pieces and over time.

That night, on the walk back to Marguerite's spacious suite of rooms, after he took Hélène in his arms and tried to comfort her, Thomas could not see that there was anything he could realistically do to help Hélène out of her predicament. Truth be told, or so he said to himself more than once on the walk, poor Hélène has made her bed and had to lie in it. He didn't say that or anything like it while he was still at her place. Instead, before he set off into the night he held her shoulders firm and tight and bestowed a few parting words of encouragement and a chaste kiss on her troubled brow.

Over the next few days though, Hélène's lot in life, and of course her pretty face and form, were never far from his thoughts. He wanted to help, he really did. Yes, he'd like to have her as his lover again, that too. He really would. But he couldn't see how he could rescue Hélène from her plight. He decided that he would not go back to see her until he had something helpful to say. How long that might take he had no idea.

From time to time, when he wakes up in the middle of the night or when he is walking along the Seine on his way to or from the magistrate's office, he feels like there is some looming possibility of a solution lurking just out of mind. Such a solution to the conundrum, however, does not stand and shout, "Over here, I'm over here." That's not the way solutions work.

It is two weeks later and Thomas and Marguerite are at table. They are both pleased with his new wig. It's stylish and close cropped. Of human hair, of course, with tight curls on the sides and the whole thing dusted with the whitest of white powder and smelling of lavender. A regrettable side effect is that sometimes the powder floats off when he tips his head forward, down into his food. So Thomas tries to keep himself especially erect. As he does so, he learns a secret of the higher born, that a rigid posture is not just about show; there's the practical side of not snowing too much on one's food.

It is while Thomas is at table on this evening that the first inkling of a solution to Hélène's predicament will come. He and Marguerite are making their way slowly but steadily through the usual stages of their meal. The good servant Simone, hunch-backed as ever, is bringing in and taking away the dishes as the evening progresses. It is a leisurely repast, which Thomas has grown used to since his marriage to Marguerite. It is a pace he did not follow when he lived alone. Generally, the meals at Marguerite's are good, though this evening's meal is not one of the better ones. The potage was nearly cold when Simone brought it in and essentially tasteless when sampled. The salad was the usual awful wintry offering. The duck was far too greasy and came with a sauce that was more than a little burned. As a result, it could not hide the fact that the duck and other meats were stringy and tough. The cook is to blame of course, but he's only filling in while Sébastien is away. Poor Sébastien's mother died in Cahors and Marguerite granted him a week away. In his absence, Marguerite has given Charles, the lackey, the opportunity he asked for to step in as chef. It hasn't been a good experiment so far. All this is to say that Marguerite and Thomas are hoping that the dessert will perhaps make them forget what has come before. They've been told that it is to be Marguerite's favourite: a fluffy batter-beaten Savoy cake accompanied by a raspberry *coulis*.

Thomas and Marguerite look at each other expectantly as little Simone brings in the sweet culmination to the meal. The servant is in her fifties and originally from Le Puy. She is adept at making and repairing lace. Simone puts the cake down and cuts two ample slices. Next she places in front of each of them their respective dishes containing the *coulis*, as well as for each a tiny silver spoon. How much each wants of the raspberry topping is up to them. You wouldn't know it from the non-committal expressions on their stolid faces but Thomas and Marguerite can hardly wait to spread the *coulis* and sample the cake. Nonetheless, it would be unseemly to start right in.

"Did I tell you, Thomas, that we've received an invitation?"

"What's that?" Thomas looks up from what he's playing at while he waits. He's killing time manipulating his dessert spoon round and round with his fingers and his thumb.

"My cousin, the Madame Dufour," says Marguerite carefully, wondering if she will catch Thomas making a sour face. "Yes, well, I know you two … let's just say you're not as fond of each other as I'd like."

Thomas says not a thing nor does his face give any more away. He pretends to be immobile in a mask. He is his old friend Collier at his best. He may not see the pale-faced fellow any more, but he remembers a thing or two about keeping a neutral expression intact. Thomas puts down the tiny silver spoon he has been twirling.

"Well," Marguerite continues, "my dear cousin will be in the country, in Brittany of course, somewhere near Vitré. It's a small château of her late husband's. Le Mesnil it's called, I believe. Sounds charming, does it not? I've never seen it in person. He used to take her there every spring for a couple of months and now it falls to her to go alone. It seems Monsieur won't be making the trip this time."

Marguerite makes big eyes, hoping to encourage Thomas to laugh at the joke. Thomas does not quite laugh, but he does contribute a sputtering noise to show that he understands the humour in what she's said.

"She'll be there a couple of months seeing to this and that. Whatever that is in a country life. I wouldn't be surprised if cousin tries to sell the thing. Anyway, she insists that we come visit her so she's not completely cut off from the world. I've not answered her yet, not with certainty, but it is an obligation I have. That we have."

Thomas purses his lips.

"Who knows, it might be tolerable. A few days in the country. Brittany. What do you think? Shall we have an idyll at our cousin's Le Mesnil?"

Thomas knows better than to say no. So he doesn't say a thing. Instead, he inclines his head twice in Marguerite's direction slowly and decidedly. It's a wordless way of communicating that he has picked up from the great magistrate he works for as senior clerk. He's curious if it will work with his wife. It's to indicate without saying the words that yes he's willing to go to the annoying cousin's château somewhere sometime, as yet another of the growing list of things that he does for his wife. He occasionally wonders if she notices or simply takes him and his acquiescence for granted.

"It won't be too bad," Marguerite replies to the vague nods coming from her husband, "you'll see."

"Of course," comments Thomas at last. "A few days, I suppose. We should, should we not, after all." He points his small silver spoon at the plate with Savoy cake in front of him. "Shall we sample?"

"Here's hoping the end to the meal is better than all that came before." Marguerite dips her spoon into the dish with the raspberry *coulis* and drizzles it across her cake.

Thomas does the same, only in Thomas's case he finds his thoughts are suddenly elsewhere. As he spoons the tart sauce onto his slice of cake he thinks of the few whole raspberries that are floating in the pale red *coulis*. The berries must come from some icehouse where they've been kept chilled, no frozen, since last summer. Completely out of the blue, an image of naked Hélène and her raspberry-like nipples flashes through his mind. It sends a message to his loins. "Might come up with something," Thomas mumbles to the table aloud.

"Come up with something? Whatever do you mean?" Marguerite lowers to her plate the small square of cake she is holding aloft, inches from her mouth. Her jaw lowers as she stares at her husband. Then she notices what he has done with his plate. It's covered in a wet blanket of the *coulis*. "What are you doing?"

Thomas glances down at his plate. Too late he sees that he has spooned far too much coulis upon his piece of cake. It's a dessert gone completely red and there's a line of drizzle across the linen tablecloth connecting his plate to the dish with the sauce. He takes his napkin and covers the red line he's made across the tabletop.

"My heavens," says a stunned Marguerite. "I was asking you something. You said, 'something might come up' … oh never mind." Marguerite blinks away her husband's absent-minded mess on the other side of the table. She brings the fork to her mouth and finally tastes the dessert.

Thomas follows suit, and no sooner does he have the mix of sweet and tart running across his palate than his thoughts again swing back to Hélène. The Hélène he recalls is not the courtesan of two weeks ago but the younger girl he knew in the roadside inn in Évreux. He pictures the two of them standing naked back to back upon the mattress in the storage room, their buttocks pressing together, each with their arms backward around the other's belly.

"Ass to ass is holy backwards kiss," he'd bellowed like a preacher in a pulpit.

"Shush, that's blasphemy," Hélène whispered over her shoulder.

"Who cares?" Thomas said as he spun round. She did the same and facing they lavished kisses on each other's mouths and chests while their hands probed and tugged.

Marguerite glances over to see if Thomas is enjoying the cake, or if he perhaps finds it a tad too tart, which is her assessment. She is surprised by the faraway, delighted expression on her husband's face.

"Something amusing?" She squints at her husband, suspicious about what's going on. She can't believe a slice of Savoy cake and *coulis* can all by itself bring a look of satisfaction like that. It has to be a recollection. And her guess is that it's of a woman who is not herself.

Thomas stops licking his lips. He finds a focus on his wife. He wonders how much she can guess of what's been running through his mind. He brings a hand to his lap to settle what is rising up.

"The raspberries, good are they not?"

"Hmm," says Marguerite, discerning a lie, but one she leaves alone. "They're all right."

"It's like having summer all over again."

"So you say."

One of the candles in the candelabra in the centre of the table starts to gutter. Thomas glances toward Marguerite. She is staring downward, glumly at what she has decided is a beginner's mushy attempt at cake. Her husband's gaze goes back to the candle that sputters and spumes. When the flame extinguishes itself, the first piece of the puzzle about Hélène's situation takes shape in Thomas's mind. He blinks at the simplicity of the idea. Have my cake and eat it too, he thinks. He silently mouths the expression a second time, ensuring his lips barely move.

The sound of footsteps on his right makes Thomas glance round. It's little Simone padding quietly back into the room. She stands quietly, waiting to clear away the plates when the dessert is finished. That's when for Thomas the next puzzle piece falls into place.

—

When Hélène hears Thomas explain his plan she agrees to go along. She's hardly enthusiastic about it because it sounds more like a possibility of a possibility. But it's better than nothing at all. As she waits for Thomas to implement his end of the arrangement Hélène continues to ply her trade. She has to make ends meet. Still, she agrees to get together with Thomas once a week, as long as the rendezvous does not involve sex and is not in her rooms. She has to keep separate the different parts of her life. Except when it's too chilly and damp, Hélène prefers the meetings to be outdoors. She especially likes the Place Dauphine. She likes the enclosing square and knowing that the reassuring statue of Henri IV is not far away. When the weather does not cooperate, however, they meet in the entrance to a church. Saint-Julien-le-Pauvre is one they've used twice. Thomas suggested it and seemed to think it amusing, though he never tells Hélène why that might be.

Wherever they meet, the rendezvous is brief, business-like even. Thomas gives updates on what he has done so far and that's about it. Hélène rarely has much to say, though she does occasionally nod her approval at this and that. Once in a while she suggests something specific he might want to consider to improve on his plan. A few times Thomas pleads his case that maybe she should begin to show him her favours, to remind both of them of the affection ahead that they will eventually share.

"You know," says Thomas to begin one meeting in the Place Dauphine, "this place, where we meet, it's called the sex of Paris?"

Hélène gives a quizzical look. "Why's that?"

"Its triangular shape."

"I see," she says. And then shakes her head. "No."

"Not even just to stroke the kitty?"

"Especially not the kitty. Not until … not until things are done."

A week later, both of them soaked from the pounding rain and standing just inside Saint-Julien-le Pauvre, Thomas whispers in her ear. "I can't see how a little something would be so wrong. I can be quick."

"Look," Hélène whispers back, "there will be no slippery dip until I say. You just do your part, all right?"

Thomas's eyelashes flutter. He thinks "slippery dip" is charming in a dirty sort of way.

"For this scheme to work," she continues with raised eyebrows and a quick darting look, "we need a rabula rasa."

Thomas hears "rabble rouser," which makes no sense. "What's that?"

"It's Latin for clean slate."

"Oh, *tabula rasa*."

"That's what I said."

Thomas is about to say something, but Hélène warns him with her eyes to leave it at that.

"I wasn't always wrestling naked with Voltaire. We talked ideas as well. I know who John Locke is, for instance. Besides being a dead Englishman. He wrote about a social contract in which we governed give our consent."

Thomas gives Hélène a smile of genuine surprise. "Well said," is all he can reply. The woman is a marvel. He cannot wait for them to be together again, and apparently for more than just sex.

The plan is this: Thomas is taking and hiding a piece of jewellery from Marguerite once a week for as long as it takes. When Marguerite notices that they're "missing" – she hasn't yet – the objects will turn up in the small *cabinet* where the hunch-backed servant Simone sleeps. Simone will be fired and Hélène hired in her place. Its simplicity is its beauty, Thomas tells Hélène each time they meet, earnestness in his eyes. He does not mention that his inspiration for the little plot was to have cake and eat it too. There's no need to tell Hélène that she is his cake.

Whether it might be right or wrong to dismiss Simone, a loyal servant to Marguerite for eleven years going on twelve, is not something Thomas and Hélène speak of at all. Thomas does quite like Simone, and not just for her deference and her noticeably clean hands. They occasionally exchange small jokes, or smiles at the least. So he regrets that the hunched-over servant has to go. However, there is an axiom he's heard that applies in this case. For someone to rise, someone else has to fall. It just happens in this case that the someone is little Simone.

—

Thomas carries out the small thefts the plan calls for – a necklace of silver with precious stones of pale blue and dark green, a ring with onyx, a cameo miniature, and a pearl-coloured comb – while Marguerite is out of the house or at least preoccupied in a faraway room. None of the objects lies out in the open, which would mean they might be too quickly missed. Each has its own little box or velvet sack. Along with dozens of other jewels Marguerite possesses, they normally reside deep within the inlaid wooden box atop the dressing table near her mirror. Only once was a swift removal by Thomas nearly caught soon after it happened. As luck would have it, it was the servant Simone herself.

She was coming down the hall with an armload of linen when she saw Thomas coming out of Madame's room.

"Monsieur, can I help you?" she asked with her head tilted to one side. She was clearly puzzled as to why the master would be exiting his wife's room in the middle of the day.

"No, why?" he replied in a hurry, avoiding her curious gaze.

He turned and hurried the other way, and knew instantly that such flight was a mistake. It was an admission of guilt. Yet at the time he felt a surge of heat in his face and chest and felt compelled to turn and walk quickly away.

But there was no harm done, as far as Thomas knows. Simone did not mention the incident to Marguerite. He still has all the taken objects. They are hidden in the bottom of his own trunk, waiting for the moment for implementation – the transfer to Simone's room – to be just right.

—

"Thomas?" says Marguerite, knocking on the door to his bedroom. "Thomas?"

Thomas opens the door wide.

"Yes, my love."

He bows like a courtier just for fun. He's been busy for an hour or more, composing the opening paragraphs of an essay on the need to balance ambition with discretion and tact. He thinks it's going well. When he is satisfied with it he will send it off to Gallatin to ask for his comments.

There is no smile on Marguerite's long face. Her expression is grim, like she may have just learned about the death of a relation or close friend. Or, it suddenly hits Thomas with a sinking feeling, has she discovered that she's missing certain objects from her room? Oh pray to God not. He has not yet hidden them where they are supposed to turn up.

"Come with me, husband, will you please?"

"Of course."

His voice is as shaky as he feels. Has he ruined his own plan by leaving it too late? They are off, striding toward Marguerite's room. Thomas feels his heart race on ahead of the rest of his body, thumping like a drum.

"There."

Marguerite waves a hand at the small dressing table near her mirror. It is the table that holds the inlaid wooden box that contains her jewellery, combs and hairbrushes, makeup, rouges and wig powder. It is the table Thomas has gone to four times already. He makes his face as impassive as he can.

"What is it?" he asks softly.

"There." Marguerite points as if the air coming from her finger were making a visible line to some object. "Can you not see it?"

"Something, something is missing?"

"Missing? Can't you see? The droppings. Right there." She grabs Thomas by the elbow and bends him over so he can study the floor beneath the dressing table. He sees what looks like grains of rice, only smaller and darker. "We have mice," Marguerite announces.

"Mice? Oh mice. Yes, I see."

"You see? Honestly. It's up to you to find someone to look after this. And today." And with that, Marguerite turns and is gone.

"Take care of it I will," mutters Thomas. His lungs send out a gush of air. Yes, take care of it he will. He happens to know an exterminator. Well, he doesn't know him personally, but he's heard a clerk in the magistrate's office speak of just such a man. He'll ask for his name and address.

Thomas glances back at Marguerite's small table as he heads for the door. He looks up to the ceiling and the unseen sky beyond. He understands that what has just happened is a warning, a sign. He's running out of time. He cannot delay any longer. If the plan is going to work, the stolen objects must be noticed as lost and then found hiding in Simone's room.

—

Hélène scrunches her cheeks. She's practicing. Practicing in front of Thomas as they sit in the Place Dauphine how her face should look when she knocks on Marguerite's door the next morning. What she is to say and how she is to look saying it are important, the most important parts of the plan. She has to win over Marguerite with her smile and her pretty face. She must seem to be a trusted servant heaven sent.

Hélène laughs to hear Thomas put it that way. He waves away her mirth and continues the preparation. She is to be polite. They will exchange meaningless pleasantries. Hélène has to smile sweetly no matter what is said. Marguerite will tell her that she has no opening for any position in her household. "That is understandable," Thomas instructs Hélène to reply. And then to say: "Nonetheless, here is a letter of reference just in case the situation should change." The letter is Thomas's handiwork, written in what he judges to be a woman's meticulous handwriting and elegantly phrased point of view. The letter is from an imaginary former employer of Hélène's, a Madame Tyrell. Choosing the name brought Thomas a smile. In any case, the fictitious Madame Tyrell has written a glowing reference letter for Hélène. Hélène is to hand that letter over, curtsey, give another sweet smile and be gone. "From that seed," Thomas intones like he's saying something profound, "a future life will grow."

Hélène rolls her eyes. She gets up from the bench. "Maybe you're missing your calling," she says to Thomas. "Maybe you should be a preacher." She thinks again. "Or off writing plays."

Thomas says nothing. He looks away and exhales a long breath.

Hélène walks away from him, strolling around the square.

"Tomorrow then?" says Thomas, approaching Hélène as she stands motionless staring at a line of trees. He leans forward and gives his soon-to-be secret servant lover a kiss on the cheek.

"Tomorrow it is."

—

"No," says Thomas, his face filling with mock shock. He has to make sure he hides his relief. "No. Are you sure?"

"I am, Thomas, I am. I checked and re-checked."

Marguerite's cheeks are flushed to near purple and red. The eyes are astir, flashing this way and that. The voice is hurt and confused.

"They're nowhere to be found. My comb, the miniature and a ring."

"Nothing else?"

He's wondering about the necklace, which he also removed. This morning, when Simone was busy in the kitchen with a chore, he placed all four items beneath the ribbons in the wicker basket that sits on the shelf in the servant's tiny room.

"What do you mean nothing else? That's enough surely. My ring, my comb and the miniature. They're gone." Marguerite stares at her husband, eyes demanding an answer.

In a few months' time, at her cousin's château near Vitré, staring into a crackling fire, Marguerite will recall Thomas saying "nothing else?" That recollection will then cause Thomas some pain. In the heat of this moment, however, Marguerite makes no more of Thomas's slip of the tongue.

"Of course it's enough," says Thomas. "It's terrible."

Thomas pauses. He leans back to look more closely at his wife. She is even more upset than he imagined she would be. There's a vein protruding blue on her forehead and another pulsing violet on her neck. He's not noticed either before. He doesn't want her to have a chest attack, clutching at a pain that could kill her dead. Still, he holds off for just another moment. The vague incriminating accusation of Simone, it has to wait just a little longer.

"Let me help you. What do you think we should do? There are so many places to look. You've checked your room?"

"Of course I've checked my room."

"There's the salon, the cabinet, the kitchen. Do you," he hesitates a beat, "I mean do you think we should perhaps check the servants as well?"

Marguerite tilts her head his way, the eyes narrowing.

"Search their quarters, I mean," he explains. "One hears about this sort of thing. It's the servants after all who have access to all of our things" Thomas leaves it at that. He's said enough.

"I suppose," says Marguerite.

The two words are said low, so the implicated servants of her household will not hear. All of a sudden her eyes are scanning the hall where she and Thomas are walking. She looks as well to the doors and doorways beyond. Thomas does not know if the scan is because of what he's suggested or some doubt she has about him saying it. Marguerite's gaze comes back to her husband. She's shaking her head.

"I can't believe it, I can't. Simone has been with me forever. It can't be her, it can't. Sébastien is still away. And Charles is a terrible cook but other than that he's loyal. Besides, he has no reason to ever go in my room. And as for dim-witted Marie-Angélique, why she …"

"Of course."

Thomas does not see the point in all the talk, running through the staff one by one. His hand makes contact with Marguerite's wrist. He is keeping his eyes as calm as he can. He is breathing like there's nothing wrong.

"A formality, that's all. Once we've checked the servants' quarters then we'll know for sure. Unless you want to call in the authorities right now? It might be best if we handle this ourselves, don't you think?"

"Go ahead." Marguerite looks for a chair. "You do it. The search. I'll be right here." She is waving at the wooden hall chair beside the narrow table and the vase with its winter display of dried flowers.

"No!" The word comes out much louder than Thomas wants. He brings his voice down. "No, please, it's best if we do the search together. Please, please come along." Thomas reaches out and tugs at her arm. "They're *your* servants after all. You need to … to be there as well."

The distraught Marguerite allows her hand and the body attached to it to be pulled up off the chair. She has a terrible sour taste in her mouth, but agrees with her husband that yes, she should be there to check out the servants, to see if one might be a thief. And better that she and Thomas do it by themselves. The last thing she wants is for the authorities to learn of the theft and word of this episode get out.

Thomas leads Marguerite down the corridor. He is changing the plan as he walks. No longer will there be a false *piste*, there's no time for delay. He's taking her straight to the tiny *cabinet* where Simone has a bed. They are going to search the room and find the objects he placed there but two hours ago.

As he puts his hand on the latch he wonders if Marguerite will later wonder how it was that her loving husband knew just where to look. It's too late now. They are in Simone's room.

—

"Can you believe it?" asks Marguerite of her husband after the sad drama is over.

"Terrible, to be sure." Thomas looks around the room to see if there is a decanter containing some wine or spirit to drink.

Simone, the slightly hunch-backed middle-aged thief has been made to pack up her things, dry her sobbing eyes and be off. Simone surprised Thomas when she didn't protest more than she did. He feared she might even point a finger in his direction. Instead, the poor woman almost made it easy. She simply looked at her mistress after the objects were found in her things and said there must be some mistake.

That allowed Thomas to intervene: "Mistake! Theft from your master is no mistake." It was funny, he recalled later, he didn't feel a thing speaking that line.

Simone narrowed her eyes at Thomas when he spoke, but she held her tongue.

After that, Marguerite had no choice. With a wavering voice she told Simone she'd better pack up and go. She would not call in the officers of justice if the woman left right away. Thomas suggested they give her a reference letter, despite her crime, acknowledging the years of service. There was no need to mention the theft, he added. It was a slip-up he was sure that Simone would not repeat, a lesson having been learned. Simone kept her eyes lowered. Her sniffles were there for all to hear. Marguerite smiled at her husband's kindness. She sat down and quickly wrote a few words to give to poor Simone.

"I can still barely take it in," says Marguerite after the door is closed. Simone is now ten minutes out the door and off to who knows where.

Thomas shakes his head and shrugs. It's the best he can do. He does not want to take the lead in damning Simone, and he thinks it best to let his wife sputter on. While Marguerite says more about the betrayal from the servant, Thomas heads over to the sideboard intent on finding a bottle of something to fill a glass. He finds a burgundy. Yes, this is what he needs. He holds up the squat bottle in his wife's direction. He's hoping that if she joins him in a drink it might make the day go by better than it is at present. A shake of the head is Marguerite's only reply.

"I wonder if there's more." Marguerite puts a hand to her brow. "If she's taken other things over the years."

Thomas takes a sip. "We'll never know, I suppose."

"Do you think her wages were too low? Did that make her steal?"

"Good God, no." Thomas puts down his glass and goes over to where Marguerite is seated. He places himself beside her and takes her hand. "Thieves are born not made." It's a comment he heard the magistrate make in the office the other day.

Marguerite is startled. She looks at Thomas like she's never seen him before. "Born not made?"

"What I mean is," says Thomas, seeing he may have taken a wrong path, "our little Simone was well treated. You looked after her very well. But she betrayed you. You would never have guessed that she would … well, she didn't seem the type. But don't blame yourself, my dear wife. Such things happen."

He hasn't answered her query at all about "born not made," but he thinks he'd better leave his remarks as they are. There's no sense in overdoing it by saying too much.

"Are you sure you wouldn't like a glass of red? Perhaps only a half?"

Marguerite nods that she has changed her mind. She holds up her thumb and finger to indicate just how much.

"Here you go."

Thomas hands his wife a small goblet of red wine. He does not retake his seat beside her but goes to stand by the fireplace. In the turmoil of the morning, it's not yet been lit. It is usually Simone's job to start the fires in whatever room he and Marguerite are to be in. Thomas could do it easily enough himself, but that's not the point. One of the benefits of climbing the ladder is to not have to perform the tasks of those on the rungs below.

He'll have to get one of the other servants to look after it. But that can wait. He turns to his wife, who is staring vaguely into some distant place above her goblet of wine.

"My dear," he says as offhandedly as he can, "do you think you'll be able to find someone … someone to replace the one we've dismissed?" Thomas thinks it best not to use Simone's name anymore.

Marguerite closes her eyes as if that might lessen some pain. As she re-opens them the voice that comes out of her is exhausted.

"The city is filled with servants. It's not the finding one that's difficult, it's finding one you like and can trust." Her gaze swivels to her husband. She seems to be asking Thomas if he wants to add anything to that.

"Exactly," he intones. He extends an arm to run his fingers along the line of mortar that runs between the course of limestone that makes up the front of the fireplace.

"They can be saucy." Marguerite begins a long list of servant weaknesses. "Spread gossip. Break things. Lazy. Crude. Unkempt. Ill-trained. And as we have seen, even steal from you." She covers her eyes with her free hand.

Thomas goes to his wife. "You should go lie down, Marguerite."

For an instant, an instant that comes and goes between two ticks of a clock, he wonders if maybe he should not have done what he has done. Was there another way to help Hélène that didn't require getting rid of Simone? No, he decides not.

"You can think about finding a new servant later on. I'm sure that someone suitable will come to mind."

"Yes, I should get some rest."

And with those words of quiet resignation, Marguerite pushes to her feet. Thomas accompanies her out of the room, lending soothing words all along the way to her room. He cannot help but think that the little incident has aged the woman in front of his eyes. The hurt of Simone's betrayal is carving fresh lines on her face. She now looks every bit twice his age.

—

It's not until the evening of the fifth day that Thomas hears what he wants to hear. That's when Marguerite tells him that she has engaged a new domestic, a lovely young woman named Hélène. She'll be taking the place of the disgraced Simone. Thomas's eyes sparkle when he hears the news. He and Marguerite are at table. He celebrates by taking a brioche from the basket and cracking it like he's not cracked any roll or pastry since he was a child. The crumbs scatter and fall where they will.

"Sounds good, my dear," he says, taking a small bite.

It is all he can do not to stand up and shout. The plan has worked exactly as intended, which is surely a first. He does find it a little odd that Hélène has not reached him somehow and let him know the news first rather than hearing it from Marguerite. He supposes his soon-to-be lover didn't want to risk any contact that could put the arrangement in doubt. That was smart on Hélène's part, he decides. It also explains why Hélène did not show up two days ago at the usual rendezvous at the Place Dauphine. She's being careful. Not risking them being seen together. Thomas cannot fault her for that.

So he is about to get what he wants: his cake and eat it too. A secret young lover under the same roof as his wife, whose roof he duly acknowledges is really all hers. Thomas will continue to respect Marguerite. She remains a lady he holds close and dear, who gave him a marriage that advanced his standing and career. It's just that Thomas needs someone closer his age, someone lithe, with smaller breasts and a waist that is still firm. Hélène. Now, it's worked out.

Yet, thinks Thomas as he gives the brioche another small bite, he will never embarrass Marguerite by being open about Hélène. He sees some men promenade their mistresses around as if there was nothing wrong with what they do. Thomas is not of that sort. He will keep his second relationship secret. It will be his hidden treat. He and Hélène will make sure they are discreet. Marguerite must never find out. Where and when he and Hélène will satisfy their longings remains the only detail to work out. There is his room of course, which Marguerite never enters without a knock. And Hélène will probably have the little *cabinet* down the corridor, which used to be Simone's. They might even try some other places, just for a change. For instance, in the little storage room with a *paillasse* on the floor for old time's sake. The challenge to remain undetected is a conundrum he will enjoy. They will learn to delve and span in silence, no cries or moans. Just the slap of two bodies having their way.

Thomas savages a bite of the brioche, finishing it off.

"Have you not eaten all day?" Marguerite asks. "You're eating like … like I don't know. Like someone who has not eaten in a month."

"I'm sorry. I guess I was lost in thought."

"What were you thinking about to bite the roll like that?"

"Be right back."

Thomas gets up and heads for the small room with the nearest chamber pot. It's a place Marguerite has taken to calling the place of easement. Thomas doesn't have to go badly, but he wants to finish his thought and to do so by himself.

What more does he want from this life, Thomas asks himself after he's closed the door and unbuttoned his breeches. To write. And for people to read what he puts on the page. When exactly that will come he has no idea, but the pile of his manuscripts is beginning to mount. As he begins to piss his mind goes blank watching the yellow stream circle round the inside of the pot. Eventually, he supposes, his desire for Hélène will abate. It's in the very nature of wanting something that obtaining it is never enough. Something else always comes along. But there's no sense in worrying about any lost desire for Hélène as of right now. The growing stiffness in his hand is proof of that.

Thomas does up his buttons and puts the lid on the pot. The servants will empty it later on. "Oh," he says aloud as he lifts the latch for the door. Hélène will soon be one of those. It could be her that has to clean up what he and Marguerite leave in the pots. "Shit," says Thomas, not liking that thought. He wonders if Hélène has also realized that.

—

Thomas is at work in the magistrate's office when back in Marguerite's household the new female servant arrives to start life as a domestic replacing the thieving Simone. He is missing Hélène's arrival and how she and Marguerite begin to establish how things will proceed. Thomas has an entire day to get through before he goes home and sees how Hélène is working out in reality as opposed to in his imagination.

He flips through a folder containing dozens of documents from a murder case – the magistrate asked him to organize and summarize the contents – yet he finds his focus and attention will not bear down. He recalls Marguerite's comment last night at table that the new girl was energetic and was coming with an excellent reference. That brought a smile. He'd crafted those words over and over until they were just right. "Good to hear," was all he said.

Thomas stands up from his desk. Instead of making sense of the murder case and summarizing it in as few words as possible, he is drawing a blank. It's because he knows that he is only a half-hour walk away from Hélène. He imagines her settling into the *cabinet*, unfolding her things.

Thomas tidies up the folder by putting all the documents inside. He ties the string and closes it up for the day. He'll get to it tomorrow instead. His head will clear. For the rest of this day, he decides to turn to something that does not require him to think. He spends the afternoon going to one after another of the subaltern clerks. It's a duty he usually avoids, though the magistrate has listed it as one of his responsibilities. At each stop he goes through whatever dossier the junior clerks are working on. One by one he tells each of them what it is that he is doing right or wrong. Someone has to pay for the long wait to see how Hélène is faring with Marguerite. He figures the misery might as well be shared with the junior clerks.

By the time Thomas gets home in the evening the light is nearly gone from the sky. The day's azure has gone deep and dark blue. It's almost black overhead. Yet there is still a strip of light, a band of what looks like pale amber along the horizon above the Seine. Thomas takes it as an auspicious sign. As he climbs the steps of the building to reach Marguerite's apartment on the first floor, Thomas reminds himself to be calm. He does not want to give the whole thing away. He has to be natural. He cannot seem overly happy. Still, it's hard not to wonder how soon and where he and Hélène will have their first slippery dip.

The moment he enters the apartment Thomas hears the singsong of voices in the salon. His wife and his lover are in an animated conversation. There is laughter back and forth. His head tilts back. He blinks in surprise. A mistress and her servant do not talk nor laugh like that. With a creased brow he wonders whatever is going on.

He heads right away for the salon, then stops. He takes off his greatcoat and throws it on the chair in the hall. There's a bright flicker coming from within the salon. It looks as if more than the usual number of candles are lit. That usually means his wife is entertaining. Yet the only other voice Thomas hears is Hélène's. What's going on? Entertaining a new servant? Thomas pushes wide the salon door and strides into the room.

"There he is." Marguerite has amusement on her face. "Oh, do come in, Thomas, do."

She puts a hand to her chest as she stands up from the divan. She comes to take Thomas by the elbow.

"Hélène," she says, turning to the young woman seated in the red upholstered chair on the other side of the room, "I'd like to introduce you to my husband. This is Thomas Pichon."

Hélène half rises. She curtseys from the front of her chair. "Monsieur. Delighted," she says. The smile is slight, a little cautious, yet it tells Marguerite that Hélène is pleased to make her husband's acquaintance for the first time.

"What is it, Thomas?" asks Marguerite. "You look shocked. Are you all right?"

"I'd forgotten about … about the new servant being here." Thomas's body has gone stiff. His eyes are as wide as they can be. Hélène is dressed in finery such as he has not seen her in ever before. "Forgotten she was to start today. That's all. Hélène, is it?" he mumbles.

Thomas avoids making repeat eye contact with her. He concentrates instead first on the area where her dress hangs down and touches the floor. As he looks up he sees what Hélène is wearing from foot to head. She's not dressed like any servant Thomas has ever seen. She's attired like, and holding her hands and head like, she belongs in a salon. In her silk and satin, and the lace cap atop her coiled-up hair, Hélène could be a lady, someone much like his wife. Thomas's face cannot mask his surprise.

"You must be coming down with something." Marguerite clutches Thomas's elbow. "Sit down right here."

"All right, I do feel … I'll be all right in a moment." Thomas steals another look at Hélène. Marguerite is adjusting her own dress, eyes elsewhere, and Hélène makes a pretend startled face for Thomas, then smiles like it's a silent laugh.

"Wait till you hear," says Marguerite, seated back on the edge of the divan. She is facing them both, husband and newly engaged Hélène. "Are you sure you're all right? You looked shocked a moment ago and now it's like you're cross."

"Fine, I'm fine."

Marguerite settles well back on the divan. She glances once at Hélène before she starts. Hélène smiles sweetly at her in return. The room is aglow. Marguerite has half a dozen candles lit, as if she were entertaining the entourage of the child king. The pale grey walls and the three seated faces dance in the flickering light.

"Well, Hélène here has quite the story. To begin, she is originally from near Lyons."

"Is she?" Thomas feels his body start to shrink.

"Yes, and listen. Her father is, I should say *was,* he was a noble. An *écuyer.* Yes, you're as surprised as I was, I can see. I thought she was just a servant when I first met her, a pretty but nonetheless ordinary servant. Well, she's not. Barely a month after her birth her parents died in an accident. The diligence they were riding in, it plunged into the Rhône. It was tragic. She was their only child. And what's more she was with them at the time of the accident. A passing farmer rescued her from the river. You don't look yourself, Thomas. Are you chilled?"

"No."

"Well, all alone in the world she was, just like that. Do I have it right, Hélène?"

"But of course." The servant – is she still a servant or has she become something else? – sneaks a peek at Thomas. He's sure that's laughter he glimpses in her eyes.

"Well," continues Marguerite, "without any family to look after her, and her true heritage not known, the poor thing was taken in by the farmer and his wife. And that's where and how she was brought up. Like any other ordinary peasant child."

Marguerite glances again at Hélène. The servant cum visiting lady nods approval and urges with a hand gesture for Madame to keep on.

"Her family name and her claim to whatever inheritance might rightfully have been hers, it vanished in the river with the accident. The farmer who saved her life had accidently taken away the child's true place in society. It could be a novel, I swear. Poor Hélène grew up in simple surroundings, as I have said, and once she became old enough she went out into the world. Into service, of course, not knowing who she by birth really was. And that's where she has been ever since. Can you imagine? I mean, Thomas, really, can you imagine?"

Marguerite looks to Hélène for fresh confirmation. Hélène smiles in return. Marguerite next turns to Thomas, as if expecting him to make his own contribution to the wellspring of sympathy and understanding in the room.

"How do you know all this?" His tone and narrowed eyes suggest that he is not yet convinced. "It sounds...."

Marguerite winces. Hélène lowers her gaze to study her hands, which are now clasped in her lap. The finely dressed servant strikes a pose of silent prayer.

"Oh, Thomas," says Marguerite.

"I'm sorry," the husband says. He cannot very well claim to know the truth about Hélène, because then Hélène would likely tell Marguerite all the rest. The would-be lady has caught Thomas in that. "I don't know what to say," is the best he can do.

"Nor do any of us," says Marguerite, "but we have some work to do on her behalf, that much is clear."

Thomas sends a fierce squint in Hélène's direction. It's a look Marguerite doesn't catch.

"Well, I don't mean to keep you," says Marguerite as she gets up. Thomas turns to his wife with blinking eyes, and after a delay rises to meet her as she comes his way. She takes her husband by the elbow and steers him to the door. "I wanted you to meet Hélène, that's all. She'll be in service with us for a while, well, a light duty of course as my lady companion. More importantly, we have some paperwork to find to support her story. To show that she's been wronged. We are going to set things right, mark my words. Set things right. Secure her lost birthright. Find her a husband. We'll enlist our cousin, Madame Dufour, for that. And perhaps your patron, the magistrate, will give you advice on how to proceed."

Thomas opens his mouth to say something but there's nothing he has to say. He barely glimpses Hélène again before he's out the door. It isn't exactly a push from Marguerite, more of a guiding touch. Whatever it is, in no time at all Thomas finds himself out in the hall. He sees his greatcoat spread out across the wooden chair. He shakes his head at that choice. He wants to feel completely enwrapped. He goes a little further on, to where his rarely used cloak waits on a peg.

—

There's more than a slight chill in the air as Thomas emerges from the building into the night. He is more than a little dazed. He does not want to think about what just happened. Hélène has played a trick on him. He has to let it sink in. To do that he has to walk. He has to let his head empty out. Only then will he allow any thinking about Marguerite and Hélène creep back in.

Somehow it has turned bitterly cold over the span of the quarter hour he was inside. It may be spring according to the calendar, but it feels like winter out here. He's glad he brought the cloak. Round his shoulders he pulls it tight. He could have used a hat, but his white-powdered wig at least is snug. He'll warm up as he walks along.

Maybe it's always like this when it's the death of one season and the birth of another. The old will not just go away. It has to hang on to have a final say. The Seine is certainly showing it. Thomas stops to watch the river give up its warmth to the air.

A blanket of mist is issuing from the flowing dark water as it courses by. Funny, the Seine is the main constant in this city yet it's not constant at all. On and on it flows.

Thomas sets off at a slow pace as if he's measuring his steps. "Don't I wish?" he scoffs. No, he's not measuring anything. He simply isn't sure where to go. What he wishes is to be able to stroll with purpose and to some destination. For the moment he has neither. So his pace is a scuff and a shuffle to begin.

Somehow, God only knows how and why, somehow his plan went wrong. Of course, it's Hélène who sent it astray. She made a fool of his intentions with that storybook story of hers. She took her own life, losing her parents in one river, and dressed up as a complete lie in another river. And with noble parents to boot. Then there's her clothes and her bearing to go along with the pretense of being someone she's most definitely not.

Fair enough, Thomas supposes. His body concedes the point with a grimace and a shrug. He picks up his pace. Maybe he had a come-uppance headed his way for wanting just a bit too much. Maybe all one is supposed to have in life is a thin slice, a single piece at a time. If so, his scheme is lost. Thomas rubs his hands together. The friction brings a bit of warmth. He has to find a way out of this unexpected box.

Two young men with strutting walks and long bats in hand round the corner up ahead. Thomas slows down to peer at them. The bats make him nervous. They can be up to no good. The bats are weapons, nothing else. Thomas makes out that both of the young men are wearing the turned-up cloth caps a person normally only wears in their rooms when in a state of undress. He's heard about these two. The "nightcap thugs" they're called. They roam the streets looking for people to strike down and rob. Thomas would have expected to see them much later and in a different part of the city, but there they are. He's not about to find out what they have in mind. The two have not seen him so Thomas spins round and sets off back the way he's just come, to the other side of the river, along the Quai des Augustins.

As he crosses the river on the narrow footbridge he hears a dog barking. Then shouts. The sounds are coming from somewhere to the west, out of sight by a street or two. There are other footpads about. He'll not go anywhere near there either. Paris in the dark is a much more dangerous place than it is by day. He will not venture into the twist and turn of night-cloaked streets unless there's some purpose in play. At the moment he sees none. The barking and yells sound to him like there's a theft or a beating in progress, maybe even worse. Someone is murdered in Paris every second night or so. He has enough to worry about with the confusion surrounding Hélène and Marguerite. He doesn't need any more than that.

He decides he'll follow a criss-cross route back and forth across the Seine. Right bank to left bank then left to right and so on as long as it takes. He'll make a circuit until he's back where he began. He has been on each of the bridges over the past twelve years but never woven all together in a single walk. He's curious to see how long it'll take to do all the loops. An hour, maybe two, he guesses. Their names spring to mind, a checklist he has to complete: the Pont de la Tour, Pont Marie, Petit Pont, Pont Grammont, Pont Saint-Michel, Pont Nôtre-Dame. There might be one or two more. The walk will empty out his head of all his troubling bits, making room for solutions to appear. When the circuit is over and he's back on the Pont Neuf, the bridge closest to his home, the green king Henri will signify that it's time to go back to the rooms. Back to where Marguerite and Hélène are apparently becoming friends.

The footsteps add up, and just as Thomas expected, they empty out his cares. Crossing the building-lined Pont Saint-Michel, its rickety wooden structures on both sides and overhead, he focuses only on his stride. He avoids the contents of emptied chamber pots as he hurries by. The outstretched appeals of homeless beggars, children as well as adults, receive from him not even a glance. It's no different on the second bridge, the equally built-upon Pont au Change. That's one whose name he had not recalled. His pace is good. He surges past the slow walkers and the cripples who call out for donations. His head at last is completely clear. The worry about Hélène double-crossing him and what harm her phony story might bring is gone. So too is the concern that Marguerite might uncover what he did to little Simone. His wife will not find out about that. The fired servant is gone.

It's nothing but send the warm air out and bring the cold air in. The chest expands then it falls back. The legs are good. The hands finally have some warmth. The cloak is doing its job. There's heat beneath his arms and down his back. Funny how sweat begins, like tiny, hot insects emerging from the skin. Now that he's warmed himself he has to keep going. He doesn't want to chill.

It's not until Thomas is halfway across the third bridge, the Pont Nôtre-Dame, that something new in his head stirs. He recalls that he has not yet answered Gallatin's latest letter from London, maybe not the last two in fact. He's been distracted, busy with plans. He owes his distant friend a reply, that's certain. It's an obligation, a kind of friendly debt. He's not sure what to tell Gallatin about his own life, but something will come when he sits down with quill in hand.

Until an hour ago he might have bragged about having a lover-cum-servant along with a devoted wife. Not that Gallatin would approve. He's a defender of the one-woman approach to life. The bastard should have been a priest, except he hates everything about the Church. An odd fellow to be sure. Which is why Thomas must like him so much. He should go see him in London some time. In any case, given what's happened, with Hélène's concocted story and Marguerite's blind acceptance of it, Thomas will not say a word about that part of his life. Instead, he'll write about an essay he has in mind. Gallatin would prefer that topic. The essay will be about how good and bad are not really fixed. How the distinction shifts according to the context. Killing is bad, except in war, when it is good and much rewarded. Could it not be the same with the other rights and wrongs? He'll have to find at least one more example to prove his point. None come to him as he steps off the Pont Notre-Dame. He'll think more about it some other time.

Maybe Thomas will send Gallatin some news about their mutual scribbler friends of days gone by. He bumped into Tinville and Caylus in a cabaret a couple of weeks ago. It was the first time in nearly a year he'd seen any of the old crowd. He listened to their usual tales of woe until he thought his smiling cheeks might crack. Gallatin will want to read a few of their latest complaints. Their very examples used to convince the two of them, Gallatin and Thomas, that they were superior to the rest of the bunch. Thomas smiles. Maybe, just maybe, it was that shared sense of superiority that drew him to Gallatin and kept them friends? They both shared a sentiment of being apart and above.

Over the bridges Thomas goes. Along the streets atop the embankments that connect each bridge to the next. Past sleeping houses cloaked in dark. Past looming buildings where there are shouts out the windows and candles and lamps burning bright. Not once but twice the contents of chamber pots rain down just ahead of his hurried path. The flying piss perfumes the air with an acidic touch. Thomas doesn't give the smell a thought. He's lived in Paris long enough to know not to inhale until it's safe. He has more serious matters on his mind than stinking air. He has to keep the other senses fully awake. To venture into the city at night he especially needs his eyes and ears. Cutthroats can be always about, in shadows, round corners, or maybe running at him from behind. The glimpse he had earlier of the nightcap thugs with their bats was reminder enough of that.

He sweeps across the Pont de la Tournelle, which like the Pont Neuf Thomas appreciates for its openness. No hideaways on it. He is partway across the next bridge, the Pont Marie, when he halts. Before he enters the section where the buildings overhang and create a sort of lurking wooden cave, he looks over the stone rail to the river running underneath. Through the gloom – there are no lamps hanging near enough to cast sufficient glow to the embankment – he spies a set of stone steps that go down to the water. It occurs to him that it being night and with no boatmen around, he could easily go down the steps and get in one of their small, sharp-pointed boats. He has a knife in his pocket. He could cut the tether and liberate any one of them. Up or down the Seine he could go, inland or to the sea. To the sea. As far as Le Havre. Then he'd hire someone to take him across the Manche to England. He could go live with Gallatin. He'd leave the disappointments of Paris behind. Start again in London.

But then he'd be leaving behind all that he's gained, would he not? And just what has he gained he could not afford to lose? Is there any particular part of his life he could not find as good somewhere else?

Frustrating Hélène comes immediately to mind. What will that unpredictable, mischievous woman do next? Thomas cannot help but smile. She would not, could not let herself be dependent on him. She had to come up with something that keeps him at arm's length. And what a story she came up with. She's like a line of poetry that has no rhyme.

A few lines of verse drift into Thomas's ears.

Who tends a garden that will grow no rose?
Who lives a life that fills only with woes?

Who aspires for poetry
Yet settles for prose?

Thomas's face pains at the lines. He doesn't even give a thought to writing them down. They ring too close to the bone. He's twenty-seven and what has he achieved? At best a middling level of accomplishment and comfort. And who knows but that he might already be halfway through his allotted span of years. Thomas rubs his chin. There are times, and this is one, when he wonders if he truly has it in him to become the someone he once thought he'd be. Does he not owe it to the poetry within him to at least try and find out? Surely, he could do what Gallatin has. He could away to a new setting and give it a try.

But Gallatin did not run away in a huff, did he? He made arrangements, and well before he left. That's what Thomas needs, a leap, yes, but at the same time a leap of reasonable certainty. Maybe it's London like Gallatin, or maybe it's the Low Countries or one of the German states. Or God forbid, one of the wilderness lands France has come into possession of overseas.

He has talent. He could be of use to others. Why place limits on himself?

Thomas's feet begin to move all on their own. His hands, chest and legs have gotten cold. His body is asking to be in motion. Back into warmth. To be able to think more clearly. He's not sure how many more bridges he has to cross, but there can't be too many. The buildings of the city start to thin out in the area up ahead. His promenade to clear his head will soon reach its apex. It's not long until he begins the journey back. Back where? To Marguerite, with Hélène making things confused, or off to a fresh other land?

He resumes a marching pace, sucking in the air he needs. It doesn't stink so much out in the open areas. The cold air is colder, and cold air does a better job than warm air at keeping away vapours and ills.

Thomas finds the darkness of this night a comfort, a covering surround. In fact, he has to admit that he likes any night despite the risks. Except for once, and that was in the middle of the day, the thieves and brigands have always left him alone. It's at night when a solitary man like himself can really be himself. Away from the bustle and chatter of others. Is that a weakness in him or a strength? A strength, he decides, definitely a strength. I'm at my best when I'm all alone.

Thomas is six strides onto the Pont de Grammont, the last bridge, when he starts to feel a little undone. A spinning sensation in his belly is radiating weakness down his legs. His pace slows. He is feeling shaky. Then it comes to him. Since midday he's not had a thing to eat. He was a little hungry heading home from the magistrate's office but then came the encounter with Hélène and Marguerite. He never got so much as a bite. He left the apartment in a hurry and he now pays the price.

Thomas goes over to the rail and comes to a stop. Through the dark he can just make out the outline of the immense stacks of cordwood on Isle Louvier, to which the Pont de Grammont leads. There are at least fifty stacks of wood. No, maybe there are a hundred or more. The sentry for the compound is standing thirty paces farther on, at the other end of the bridge. He's keeping any intruders thinking of stealing their heat away from the woodyard on the isle. He gives Thomas a stern look. The sentry taps the musket strung over his shoulder then points with his free hand at Thomas to make sure the stranger approaching on foot gets the warning. Thomas has to smile. Does the fool think he's come to steal an eight-foot length of wood? And carry it away with an invisible horse and wheeled cart? Thomas blows a kiss at the man. The sentry spits and brandishes his musket with both hands. At no point does the sentry look away.

Thomas swings round and heads back in the direction he came. That's it, as far as he goes. He's done the bridges as planned and worked a few things out as he went. Hélène's mischief is just that, a playful game by which she hopes to speed her advance. Thomas admits he has no right to complain about that. He's done the same in his own way and will do it again if and when he gets the chance. Doesn't everyone when they can?

No, maybe not. There are those who have limits, who follow certain codes. Religion is one, though morality is the word closer to the mark. Well, so do I, thinks Thomas, hurrying along. I've never harmed anyone, at least no one I can recall. What I've done in this life so far is simply aspire to independence outside of any other person's controlling realm. Reason is his instructor, nothing else. What is that little line that Gallatin likes to preach? Let logic be your firmament and reason your guide.

Hélène's uppity new story does not necessarily mean that the two of them can't still find ways to be together, at least once in a while. She owes it to him, does she not? He created the situation that is allowing her to write her new life the way she is. If it's less frequently than he imagined then maybe that will only sweeten the game. Suspense and holding back are pleasures of their own, as he discovered a few years ago. The fact that the two of them know each other's lies and secrets is something else to keep in mind. Each has to keep the other's fabrications quiet or else. Or else they'll both sink. There is a trust in mutual lies, it would seem. So given that, why wouldn't they once in a while meet alone in her room or maybe his?

As for Gallatin's example of moving somewhere else, Thomas thinks he's figured that out as well. He'll stay put for the time being but keep his eyes peeled. He is only twenty-seven.

He should have a few good years yet. Who knows when his life will open up to become more than it now is?

A sudden gust pushes abruptly out of the west. The blast knocks Thomas to a halt. He hangs on to his wig as he watches how the wind scuffs up swirls of dust on either side of the river. He raises the hood of his cape and turns his back to the gust. The weakness in his body, the faintness he felt moments ago, is temporarily gone. His legs have renewed life. They will get him home.

As he bends into the wind, words faintly heard swirl through his head.

Advance soft shadow
Down the dark wind

Deepen the twilight
Dust of the sinned

Thomas smiles at the familiar lines. Someday he should see if they might have life on a page, in some kind of larger work. He has never yet heard them reach their end. They were interrupted first by Jean-Chrys and later by Jean Gallatin.

Shadow swing round
Out of the deep

Blanket this air
In night's soft sleep.

There. Thomas likes them well enough, though it seems odd to have "soft" twice in eight lines. Maybe it should be "night's final sleep." No, maybe not. That sounds like death. But what's wrong with that? Does death not loom over everyone and all the time? He'll have to get back home now and record the lines. He'll play with them for a while, the quill cradled in his hand.

As the Pont Neuf comes into view Thomas is struck by a bright glow in the sky that wasn't there when his walk began. Peeking above the rooftops is the rounded tip of a cream-coloured moon. It's on the rise, its corona of illumination lighting the way, brightening the city's countless rooftops and spires an inch at a time.

Stopping on the bridge, one hand on the cold stone rail and the other fingering the silk-lined *mouchoir* in the pocket of his *veston*, Thomas is for a moment transfixed. He is once again a boy in sock feet. Only not in his attic room in Vire but wandering through the woods. The trees are tall and straight. A blanket of snow. The ground is frozen. It resounds like a drum. He hears the footsteps of others, quiet and soft to begin, then a menacing thrum. The boy turns round. His breath paints the air in the snowy woods with steam. A large dog is coming. No it's not one dog, it's many. No, it's a pack of wolves. Their bodies lean and stretched. Snarls echo off the trees.

Thomas shivers. He averts his gaze from the moon and the memory it brings. He glances up at the equestrian statue of Henri IV. "Better get back," he mutters to the king. A last look at the river coursing down below.

The final steps back toward Marguerite's place are grudgingly and slowly begun. The rapid footsteps approaching from the other side of the bridge are only faintly heard.

Thomas squints but continues on, angling his head to hear better as he begins to pick up the pace. Nearly too late he turns to glance back over his shoulder. There are two bats upraised maybe twenty feet away. And fierce faces beneath two nightcaps coming at a near silent run. They are after the solitary man foolishly out for a nighttime river walk. They will take his purse and have a bit of whacking fun. Where they were approaching as stealthily as they could, now that Thomas has spotted them there is no holding them back. They advance side-by-side in a full run. He sees their angry faces before his ears process their threatening gasps and grunts.

Thomas takes off. The thugs are right behind. A wasted blow from one of the bats makes a whoosh as it strikes his windblown cloak.

Thomas unclasps the cloak. He half throws it as he lets it fall behind. He hears them curse at the sudden billowing obstacle and hears what he takes to be a thud. He hopes and prays it's made one or both trip. He tells himself not to glance round, yet that's exactly what he does. Yes, one of the runners is down, holding on to his knee. There is now only one attacker but he's closer than before. He's gone round the cloak and is only a few feet away. A surge goes into Thomas's legs.

He feels a hit upon his shoulder. It hurts like a fire burn but the pain has come and gone. Since it did not knock him down it spurs him on. He figures that to swing a bat means the thug likely had to break his stride. That gives Thomas a chance to widen the gap. A second blow comes low down on his back. It hardly burns at all. That means that Thomas is for the moment getting away.

Thomas reaches up and yanks at his wig. It's attached more snugly than he wants. It comes free at last but at the cost of a bit of foot speed. Thomas takes another blow, this time high up on his back. The thug is closing in. The next blow will likely be upon his head. As he has no purse on him to lose, it occurs to Thomas that the angry thug might just decide to beat him to death to make up for the wasted run.

Thomas sends his wig backward. He hears a sputter then a cough. And the slowing of the footsteps coming behind. Thomas looks over his shoulder and slows down as he does. The man who was chasing him has stopped. His face is whitened from the powder that was amply sprinkled this morning on Thomas's wig. He shakes a fist at Thomas as he gives up.

Thomas does not stop. He continues to run, though at a slower pace, all the way to the building where he and Marguerite, and now Hélène, live. The blows upon his shoulder and back he begins to feel. In fact, they hurt a lot. He'll have bruises, for sure. But what are bruises compared to what might have been? There's nothing like a risk of loss to sweeten one's appreciation for the good things one has. Thomas cannot stop from smiling as he uses his key to open up the door to Marguerite's suite of rooms.

"Well, there you are." Marguerite's face is stern. "I was getting worried."

Thomas does not lose his mood. He's pleased to be welcomed home, even if it is by an angry face. Besides, sternness is just who Marguerite is. Stern faces, it occurs to Thomas, come with the aging process. It's a part of knowing that one's days are numbered and the number is getting smaller all the time. He supposes he'll get a stern face of his own one day.

Coming into the hall out of the salon comes Hélène. She sends a concerned look to Thomas but not a spoken word. Marguerite does enough talking for everyone.

"You're all a mess, Thomas. Your hair, your clothes. You're perspiring like a … like I don't know what. You'll have to clean up." Marguerite turns to Hélène. "Would you ask one of the men servants to heat up some water, please?"

"Of course." And Hélène is away.

"As for you …" and thus begins a fairly long discourse from the worried wife.

Every so often, when and where he thinks it necessary, Thomas inserts a few words of his own. He does, for instance, eventually explain that he went out to get a bit of air in front of the building and was immediately attacked by a gang of thugs. He thought that sounded better than admitting what really sent him away and the conclusions he drew. Right in front of the house it happened, he said. The large gang chased him all over the city, all along the river, over half its bridges, before Thomas was finally able to make it back home.

"Poor darling." Marguerite smiles enigmatically.

Thomas wonders if she knows that he sometimes has a tendency to embellish or even to just make things up.

"I was fast and I was tough."

"Of course you were."

And so the rest of the evening unfolds rather pleasantly for Thomas. He is treated as someone sorely wronged, someone who needs special care. That includes a little treat in his bedroom. Marguerite does not want the man to hurt himself any more than he already has. So instead of him coming to her in the usual way, she goes to him in his room. And she is pleased to do most of the work.

With Marguerite gone back to her room afterwards, Thomas fights off falling right away into sleep. He would like to reflect a little bit about where he is in his life and what it all means.

It's not easily done. The call of slumber this evening is strong. It's been an eventful day. His body twitches and trembles on its own. To stay open the eyelids require a fight. Only for a short while is Thomas able to stay awake.

He is given to concluding that as much as he would like more and better than what he has, what he has is not so bad after all. He'll stay the course. Keep his aspirations he will, but he'll also see what fresh opportunities come along. No life is completely under anyone's control. That's clear. It's more like a river, the Seine and countless more. The lucky ones are those who find the current and move along with its onward flow.

FIN

Acknowledgements and a Few Notes

The idea to write this novel first came to me more than a quarter century ago. I recall the moment. I was reading a section of a document dating from 1778 when the words on the page literally made my head snap back. I thought: there's a novel in that. Now, after an excessively long gestation period, there is—at least, the first of what could surely be several novels that tell the story of my central character Thomas's journey through life.

Prior to turning to fiction I had a pretty long career as a historian whose specialty was the 18th century. Much of it was spent with Parks Canada, where I was fortunate enough to work for a long stretch at the Fortress of Louisbourg National Historic Site on Cape Breton Island. For those who don't know it, the Fortress is a partial re-creation of an entire 18th-century French fortified town. It's *la France outre mer*, Cape Breton-style. My exploration of the history of Louisbourg, and by extension of the 18th-century French world from which Louisbourg sprang, laid the conscious and unconscious groundwork for this novel. I can never fully express my gratitude to the many colleagues and predecessors at the Fortress who made that place such a great research venue during the twenty-three years I worked there.

Having a background as a professionally trained historian specializing in the 18th century is a great help when writing a story set in the 18th century. The historian's discipline, however, only takes you so far. One is not supposed to make up characters, invent dialogue and twist timelines and events according to the demands of a plot. It was quite an education for me as an apprentice novelist, and my apprenticeship goes on.

The document that sparked my desire to write this novel was written by one Thomas Pichon (1700–1781) near the end of his life. Anyone interested in reading that letter for themselves can find it on pages 25–26 of John Clarence Webster's *Thomas Pichon, "The Spy of Beausejour,"* published by the Public Archives of Nova Scotia in 1937. A few lines from the 1778 letter are also extracted and presented in T. A. Crowley's short biography of Pichon in the *Dictionary of Canadian Biography* (now available online).

In the summer of 1985 my wife, Mary and I took our three kids to live in France for three and a half months. We selected Normandy, in part because it allowed me every so often to go to Vire, Pichon's hometown. Vire is also where Pichon sent his many papers and books after his death. That collection is in the care of the local municipal library. I went through much of the Pichon collection and consulted various books, articles and images of early 18th-century Vire. I wanted to be able to depict the setting for the early part of the novel as accurately as possible. I would like to acknowledge the assistance I received from the staff of the Bibliothèque municipale de Vire who were there in 1985. Today's Vire is a lovely place, but it is not the Vire of Thomas Pichon's era. American and German tanks laid waste to much of the town in a ten-day battle in 1944. There is still the clock-tower gate and a few churches, but most of the rest dates from after the Second World War.

In the winter of 1988, I carried out more research in France. Thanks go to Mary's parents, Marg and the late Les Topshee, for looking after the kids. That allowed us to go overseas *sans enfants*. I also thank the Canada Council for the Explorations grant they awarded me to undertake that in-depth research trip. It has been a long time coming, but the material gathered on that trip is finally surfacing in this novel and will continue to do so in however many more books it may take to tell the whole story.

I could not begin to list all the books and articles I have read about 18th-century France that have shaped my understanding of that era. Readers interested in such details should consult the bibliographies in my history books, especially *Life and Religion at Louisbourg* (McGill-Queen's University Press, 1996), *Endgame 1758* (University of Nebraska Press and Cape Breton University Press, 2007) and *Control and Order in French Colonial Louisbourg* (Michigan State University Press, 2001).

One particular source for this novel deserves a special mention. Its author is Geneviève Menant-Artigas and her study is called *Lumières clandestines. Les papiers de Thomas Pichon*, published by H. Champion in Paris in 2001. The book is about Thomas Pichon and his intellectual world. Her research and analysis was most helpful, though in the end what I have written is fiction, not history. From my perspective, there are now two Thomas Pichons. The historical personage, about whom Menant-Artigas writes, and the fictional creation I have penned. The two figures have a lot in common—parents pressuring them to enter the church, an early aspiration to pursue medicine, a move from Vire to Paris at age fifteen, an attraction to the sensual side of life, a penchant for writing and stretching the truth, and a close (maybe even marriage) relationship with Marguerite Salles—but there's an awful lot in the novel that comes out of my imagination and not from any documentary source. Hélène, for instance, is a complete invention. Jean Gallitin is a name I borrowed and gave form and flesh to, but all I really know about him is that he was one of the real Thomas Pichon's many correspondents.

Turning to the setting for the latter two-thirds of the book, there are countless books, articles and images on early 18th-century Paris. The idea that Thomas might have been a part-time "fly" for the Paris police came to me when I recalled Alan Williams's study *The Police of Paris, 1718–1789* (Louisiana State University Press, 1979), a book I read maybe thirty years ago. The character Jacques whom Thomas and Gallatin encounter in the tavern outside Paris's walls is based on Jacques-Louis Ménétra, author of *Journal de ma vie* (edited by Daniel Riche and published by Albin Michel, latest edition, 1998). Illustrations of that tavern, known as Au Tambour Royal or the Ramponeau Inn exist and guided my description of the scene.

To assist me in visualizing overall Paris at the time of this novel, the famous 1734 bird's eye view known as the Plan de Turgot was incredibly helpful. The many sections of the plan have been scanned and made available on the Internet. If you're in Paris, I highly recommend a visit to the Musée Carnavlaet, the official museum on the history of Paris. It is a treasure trove. Though like Vire, Paris has much changed since the early 18th century, there are a host of sources that enable one to revisit that period. Books, paintings, engravings and museums offer glimpses into this or that aspect of Paris life. I carried out a useful research trips to the city in 2011 and 2012 to finalize many details.

As for the process of turning an idea for a novel into a manuscript and then a manuscript into a book, I would like to thank the following: Sandy Balcom for suggesting books to re-familiarize myself with early 18th-century furnishings; Stephen Brumwell for planting the germ of an idea that a trilogy might be a better way to go than a single book; CBU Press for their enthusiasm for the manuscript and eagerness to turn it into a book; Kate Kennedy for being a terrific editor; Elizabeth Tait for pointing me toward books on the clothing of the period. Any erroneous descriptions found in the novel are entirely my fault.

I close by acknowledging the most important person in my life. That is Mary Topshee. Mary has been a part of my life almost as long as I can recall. Without Mary, I doubt this book or any of the non-fiction titles I have written would exist at all.

A. J. B. Johnston, Halifax, Nova Scotia

Previous books by A.J.B. Johnston

1758 : La Finale. Promesses, Splendeur et Désolation Dans la Dernière Décennie de Louisbourg. (Presses de l'Université Laval, 2011)

Endgame 1758. The Promise, the Glory and the Despair of Louisbourg's Final Decade. (University of Nebraska Press and Cape Breton University Press, 2007)

Grand-Pré, Heart of Acadie / Grand-Pré, Coeur de l'Acadie. (Nimbus, 2004; co-authored with W. P. Kerr)

Louisbourg, An 18th-Century Town (Nimbus, 2004 [1991]; Co-authored with Kenneth Donovan, B.A. Balcom and Alex Storm)

Storied Shores: St. Peter's, Isle Madame and Chapel Island in the 17th and 18th Centuries. (Cape Breton University Press, 2004)

Control and Order: The Evolution of French Colonial Louisbourg, 1713-1758. (Michigan State University Press, 2001)

Louisbourg: The Phoenix Fortress / Louisbourg, Reflets d'une époque (Nimbus, 1997)

Tracks Across the Landscape: A Commemorative History of the S&L Railway. (University College of Cape Breton Press, 1995; Co-Authored with Brian Campbell)

Life and Religion at Louisbourg, 1713-1758 (McGill-Queen's University Press, 1996) / *La religion dans la vie à Louisbourg (1713-1758).* (Environnement Canada, 1988)

From the Hearth: Recipes from the World of 18th-Century Louisbourg. (University College of Cape Breton Press, 1986; co-authored with Hope Dunton)

The Summer of 1744, A Portrait of Life in 18th-Century Louisbourg / L'Été de 1744: La vie quotidienne à Louisbourg au XVIIIe siècle. (Parks Canada, 1983)

Defending Halifax: Ordnance, 1825-1906 / La défense de Halifax: artillerie, 1825-1906. (Parks Canada, 1981)